Readers love HEIDI CULLINAN

Second Hand

"I loved this book and am so glad I got to spend time with El and Paul."

—Diverse Reader

"This was an enjoyable read with a very satisfying happily ever after. I loved seeing Paul come into his own and choose El above all others."

—Open Skye Book Reviews

"I can always count on Marie Sexton and Heidi Cullinan, and combining forces they create a great one in *Second Hand*. If you're in the mood for something sexy and sweet, a feel-good romance with humor and a great message, this is the novel for you."

—Kimmers' Erotic Book Banter

Family Man

"...*Family Man* was everything I love in one book. Seriously. It was absolutely adorable!"

—Birdie Bookworm

"*Family Man* by Heidi Cullinan and Marie Sexton is the epitome of a comfort read."

—Gay Book Reviews

By Heidi Cullinan

With Marie Sexton: Family Man

COPPER POINT MEDICAL
The Doctor's Secret
The Doctor's Date

TUCKER SPRINGS
With Marie Sexton: Second Hand
Dirty Laundry

Published by DREAMSPINNER PRESS
www.dreamspinnerpress.com

THE DOCTOR'S DATE

HEIDI CULLINAN

DREAMSPINNER PRESS

Published by
DREAMSPINNER PRESS

5032 Capital Circle SW, Suite 2, PMB# 279,
Tallahassee, FL 32305-7886 USA
www.dreamspinnerpress.com

Mass Market Paperback ISBN: 978-1-64108-066-8
Trade Paperback ISBN: 978-1-64080-853-9
Digital ISBN: 978-1-64080-852-2
Library of Congress Control Number: 2018907092
Mass Market Paperback published June 2019
v. 1.0

Printed in the United States of America
∞
This paper meets the requirements of
ANSI/NISO Z39.48-1992 (Permanence of Paper).

For Amy
because you also deserve all the happiness

THANKS TO

DAN AND Anna Cullinan for putting up with the year from hell, my patrons for putting up with me whining about the year from hell and for supporting me, particularly Marie and Rosie, and above all, thanks to Tom and Nina Cullinan for being so understanding about me writing the last few scenes at their fiftieth anniversary party. I'm sure that was part of the magic.

PROLOGUE

ERIN ANDREAS was thirteen when he fell in love.

One of his mother's interns dropped Erin off at the Mayo Clinic, leaving him at the curb in front of huge glass doors with no further instructions on how to reach his father. Erin asked for John Jean Andreas at the main desk, but his father wasn't a patient, and no one had time for the shy teenager who didn't know where he was supposed to go.

If he's expecting you, you'd better find him. If you don't show up, he'll get angry.

The thought of his father's anger was far more terrifying than being lost, so Erin wandered, hoping somehow he would end up in the right place. All the while, he racked his mind for a clue. He was pretty sure his father's friend was here for surgery. Some kind of cancer. He glanced around, hoping for a map, but he didn't see one. Could he ask which building handled cancer surgery at an information desk?

Maybe he should go back to where he'd been dropped off. Except he wasn't sure how to get there.

Erin crouched beside a pillar, breath coming too fast, the tightness spreading through his body. His father would be so angry….

"Are you all right?"

As Erin blinked the world into focus, a boy his age appeared before him. Taller than he was by a few inches, and broader, though it didn't take much, as broom handles were thick next to Erin. Dark, tousled hair, in contrast to fair, lightly freckled skin, and brown eyes that bored into Erin, seeing everything. Erin's hair was wild too, but in a messy, embarrassing way. This boy's hair was… dangerous.

"Are you all right?" the boy asked again.

Nodding, Erin pressed his hands against his clothes. "I—I'm lost. I'm trying to find my father. We're visiting someone."

The boy scratched his chin. For some reason this drew Erin's attention to his mouth. The boy had thick, pretty lips. "Do you know what department the person you're visiting is in?"

Lips. They looked soft, like little pillows. Belatedly Erin realized the boy was waiting for an answer, and he blushed. "I—I… cancer, I think."

"Oh, I can take you—" His gaze shifted to something behind Erin, and his entire demeanor changed, his face going pale, his expression stony. "Sorry, I have to go. You want the third floor."

As quickly as he'd come, the boy was gone. Erin didn't even know his name.

He went to the third floor as the boy suggested, but there wasn't exactly a sign saying, "Cancer is here," though there should have been. Wasn't there a different name for it? He couldn't remember it. It started with an *o*, maybe. Erin thought he would ask at one of the desks, but they all had lines of patients at them, so he sat in one of the waiting areas and drew his knees toward his chest.

He was quite late now. His father was going to be so furious.

"What are you doing?"

Glancing up, Erin saw a young girl blinking at him. She wore a yellow sundress and had her natty hair in pigtails sticking out like cotton tufts on either side of her head, and she held a large picture book. She didn't give him much time to answer before she continued speaking.

"I'm waiting with my mom and my grandma and my brother. My dad is coming up later after work and bringing my aunt. My uncle is having brain surgery. I brought a book. Why are you here?"

Erin lowered his legs to the floor. "My father's friend is having surgery, but I can't find my dad."

The girl hugged the book and shifted her hips so her skirt twirled from side to side. "You should sit here with me while you wait for him. You can read to me."

The information desks were still full of lines. "I'm not sure where I'm supposed to wait, though."

"Come on already."

He was going to argue more, but she pulled him from the bench, leading him to a different section of the waiting area, where a tall woman and an older woman approached them, looking stern.

"Emmanuella Grace, where have you been?"

The girl smoothed a hand over her pigtails. "Mom, this boy is lost."

Emmanuella's mother appeared to be highly suspicious of this story. The grandmother came forward on a cane and scrutinized him over the top of her glasses, which had a glittering gold chain dangling from each end of the frame. "Land sakes, child, you don't look like anyone's fed you in weeks. And what is going on with your hair?"

Reflexively, Erin touched his unruly, kinky, sandy curls that did nothing but frizz.

Emmanuella's mother folded her arms over her chest. "Where're you supposed to be?"

Erin tried not to let his panic show. "My father is here, but I don't know where. They didn't tell me how to find him when they dropped me off. I thought maybe he would be waiting for me, but he wasn't, and I can't find him."

Emmanuella's mother muttered under her breath and cast her gaze at the ceiling.

Erin fixed his gaze on his shoes. "I'm sorry."

Emmanuella was undaunted. "See, Mama? He needs me."

Daring a glance upward, Erin saw Emmanuella's mother nodding at him, lips flat. "You sit with my mother and Emmanuella, and I'll find your father. What's your name, and what's your father's name?"

"Erin Andreas, ma'am. My father is John Jean Andreas."

The woman's face became a stony mask.

Emmanuella's grandmother chuckled darkly. "Don't that beat all."

Erin worried he should maybe apologize again.

Emmanuella's mother sighed. "All right. I think I know exactly where your father is. Wait here. I'll be back soon."

She left the lobby, and as soon as she was gone, the grandmother sat beside him. After opening her large purse, she produced half a sandwich in a bag and gave it to Erin.

"Eat this, boy. When Nicolas returns, I'll send him out to get you some milk. Maybe something sweet too, if you eat all of your sandwich."

Erin peeled away the cellophane. The sandwich smelled strongly of mayonnaise, mustard, and onions. He'd never seen anything like it.

Emmanuella nudged him with her elbow. "Go on, eat it, don't stare at it. Haven't you seen an egg salad sandwich before?"

Erin hadn't, but he didn't want to say so. He shoved his uncertainty aside and took a bite. His eyes widened. "This is good. Really good."

Emmanuella beamed with pride. "Grandma Emerson makes the best egg salad sandwiches."

He finished it quickly, and while he ate, Emmanuella settled in beside him, opening the book on his lap. "When you're done eating, let's read this book together. I can read it, but I'm slow, so it's better if you do most of it. My brother Nick won't. He says it's too girly." Emmanuella smiled at Erin. "But you look a lot like a girl, so you won't mind."

"Hush now," Emmanuella's grandmother said.

Erin was used to being told he was girly. "I'll read your book." He wiped his mouth with his fingers. "I think I need to get a drink of water first, though."

"I'll get it for you." Emmanuella popped off the chair, beaming. "They have cups by the water fountains here. I'll bring the drink to you."

She ran across the room—until her grandmother scolded her and told her to walk—hurrying with the paper cup full of water. As Erin drank it, Emmanuella studied his hair.

"Your hair is too fuzzy. You don't use enough grease on it."

"White boys can't use grease." Grandma Emerson was reading a book now. "Though he could stand to wash less and simply use conditioner."

Erin blinked at her. "Would that work?"

Emmanuella's grandmother shook her head. "Sometimes I wonder if white mothers teach their children anything."

Erin's certainly hadn't taught him much, and now she didn't even want to live with him. "Thank you. I'll try it."

Emmanuella tapped his leg impatiently. "It's time to read my book."

The book was a fairy tale of sorts, a story about a princess who was kidnapped by an ogre king and held in his castle until the prince appeared, sword in hand, to slay the ogre and rescue her. Emmanuella knew the story well, interjecting occasionally when she recognized words or remembered certain parts. She also added her own commentary.

"The ogre king is so ugly." Then, on another page, "You're like the princess, see? You have the same hair and the same nose."

This got another reprimand from her grandmother.

Erin didn't mind, though. Besides, he felt like the princess in the castle a lot of the time. Except he didn't agree—the ogre king was a bit rugged, but he wasn't ugly. Erin preferred him to the prince, to be honest. He looked similar to the boy he'd met in the hallway earlier, which probably helped make Erin partial to the ogre king. In fact, Erin was disappointed, because he could tell how the story was going to end, and he didn't want the ogre king to die. He wanted….

He stared at the scowling ogre king—muscled and swarthy, dark hair wild, glaring out at Erin. Erin's chest felt funny, and so did his stomach.

He wanted….

"Who's this guy?"

Erin blinked, his focus shifting from the fear inside his head to the unknown in front of him. A boy about his age, maybe slightly older, stood above his chair, glowering. Erin shrank into his seat as Emmanuella's grandmother swatted the newcomer.

"Nicolas Beckert, mind your manners. Where have you been all this time? Did they move the cafeteria to the moon?"

"I ran into Owen Gagnon. His dad dragged him here, I guess, and he's angry. I figured somebody had to calm him down." He turned to Erin, casting a protective glance at his sister. "I'm Nick Beckert. Who are you?"

Erin did his best to sit up straight and hold out his hand without knocking the book off his lap. It didn't work, because the book slid and he had to grab it, and he ended up looking like an idiot. "Erin Andreas. P-pleased to meet you."

"Aw, hell."

"I will wash your mouth out with soap." Emmanuella's grandmother pulled her wallet out of her purse. "Go back to the cafeteria and get some milk. Whole milk, and some cake. This boy is too thin."

"*Grandma.*"

"Don't *Grandma* me. You do as you're told."

Nick clenched his fists at his sides. "I don't want to give *him* milk and cake."

"It's clear to me you want a whipping as well as a mouth full of soap." She handed him a bill. "Now go and get—"

"*Erin.*"

Erin's grip on the book slipped at the sound of his father's voice. The egg salad sandwich in his stomach turned over as he stumbled to his feet, fighting the urge to cower, knowing he had to stand up straight or it would be worse. So much worse.

John Jean Andreas towered over his son, his displeasure coming off him in tight waves. "Why are you here clutching a picture book? You were supposed to meet me, and now I've had to come find you."

Erin was cold to his bones, but he dared not let himself tremble. He wished he hadn't eaten. "I'm sorry, Father."

"He wasn't causing any trouble." This came from Grandma Emerson, speaking with a firmness that almost made Erin more nervous of her than he was of his father. "Poor child was lost and hungry. We were happy to help him out."

"Mama." Emmanuella's mother's voice was sharp with warning.

Grandma Emerson ignored her, easing into her chair. She patted Erin on the small of his back. "You go on, young man, and don't keep your father waiting. Thank you for reading so patiently to Emmanuella."

Erin walked toward his father, who was already leaving. At the last second, Erin remembered himself and turned. "Thank you for the sandwich."

Grandma Emerson nodded, then waved him on.

As soon as they were out of earshot, his father started in on him.

"What did you think you were doing? Why didn't you come directly to me?"

Erin wanted to hunch his shoulders, but he knew he couldn't without getting yelled at, so he simply kept his gaze down. "I'm sorry. I didn't know where you were. It's so big."

"For heaven's sake, it's not as if we're in the Damon Building. This is only the St. Mary's campus."

"I'm sorry."

His father pursed his lips and smoothed his hands over his suit. "It's fine. I don't like how *they* had to find you for me, but it's done now." John Jean pushed the button for the elevator. "Stay away from the Beckerts. Collin Beckert has finally muscled himself onto the St. Ann's board, but if we have our way, it'll only be temporary. Christian's cancer is supposed to be treatable, but… well, we have to tread carefully. Don't muddy the waters for me."

This must have been why Nick's family reacted coldly when they'd heard Erin's name and his father's. It was another one of his father's work things, something to do with the hospital in Copper Point. It always had to do with the hospital. All Erin could think of, though, was Emmanuella's kindness and Grandma Emerson's egg salad sandwich.

Erin wished he'd gotten to know Nick better, even if Nick didn't like him. Maybe if he'd spent more time with him, he could have changed his mind. People in Copper Point were kinder than the other people at boarding school. Erin longed to meet boys his age and have them over while he was on break. Just one friend would do… but it never worked out.

His father led him to another lobby area, where they sat down to wait. His father read the newspaper, and Erin perched quietly beside him, doing nothing.

He didn't know why he was there, but he knew better than to ask questions. His father would tell him what to do when it was time. He did his best to concentrate on being still and ready for whenever his father would want him.

Except it wasn't easy, because he kept thinking of Emmanuella's picture book and the ogre king. More specifically, his reaction to the ogre king. What did it mean? *Did* it mean anything? It terrified him, but he didn't know what to do with his emotions. He'd had all sorts of strange feelings lately about a lot of things. He didn't want to do *anything* with them, but it was as if something had awakened in him, and though he didn't understand it yet, he was pretty sure it wasn't good. Like how he kept thinking about the ogre king, wishing he had someone strong and bold in his life to burst in and take care of everything.

Maybe the ogre king would care for him too.

Erin swallowed and ducked his head, cheeks heating.

His father's sharp flick to his knee brought Erin upright, dispelling thoughts of the ogre king. His father kept his gaze on the far wall. "I'm going to check with the nurse to see if Christian is ready for visitors yet. When we go in, I want you on your best behavior. He'll be impressed you've come along, so make sure you don't stand there like a fool. Be intelligent. Ask polite questions. Look interested."

Erin still didn't understand, but he didn't dare ask for clarification. He'd have to figure it out. Closing his fists nervously against his thighs, he nodded. "Yes, Father."

John Jean rose. "Stay here."

Erin didn't allow himself to relax until his father disappeared around the corner, but even then he only allowed himself a sigh, not easing his posture. Moments later Nick came toward him from the other direction, holding a container of milk and a piece of chocolate cake on a plate wrapped in plastic.

Erin's whole spirit lifted, and he hoped the smile on his face wasn't goofy. "You came back."

"Here." Nick held the milk and cake out to Erin.

Erin took the items, glancing at the place where his father had disappeared, but the hallway in that direction remained empty. "Thanks." He couldn't drink or eat, not with his stomach this queasy, but he couldn't throw anything away until Nick left. Not that he wanted Nick to go.

Nick sat on a chair opposite Erin, eyeing him uncertainly. "Your dad is scary."

Erin stared at the food in his hands, not knowing what to say to that. Not out loud.

He can be scary, yes. But he's my father, and he's the only parent who cares about me at all. Even if he's a little mean sometimes, I can't afford to lose him, or I won't have anyone. And I'm terrified of being alone.

No. He definitely couldn't say any of that.

A lump formed in Erin's throat, and he scraped his thumbnail along the side of the milk carton.

Nick shifted uncomfortably. "Are you really okay? Because… well, you seem like you're scared."

When Erin remained quiet, Nick blushed and stood up. "I know it's not my business, but I wanted to let you know, if it's not your dad making you scared, if it's bullies in Copper Point or something like that… I'm not much help, but there's a guy you might want to look for."

Erin blinked. "A guy?"

"Owen Gagnon."

Owen Gagnon. "The person you were talking to in the cafeteria?"

Nick nodded. "Owen's always on the streets, getting in fights. He's pretty rough around the edges, and a lot of people are scared of him. He'll defend you if you're getting bullied. Especially… somebody like you."

Erin clutched the milk carton. "What do you mean… someone like me?"

Nick averted his gaze. "You know. Someone… frail. Quiet. Nervous. Who looks a little girlish and will read picture books about princesses."

Erin's reaction to the ogre king came back to him, and he panicked. "I'm not—I—"

Nick held up a hand. "It doesn't bother me, okay? I'm just telling you. If you're in town and you're ever in trouble, look for Owen. And good luck with your dad."

Still holding the milk and cake, Erin watched Nick leave. He didn't know what to make of anything Nick had said. He wasn't sure if they were friends yet or not.

"Erin."

His father's voice jolted him out of his woolgathering, and he stood, discreetly tossing the food onto his chair. "I'm coming." He smoothed out his suit and hurried across the lobby toward the doors leading to the patient rooms.

What Nick had said about Owen, the rough-around-the-edges bully-beater, rolled around Erin's head. Owen Gagnon. Erin liked the name. Would he really help Erin simply for asking? Because he was a hero who stood up to bullies?

Would you defend me against my father too?

"Stop falling behind."

Erin shuffled to catch up, pushing his daydreams aside. He shouldn't think about that anyway. He needed to focus on getting on his father's good side, not finding someone to stand between the two of them. Also, he rarely left the house in Copper Point when he was visiting except to go where his father told him—he wasn't going to run into this Owen person. And even if he did, even if he wanted it, no one could protect him from his father.

"William." Erin's father clapped a tall, broad-shouldered, and handsome man on the back. "You devil. I didn't know you were coming."

The tall man put a hand on John Jean's forearm and winked. "Can't leave our dear company chairman all alone now, can we?" He saw Erin, and his eyes widened. "This your boy, John Jean? My God, but he's grown."

Erin scurried forward, awkwardly introducing himself to the stranger, after which his father finished speaking for him. "Yes, he's thirteen now. Erin's at

Trinity Academy in Sault St. Marie and getting top grades. Can't keep his nose out of a book."

William rubbed his chin. "They have a decent music program? Maybe I could ship this one over there."

"I'm not going to Canada."

The sharp retort startled Erin, and it wasn't until William moved that Erin saw him, the boy from the hall, the one who had started to help Erin before he ran away. The one who looked like the ogre king.

He wasn't much of a king right now. More of a wiry, lanky boy sitting in the corner, legs drawn in close, dark head bent over a handheld video game with the sound off. Still, Erin's heart beat faster at the sight of him. He couldn't believe they'd met again, here.

As William regarded his sullen son, his perfect smile slipped, his expression going dark. "What did I tell you about putting that thing away, Owen?"

Owen. Erin straightened, staring at the boy with new eyes. Was this Owen Gagnon? The bully killer?

The one who would defend me? Was his ogre king and potential defender one and the same?

Owen unfolded from the floor, looking as liable to eat you as save you. Not a hero at all. Dangerous.

Beautiful.

Wheels clicked in Erin's head as he understood what his reaction to Owen, to the ogre king in the story, meant. *He's wild and menacing and handsome, and I want him to want me the way I want him.*

Their eyes met briefly, and for a moment Erin couldn't breathe.

This is who I want to rescue me from the castle.

"We'll see you later," John Jean said to William, ushering Erin inside.

Except they hadn't seen the Gagnons later. They weren't in the hallway when Erin and his father finished their visit with Christian West, and though Erin went out of his way to search for Owen in town, he didn't see him the rest of that break, or the next.

Erin was disappointed, but he didn't let himself dwell on Owen Gagnon, Nick, Emmanuella, or thoughts of ogre kings. Once he returned to school, he learned to dodge the bullies on his own. He told himself he didn't mind being alone, that it was fine staying in the shadows where no one could see him.

He was almost able to believe his own lies, until a full year later when, while home for a break, one evening Erin came downstairs to find something to eat and encountered the most beautiful violin playing he'd heard in his life.

Ever since Erin's mother left, the main part of the mansion was off-limits, rented out or made over for the museum tours, and Erin had no problem staying away when other people were in the house. Whatever was happening right now, however, was so incredible he had to peek. The sound of the violin lured Erin helplessly forward, compelling him to sneak into the shadows of the parlor.

He drew aside the curtain… and there was Owen Gagnon, bright and shining as he played violin for Copper Point's wealthiest citizens.

Oh, but he'd gotten so much more handsome since the last time Erin had seen him. He was especially beautiful as he played. There were other strings as well, but Owen sat in the center of the group, the youngest member there, the soloist. Playing with his eyes closed, he swayed in his seat, his messy black hair whipping as his bow flew across the strings.

Erin never wanted the music to end.

Diane, the caretaker of the museum section of the house, poked a feather duster in his face as she caught Erin gawking. He retreated, but to his surprise, Diane didn't scold him for being where he shouldn't.

"Good, isn't he?" She looked wistful. "He's always in trouble, unless he has that violin in his hand. They say he could get into any music college he wanted."

Erin could believe it. He lingered until the concert was over, wanting to reach out to Owen. But while watching Owen hobnob with guests during the after-party, Erin became too intimidated to step forward. This was a king, yes, not an ogre before him, and kings never spoke to Erin.

Losing his nerve, Erin ended up going to his room without so much as catching Owen's gaze.

It wasn't until he was home during the summer of his junior year and heard the scandal of Owen's abandoned music scholarship that Erin knew something had gone wrong. Erin only heard bits and pieces of rumors, as isolated as he was, but the result was there would be no music school for Owen, period. Apparently he was going to college to be a doctor.

Erin wished he had the courage to find Owen and ask what had happened.

He had no reason to do so. Owen was a boy he'd seen twice, whom he'd barely spoken to. Except Erin couldn't get him out of his mind. Part of him still harbored silly thoughts from what Nick had told him at

Mayo Clinic, how Owen was good at chasing away bullies.

Maybe… maybe this one time, Owen needed Erin to help *him* chase them away.

When Erin learned Owen liked to hang out at Bayview Park at night, he took walks there too in hopes of running into him. He found him, except he walked past him five or six times, too nervous to attempt an approach. It was on the seventh night when, without Erin having to orchestrate anything, they nearly ran straight into each other.

"Oh." Blushing, Erin stepped out of the way, but he tripped over his feet and almost crashed backward.

Owen caught him. "Careful. You okay?"

This is just another boy. He's definitely not the boy you've made him out to be in your head. God help him, but Owen had aged well. He was even more handsome, in Erin's opinion, when he was troubled. His hair had lightened over the years, and the tips had burned blond from the sun. He still had an aura of sadness about him, and it drew Erin in the most.

Owen smiled at him, sorrowful, shy… and Erin was lost.

Erin needed to say something. He stammered around a reply. "I—I'm fine. S-sorry."

"I keep seeing you around. Are you new here?"

Was this flirting? Erin tucked his unruly hair behind his ear, scolding his own thoughts. For heaven's sake, this wasn't flirting. It was polite inquiry. "I… no. But I'm not usually in town. In fact, I go back to school next week."

"Me too. I mean, I leave for college." Owen folded his arms over his chest and rubbed his toe awkwardly in an anthill along the sidewalk. "I never saw you in school. I'd have remembered you."

I'd have remembered you. That was flirting. No question about it. Erin couldn't breathe.

In this moment, dizzy from lack of air, lost in wonderment, finally noticed by someone after years of loneliness, Erin Andreas acknowledged he was in love. He admitted he had been, honestly, since Owen had stopped him in the Mayo Clinic hallway and asked him if he was all right.

Erin forced himself to inhale, fought through his awkwardness, trying so hard to speak the words in his heart. *It's because I never got to go to school here, but I wanted to. Perhaps we can exchange email addresses. Or phone numbers. Maybe the next time we're both in town we can walk along the bay together.*

"I—"

"Hey, Owen, what the hell are you doing?"

Erin startled, and Owen turned toward the road, where a car had slowed down. Heart sinking, Erin noted how Owen's expression shone like a sun as he waved to the person who had called out to him.

"Sorry, my friends are here to pick me up. What were you saying?"

Nothing. I wasn't saying anything at all. Erin forced a smile. "It's okay. I don't want to keep you."

Frowning in confusion, Owen hesitated. Then he nodded. "Well, I'll see you around."

Erin waved halfheartedly. As the door to the car opened and Owen climbed in, Erin heard, over pulsing house music, "What were you doing with Erin Andreas?"

Owen drew back in surprise and glanced Erin's way.

Blinking rapidly, Erin hurried in the opposite direction, and he never went to walk by the bay again, not that break or any other.

He wasn't a princess after all, and not even an ogre was going to come rescue him.

Tucking his love deep into his heart, Erin put everything away: his longing for a partner, his whimsical dreams of princes and ogre kings. He dismissed his desires for connection, forgot he'd ever had them. He became self-sufficient and competent, focusing on pleasing his father and furthering his career, his family's name. He told himself he'd never fall for anyone, and for a long time, he was able to uphold his vow.

Then one day Erin returned to Copper Point for good, and the ogre king was already there, waiting for him, guarding the castle Erin was meant to conquer. Owen the Ogre was just as boorish and terrible as the fairy tale had warned, destroying Erin's orderly life with a cheeky wink and grin.

Making Erin fall in love all over again.

CHAPTER ONE

WHEN OWEN Gagnon's friend Simon came by his house and asked him to be part of the hospital bachelor auction Valentine's Day fundraiser, he simply snorted and resumed arguing on an online political board.

Unfortunately Simon wasn't easily deterred. "Come on. We're short so many volunteers, and it's for a good cause. We *need* this cardiac unit."

Owen continued to type. "Then you and loverboy sign up."

"Hong-Wei and I can't. They want unmarried men."

"You and Jack aren't married yet." Owen waggled his eyebrows. "Get on the stage, and *I'll* bid for you."

Simon swatted him. "They don't want married *or* engaged men. Jared's already said yes. I need one more volunteer and I'll have met my quota for the committee."

"This is sexist as hell, only asking men. Why can't they do a gender-neutral auction?"

With a sigh, Simon sat beside him. "I know, but I've about sprained my back trying to yank the rudder on this ship so we stay away from insensitive areas. You wouldn't believe some of the racist, sexist, homophobic things these people wanted to do for a fundraiser."

"I would absolutely believe it." Owen ran a finger down Simon's nose. "Which is why I'm steering clear."

"*Please, Owen.* I didn't ask you to be part of the entertainment committee like I did Hong-Wei. I just need you to stand on stage for ten minutes while people bid on a date with you for charity."

Owen closed the laptop. "First of all, Jack loves performing, so it's no hardship. I assume your fiancé is playing with his damn quartet?"

"*You* could be in the quartet too. Ram keeps saying he'd make it a quintet if you came in as the other violin. He can play cello and double bass too." Simon bit his lip. "I don't know the whole story on why you don't want to play anymore, but it *has* been a long time—"

Owen held up a hand, unwilling to let Simon see how the simple mention of the violin made him queasy. "I'm not joining Ram's strings club, and I won't be auctioned off for a date. Don't start a sob story about the cardiac unit either. No one is going to bid on me if you put me on the block."

Simon's blush said this hiccup had occurred to him. "It's not only for dates. People can ask for favors or things. Plus I have a plan."

Oh hell. "Absolutely not. I'm not standing on stage so you and Jack can pity bid on me or so some nurse's aide can get revenge."

"*Owen—*"

Rising, Owen went for the door, grabbing his coat on the way. "I'm going to work."

"But we don't have surgery until ten today."

"I'm going to sit in the lounge and glare at people until your hubby needs me."

This was exactly what Owen ended up doing. The house he shared with Jared—which he used to share with Simon and Jared, before Simon went and fell and love—was only a mile from St. Ann's Medical Center, and three-quarters of a mile from the condo where Jack and Simon lived. It had snowed again the night before, bringing the on-the-ground total to a foot and a half. Damn lake effect snow anyway. The temperature was in the midtwenties, which for the end of January in northern Wisconsin was practically balmy. He considered walking, but since half the sidewalks were undoubtedly still not cleared, he drove.

He met Simon's fiancé, Dr. Wu—Hong-Wei to Simon, Jack to everyone else—in the parking lot. Jack was huddled into his hat and scarf and shivering. "Owen, how are you not freezing?"

"Because this isn't cold."

Jack, born in Taiwan and living in Houston until last year, grunted as he hustled to the door. He held it for Owen, which was nice of him.

It was also suspicious.

Owen cast a side glance at him. "You're here early for Monday. Since you didn't have call this weekend, you don't have any patients to see in rounds."

"Need to go over a few files before surgery."

Something fishy was definitely going on, and Owen was sure Jack was here because Simon had sent him to fulfill the mission he'd failed on. "I'm killing some time before surgery, so I guess I'll see you later."

Jack waved as they parted ways, Owen heading for the elevator, Jack the clinic entrance.

In the lounge, Owen surveyed the paper over coffee, reading the minutes of the most recent hospital board meeting, scanning an editorial that questioned where the funding had gone for the proposed cardiac program. Two of the visiting specialists were in the room with him, the speech therapist and the podiatrist. They were having a pleasant chat near the soda machine, but after a glare from Owen, they changed it to a hushed conversation. Two family medicine doctors entered, guffawing about something; then one of them shushed the other. "Gagnon's here."

Owen smiled behind his paper. He enjoyed his reputation as the resident pariah. It allowed him to live his life in peace.

The door opened again, and this time Jack entered. Owen groaned and slid deeper behind his paper.

Jack waved at the other doctors and returned their polite greetings before settling beside Owen. "Don't mind me." He tugged at the edge of the local news section. "Anything good?"

"The usual nonsense. Someone is up in arms about the cardiac unit, convinced the fundraiser won't bring in enough money because there's some kind of backroom conspiracy. Someone wrote a letter to the editor about the mine ruining the environment, and someone else wrote how we need more jobs. Then there's one complaining about whoever is kicking over his garbage cans."

Jack looked bemused. "I'll never get over small towns."

Owen pretended to read the paper a little longer, then folded it. "I'm tired of waiting. Ask me to take part in the auction so I can tell you no."

Jack stared back implacably. "I wasn't going to ask because I knew you'd say no."

"Seriously, you can stand down. Obviously I'm not going to participate, but I'll help Si find someone to fill his quota."

Jack shrugged. "Don't worry. I'm looking."

"You don't need to. I can do it, I said."

Jack glanced around the room at the other doctors, who regarded Owen with unease and Jack with respect bordering on awe. "I think it'll be better if you leave it to me."

Oh, now Owen was going to find Simon's last person *for sure*.

He left the lounge and wandered the halls, ignoring the way the nursing staff scuttled away from him. That was nothing new. He scanned every man he encountered, doctors and nurses both, for potential bachelor auction candidates. He was immediately hampered, though, by several factors. Jack was right, his pariah status did him no favors. Also, he had no idea who was already roped into the thing or who was working the night of the fundraiser and therefore was out of commission.

The thought of Jack's knowing smirk sent Owen grumbling to the third floor and the administration offices, where he tried the most obvious and therefore clearly stupid get, the hospital CEO, Nick Beckert.

Beckert was in his office, and he happily waved Owen inside. He grinned sadly when Owen asked if he could pin him down for the auction. "I was the first one they put on the list, I hate to tell you. But why are *you* asking me? I didn't think you were on the recruiting committee."

"I'm not. I was recruited, and I'm trying to find a replacement."

Nick lifted his eyebrows and whistled low. "Good luck. From what I hear, everyone else has either been called up, is on shift, or is ineligible."

Good grief. "How is that possible? Also, why is this limited only to men, by the way?"

"Because the planning committee is short on imagination and big on words like *traditional values*. If I'd known you were this invested, I would've put you on the team."

Owen held up his hands. "I'm fine helping find the last victim, thanks. There's got to be at least one single male who isn't on shift. I need to know who's already signed up and who isn't eligible."

"You'll need to talk to Erin."

"Speaking of Andreas, how come he's not on the list?"

"Ineligible."

"On what grounds?" Owen sat up straighter. "His father didn't finally coerce him into an engagement, did he?"

"No. But he's recused as a committee member."

Owen eased back, annoyed at his heart for kicking up a notch at the idea of Erin engaged. "That's ridiculous. Why can't committee members be on the auction block?"

"I did tell you this was an interesting group. The only rudders we had were Erin and Simon, and Erin wasn't supposed to participate, simply ensure the evening ran smoothly." Nick grimaced. "Between you and me, it's just as well he couldn't be asked to be auctioned off. His father would have arranged for something uncomfortable."

True. After all they owed Erin for, Owen would have ended up bidding on him to get him out of his father's clutches, which would've made Erin furious.

Actually, now Owen was mad he couldn't do this.

Owen sighed. "This whole Valentine's Day fund-raiser is ridiculous. Why aren't they doing a tired old dinner on a random weekend in March the way they usually do?"

"Because *someone* stood up in front of the board and declared we were going to do things differently. And now we're doing things differently. All of the things. Incredibly differently." Nick pushed his glass-es higher on his nose. "Now if you'll excuse me, I have a mountain of work to finish before the board meeting."

Owen wanted to sit and argue with Nick longer, but he knew he'd get nowhere. The hospital CEO was cautious, though Owen understood why. He'd been brought on after the former president embezzled mon-ey from the hospital, but his predecessor had been chummy with the present hospital board, so they re-sented Nick at every turn. Additionally, his family had moved to Copper Point when he was young, and his father had joined and left the board in a scandal in the nineties. Though Nick had done everything he could to prove himself, plenty of people in town still saw him as a member of an enemy camp. Nick couldn't help Owen. He had enough work to do helping himself.

Owen could feel the writing on the wall about this stupid fundraiser. He was annoyed, and he wanted to argue. He wanted to snarl at someone without having to worry about being polite. If he was called a demon or a dragon or a devil or a monster or an ogre, he wanted it to be done with a glint in his accuser's eye, not a tinge of fear.

In short, he wanted to spar, and he knew exactly who he needed to see.

Simply pushing his way into Erin Andreas's office, taking in the ridiculously neat room, gave Owen a satisfying rush of annoyance. Nick's office was tidy, but it had a reasonable amount of lived-in clutter: overflowing inboxes, forgotten coffee cups, unopened mail in piles on filing cabinets, yesterday's blazer folded in a casual heap over the arm of a chair. Not Erin's workspace. It looked as if someone had gone across the bookshelves with a ruler and made sure the books and binders lined up, not a single one of them sticking out farther than the other, the decorative knickknacks on top drab and soulless, yanked from some design catalog—but perfectly arranged. There were three plants in the window spaced evenly across, neatly trimmed, not a dead leaf among them. The desk was clear of everything but Erin's ubiquitous laptop and a wire pencil holder—containing only crisply sharpened pencils—a pencil sharpener devoid of shavings, a desk lamp tilted at a ninety-degree angle, and of course his inbox.

The papers and files inside of it were stacked in such incredible alignment they looked like a single unit.

In the middle of the scene was the man himself, Erin Andreas, human resources director. He'd arrived almost two years ago to work at St. Ann's, but in the mindset of Copper Point, he was still *new*, especially since the previous HR director had held the position for twenty-five years. Erin wore the same prim heather gray suit he always did, with the same pristine white shirt. Only the tie changed, and not much. Today it was dark gray, almost black. It didn't suit him at all, though it did match the desk. The suit choked Erin's petite frame and made most of his body blend into his desk chair, giving the illusion he'd been strapped into it by invisible threads.

The only thing about the man that didn't fit the corporate image was his hair, which was curly and too long, resting in unruly ringlets around his ears and brushing his collar. The ringlets shone in the fluorescent overhead lighting, and as always Owen had the juvenile urge to tug at one and make it bounce. He managed to refrain, but his gaze trailed them, and he knew a whisper of delight as one caught the edge of Erin's collar and another *boinged* against his eyebrows as he lifted his head.

A kick hit Owen in his belly as his opponent's eyes ignited with fire. *Finally.*

Erin pursed his lips. "Is there any hope you will ever learn to knock?"

Owen shut the door and plunked with deliberate heaviness in the chair opposite Erin's desk, knocking it out of its careful alignment. He purred inwardly as Erin's annoyance ticked up a notch.

He kept his pleasure from his face as he laced his fingers over his chest. "What's going to change if I rap my knuckles on the door?"

"I'll tell you to go away because I'm busy."

"Precisely why I don't knock."

The curls *boinged* again as Erin leaned over the top of his computer. "Did you have some purpose in coming here today, or is this playground-bully routine your way of telling me our resident anesthesiologist needs more work assigned to him?"

Oh yes, this was precisely what Owen had come for. Narrowing his eyes, he gave Erin a thin, menacing smile. "I have a bone to pick with you about this ridiculous auction."

Flinching, Erin lowered his eyes to his computer screen. "I don't have any authority over that. I'm only on the committee."

Owen hesitated, thrown off his game. Okay, what in the hell was that about? This was decidedly not in the script. Thinking he must have stepped in something without realizing it, Owen softened. "I get the concert, the overpriced dinner, the usual crap. Where in God's name did this auction come from, though, and why is every single male roped into it whether they want to be part of it or not? I'm the last person you want up there. I'm either going to be laughed into the wings or bought up by a cabal of nurses with a grudge."

This was Erin's cue to tell Owen to stay out of committee business unless he wanted to sign up and do the work, to remind him everyone in the hospital had to volunteer, to point out he could do this duty since he hadn't signed up to do anything else. Any of those responses would have been fine and given Owen an excuse to snarl in response again. He was *ready* for them.

Instead Erin… paled. When he spoke, he didn't sound irritated half as much as he sounded nervous. "I don't have time to entertain your pointless questions right now, Dr. Gagnon. If you don't mind, I want to finish preparing for the meeting. I'm certain you have somewhere else to be."

Owen was so stunned he had no idea how to respond, could only gape at Erin, who in turn stared at his laptop screen, face flushed.

No acrid rejoinder. No demands Owen leave his office with a heat that said, in fact, he wanted him to stay and keep shouting until they nearly burned down the hospital. Nothing at all.

This was… weird.

There was no denying Erin had been off his game for some time, a little more frazzled around the edges, slightly more inward than normal. It was easy to pinpoint ground zero for his transformation: *he'd* been the person who'd stood up in front of the hospital board, after all. Except he hadn't stood. He'd sat defiantly in the middle of the hospital cafeteria, waiting for his father—the hospital board president—to gut him after Erin sent a particularly nuclear staff memo.

This reaction was different, though. Was it about the committee? Owen frowned at Erin, disquiet settling in his gut. Everyone in the hospital rejoiced at the freedom Erin's reversal of the policy had granted them. How much of the cost had come on Erin's shoulders?

Had everyone ignored that and left him to face dragons alone? Had Owen done that too?

Well, now he felt like an ass.

Erin glanced up from the computer, saw Owen regarding him with concern, and immediately swapped his hollow expression with an icy glare. "Why are you looking at me like that?"

The disdain was such a relief Owen had to suppress a fist pump. He wanted to ask Erin what was wrong, but he was smart enough not to make a direct line of questioning. "What's your meeting about?"

Internally he winced—well, that wasn't a direct question, but it was a ridiculous angle to take. The delivery was too bald, almost politely inquisitive. Now Erin regarded him warily, as if he were a snake about to strike. "My office is not a social lounge. If you don't have business with me, please leave."

Nice save. Owen leaned forward so his elbows rested on his knees. *Think of another topic. Another topic, anything, anything....* "This Valentine's Day auction is a mess. There's got to be time to kill it."

What the fuck was with him? Totally the wrong tone, completely the wrong approach, and the *dead worst* thing to bring up.

Maybe it would be okay. Maybe he'd pissed Erin off with this out-and-out begging. Maybe he'd fix Owen with an icy smile and tell him off as he'd never been told off. Then everything would be normal again.

Erin shrank into his chair, color draining from his face as he lowered his gaze, his voice going quiet. "The auction is nonnegotiable."

An ill wind blew over Owen's neck, and he forgot all about fighting, all about delicately dancing around the topic. "Erin, what is going on with you?"

Erin iced over and aimed a long, slender finger at the door. "Leave."

"Why are you closing up like this every time I bring up the auction? Why are you barely fighting with me?"

Why do you look so... lost?

Erin said nothing, and Owen angsted in a conflicted private storm, at a loss over what to do. He'd sparred with Erin since he'd come to St. Ann's, and they'd never been anything close to friends, but it wasn't as if he didn't care about the man as a human being. Particularly since that stunt with the memo, Owen had begun to rethink his stance on Erin Andreas entirely, because clearly this man whom he'd thought of as aligned with the old guard on the board had been an ally all along. For some time now, Owen had wanted to know what other secrets this man was hiding, but it was difficult when their entire relationship was built on arguments.

Looking at Erin now, feeling the fractures in him, Owen had never been more motivated to craft a bridge toward a new understanding between them. What could be the problem? Maybe if he nudged him in the right direction, Erin would loosen up and tell him what was going on.

It wasn't hard to guess what the problem likely was, the more he thought about it.

"Your father." Owen hesitated, trying to figure out what to add, then decided that was enough to get started.

Erin didn't loosen up. "At whatever point you'd like to leave, please do so."

Owen was so frustrated. "I just want to help. Let me help. You don't want help?"

He didn't know if it was an improvement or not, but Erin wasn't frozen or hollow-looking anymore. He was coldly furious. "Why would I want *your* help?"

Yikes. Also, ouch. Owen rubbed his cheek. "Harsh."

Erin gathered a pile of papers and shuffled them, banging the bottoms with excessive force against the desk. "I'm perfectly fine."

"That is the biggest line of bull I've ever heard. You're completely wooden, you can barely maintain eye contact with me, and you get weird every time I bring up the auction. Usually you can argue with me until we're both blue in the face, but you can't keep up more than a few lines of banter today. Something is wrong." He pursed his lips. "It's got to be your father."

For a moment Owen had him. Erin had softened—and looked at him—when Owen pointed out he couldn't maintain eye contact, and just before the end, he seemed almost ready to, if not confess the problem, at least admit there was one.

The second Owen said *your father*, though, he lost him. His cool, dead mask sliding back into place, Erin averted his gaze again. "Leave, or I'll tell the entertainment committee you've volunteered for a violin solo."

Owen drew back as if he'd been slapped.

Rising, he pushed Erin's desk light into the most obscene angle possible and exited the office without a word. If he was going to play that kind of dirty pool, he could damn well save himself.

ERIN DIDN'T look away from his computer screen, acutely aware of the place Owen had occupied, of his scent lingering in the room. Owen's shocked expression echoed too, burned on Erin's mind.

He hadn't meant to make him *that* upset.

After fixing the lamp, Erin resumed his mindless moving of the cursor across the screen, not reading the report open in front of him. Goddamn Owen, finding the one topic Erin didn't want to talk about. He didn't know why he should be surprised, as this was the man's specialty.

Something was off about him, though. What was all that about, saying he wanted to help? Erin's cheeks pinked in memory. Had that been some advanced level of teasing?

Had it been flirting?

Closing his eyes, Erin shook the nonsense out of his head. *Don't be ridiculous.*

He didn't know what to make of Owen so doggedly bringing up the auction and Erin's father.

A knock on the door startled him. The door was open, but Nicolas Beckert always knocked. "Hey." Nick's expression changed to concern. "You okay? I saw Gagnon go by looking ready to murder someone."

Erin smoothed his fingertips across his desktop. "It's fine. I'm fine."

What a lie.

Nick came into Erin's office fully, though he didn't sit, only lingered at the doorway. "Everything is set for the auction?"

Good God, everyone wanted to talk about it. Well, Erin didn't mind half as much with Nick. "More or less. We have most of the bachelors lined up, as well as the pre-event entertainment, and the decorating committee is doing well. The food and venue came in under budget. Tickets are selling."

"And how is your dad feeling about it?"

Of course Nick went right for the jugular. "He hates it and tells me every day how it's going to be a disaster because we didn't do the usual event."

"Do you point out we revamped it so it was more accessible to the whole town, not only the elites, and that this vision fits in line with the rest of the hospital's goals?"

Erin stared at his hands. "I… tried."

Pursing his lips, Nick folded his arms over his chest.

Erin's gaze flitted past Nick, landing on the ceiling. "He has concerns that the higher-end donors won't make contributions since it's a lower-class event."

"Which is why there's a private reception at the Andreas mansion first, and we have a VIP section reserved for them here."

"Yes, but he doesn't think this will be enough." Erin held up his hands as Nick glowered again. "I know. I don't think he's being fair. I want to try our way. I'm nervous, though. Because if we don't bring in enough money and we can't pay for the cardiac unit, I don't know how I'll live with this."

For several seconds Nick didn't say anything. The sunlight from the window caught the hospital CEO just right as he leaned against the wall, making his dark skin gleam and highlighting his broad shoulders.

Nick had always been handsome, kind, and competent. He'd been standoffish when they were young, but they'd shared the trenches in college and in the years that followed as they fought their respective battles. Now they worked well together and respected each other. They had trust. Which was vital these days, with everything they were going through.

If only it would be enough to get them through this without losing their jobs.

"I'll have Wendy make sure we put as much effort as possible in promotion, reaching beyond Copper Point to the neighboring communities we serve," Nick said at last. "And if somehow we don't meet our goal, we'll make up the difference with smaller events after. Because I think it's worth doing this type of outreach for more than the money. The auction isn't my favorite type of event, but I'm willing to play along and rake leaves as community service to promote the hospital. I want as many of our doctors, nurses, and other staff members doing the same. If I had my way, everyone would participate, but the sad truth is there are serious safety issues with women getting auctioned. Men potentially as well, but this feels like the more manageable route. In the future, perhaps we can find a fundraiser that meets all our needs."

Erin didn't know how to respond to such a speech, so he simply nodded. He withdrew a hand from the desktop, though, and as it rested on his thigh, it curled into a frustrated, helpless fist.

Pushing off the wall, Nick adjusted his suit. "The board meeting will start soon. I'll go in early and do the glad-handing. You seem like you could use a few minutes. Want me to bring you a cup of coffee?"

Erin held up a hand. "Thank you, I'm fine. I'll be along as soon as I finish this."

Nick nodded in acknowledgment. "As you wish. Thanks for all your help."

Alone, Erin replayed what Nick had said about the fundraiser and why they'd done it the way they had, all things Erin completely agreed with. The trouble was that his father didn't, and he continued to make his displeasure plain, in addition to his expectation that Erin would fix it.

I just want to help. Let me help. You don't want help?

Every standoff with Owen felt like a siege, and if Erin lost the battle, the torch Erin had carried since adolescence would be exposed. This particular exchange felt dangerous in new, more terrifying ways. Normally Owen simply insulted Erin and exchanged barbs. He'd never offered to assist.

What if Erin had said, *Yes, I'd love your help*? What would Owen have done?

Stop it. Pursing his lips, Erin dragged himself out of his ridiculous thoughts and back to the meeting notes on the screen in front of him. He only had a few things to finish and he could join Nick in the boardroom—

"I see from the flyers posted all over the hospital you haven't done as I told you and changed the arrangement of the event."

The cool, crisp tones of John Jean Andreas's voice cut across the room and made Erin startle in his seat. "Father." He rose, closing the laptop, trying to adopt a proper posture. "I didn't realize you were stopping by before the meeting. It's good to see you."

His father closed the door as he entered the room, glancing around with his lips pressed thin in his ever-present expression of disappointment. He ran his fingers along the edge of a bookshelf, rubbed them together as if to dispel dust, then adjusted a figurine. "I thought I'd stressed to you the importance of St. Ann's image at these functions, but I clearly didn't put enough effort into my explanation."

There had been so much effort in it that Erin hadn't been able to eat dinner last night or breakfast this morning. He willed his hair to catch the beads of sweat forming on his brow. "I'm sorry, Father. As I said, it isn't entirely up to me what happens at—"

"And as I said to *you*, as someone who will one day lead St. Ann's into its future, it's *your* job to make sure every single breath taken at this hospital follows the vision of the Andreas family. We may not own the buildings any longer, but this is still our legacy. It's our duty to protect it."

What was he supposed to say to his father when he was like this? "Nick runs the hospital, and I'm happy to serve under—"

"The only reason that man is CEO and not you is because you refused to take the job. It's your duty to take responsibility and groom yourself so you can take his place when the time comes."

Erin nearly fell out of his chair. "Take Nick's place? Dad, what are you—?"

"These are desperate times." Erin's father loomed over his desk, glowering, his face in shadow, eyes wide with a determination that made Erin's insides squirm. "Every member of the board is reaching an age of retirement, and we're all looking to groom our replacements. They're considering their sons, their younger business partners. I can't have you dragging your feet as my heir."

No, the room wasn't spinning, but Erin had to grip the edge of the desk to maintain his equilibrium nonetheless. Erin was supposed to take over his father's position on the board as his heir?

A faint flicker of something like hope bloomed inside Erin. *He sees me as someone worthy to succeed him?*

His father huffed and stared out the window. "It's enough of a shame that you helped out that woman in our way. I don't know what other wild ideas you have cooked up, but I'm here to tell you that you'll toe the line from now on."

Ah, so no, he didn't see Erin as worthy at all, simply his only option. That was more familiar. And by *that woman*, his father meant Rebecca. Now everything made sense.

Rebecca Lambert-Diaz had been elected to the board last fall in the shakeout after Erin's memo, and according to Erin's father had been causing nothing but trouble. Erin liked Rebecca, however. He'd known of her since he'd joined the staff two years ago, seeing her at official functions as the wife of St. Ann's resident OB/GYN, Dr. Kathryn Lambert-Diaz, but now he was getting to know her on her own merits, and she had plenty. She brought new life and vibrancy to a board whose members had stood for ridiculously long numbers of terms. She was also the single woman of color on an otherwise all-white and all-male board in a town whose diversity rate was higher than its neighbors because of Bayview University. Rebecca asked good questions, pushed buttons Erin had worried were too rusty and unused to work, and best of all, frequently sided with Nick in his efforts for change. She managed to bully the majority into letting him try things out, something that had never happened before. She had the good-old-boys club, if not running scared, adequately ruffled.

The fact that Erin was too stupefied to reply didn't seem to bother his father, who simply continued with his monologue. "It's probably too late for you to get the event altered at this point—I count this as a failure of yours, so you understand—but there's plenty of battle ahead. If by some miracle you manage to meet the target funds for the cardiac unit, I'll walk you step by step through how I want future doctors recruited." His lip curled. "I don't want any more ideas about diversity. We have more than adequately filled those slots."

Horrified, Erin opened his mouth to object, but all he could do was squeak.

His father, paying no attention to him, gestured vaguely into the air, looking pleased with himself. "The cardiologist will be a man. A white Midwestern man from a good college. I suppose he could be from the South, so long as he isn't brash. The East Coast could be all right, but none of those liberals. We need to reestablish our core Copper Point values. What's more important than the *heart* of the hospital?"

Erin pressed his hands to his cheeks. This wasn't happening. This seriously wasn't happening. Where did he start with his objections? The white supremacy? The sexism? The complete lack of understanding of how desperate they were when they courted doctors to come to a remote area and often relied on recommendations from physicians already present, which as he'd pointed out with his classic racism was a uniquely diverse group?

Who was he kidding? How was he going to get his father to listen to anything he said when he'd never managed to do anything more than meekly obey him his entire life?

Except for the time I posted that memo.

John Jean continued his lecture. "This will all work out. In the meeting today, I expect you to make it clear you back us if that woman steps out of line again. Oh, and I'm going to talk to Christian West and see if his youngest daughter would be open to dating you. She's shyer than you are, so I think you could handle her. I'll have Christian set up a meeting at the country club."

This, finally, jolted Erin out of his frozen state. "I—I can't—I don't want to date—"

"I'd better head down and see what trouble the boys are stirring up." John Jean adjusted the lapels of his suit and nodded at his son. "Don't be late to the meeting. It doesn't give a good impression."

His father exited his office. Erin stared at the closed door for several seconds, then lowered his forehead to the top of his closed computer.

Unfortunately, between Owen, Nick, and his father's interruptions, Erin didn't have time to dwell on anything. Righting himself and opening his laptop, he hastily finished the meeting notes, fired them off to Nick's assistant, then organized the files he needed to take to the meeting and headed down the hall.

He didn't make it four feet before a bright voice called out his name. "Erin!"

Turning around, he saw a young woman with long dark hair, a bright expression, and a smile hiding knives. As was her habit, she wore a deep-red coat that matched her lipstick. Rebecca always wore red to the courtroom, Erin had heard, fueling the rumor the color represented the blood of her enemies. She wore the color to every board meeting as well.

Rebecca waved a breezy hello at the elderly white men casting cold stares at her as they shuffled into the meeting room, then gave Erin a much warmer greeting. "It's so good to see you. How have you been?"

"I'm well, thank you." Resisting the urge to glance around and make sure his father wasn't watching, Erin inclined his head politely. "How is your wife?"

"Getting ready to admit a soon-to-be mother as we speak, so she's happy as a clam." Rebecca swept her hair away from her face as she shrugged out of her coat and draped it over her arm. "I wish I'd been able to get in with enough time to grab a latte from the gift shop. I want to catch up with you after and treat you as thanks for helping Kathryn get coverage last weekend. Plus I'm going to drown you in photos from our getaway. We had so much fun. It's been ages since I saw her smiling like that, and it's all because of you."

Erin blushed. "It's nothing, really. Just doing my job."

Rebecca wagged a finger at him. "But nobody does their job as diligently as you. Kathryn has always said so, and now I've seen you in action, so I can attest to this truth myself." She winked. "You know, to hell with it. They can't start the meeting without us. Let's go get some coffee now."

Before he could so much as draw breath for protest, she dragged him off, binder, laptop, and all, hauling him away at a breathless clip. She bypassed the elevators entirely and led him to the stairwell.

"This way is faster," she said as she pushed through the door.

As soon as they were alone on the stairway, she let go, stopping to face Erin. Her demeanor relaxed significantly, and she favored him with a patient, kind smile. "So, I am going to get you a coffee, but mostly I wanted to pull you aside and talk with you."

Erin closed his hand over a cold air return pipe. If anyone else tried to talk to him today, he was jumping into the bay.

Sensing his mental overload, Rebecca held up her hands and gentled her tone even further. "I'm not trying to put you on the spot or pressure you. In fact, it's exactly the opposite. You're in a real box with your father and the rest of the board, but I know in your heart you side with Nick and want to move his agenda. All I wanted to do, in addition to sincerely thanking you for helping Kathryn, was tell you not to worry. I understand having to play the middle to get to the place you want to go in the long run. I'm not going to take any offense. That's all, really. Just wanted to make sure we were clear."

Play the middle. Erin's cheeks burned. How was he supposed to tell her she'd seriously overestimated his political maneuvering abilities? *Sorry, I'm not playing a deep game, I'm actually this inept?*

She winked. “Anyway, I’m going to run down and get you a coffee now. I’ll probably be late, which will give them something to bitch about. I do like making people happy. What’s your poison today, Erin?”

Vodka, neat. He pressed his hand to the side of his aching head. “Maybe an herbal tea.”

“One herbal tea coming up.” She patted his arm. “Get your game face on and go in there. Don’t let the patriarchy get you down.”

He waited until she disappeared, then shut his eyes, clutched his computer and binder to his chest, and slid down the wall.

He didn’t want to go to this meeting. He didn’t really want to go home either, because there was probably something going on in the front of the house. He didn’t know where he’d like to escape to, but he craved it desperately. Somewhere safe and warm and free of people who thought they knew who he was, who insisted he do or be things he wasn’t, that he couldn’t embody. Rebecca thought he was someone he wasn’t, his father demanded he be his surrogate, and Nick failed to understand Erin couldn’t be as amazing as he was.

Owen didn’t ask me to be anything I wasn’t. In fact, he asked if I wanted help.

Erin shut his eyes tight and buried his face in his things. He had to stop thinking about that. Owen hadn’t meant that the way Erin kept insisting on taking it. Owen had come to complain, to fight with him as he always had.

How could Owen help? It wasn’t like he could storm the boardroom and take on Erin’s father.

At the same time, it had been Owen who'd helped Erin indirectly before, when he'd written the memo. Everyone assumed he'd done it to keep St. Ann's from losing its surgeon. That had been a convenient smokescreen, yes, but the truth was he'd rescinded the policy forcing the surgeon and his fiancé to leave because their friend the anesthesiologist had threatened to follow.

What, you plan to tell him that? Confess your bravest moment hung on such desperate foolishness? On unrequited love? A childhood crush a grown man can't shake? Oh yes, tell him, so he can laugh in your face.

"What are you doing here?"

Startled, Erin lifted his head. There was Owen, as if he'd been summoned.

When Erin gaped at him, Owen put his hands on his hips and glowered. "I thought you had a board meeting. Did they move it to the stairwell? What the hell is going on?"

Erin couldn't do this anymore. He couldn't argue. Couldn't speak. Could only stare up at Owen, even as part of him banged on the inside of his head, a prisoner desperate to escape.

Please—please, help me!

Crouching, Owen held the back of his hand to Erin's forehead, then pressed two fingers to his neck to find a pulse. "No fever. Heart rate slightly elevated, but nothing significant. Skin somewhat pale, and you seem like a plant that could use a little more watering." He lifted a bag from the floor beside him and shook it in front of Erin's face. "It's got a sandwich, an apple, and a large bottle of water in it. I know you have to get to your meeting, but I'm going to text Nick, and if he doesn't give me a report of you eating at least half of this and drinking this *entire* bottle of water, I'm going to spoon-feed you personally after my afternoon surgery. Is this clear?"

Eyes wide, Erin nodded.

With a grunt of satisfaction, Owen gripped Erin's elbow and hoisted him upright, though somehow during this process he also stole the binder and computer from Erin's arms. He continued to talk as he led Erin out of the stairwell and down the hallway. He also didn't let go of Erin.

"I'll join your auction and won't complain about it, so if that's what you're worried about, stop. Don't even joke about me playing an instrument, but if there's anything else you need me to do, sign me up and I'll help. You only have to ask me. Or tell me what I'm doing. This one time, I won't put up a fuss. In return, though, you're going to eat and drink water regularly, and sleep, and if you won't talk to me about your problems, find someone you can. All right?"

They were at the door to the meeting room now, and Owen passed Erin his binder and computer, but he loomed over him, all but backing Erin against the wall. *This is like the high school romantic drama I never got to have, down to the cute boy carrying my books for me.*

Just when Erin was about to chide himself for his thoughts, Owen reached up and tugged lightly on a curl beside Erin's face.

Erin forgot to breathe.

Owen righted himself, rubbing the back of his neck. "You—had something in your hair. Anyway.

Remember what I said about eating. And about being stressed. And sleeping. And asking me for help," he called over his shoulder as he hurried down the hall.

Still in a daze, Erin entered the meeting room. He could see his father trying to get his attention, but he ignored this, quietly sliding into his place beside Nick. He opened the bag Owen had given him and saw his favorite deli sandwich inside, along with his favorite type of apple. There was yogurt too, also the brand he preferred, but it had a sticky note on it that read *dessert, only eat if you finish everything else.*

Erin couldn't help a smile.

Beside him, Nick laughed. "About time. I think that's the first smile I've seen on you all day. Maybe all week."

Erin ran his finger over Owen's note, glad he wasn't having his pulse read now because it had to be racing as the decision, as wicked and wild as the memo impulse, formed in his mind.

If there's anything else you need me to do, sign me up and I'll help. You only have to ask me.

No, Owen wouldn't have to lift a finger. Erin would take it from here.

Because he was going to bid on Owen Gagnon's bachelor auction. And he was going to win.

CHAPTER TWO

As Owen feared, the bachelor auction was ten thousand times more complicated than he'd anticipated it would be. It began when he asked what he'd be expected to do for whoever won his bid, and wanted to know what it meant that his dates could buy him for "experiences."

"It means you'll do whatever you're asked, within reason," Simon explained. "If a little old lady buys you and wants you to rake her leaves, you rake her leaves. If she wants you to shingle her roof… well, we actually have a clause naming it out of bounds. You might clean out some gutters, though."

When Owen pointed out there was a world of difference between raking leaves and clearing gutters, Simon dropped the next bomb. Apparently the level of service each bachelor was expected to perform was directly proportional to the amount of money bid on him. Which meant someone could bid on him for retribution and have him at their beck and call.

"Don't worry, we plan to be the ones to bid on you," Jack assured him with a wicked smile. "You'll only be beholden to *us*."

Owen grumbled at him and stalked away.

For all Jack's teasing, he trusted the man. Jack viewed this as Owen helping Simon, and Owen had a feeling his stepping up to help Jack's fiancé wouldn't go unrewarded. If someone did try to bid on Owen for payback, Jack would come to his rescue. Everything about this fundraiser had Owen itchy, however.

Especially when the fundraiser snared Owen in the worst possible way.

The Copper Point Quartet was slated to play at the auction, and its presence was a huge draw. It was a community-based gathering of amateur musicians headed by Ram Rao, the director of music at Bayview University. He was the choir director, not the orchestra conductor, but he'd always dreamed of having a town quartet, and last year he realized his dream when Jack filled in his missing violin slot. Ram dogged Owen for years to join them until Jack arrived, and though Jack teased him about beating him out of his spot, secretly Owen was relieved. The competition to see who was the better player would never happen, not unless it was Owen's punishment in hell.

Little did he know how near those fiery gates lurked.

Four hours before the fundraiser, Ram came down with the flu. Full-blown, aches and pains, fever, coughing-until-he-vomited, so-dehydrated-he-had-to-be-admitted-to-the-hospital flu. As soon as Owen got home from work—early, in deference to the auction—the three remaining members of the quartet, plus Simon, showed up to beg Owen to take Ram's part.

Owen all but slammed the door in their faces. "Absolutely not. Put on a recording or something. Put Jack on the piano. Or have a trio. A duet. Literally anything else."

He wasn't ready for Simon to get on his knees. "*Please*, Owen. I'll get you out of the auction if you do this."

Owen pursed his lips. "How, exactly? I'm listed on the program, and you've done nothing but tell me how you had no one else to fill my spot. Anyway, I'd let myself be auctioned twice to get *out* of playing. I've told you before I don't play any longer. I haven't touched a violin in years."

"But you won all those competitions in high school, and you had that scholarship." Simon clasped his hands together. "*Please*, only for this one hour. We're desperate."

"The songs aren't difficult, and it's second violin. I can practice with you if you want," Jack said.

Amanda and Tim, the viola and cello of the group respectively, nodded in agreement. "We'll all practice with you." Amanda lifted a cloth instrument case. "Ram sent over his violin, and I have the music too."

Owen wanted to wrench the music out of her hands and toss it into the air. "You seriously couldn't find anyone else who could play? Isn't there a college full of musicians in town?"

Tim shook his head. "The Bayview University Orchestra is away at a festival this week. Possibly there's someone in the student body who knows how to play who isn't involved, but I don't know who they are, and I don't know how to find them this fast. The high school doesn't have an orchestra, as you well know."

Owen stared at them, his friends and the friends of his friends, begging and pleading, and he was angry, more so because he couldn't be upset, not without them wanting to know why being asked to play bothered him so much. Which was why he didn't shout at them or argue any longer. He went to his room, closing the door.

He wasn't surprised when it opened not long after, nor was it a shock to see it was Jared who had come for him. Jared didn't have to be told why he was so upset. He didn't know the whole story, but he understood part of the reason Owen didn't want to so much as touch a violin, would never insist enough time had passed and he should move on.

Right now, though, Owen didn't want to look at Jared either. He remained seated on his bed, facing the window.

Jared stayed at the entrance to the room, waiting patiently.

Owen's hand closed in a loose fist. "I don't want to talk about it. And I'm not playing in the quartet. End of discussion."

"The thing is, they're in a bind." Running a hand through his hair, Jared sighed. "I'm going to need something to tell them. I don't know what you want me to say or not say. You know clamming up won't work."

Owen shut his eyes, the thick, old feelings welling up inside him. No, it wouldn't work. Except the problem was, he didn't want to tell Jared, or Simon, or Jack, or anyone anything. But Jared was right. Unless he caved and played, he'd have to explain.

Which hell was worse?

He stared at the ceiling. "Bring me the violin. If I can keep myself together enough to get through a piece, I'll do it. But the price is those guys have to buy my auction no matter what it costs, and I don't have to do a damn thing in return. They're renting me in advance. And nobody asks me why I don't like playing. Today, or ever."

"I'll pass the word along."

They sent Simon in with the violin. Contrite, abashed, he apologized over and over and thanked Owen when he deposited the instrument on the bed and then left the room. Owen ignored the thing for several minutes, pushing away the rage and other helpless, hopeless feelings the day had already managed to inspire.

It's just a stupid instrument. You'll probably suck. It's been about seventeen years.

Except it didn't seem like seventeen years as he unzipped the case and removed the wooden body from the protective cavity. It felt….

He shuddered. It felt like going home and finding a knife waiting for him.

Shoving down the bile and the pain, he attempted to play.

Oh, he wasn't what he used to be, no, but he wasn't bad. The bow was comfortable and familiar in his hand. When he moved it over the strings, the sound didn't jar him or set his teeth on edge, only leaked something slow and cold into the edge of his soul.

Yes, he could substitute in their damned quartet. All it would require was to take on a few more scars.

They were joyous when he told them but confused when he declined to practice with them outside of a quick run-through at the community center before they went on stage. "You get what you get" was all he would tell them, and when Jared and Simon tried to console him, he snarled, got into his car, and drove off. He ended up walking along the bay, shutting his eyes as he followed the path along the greenway, letting the wind from the water whip around his ears.

Jared was pacing the living room when he returned. Owen had nine missed calls from Simon and Jack, and Tim had apparently stopped by the house twice.

"Hurry up and get dressed." Jared, already wearing his tuxedo, gestured at Owen's room. "Or are you punishing everyone for making you do this by arriving late as well?"

Owen flipped his housemate off as he climbed the stairs. "You're giving me a ride. I'll behave while I play and during the auction, but I intend to start drinking the second they slap a sold sign on my ass."

"Then hustle, because I'm leaving in five minutes."

They were late, of course, but everything was fine. The auction rehearsal was simple. It took Owen and Jared thirty seconds to get the gist of where to stand and how to comport themselves while they were in the spotlight and how they should thank their bidder. The fact that Andreas seemed annoyed by their delayed entrance was a bonus. He was his old self again, no longer haggard and wan. Whether it was the sack lunch and threats that did the trick, or something else entirely, Owen was just glad to see Erin not looking like he was about to walk the plank.

Also, Owen was pretty sure Andreas did a double take when he saw Owen in his tux. Grinning, Owen adjusted his tie. *Still got it.*

The quartet run-through was no big deal. Owen only stumbled in a few places. The difficult part was how they effused over him and told him he should join them more often.

"It's a one-day occurrence." He kept his gaze tightly on his music. "So do we sit here until it starts, or can I go get some air?"

Jack raised an eyebrow at him. "Is this air going to be relatively close to the community center?"

Owen waved an annoyed hand in his direction. "I'll return well before the show starts, and I'll keep my phone on."

He left Ram's violin on his chair and ducked away from the chaos of setup before anyone else could attempt to speak to him, whether it be to chastise him for his rudeness or attempt to soothe his brusqueness. Neither effort was welcome.

God help them if they complimented his playing.

He wanted to go outside, but the rear door opened onto the parking lot, which was filling with guests. Owen didn't have patience for people right now. He needed ten precious minutes alone, away, in silence, with the gulls at best for company. As with everything about this event, what he ended up with instead was a shitty compromise, a cramped corner in the dark, sitting on a pile of tarps as he stared at last summer's community theater backdrops, trying in vain to calm himself.

"Thank you for filling in for the quartet. I know you said this was the one thing you didn't want to do, and I appreciate the lengths you've gone to in order to make this event a success."

Owen turned toward the intruder's voice. Erin Andreas stood five feet from him, at the edge of the narrow space Owen had wedged himself into. He appeared prim and crisp as ever in a suit no different from the ones he wore to work, which meant it was completely unflattering and seemed to be sucking out his soul as Owen watched. If it weren't for Erin's hair playing about his head in wild tendrils, he'd look as if he'd been pressed from a mold for corporate executives who don't want to draw attention to themselves.

Had Erin come to fight, Owen might have welcomed him. But Owen didn't have the strength to start anything, and Erin was never the instigator. In fact, he was too close to that uncomfortably subdued mode from his office again, and Owen was seriously not in the mood for it.

He kicked at a folded-over piece of tarp. "I didn't do it because I'm a team player. I did it because Simon wouldn't get off his knees, and Jack swore he'd mortgage his condo to buy my date as payback if he had to."

"He—what?" Erin came around to stand in front of Owen. He looked like someone had punched him in the gut. "You… you did… what?"

Owen shot a withering glance at Erin. "Don't go high and mighty because we fixed my results. It's not as if anyone was going to bid on me anyway. The worst-case scenario is someone's revenge plot gets foiled, Jack's out some fun money, and the hospital gets the funds it needs for the cardiac unit. And I get left alone. Which, speaking of, I'm sure you have somewhere else to be."

Erin only stared at Owen, dumbfounded. Hell, he almost looked hurt, which made no sense whatsoever. Unbidden, Owen remembered Erin in the hospital stairwell, so lost and alone.

No. He seized his bleeding heart with both hands and tossed it as far as he could.

Erin made his own recovery, whatever emotions he'd been experiencing neatly packed away as he smoothed his hands over his clothes. "I'll be going, then." Except as he left, he stopped near the stage door. "You sounded as good as I remember, by the way."

As soon as the door closed, Owen kicked the curtain, though without any strength. He clung to himself, weak and turned inside out. *Goddamn compliments.* The words were barbs, hooked into him and digging, not letting go.

You sounded as good as I remember.

Shutting his eyes, Owen hugged himself tighter and spiraled into the nightmare of his own mind.

By the time Owen went out to join the others, he had himself somewhat stable, which was good, because the community center was packed with people. The multipurpose room attached to the stage held no traces of being a gymnasium; the committee had transformed it into a glittering small-town centerpiece landing somewhere between high school prom and wedding on the tacky-decorations meter, leaning heavily of course on red and pink hearts. Owen couldn't bring himself to mock it too much, though, despite all the personal headache the event dragged in its wake. Every other year this fundraiser had been held at the country club, and the same local elite had gathered to deposit checks into the hospital coffers.

This year the event was in the center of town, in an accessible building at accessible prices, and it was packed to the gills. Yes, the tickets were still a bit of a bite for some people at thirty-five dollars a person, but the fact that you could see the elliptical machines through the glass on the far side of the room where the decorative paper had slipped made the middle class of Copper Point feel less self-conscious about attending. There were silent auction items strewn about the room, ranging from luxurious to silly and fun. As Owen took his place with the others on the stage, he saw nurses and students from the university in the audience. It was the first time he'd ever witnessed such an occurrence in all the years he'd attended these fundraisers.

If he were simply sitting in the audience sipping cheap wine with the rest of them, he'd applaud the committee's efforts.

Instead, he tuned Ram's violin and flattened his thoughts as much as possible. He reminded himself all he had to do was get through playing, then remain on stage long enough for Jack to keep his word. When the bow quivered, he imagined himself standing there, the spotlights on him, Jack and Simon with their paddles raised. He watched himself leave the stage with a salute and join them, where they waited with the bottle of Scotch Jack had sworn he'd smuggle in.

Soon. It'd be over soon.

The spotlight went up, and the Copper Point Quartet played with its substitute second violinist. They performed pop music arranged for quartets, and the crowd ate up every moment. Owen did his job, hitting the notes, sitting quietly as they bled out of his soul. Owen managed to hold his own so well his temporary quartet members showered him with compliments as they finished the first set of songs.

"Wow." Amanda beamed at him. "I can't believe you haven't played in seventeen years. You're fantastic."

"You're doing great," Tim agreed. "You're as good as I've heard you were."

Owen stared so hard at the center of his music he was surprised it didn't burst into flames.

Jack looked ready to say something, but whatever it was got lost as Erin swept up to them, standing between Owen and the stage. The light hit him from behind like a halo, and Owen couldn't see his expression. "Everything sounds perfect. Thank you. Once this next set is done, we'll transition into the auction, and the four of you can take your seats in the audience." He paused, glancing at Owen. "Three of you, at any rate. Thank you once again, Dr. Gagnon, for being such an exceptional team player this evening."

You play as beautifully as I remember.

Owen propped the violin on his leg. "Whatever."

His neck broke out in gooseflesh and his hair stood on end when Erin pressed his hand on his left shoulder.

Owen shook off the touch and swallowed, gripping the neck of the violin tighter.

Jesus, he seriously couldn't wait to be drunk.

The last set dragged on much longer than Owen cared for, but he got through it one note at a time. He distracted himself from the dull horror of playing by being irritated over Erin's touch of his shoulder. Erin hadn't touched him before.

Whatever. He didn't care if Erin never looked at him again, so long as he could get the hell off this stage.

Soon enough, he managed it part of the way, stiffly half bowing with the quartet before abandoning his instrument and disappearing behind the curtain to join the rest of the bachelors, including Jared.

Jared waved at him and patted a space beside him on the wall. "Good job, Crankypants. You made it through. I warned people not to compliment you, but feel free to snarl at anyone who doesn't listen."

Owen shut his eyes. "Can I go first and get this over with? I want a drink."

"Unfortunately they've assigned us numbers. I'm number eight. You're number seventeen."

"*Hell.*" Owen shrank into a crouch.

Jared reached into his jacket, lowering himself to Owen's side. "Here." He handed Owen a bottle. "I thought it was overkill, but after interrogating Simon and me to figure out why you were behaving the way you were, Jack wrote this script for you and had the hospital pharmacy fill it, making me bring it just in case. It's a handful of Xanax. Don't take enough that you're too stoned to stand, but maybe enough so you can remain upright without sweating."

Owen checked the dosage, popped the lid, and dry swallowed a tablet. He hadn't taken a short-term anxiety med in years. He was pissed that he needed to, annoyed Jack had noticed he was so off his game he required medication, but he was also grateful.

Jared grimaced. "Jack regrets making you play."

Owen rubbed his thumb over the top of the prescription bottle. "I don't want to talk about it."

"Trust me, the message has come through loud and clear. All I'm saying is, don't worry, we've got you, okay? You're not going to have to do anything more tonight except stand on the stage long enough for Jack to pay up. I'm chipping in too if it comes to it, but I can't imagine it will."

"Just pay for the booze." Owen willed the Xanax to work faster. "Why didn't Jack give me this before we played, anyway?"

"He was afraid you'd fuck up."

Owen snorted. *No, idiot. I'd have played ten times better.*

Whatever. It was over now, and he was never touching a violin again. For tonight, the damage had been done. He'd put the instrument down, but he still felt it in his hands, heard it in his head. Stirring up things he'd buried for good reason.

He could see her. *Hear* her. He hadn't spared his mother a thought in years, and now she reverberated, starring in the memory that made him want to curl in a ball and vomit. It didn't end there, though. Older ones began, tinged with the darkness of that day. All the times he trudged across the snow with the violin case clutched in his hand, his house in the distance, wondering if he'd hear her at the piano or hear his father shuffling across the kitchen, searching for another beer. He saw her profile at the piano bench as he played beside her. He saw himself crouching underneath it as he watched their arguments from between the legs.

Broken glass. The broken legs of the piano bench. The jarring discord of her back as it hit the keys, the crunch of his first violin when it slammed against the wall.

The day he'd come home from high school and she'd been sitting at the piano, waiting for him, her back in profile at the bench as she played, then stopped. *Come here, Owen. I have something to tell you.*

Owen reached for a second Xanax. He could push most of the memories away, but his mother sitting at the piano with her back to him lingered like something out of a horror film. If she turned around and gave him that haunted smile, he was a dead man.

Jared held out his hand. "Give me the bottle."

Owen tucked it deep inside his interior vest pocket. "Go to hell. And never let anyone ask me to play again. Not if it's the only way we keep the world from ending."

By the time the auction kicked off, so had Owen's drugs. He didn't have any more memories playing on repeat, and he didn't feel haunted any longer. He still felt raw and peeled back, but he was more objective about it, as if observing himself on a hospital gurney. *Adult male, age thirty-four, acute anxiety attack brought on by unwanted remembrance of bullshit past. Vitals are stabilized, but recommend patient be placed in front of a bottle of Scotch and more Xanax and left alone until he forgets he ever knew how to play violin in the first place.*

When Owen chuckled, Jared poked his arm and held out his hand insistently. "Seriously, give me the fucking bottle."

Owen did, mostly because at that point he had no need for it. She wasn't drifting through his mind anymore, but if she did, it wouldn't matter. God bless alprazolam.

Jared made him stand to prove he wasn't going to act drunk on stage—it was going to be a near thing, but he could fake it. "You're a mess," Jared said as he went off to be auctioned, and then it was Owen alone, glaring at the other bachelors for fun except when he wanted to laugh at them instead. He was freaking them out, so he stared at the wall, which thanks to the drug had become suddenly interesting.

At last they called his name, and honestly Owen thought someone should give him a medal, because instead of stomping out like a cloud of doom, he sauntered onstage with a cheeky salute. Jared, seated by a beaming elderly woman in the front row, gave him dirty looks, but Owen didn't care. He rocked on his heels and waited for them to finish his introduction so the bidding could get over with and he could get out of here.

"Bachelor number seventeen." The middle-aged woman Owen recognized as Mimi Roberts, the wife of one of the clinic doctors, gave an annoyingly knowing and theatrical wink to the audience. It would have bothered Owen normally, but he was too spent and high to care. She lifted her card and read, "Dr. Owen Gagnon, local boy through and through, who left Copper Point to get his degree, then returned to be our first and only anesthesiologist. He may be short on charm at times, but he's long on loyalty, and he's always ready to help a good cause."

Cripes, who wrote these intros? He cast an eyebrow at Simon, but his friend was too busy staring at the emcee, paddle primed. Owen relaxed.

Oh, and there was old asshat John Jean Andreas, sitting with the other stuffed shirts from the board. Owen was surprised the jerk wasn't tormenting his son, or at least keeping him on a short leash. Must be in the middle of greasing the old-white-man society wheels—

Owen's blood chilled, curdling when Christian West leaned over to speak to John Jean, smile glinting in the dim light. After shutting his eyes on a long blink, Owen dove deep into the sheltering embrace of the Xanax and averted his gaze.

Mimi beamed at the audience. "As with all our bachelors, we'll start the bidding at one hundred dollars, but I'm sure we can get—"

"Two hundred," someone called out, and it wasn't Simon or Jack. Oh hell, it was a clutch of drunk nurses with their pooled money on the table. *Shit*, this was exactly what he'd been afraid of—

Simon's paddle whipped into the air. "Four hundred."

The crowd erupted in murmurs, and Mimi clucked her tongue. "My, my. What an exciting beginning. It's so good to see bidders enthusiastic, but as a reminder, we don't need to jump up with quite so much drama this quickly—"

"Ten thousand dollars."

Now the room was a wall of sound and a sea of chaos, people standing and trying to figure out where the bidder had come from. Owen recognized the voice, but he was sure he had to be wrong. He hadn't heard someone bid *ten thousand dollars* for him.

Except someone had, and once again, it wasn't Jack or Simon, who were pale and conferring with one another desperately as Jared extricated himself from his date and rushed to their table.

"Well." Mimi laughed nervously into the microphone. "Someone certainly wants a date with you, Dr. Gagnon. I can't see who it is, but I can't imagine anyone else is going to top—"

"Um, eleven!" Jared's voice broke as he held up Simon's paddle and arm at once. Visible sweat was running down his face, but Simon and Jack nodded at him, their jaws set in determination.

"Twenty-five thousand dollars. I bid twenty-five thousand dollars for a date with Dr. Owen Gagnon, and I'm prepared to go *much* higher if need be."

This time there was no mistaking the voice. Owen had known it before, but his brain had issued flat denials. He couldn't get out of reality, though, when Erin Andreas walked down the aisle, holding his paddle high as the room whispered and gasped around him. Jack and Simon argued, panicking, and Jared shook his head. They were out of the running.

Owen collapsed on the edge of the stage, staring at Erin as he calmly closed the distance between them.

Well. Owen didn't know what the hell was going on, but he did know he was going to need the bottle of Xanax back.

ERIN IGNORED the whispers and rushes of sound around him, keeping his focus on the man he'd emptied his accounts for. The man who appeared to be either high or drunk or possibly both, who sat on the edge of the stage, tugging his tuxedo shirt free from his cummerbund.

Who looked stunned and… pissed. Erin had been prepared for the former. The latter was throwing him off his game.

Every other bachelor received a round of applause once the bidding was finished, then bowed to whoever had claimed him and exited the stage to sit with his date in the audience. But Mimi hadn't closed the auction yet. She was staring at Erin with her mouth open. Dr. Wu and Dr. Kumpel conferred madly as Simon Lane punched at his phone with trembling fingers. Erin forced his attention away from them, telling himself he needn't worry. They couldn't match his number. Not with Wu and Lane planning their wedding. Kumpel could, possibly, but he was so hesitant with money. The roof on the house he co-owned with Gagnon and Lane needed new shingles, and they still had to sort out Lane's section of the mortgage.

As he passed the VIP tables where the board sat, he deliberately didn't make eye contact with his father, but he felt the cold fury of the stare nonetheless. That anger he'd anticipated, though he hadn't worked out how to deal with it, too focused on his goal.

Later. He'd deal with it later. First he had to finish this.

Erin waved his auction card at Mimi. "Ms. Roberts, would you mind terribly closing my bid?"

"Oh. Yes." She touched her hair, glancing at the crowd, at Owen, at the table where the board sat.

At Erin's furious father.

Erin's breath caught. *No. She can't possibly think of letting him override this.* He cleared his throat and stepped closer. "*Ms. Roberts?* Is there a problem?"

Startling, she smiled faintly. "Of course not. Since there are no more bidders, it does appear you have won." She tapped her rhinestone-encrusted gavel onto the podium. "Dr. Owen Gagnon, bachelor number seventeen, sold to Erin Andreas for twenty-five thousand dollars. Dr. Gagnon, please join your date."

Though the hesitant beats ending their auction could barely be heard above the whispers of surprise, they brought Owen to life, lifting him out of his stupor and focusing his fury on his purchaser. There was something seriously off about Owen, something more than had been wrong when Erin had spoken to him backstage. The cold woodenness wrapped around him all day had melted away, leaving a twitchy, giddy mess.

"So." Owen kicked his feet to the point that one of his shoes was in danger of falling. His shirt was completely untucked from his trousers, his bow tie askew. "This is a surprise."

Erin did his best to keep his cool. "We should take our seats."

Owen ignored his request. "That's a lot of money you just threw around on me. Jacked the price way up right away too. Didn't think to take it up by increments?"

"I didn't know how much Jared and the others were prepared to bid, and I didn't want to waste time."

"Ah." Owen grinned at Erin like he wanted to grind him into powder. "I shouldn't have told you my plan."

Thank God he had. Erin had barely organized his assets in time. "Are you planning to come down from there anytime soon? They have more bachelors to auction, and you're making a spectacle of yourself."

He snorted. "No, that would be *you*, Mr. Twenty-Five Thousand Dollars."

Erin needed to calm Owen down, but he couldn't do that with Mimi giving him shooing motions and the whole town looking on. He wanted to suggest they go outside and talk—Owen would yell, and Erin could give him the speech he'd prepared about why he'd done this. Unless Owen stayed angry.

Of course, if they left the room, his father would come after them. His father would come for him eventually, period. But he told himself if he could get Owen alone first, everything would be fine, because... because....

It had all made so much more sense in his head, when Owen wasn't behaving this way. He didn't understand why he was so angry. Shouldn't he think this was flattering, or at worst, funny? Why was he upset?

This isn't good.

Stepping on the panic, Erin kept his expression neutral and extended his hand. "Let's go to our seats."

Owen hopped off the stage, still glaring at Erin. "I've waited all day for a drink. Jared and Jack have Scotch for me at my table."

Erin was painfully aware the entire room was watching them. "I'll get you a beverage as soon as we sit." When Owen failed to follow him, Erin attempted to take his arm.

Owen caught Erin's elbow and drew him in so close Erin could smell his aftershave. It made him dizzy.

"What," Owen whispered, "are you trying to pull?"

For a moment Erin couldn't breathe, let alone respond. The heady scent of Owen combined with the magnitude of what he'd done made his voice waver. "I'll explain what I expect from you as my date *once we're seated.*"

Owen kept Erin's arm captive and spoke into his ear. "I want to sit with my friends."

Erin hated himself for his shiver. "I paid twenty-five thousand dollars for you. You can sit where I ask."

"You paid twenty-five thousand dollars for *me*, and you knew full well who I was when you did so. I'm sitting with my friends and drinking Scotch. You can sit with me or not."

He let go of Erin and started down the aisle.

Erin hurried to follow while doing his best to appear cool and collected, as if he wasn't wounded, as if he didn't mind being completely thwarted by the world's most annoying man.

The auction resumed on the stage, but the audience buzzed as Owen and Erin walked past, everyone transfixed on their drama. Nick cast Erin a worried glance as he passed, but Erin only gave him a curt nod and continued on.

Dropping unceremoniously into the single chair available at his friends' table, Owen reached for the bottle of liquor tucked not at all discreetly beside the vase of silk flowers. He didn't help Erin find a chair, nor did he pay him any attention in the slightest. The others glanced from Owen to Erin and across to each other, everyone clearly unsure how to handle this situation.

Erin was barely able to mask his hurt at this point. He'd spent quite a bit of money only to get this treatment. And what about that business with the sack lunch, asking if he needed help? Had that all been just a line?

What did you think was going to happen? That you'd bid on him, he'd be flattered, and you could confess your idiot feelings after all these years?

It had, in fact, been something foolish like that, yes. Obviously it wouldn't be happening now, but he at least had to get through this evening with some dignity. Fixing his gaze on the far side of the room, Erin spoke in a dry, tired voice. "Please get me a chair, Dr. Gagnon."

Owen, who had poured himself a shot, downed it and set the glass on the table with a happy sigh. "Nope."

Erin neither shifted his posture nor altered his tone. "I asked for a chair, not the *Mona Lisa*. Is this honestly the hill you want to die on?"

Owen's fingers tightened around the neck of the Scotch so tightly Erin thought he might break the glass. "I've been running for the hills ever since I got roped into this circus, and when I thought I was through the last hoop, you put up a brand-new twenty-five-thousand-dollar tent. You can damn well stand."

Simon rose. "I'll find you a chair, Mr. Andreas."

Erin remained where he was, doing his best to pretend he wasn't a spectacle. Simon returned with a chair, apologizing as he passed it over. As Erin sat,

Dr. Wu regarded Owen with concern as he poured his third shot.

"How many Xanax did you take?" Wu asked Owen.

"About six less than I needed." Owen tossed back the alcohol.

Xanax. Frowning, Erin studied Owen anew. He hadn't known him to be the type to need anti-anxiety medication as a general rule. What about this upset him so much?

Jared deftly swiped the bottle of alcohol from a protesting Owen and crouched between Wu and Lane. "He had two."

Wu pursed his lips. "Don't let him drink any more or take any additional pills."

Jared withdrew a vial from his pocket. "Way ahead of you. I need to go, as my date is waiting, but I wanted to make sure things were okay here." He nodded as he met Erin's gaze. "Andreas. I can't say I saw this coming."

Finally, part of the script Erin had rehearsed for. "Charity is important."

Owen, staring at the ceiling, chuckled darkly. "I'm going to make you so miserable."

Erin nodded to the front of the room, where the latest bachelor was joining his date. "They're nearly done. After that we have the dance of the bachelors with their dates, the announcement of the silent auction items, and everything is finished." Then all he had to do was find a way to live down the indignity of this.

Jared rose. "I'll see you all after." He aimed a finger at Owen. "Be good."

Owen grunted and turned his back on Erin.

Erin sat quietly and focused on the auction.

Once the final bachelor left the stage, Mimi called for the middle tables to vacate so they could open up the dance floor. Since their table was one of the few in the center, they had to rise, and Owen drifted as far from Erin as possible.

Erin let him go. He could feel the vultures ready to descend on him, citizens of Copper Point who wanted to feed off the juicy display he'd provided. *How unlike him*, they'd be whispering. Stiff, proper Erin Andreas spending so much money on a gay man, one who clearly wanted nothing to do with him. *What was he thinking?* That's what they were all wondering.

Well, they could keep wondering. He didn't have any answers.

Bidding on Owen should have been easy enough, but when he'd found out Owen had rigged his auction, he'd gone a bit… overboard. Looking back, he was slightly horrified at his behavior. He felt as if he'd been possessed. No one got under his skin quite like Owen Gagnon. No one else made him behave foolishly, unpredictably. He had been in love with him for so long, but ever since Erin had come back to Copper Point, he always ended up shouting at the man he'd once cherished. And though he tried to bury his old feelings, they kept resurfacing, making him do impulsive, dangerous things.

This was simply another brick in the wall. Nothing else to do but face the music and regroup the best he could—

"What do you think you're doing?"

At the sound of his father's voice, Erin jerked sideways, almost losing his balance. "F-Father. My apologies. I was deep in thought and didn't hear you approach."

John Jean's laugh was dry and biting. "*Thought.* Well it's good to know you're still capable of the action. I wondered if I'd need to have Dr. Yoshen commit you on the way home."

Though Erin tucked his hands to his sides, he couldn't stop them from shaking. He wasn't ready for this. He'd known his father wouldn't like him bidding on Owen, but he hadn't considered his father at all when he'd raised his bid so significantly. Certainly in no vision of this moment had he stood alone, humiliated and ignored by his date, out tens of thousands of dollars, with his father full of fury.

John Jean stepped in close. To the rest of the room he was smiling, but Erin heard every furious word, and each one punched him in the stomach.

"You're making a fool of yourself, and you're disgracing the Andreas name." His hand closed on Erin's elbow and squeezed. "I'm disgusted simply looking at you, and so is everyone here."

Erin shut his eyes on a long blink as he fought the pain of his father's touch. He did his best to gather himself, but it was no use. His father was right, on every count.

His father's hold on him tightened, making Erin wince. "We'll discuss this further at home. In the meantime, stay away from that man and behave with more decorum. Don't make me warn you again."

I'm a fool. I'm nothing but a fool.

"Pardon me, sir."

Erin's eyes flew open. Owen stood before him, still furious, still listing and high, but his ire was aimed elsewhere now. Not moving his steely gaze from John Jean, Owen disengaged Erin from his father with a swift, blunt chop to John Jean's wrist, and while the older man sputtered in rage, Owen collected Erin and drew him to his side.

"You'll have to argue with your son later. Right now we're in the middle of a very expensive datc."

Before Erin could finish his gasp of surprise, Owen laced his fingers with Erin's and dragged him bodily onto the dance floor.

CHAPTER THREE

THE ROOM was a dizzy blur to Erin as Owen pulled him through the crowd. His father's threats rang in his ears, and he couldn't help fearing John Jean would emerge and stop their escape. Erin could still feel his father's fingers on his elbow, thumb pushing on the exact point that promised the most pain.

But his father was only one of his problems. Why had Owen rescued him when he was clearly furious with Erin? Why had he seemed angrier with Erin's father? Erin's limbs tightened, seizing quietly. His breathing became shallow, his vision darkening around the edges.

Abruptly, Owen swept him into his arms and spun him into a dance. Erin's face was so close to Owen's chest it took an effort not to burrow into it. His forehead rested against the hard plane of muscle, the buttons of his shirt pressing into Erin's forehead, the smell of the man and expensive Scotch wrapping around him.

Owen's softly spoken words sent a shiver down Erin's spine. "Take a breath and stand up. I don't know what your dad said to rattle you, but the Erin Andreas who spits fire at me on a daily basis can surely dance with the dragon he paid so much for."

Lifting his gaze to Owen's, Erin stumbled, not ready for the intensity there. His date was furious, but he was also… protective.

Erin looked sharply away.

At the small of Erin's back, Owen's thumb moved in subtle, soothing circles. "I apologize it took me so long to figure it out, but you weren't simply trying to annoy me, were you?"

Erin clung to Owen's arms, drinking deep draughts of his scent. "I didn't want to annoy you at all."

The sigh ruffling Erin's hair was hot and smelled of alcohol, but Owen's embrace made him feel protected and surrounded. "I don't understand why you did that, but I'm sorry I was an ass and left you alone. I won't do it again."

It was difficult to breathe, and Erin's knees were rubbery. "What, ever?" he quipped, trying desperately to regain some ground.

"Not ever."

Owen had spoken all of this into Erin's ear, dipping his head to whisper as he maneuvered Erin expertly through the crowd. Between this, his unexpected overbid, and Owen's rescue, they had to seem like lovers.

How was everything a disaster and absolutely perfect at the same time?

Erin shut his eyes and turned his face so he could speak for Owen's ears alone. "I didn't mean for this to get so out of hand. I apologize for upsetting you. I didn't think it would be so offensive for me to bid on you, but I see that it is, so you don't have to do this."

"I never said I was offended. I've had my own trauma today, and I didn't expect this. I thought you were using me."

Erin drew back, rigid. "I would never!"

"I know that now. It took me a minute. And like I said, I'm sorry."

Erin relaxed. "There's no need for apology."

The song playing was a simple pop number, not suited for the type of dancing they were doing, though Owen made it work. Barely anyone was on the floor, and all eyes were on them. Owen didn't seem to care, only continued to navigate them around the room.

When the music finished and Mimi announced the bachelors and their dates should assemble, Owen kept Erin in his arms, his hand settling onto Erin's hip.

"Don't look now, but so you're aware, your father is staring daggers at us." When Erin tried to turn around, Owen stopped him. "Didn't you hear me? I'm pretty sure he's waiting for you to look at him. I think he's furious it's taking you so long."

Erin's breath caught audibly, and he would have fallen over if Owen hadn't held him up.

Owen continued, a wicked smile on his face. "You didn't have to spend that kind of money. I would have helped you for free."

Wait, what? "Help me?"

"You're after the ogre to tame your father. Completely understandable."

Finally, Erin found his voice. "I've never called you that."

Owen waved a dismissive hand. "Plenty of others have, and it's fine. I've heard it all. Dragon. Ogre. Goblin. Devil. Bastard. Rotten, nasty son of a bitch. We'd be here until midnight if I listed every name. I own all of them. I can be whatever monster you need me to be, Erin."

The music began to play, a faster swing number. Erin lifted his head to tell Owen he didn't think he was a monster, that he didn't want a savior, just a date, but when he saw Owen's intense, fiery expression, he stopped, his breath stolen away.

Owen's thumb caressed the underside of Erin's chin with a tenderness that made his knees weak. "I'll be your boyfriend, Erin Andreas."

Then, in front of Erin's father, the hospital board, and half the town, Dr. Owen Gagnon took Erin in his arms and gave him the most passionate kiss he'd received in his life.

In fact, it was the only kiss he'd ever had, from the only person he'd wished would give him one.

ERIN ANDREAS tasted soft and sweet—and he didn't know how to kiss.

Owen regretted the move as soon as he'd done it, feeling like it was too much, the slowly sobering part of his brain shouting at his high, drunk id for following the impulse. Except Erin didn't reject him. He tried to kiss him back, but with the blind panic of someone who didn't want anyone to know they didn't know what they were doing.

This man has never been kissed properly. This truth presented itself in Owen's mind, twining with the memory of John Jean Andreas looming over a pale, trembling Erin.

Erin's fingers grazed Owen's cheek, falling to his neck. He wasn't pulling away.

I didn't think it would be so offensive for me to bid on you, but I see that it is.

Gut clenching in shame, Owen slipped his hand to Erin's neck, thumb trailing down the quivering muscles, soothing them as he supported Erin's head. *Let me show you how much I'm not offended.* He opened his mouth over Erin's, coaxing him into a deeper kiss.

His hand that had drifted to Erin's waist traveled lower, cupping the curve of Erin's ass.

As the gasps of the room mingled with the swell of the music, Erin drew away, trembling. "What are you doing?"

Not quite the reaction he'd been after.

Owen spun them into the dance. He hadn't done ballroom in a while, but his brain remembered, the same way it had the violin. Shit, he didn't need to think about that either. He settled his hand more politely on Erin's hip.

What happens now?

He was still searching for the answer when Erin spoke, his voice clipped and wavering. "I think a few people heard you announce you were my boyfriend, and this performance isn't going to help that rumor go away."

"I don't mind if people think we're dating." Owen raised an eyebrow at Erin, but Erin was staring at Owen's bow tie and wouldn't look at him. "Do *you* have a problem with it?"

He hadn't known Erin could blush like this. "Wh-why would you want them to think that?"

"Because of your father, obviously."

"I didn't—I don't—" Erin stepped on Owen's feet, frowning. "I don't understand what you mean."

Owen drew Erin closer. "Everything's working fine. See? I'm right here."

"Yes, but I think you've misunderstood me. And you're making me so unsettled."

"I honestly think having us be pretend boyfriends is better than just a date."

The color drained from Erin's face. "Pretend—*what*?"

"As for unsettling you, I think it's only fair. You knocked me flat with your bid when I was already weak, then sauntered up to the stage as if you did that sort of thing every day."

Erin's trembling hand slid to Owen's chest. "I don't know why the quartet upset you so much, but I would never have let them enlist you if I'd known. I'm sorry."

Now it was Owen's turn to trip. He tried to cover his clumsiness with a wink, but that turned out to be a bad idea because Erin's vulnerable face made him dizzy.

The thought plaguing Owen since he'd seen Erin with John Jean finally bubbled to the surface. He clung to Erin and focused on keeping them both upright, on drawing one steady breath after the other.

He reminds me of my mother.

The only sound in the room was the soft thump of his heartbeat in his ears, the slow, gentle pulls of air into his lungs. He felt as if he were a bird, caught by his foot with his wings extended. If he didn't flee, he'd be dragged into everything he'd told himself he never wanted to face again. Yet even as he thought this, though his wings had yet to be clipped, he realized the chain had already been placed on his leg. He would never get Erin's terrified face from his mind. He would never forget watching John Jean grab Erin's elbow and Erin cowering before his father, trying to hide his pain, his fear.

Erin reminds me of my mother, and I can't bear the thought of him going home with a man who reminds me of my father.

Maybe this time I can save her.

Cool fingers on his face drew him out of his trance. Glancing down, he saw Erin regarding him with a worried expression.

They stood in the middle of the room, no longer dancing, only holding one another in an awkward embrace as other couples danced around them.

Owen scanned the crowd for John Jean but couldn't find him. Ignoring the stares from their onlookers, he turned back to Erin. "You live with your father, right?"

The shuttering of Erin's expression set Owen's primal instincts on red alert. "Yes. Why?"

Owen searched Erin's face. "What's going to happen tonight when you go home?"

The way Erin's walls slammed up told Owen everything he needed to know. "That's none of your concern."

"I swear to you, I can protect you. I'll keep you safe." His grip on Erin tightened, and so did the muscles of his chest. "But if you want my help, you can't stay in his house any longer. Not for a single night."

Erin pulled away. "What in the world?"

Owen held him fast. "I'll pretend to be your boyfriend and kccp your father out of your hair. That's a promise. Just move in with me. Right now."

Erin stared at Owen. "Move in—with you?"

"That's right." Grinning, Owen spun them back into the dance.

MOVE IN with Owen.

Erin was in so much shock he couldn't say a word. This was completely out of hand. Owen hadn't simply misunderstood him. He'd… run mad.

Move in with Owen. Move in with Owen. Move in with Owen.

When Erin's legs wobbled, Owen bore him up and took him away from the dance floor, leading him to the nearest table, where he glared at a bank president until he allowed Erin to sit. Erin wanted to apologize on his date's behalf, but he couldn't form words. It took all of his control to stifle the urge to whimper.

How was he supposed to move in with Owen?

The bank president and his guests vacated the table, and now Dr. Wu and Simon Lane approached, with Dr. Kumpel close behind them. All three men regarded Erin and Owen with concern.

"Did something happen?" Kumpel's gaze darted between Erin and Owen. "What was that with John Jean?"

Owen ignored him. “Can someone go get Erin something to drink? A glass of water?” His hand rested gently on Erin’s shoulder as he crouched slightly to speak directly to him. “Have you eaten? When was your last meal?”

Erin’s cheeks heated, and he couldn’t stop touching them. Owen was looking at him with so much intensity all he could do was answer his question. “I… I ate lunch. A sandwich from the hospital cafeteria.”

“So you were working too much on top of everything else.” Owen aimed a finger at Dr. Wu. “Find him something to eat.” He shifted his focus to Lane. “Get him something to drink. Juice, if you can manage it. Nothing alcoholic. Water for me too, please.”

Dr. Wu took his fiancé’s elbow. “We’ll be right back.”

Dr. Kumpel claimed the seat opposite Erin. “Are you feeling all right?” He cast a glance at Owen. “Is he treating you okay?”

Owen’s hand slid more possessively over Erin’s shoulder. “Of course I’m treating him all right.”

Kumpel raised a dubious eyebrow at Owen. “I didn’t ask *you*.”

This was the moment to explain there had been some kind of misunderstanding. How to start, though? Unbidden, Owen’s searing kiss replayed in Erin’s mind, making him flush and stammer. His shoulders slumped forward in defeat. “I—I’m fine. Thank you.”

Except for the bit where Owen is begging me to move in with him based on a misunderstanding and I’m considering going along with it.

Kumpel continued to scan Erin as if he were one of his patients, which made Erin feel acutely awkward, since Dr. Kumpel's patients were children. "Do you have secret hordes of cash hidden away, to throw around money like that for a date with Owen? Can you afford food now? Because if not, I'm making him feed you more than hors d'oeuvres." Kumpel leaned in closer, frowning slightly. "Also, you're aware you bid on *Owen*? Our Owen? A cranky, antagonistic wild card? I mean, he's loyal as the day is long and will defend the ones he loves with his life, but don't discount those first three elements."

It was absolutely too warm in the room, no question. Erin swallowed against a dry throat. "Yes, I'm aware. And I'm fine, thank you for your concern. I have plenty of money. And I only very much wanted a date with him. That's all."

There. He'd said the truth at last. He glanced at Owen, wondering how it would land.

Owen was unmoved by his confession, too busy glaring at Kumpel. "I'm *not* antagonistic."

Kumpel regarded him blandly. "Oh, yes. I see I was in the wrong on that point."

Lane and Wu returned, Lane clutching a tray of drinks, Wu with both hands carrying plates groaning with the finger foods offered on the buffet tables on the sides of the room. Lane passed Owen a bottle of water and pressed a glass of what appeared to be pineapple juice into Erin's hands.

"Here you are." Lane smiled at Erin. "They didn't have much juice, only what they mixed drinks with at the bar. I got you a bottle of water as well."

"Thank you." Erin sipped at the pineapple juice. It was tart and sweet, and it tasted good.

Dr. Wu set the plates of food on the table as his fiancé moved out of the way. "I brought enough for everyone to share, and spare plates so we could take what we wanted for our own."

Owen immediately swiped an empty plate and handed it to Erin. "Take what you like. Unless you want me to select something for you?"

Erin couldn't tell if Owen's solicitousness was part of the boyfriend package or if this was genuine concern. He wasn't sure why he didn't make more effort to object. Was he seriously going to move out because Owen clasped his hands passionately?

He couldn't think about that now. He needed to eat. He hadn't realized how hungry he was. The pineapple juice had only stirred his appetite. "I can help myself, thank you."

Everyone waited while Erin made his selections, but once his plate was full, the others descended on the remaining food like locusts. Owen went last, and as he chose his items, he hesitated, glancing at Erin. "Are you sure you have enough?"

Ducking to focus on his plate, Erin nodded. "I'm positive, thank you."

He'd barely recovered from this episode when Owen threw another grenade at him.

"Jared," Owen began, wiping his mouth on the napkin, "so you're aware, Erin's going to stay with us for a bit. I thought we could give him Si's old room."

Dr. Wu, Dr. Kumpel, and Simon Lane froze.

Erin tugged on Owen's lapel as he spoke in an insistent whisper. "This absolutely isn't necessary."

Owen's reply wasn't a whisper at all. "Are you trying to back out of my single, solitary condition?"

Now. Explain it to him now, even if you're mortified. "I'm trying to tell you, you've misunderstood—"

"Have I?" Owen's gaze drilled into Erin's, stopping him cold.

Abruptly, distinctly uneasy, Erin looked at the floor, the wall, the ceiling, anywhere but at Owen or his friends.

Owen continued speaking to the others as if Erin hadn't interrupted him. "So, as I was saying, Erin's going to be staying with us. That fine with you, Jared? And I guess Simon, since you technically still pay part of the mortgage until we get that squared away. Honestly, I suggest you regard this situation as Erin saving you a ton of money, since you didn't have to buy my auction."

Kumpel laughed, his tone full of disbelief but not upset. "I assume we don't get to ask any questions about what's going on?"

Owen popped a potato chip into his mouth. "Absolutely not."

Wu folded his arms over his chest. "He's still high. I don't think we should take any of this seriously."

"I had sobriety shocked directly into my system. You should take everything completely seriously."

Jared raised an eyebrow at Erin. "Is he telling the truth? Are you moving in with us?"

Am I? "I…."

Owen caught his hand, squeezed it, then laced their fingers together.

Something eased inside Erin. "I suppose I am."

Owen winked at him, then let go of his hand to lay it on the table, palm up, as he regarded his friends.

Jared laughed. "Look at you two." He shook his head. "I can see we're not going to get any answers right now. So, Erin. Do you need help getting your things?"

A strange darkness passed over Owen's countenance. "No."

Dr. Wu turned to Dr. Kumpel. "I feel strongly that we should help Erin collect his things."

Owen glared at the two of them. "Why, you think Erin needs protection from me?"

Wu regarded Owen placidly. "I think you're a bit too wound up and have high odds of embarrassing him and yourself. Plus, you're in no condition to drive."

They argued for several minutes over this, and Erin was so overwhelmed at this point he didn't fight any of it. Instead, he looked for his father, trying to find him in the room, checking to see if he still watched Erin. Would he come to the table? Would he make a scene? No. He'd wait until they were home alone.

The food in Erin's belly threatened to make a second appearance.

Owen's hand found his under the table again, his thumb stroking the back of Erin's hand. *I still need to explain things to him*, Erin thought.

But as the rhythm of Owen's touch brought him ease, Erin lost more and more will to speak.

Perhaps I could stay away from the house for one night. I can explain in the morning.

Was that insane? Probably. Irresponsible? Definitely. Except the longer he sat here, the more time he spent with Owen, the more he wanted to go. Wanted to run, hide. Be with Owen.

Erin pressed a hand to his temple, warding off a headache.

Owen's fingers threaded into Erin's hair, massaging his scalp, making Erin's whole body tingle.

"Enough." Owen's voice lost its combative edge. "It's fine. We'll all go, but let's do it now. Erin's tired."

Erin perked up, trying to push through the fog of Owen's touch. "I can't go yet, not as a committee member—"

"There are other committee members." Owen nodded at Simon. "Find someone else to monitor this so we can go."

Erin knew he should argue he couldn't abandon the fundraiser, but he was so exhausted. "Find Nick. Give him my apologies and ask if he could please take over."

"I'll do that." Jared rose. "The rest of you get going. I'll follow and meet you there."

Halfway to the exit, an elderly woman stopped Owen. She put her hand on Owen's forearm and patted his wrist, smiling up at him as she spoke over the din of the room.

"It was so lovely to hear you play again, young man. You're as talented as I remember."

Beside Erin, Simon and Wu both winced, looking as if they wanted to tuck Owen between them and hustle him out of the room, but their reaction was nothing compared to Owen's own. Owen didn't startle, didn't break eye contact with the woman or stop smiling, but Erin shivered as the life and color drained from Owen's face. All the sparkle, all the fire, was sucked out of him. He was the same as he'd been when Erin had found him backstage, except now he seemed… haunted.

Haunted, and trying not to let anyone else know.

"Erin, why don't you let one of us take you?" Wu suggested as they reached the parking lot. "You keep touching your temple. Do you have a headache?"

"A little one," Erin confessed. "I don't want to leave my car, though. I can manage—"

"I'll drive him," Owen cut in.

"You're high." Wu turned to his fiancé. "Simon, why don't you drive Owen, and I'll drive Erin? Erin, I know you could probably drive yourself, but let us take you. I think you've had enough excitement for the night."

"*I'll drive Erin,*" Owen said again, but no one listened to him.

Erin ended up in the passenger seat of his own car, with Dr. Wu driving him, Simon following with Owen as they went to the Andreas mansion. Jared, having found Nick and given him the news they were leaving, trailed a few blocks behind.

After a few moments of silence, Wu cleared his throat. "I don't intend to pry in any business between you and Owen. I will, though, admit the events of this evening have left me confused. Is everything all right?"

Erin almost wanted to laugh. He rubbed his throbbing temple once more. "I'm confused as well, Dr. Wu. But I'm… okay."

As he said the words, he realized they were true. *I'm okay.* A little shaky, a bit lost, but on the whole, this felt good, even inside the terror. A night with Owen, however it happened, was something he'd dreamed of all his life.

Dr. Wu nodded. "I'm glad to hear it. Though, please, out of the hospital, call me Jack."

The Andreas mansion was on the northwest side of town, in the small section of houses that overlooked the bay. One of the oldest homes in Copper Point, it was listed on the national historic registry and was literally a museum. Erin had spent his entire life in a house where two-thirds of the space was off-limits to his use because strangers were touring it or might do so at any time. It was a beautiful building filled with exquisite things. Bringing other people into it, however, was always awkward.

He directed Jack to the rear of the building, telling him to park off to the side. He'd hoped it would be empty given it was so late, but the caretaker's car was still there, ensuring this debacle would be a mess. Probably Diane had to come late because his father had entertained guests before the fundraiser.

As they got out, Jared and the others pulled into the drive behind them. Erin drew Owen aside. "So you understand, we're going to encounter a rather bossy elderly woman who is here to clean the museum portion of the house. Please don't engage with her."

Owen raised an eyebrow at him.

Jack frowned. "Museum?"

Simon answered for Erin. "Yes. The Andreas mansion is partially open to the public, since it's so historic to the area. I toured it in sixth grade and wrote a report on it. It's beautiful. I always wondered how it would feel to grow up inside of it—I thought it would feel like being a prince."

Erin had no idea what to say to that. "My room is on the third floor. If we go in through the kitchen, we can go up the back stairs and get straight to it. My suitcase should be in my closet, and there are some spare totes in the hall. Hopefully this won't take long."

The house was huge, and there were at least four places on the first floor alone for the cleaning crew to be. By rights it should have been simple for the five of them to escape unnoticed up the stairs to Erin's room, but Erin was barely inside before he heard the familiar heavy footsteps in the hallway to the kitchen.

Diane.

It was strange, because while she had been around all of Erin's life, she had remained ageless in his mind. She had come into his life grim and unsmiling, her hair not gray and yet clearly not naturally that flat blonde, singular in hue and without a solitary glimmer of shine to it, as if she were using its oil alone to polish the antique furnishings. The hair always stuck out in a strawlike shock from the top of her head, wrapped in a scarf. Large, disapproving, washed-out blue eyes peered at Erin from over the same pair of silver-rimmed glasses hung on a plastic string of beads. She wore the same pale pink smock he'd always seen her in, now worn with age, the pockets patched where bottles of cleaning fluid had pushed their way through.

She padded up to Erin and his company in her yellow house slippers, hands on her hips as the smell of wood polish and ammonia drifted from her. "And who are all these people traipsing through my house at this hour?"

Jared, Owen, and Simon exchanged confused glances with one another. Owen narrowed his eyes at Diane.

Erin put a hand on Owen's forearm and steered him toward the stairs. "I'm staying with friends for a while, Diane. They've come to help me collect some things from my room. *Only* my room," he added quickly as she screwed up her face to object.

Diane waved a microfiber duster threateningly at them. "If anyonc so much as *touches* any of my antiques, I'm calling the police."

Owen stiffened, and Erin pushed him with greater purpose out of the room.

"Seriously, who was that woman?" Simon whispered as soon as they were clear of the kitchen door.

"Diane Ketterson." Erin spoke quietly as he led the way up the narrow stairs once used by servants. "She's the caretaker for the museum. Essentially she's in charge of maintaining the antiques and keeping the place clean and ready for visitors, but she's always been… zealous about her work."

"*Militant* might be a more apt term," Jack murmured.

Erin couldn't deny that. "When I was young, my mother ran the museum, and it wasn't open as often. But once she and my father divorced, he hired Diane and turned the museum over to a local committee. I've been able to use less of my own house since then, but it only bothered me when I was younger. At this point I only come here to sleep, shower, and eat breakfast. Sometimes only to sleep."

They were at the second-floor landing now, and as Erin absentmindedly headed to the stairs for the third floor, someone took hold of his arm, jolting him out of his reverie. Blinking, he saw it was Owen who had stopped him, regarding him with incredulity.

"Are you telling me you live in this huge house, but you can't leave your room because total strangers are wandering through it? And it's been this way your entire life?"

Feeling awkward under the intensity of Owen's gaze, Erin averted his own. It sounded so abysmal, the way he phrased it. "Well, not my *entire* life, no. Only since my mother left."

Owen's expression didn't change. "When was that?"

What, did he want the year? "I was seven. Why does it matter?"

Now *everyone* stared at Erin in horror.

"I'm so sorry." Simon covered his mouth with his hand. "I remember hearing, vaguely, that your parents had divorced, and I knew your home was open to the public, that you ended up going to boarding school because of the separation, but I didn't realize… *oh my God.*"

Erin felt self-conscious. "It was a little rough when I was young, but I'm fine, I assure you." He gestured to the stairs. "Can we please continue?"

No one else objected or commented further, but now that they had brought it up, the disparity in his living space as compared to the rest of the house made Erin anxious. The exterior of the mansion, even at night, gave off a grand appearance, with the meticulously refurbished brick and elegant sconces and well-kept shrubbery, most of it evergreen in deference to the northern climate. The kitchen, despite never being part of the tour, was large and modern, well-appointed as occasionally it was rented as part of the museum through special arrangement with Erin's father, and because it wouldn't do, John Jean said, to have the kitchen appearing paltry. The second-floor landing Erin used to access his room was part of the tour, and so it was carefully arranged with antique rugs and furnishings both from the Andreas family and the Copper Point area in general. Rooms with doors ajar whispered of opulence meant to impress guests of John Jean and the patrons of the museum. John Jean's own room was down a side hallway, off-limits to the tour, but it too was full of elegance and power.

The door Erin led them through to get to his living space was narrow, same as the winding stairs. These were painted, not polished like the grand staircase from the main floor. This set of stairs wasn't cleaned as often, usually only if Erin asked or did it himself, and to his shame he caught sight of cobwebs on the ceiling and dust in the corners of the treads. The single naked bulb that lit their way was pathetic compared to the grand chandelier in the hallway. When they arrived at the top of the stairs, the tiny space crowded with storage, it was shabby and plain. This was before they entered Erin's room, which was small, cramped, and in complete disarray.

He rushed around, picking up papers, discarded clothing, unopened mail. "Please excuse the mess."

Everyone appeared uneasy—except for Owen, who was eerily stoic. Once again it was Simon who spoke. "Why is your room so small? Why are you so far from the rest of the house?"

Erin continued to tuck things away, straightening the covers on his bed before opening his drawers and pulling out clothes to set on top of the comforter. "As I said, it's because of the museum. When the committee took over, the museum expanded and absorbed my room."

Jack looked like he wanted to punch someone. "You were moved to this attic when you were *seven*?"

Erin smoothed a hand over his hair. "I wasn't here much to care. They enrolled me in boarding school right away, and initially during vacations I stayed with my mother, so it made sense to everyone, I'm sure. By the time she drifted away and my father was my main parent, my room was gone, my things were up here, and, well, it all sort of happened, I suppose." He sighed and put down the stack of socks in his hands. "Honestly, you can stop looking at me as if I'm Little Orphan Annie."

"I was thinking more along the lines of the heroine of *The Little Princess*," Jared said.

Erin blushed. "These are the former servants' quarters." He realized that didn't help his argument and busied himself with packing. "They're converted, as you can see. I have my own bath suite." Calling it a suite was such a stretch he almost winced. If any of them asked to use the toilet before they left, he'd be in trouble. "I'll grant you the situation is strange, but everyone has their struggle. I certainly have plenty of compensations and advantages. Someday this place will be mine, and if I want, I can cancel the museum tours and roll around naked in the middle of the antique rugs whether Diane likes it or not. I sincerely doubt that will happen, however." He put his hands on his hips. "I can't remember if I put my suitcase in this closet or if it's in the hall."

He knew it was in his closet, but he wanted to stop talking about his life, about his family, about his house, and whether or not he was a deprived, poor being. It was completely ridiculous. He wasn't poor anything. What truly unnerved him, though, was that while the others asked questions and cast worried or pitying glances his direction, Owen gave no reaction whatsoever.

Erin kept waiting for a remark from him. Some outburst or declaration. Especially when Owen was the one who found the bathroom. But he made no comment, not even when Erin rushed after him to try to stop him. When they met in the narrow passage, blocked in by towers of boxes and totes, Owen's expression was still flat, and when Erin looked up at him expectantly, the only thing Owen said was, "Hurry and pack your things so we can get going."

Quietly. Patiently. Not Owen the Ogre at all.

He knows I don't want to discuss it. He's deliberately not bringing it up because he can tell I'm uncomfortable.

Erin recalled the way Owen had reacted to the woman at the fundraiser, how she'd mentioned his playing and how it was as good as when he was younger, and he'd clearly wanted to discuss anything but that. Erin recalled Owen's hollow expression as Erin thanked him for taking up Ram's place in the quartet.

Oh God—Erin had mentioned something about how he sounded as good as he remembered, the same as this woman.

You made things awful. You ruined his escape from a bad evening. You said unfeeling things. You made yourself a nuisance. You've let him misunderstand. You're terrible.

Trembling, he leaned into the wall as his knees became weak.

Taking gentle hold of his arm, Owen bore him up and led him toward his bedroom. "Come on. I'll help you."

So apparently he saw himself as Erin's guardian now, the man who could see past Erin's defenses into all his private spaces, and then when Erin realized he'd been a fool and a boor, Owen would forgive him.

"I'm so sorry," Erin whispered, trying to keep the words low enough only Owen would hear.

Owen pressed his lips close to Erin's ear. "You have nothing to apologize for."

"This wasn't why I bid on you." He couldn't make eye contact and he could barely speak above a whisper, but he forced the words out.

"I know." The kisses against his hair were going to be the death of Erin. "Is this so bad, though? Do you hate being comforted?"

Erin's eyes fluttered closed. "I don't."

"Then let me do this. Please?"

What could Erin say to that? Nothing. He could only nod, allow Owen to lead him back to his room, and help him pack his things. Soon they finished, and with his odd new group of friends each carrying a load of his belongings, Erin left his father's house and drove away into the night.

This time he rode in the back seat of his car beside Owen, his head on Owen's shoulder, wrapped in the unexpected shelter of his arms.

CHAPTER FOUR

OWEN LAY awake in bed late into the night, staring at the ceiling.

From the moment he'd put down the bow of Ram's violin, he'd heard a freight train in his head rushing slowly toward him. It accelerated as Erin won his bid, accompanied by the steady *thud* of his heartbeat in his ears as John Jean took Erin's elbow. The evening had roused his nightmares from the depths of his subconscious and dressed them in tuxedos. Owen heard the familiar whistle of the train wreck coming to the station, and like a good conductor, he prepared to get on board.

At Erin's house, Owen had listened to him recount the emptiness of his life so baldly… and the train had skidded, grinding the gears and sending Owen tumbling inside of his own mental hellscape. Worst of all had been the calm way Erin had described his neglect and abuse.

Owen pressed his forearm over his eyes, letting out a slow, deep breath. He had no idea where the prescription for Xanax had gone. He didn't want more to drink, but he did want to sleep, and it was clear lying here waiting for his brain to stop eating itself wasn't a strategy that would end with him finding respite in slumber.

When he stood in the kitchen in front of the cupboard where they kept the liquor, he only ended up closing the door to the cabinet as soon as he opened it. He reached into the refrigerator instead and pulled out a mineral water.

The creak of footsteps on the living room floor announced Jared's presence before he spoke. "Grab one for me, will you?"

Owen snagged a second bottle with his index finger so two of them hung from his knuckles, then tossed one lightly to Jared. "I know why I'm awake. What's your excuse?"

"I don't know, maybe it's our new houseguest, whom you invited without consulting me, the one who bid twenty-five thousand dollars on you and then showed us his garret in the flashiest mansion in town as if it were the most normal thing in the world." He shook his head as he twisted off the top of the water and took a sip. "Seven years old. If that family weren't wealthy, it would be considered child abuse. Well, it *is* child abuse, but we both know they'd never be punished for it." When Owen glanced worriedly at the stairs, Jared waved a hand. "Oh, don't worry. The Little Princess is out like a light. I checked, naively thinking he might be unsettled after the chaos. But he's completely gone. I think we short-circuited him. His snore is adorable, by the way."

Owen leaned against the fridge for a few seconds, then said out loud what he'd needed to say to someone the entire evening. "I looked across the room when his dad was angry with him for the bid, and all I could see was my parents."

"I gathered, from the way you became the newest member of the Avengers." Jared took a long swig of water. "Is this related to why you insisted he move in with us? Can we talk about that? Please?"

Owen didn't want to talk about it, but he owed it to Jared. "It was the hand on his elbow. The way Erin went so pale. For a minute I couldn't move. Then I remembered I wasn't ten, I was thirty-four, and this time I could kick ass." He clung to the water bottle, breathing deliberately and doing his best to keep himself calm. "I couldn't leave him there. Not after I saw that."

"Owen, you need to be careful. You also need to make sure you're seeing what you think you're seeing." Jared sighed. "Though after the tour tonight and the way he gave in and went along with your mad demand so easily, I honestly don't know what to say."

"He wasn't exactly easy about moving out. More… I don't know how to describe it, except to say the way he barely put up a fight made me more determined to extricate him. That and his horrible servants' quarters. I couldn't decide if it was for our benefit or if he really believes it was fine to be treated that way."

"I don't think he knows either. Speaking of—why did he bid so much on you? That was an insane bid."

"To get away from his father, obviously."

Jared frowned. “Wait, what?”

“He bid on me to….” Owen rubbed the water bottle against his cheek, the fine details of this part of the story escaping him. “Look, it’s all about his dad, okay? He hadn’t thought his plan through very well, which was why I told him he had to move in here.”

This justification made much less sense to him sober at home than it had drunk/high at the party, so he drank his water and frowned at the opposite wall.

“This is what he told you, did he?”

Owen opened his mouth to say yes, then hesitated.

This wasn’t why I bid on you. It wasn’t for this.

Owen cleared his throat. “Look. It’s complicated. But it definitely has to do with his dad.” Erin had agreed to come live here with him. What other proof did he need?

“So you don’t think there’s any *other* possible reason than that?”

“Well, what *other* possible reason could there be?”

Jared swore under his breath. “I can see I’ve been appointed the role of something between nanny and referee. Thank you so much.”

Owen pursed his lips. “We’re not fighting.”

Jared laughed. “Since Erin took the HR job at St. Ann’s, fighting is all the two of you have done. That you think somehow this has changed overnight is a sign your Xanax hasn’t completely worn off.”

“I told you, I sobered up. But speaking of, I want another one so I have a prayer of sleeping. Where’d the bottle go?”

“I’ll give it to you in a minute. First, I want to talk some more about this mess.” Jared raised his mineral water in a mock toast. "I'm the only sleeping pill you get for the moment."

"He literally is a princess in a tower. Prince in a tower."

"Mmm, but he doesn't want rescuing." Jared inclined his head. "So this is a fake relationship, is what you're telling me?"

"Of course. This is entirely to help him with his father."

"I wonder why he wants you to be a *boyfriend*, though. There are so many ways for you to help him escape his father without that moniker."

Owen wasn't about to point out he'd been the one to propose that idea. Though now he wondered about that too. Why hadn't Erin told him where to get off? "I guess I need to ask a lot of questions tomorrow."

"You can try, but something tells me you're not going to get many answers."

Owen had the bad feeling Jared was right.

WHEN ERIN first woke, he wasn't entirely sure where he was.

He'd slept heavily, alarmingly so, and no familiar noises woke him. He had a preset alarm on his phone, but this was the first time in a long while its charms had pulled him from slumber. Usually it was the sound of someone vacuuming below him, or Diane chastising the tour guides as they arrived to prepare for the day, or someone working on the grounds that stirred him. Today he heard nothing but the gentle tick of a clock he didn't recognize.

Rolling over, he saw the room in the dim light of early morning and remembered.

Oh, yes. He was at Owen Gagnon's house, in Simon Lane's old room.

It didn't have much in it, since Simon had moved in with Jack Wu several months ago and taken nearly everything with him. The only items remaining were the stray odds and ends he didn't want but couldn't quite throw away. What appeared to be a bin of mementos was stacked on top of another of clothes and scrubs from another hospital and several pairs of shoes. There were a few framed posters on the walls, and a bulletin board with an outdated calendar pinned to it.

The closet was full of Erin's clothes now, his suits and shirts carefully hung there by Jack and the others, his dress shoes lining the floor. Boxes and totes of more casual clothing stood beside the dresser, which Simon assured him was cleaned out and ready for his use. Jared had told him to help himself to anything in the kitchen cupboards and fridge and promised to show him the essentials, such as how to run the coffee maker.

Erin wondered where Owen was this morning.

By rights Erin should go into work, but… well, honestly, he would probably take the day off, considering everything. After making a quick call to his assistant, he slid out of bed, then moved the curtain aside at the window.

It had snowed overnight, several inches, enough that school was likely cancelled and the hospital's surgery and shift rotations were in chaos. Owen and Jared's house was on the street, as opposed to his father's, set back on a long drive. Erin watched neighbors clearing their drives and heard the occasional plow.

Though he'd resolved to stay away from the hospital, he wasn't certain what he was meant to do with himself. If he were at home, he'd be sitting with his father in the kitchen, listening as he droned on about whatever he deemed important. Today would have been supremely uncomfortable. He wondered what his father had done when he discovered Erin wasn't there.

Perhaps he'd sent a message. When Erin checked his phone, the only notices he had were from hospital employees needing things.

One was from Nick.

Are you all right?

Erin tapped out a reply. *I'm quite well, though I took the day off. Want to meet for coffee later today?*

Coffee sounds good. What time?

I don't currently have any plans. He glanced at the door to his room, felt a flutter of butterflies, and amended his text. *I should check in with my new housemates. Shall we say afternoon, once the roads are cleared?*

One o'clock?

Sounds perfect.

I'll come pick you up, armed with many questions.

Erin realized he'd mentioned new housemates to Nick but not who they were. *Do you know where I am, though?*

Erin, the entire town knows exactly where you are.

Oh.

Erin lowered the phone and stared at the door, his heart beating faster.

He felt strange greeting his housemates in pajamas, so he combed his hair into the most presentable state it would allow and threw on a pair of jeans and a sweatshirt, as well as a thick pair of socks. Owen's house was warmer than the Andreas mansion, but it was still an older home with hardwood floors in abundance, and he could tell he would need to find his slippers as soon as possible.

He had to organize his entire room, he supposed. Well, he'd do that later.

The smell of coffee and some kind of sizzling meat announced the presence of at least one person as Erin entered the hallway, and by the time he passed the bathroom he heard voices too. He assumed the two bedrooms he could see on the opposite side of the open stairway were his housemates'—both doors were open.

He wondered which one was Owen's and which one was Jared's.

He wondered what he should say to them when he went downstairs.

As he approached the kitchen, treading as silently as possible on the creaky floor, he listened to their conversation, which turned out to be an argument. Not much of a surprise, given Owen was involved. It seemed to revolve around who was going to remove the snow on the driveway and the sidewalk.

"I'm telling you, I did it last time." That was Owen.

"And I'm telling *you* the last time didn't count. It was as much of a dusting as this one. I did the ten-inch disaster after New Year's."

"What, so you get to sit everything out until the next blizzard? Forget it. That's never been the arrangement. It's always luck of the draw."

"Well, that was when we had three people. Now you keep getting the lucky draws, and it's pissing me off."

"So it's my fault you have crap luck?"

"I'm saying we have to rethink the system." Jared paused. "Though we have three people again now. Maybe my curse will be broken at last."

Erin stopped short and held his breath. He'd never shoveled snow in his life.

"Oh, no. Forget it. Even if Erin knows how to run a snowblower, which I doubt, I'd worry the wrong push would suck him under and blow him through the chute along with the snow."

Erin blushed.

Jared sighed. "For crying out loud."

"Well obviously not, but seriously, our blower isn't self-propelled, and you know as well as I do once it's over six inches it's like pushing a dead heifer. If he carries more than one three-ring binder at work, I take them away from him because he looks like he's straining."

Erin clapped a hand over his mouth. *Oh my God.* Owen *did* take his binders away from him, annoying Erin all the way to whatever meeting he was attending.

That… that was… *intentional*?

"Fine. You can have his turn at snow removal if you think it's too much for him."

"*That's a dick move*."

Jared's only reply was a wicked laugh. Owen said nothing more, and after some rustling of clothing and stomping, a door slammed. Shortly afterward, the gentle whirr of a gasoline engine began in the garage.

Erin gave a quiet yelp of surprise as Jared stuck his head around the corner and smiled at him. "Good morning. Cup of coffee?"

"I—I—" Erin's gaze darted around as he tried to come up with an excuse for eavesdropping, and failed.

Jared waved him into the kitchen. "Owen already gave me a lecture about how you like your coffee, which is apparently with half-and-half and two sugars, but we only have skim milk, so I hope it will do."

Erin felt dizzy. "How does Owen know how I take my coffee?"

"Honey, I don't ask the questions, I just write down the grocery list. Oh—I wanted to tell you. The fourth step on the stairs creaks. Which is how I knew you were there. Normally I think Owen would notice, but he's a bit too amped."

Erin pulled out a stool from the island and sat on it before he wilted onto the floor. "Is Owen… all right?" He glanced at the clock then straightened in alarm. "Aren't you both late for work?"

"I had a light morning as it was, and the snow cancelled more of my patients and all the morning surgeries. I'll go in and see a few patients and do rounds later. But don't worry about me, Mr. Moneybags." Jared passed a cup of coffee to Erin and leaned against the counter. "Okay, I need a straight answer. What's going to happen between you and your father because of this? Owen said something about you asked him to pretend to be your boyfriend to deliberately upset him, and he spoke as if you needed his protection." The edge in Jared's voice sent goose bumps across Erin's skin. "Did you knowingly put yourself and Owen by extension in danger?"

Startled, Erin put his mug down. "I—what? No, that's not… but is that why he thinks I…?" His cheeks heated, and he put his hands against them as if this were some sort of camouflage. "I knew he misunderstood, but I didn't realize it was this out of hand."

"So you didn't bid on him in some wild scheme to get back at your father?"

"Of course not. I don't even understand how that would work. It will anger my father, yes, if he thinks Owen and I are going out, because he doesn't like him and he thinks I'm straight, but I'm not sure he'll believe the story. He'll be more upset about me moving out."

Jared raised an eyebrow. "Owen's showstopper kiss helped the relationship story along significantly, as well as his gallant rescue. People have always wondered if you were gay, but now they don't have any doubts. Your father's going to look like the king of denial if he doesn't believe."

"How do you know all this?"

"I'm at the center of the Copper Point gossip hub. They're not sure why you bid so much money, but they're impressed by the latest St. Ann's romance."

Erin pinched the bridge of his nose.

Jared didn't let up his line of questioning. "If you weren't trying to make your father angry or escape him or whatever delusion Owen has, why did you let him move you out of your house?"

"I think I got a bit caught up in the moment. I hadn't meant to bid as much as I did and…." Visions of Owen sweeping him away, staring his father down, whispering vows in his ear made Erin dizzy. "Well, staying here a night or two won't hurt anything. It'll give me time to properly explain things as well, away from the chaos, with everyone calmed down."

Jared folded his arms. "You don't know anything at all about Owen's family, do you?"

"I don't know much, no. I assume this is an oversight I should correct?"

"Yes, but I can't give you the answers you need, unfortunately, without breaking his confidence. That said, a talented HR director should be able to uncover some details." Jared picked up an oven mitt. "Bacon? Eggs? Owen made both and insisted I keep some ready for you in the oven."

Erin was about to say he wasn't hungry, but the words *Owen made* and *insisted* subdued him. "Please. Thank you."

Once he'd given Erin his food, Jared discreetly left the kitchen, and the second he was gone, Erin had his phone out and Google open. He didn't know the names of Owen's parents, but it didn't take him long to discover them. His father was William Gagnon, vice president of operations at Weber Mining & Minerals until he'd left the company and relocated to western Minnesota. His mother was Dr. Eliza Robinson, a celebrated violinist in her day before she'd married and taken a teaching position at Bayview University. She'd helped build the orchestra program there, small as it was, and the Robinson Rehearsal Hall was named in honor of her efforts. She retired unexpectedly early in 2002 and moved to Ann Arbor not long after to live with her sister.

Erin frowned. How old had Owen been when she left?

He put the phone down, arrested by a thought. He'd always assumed Owen had returned to Copper Point because of family. There were no Gagnons in town, though, except for him. Was Owen's mother's family here? Why *had* Owen come back?

According to the online archives of *The Copper Point Gazette*, Owen's father was a shining, upstanding citizen, his mother was a model professor beloved by everyone at the university, and their marriage had appeared perfect. Their divorce must have been a real shock. In fact, he vaguely remembered his father mentioning something about it at breakfast on a break.

Erin found more notifications of Owen Gagnon's upcoming violin recitals than anything regarding Owen's parents. Countless photos showed Owen holding his violin and receiving awards. Always standing by his side was a beautiful, smiling woman the captions explained was his mother.

One article said Owen had a prestigious full-ride music scholarship at a college out east Erin recognized as renowned for accepting musical prodigies. Yet it wasn't a violin virtuoso out blowing the driveway. It was an anesthesiologist.

Erin now remembered the gossip surrounding Owen that summer Erin had longed to talk with him while he wandered the greenbelts of Bayview Park. Apparently he'd had a lot on his mind during those walks. And Erin had been the fool attempting to make a friend.

Erin pulled up the photo of William Gagnon again. He looked only a little like Owen, but enough that Erin could find the son in the father's face. Owen had his mother's eyes, but he had his father's smile. Cheeky. Reckless. Slightly sad.

Staring at the stranger in the digital image, the man with a proud arm around his beaming wife, Erin couldn't figure out what he was supposed to be looking for here.

He was about to give up when he found it: a single line in the public records section three months before William and Eliza filed for divorce. *William Gagnon, charged with third-degree domestic assault.*

Erin stilled.

He searched the public records more carefully, backward and forward, but all he ever found beyond that was another notice saying the charge had been dropped, notably around the time of the divorce filing. Yet that initial charge burned in Erin's mind, telling him with certainty this was what Jared had meant for him to find.

Had this man hurt Owen's mother?

Had he hurt Owen?

How much more had he hurt either of them than was in the police report? The mere whisper of the thought hurt Erin's heart enough he had to press his hand to his chest.

Owen came in, stomping snow from his feet. Erin closed the browser and set the phone facedown on the table in front of him, and as he held his cup of coffee in his hands as a sort of shield, Owen smiled at him.

Cheeky. Reckless.

Slightly sad.

"Hey. You're awake." Owen stomped a few more times, toed out of his boots, and hung up his coat on a peg beside the door. "Oh good, Jared got you the food. And coffee, I see. Sorry about the half-and-half."

Erin clutched the mug tighter. "It's fine. Thank you."

"I thought we could go grocery shopping later to make sure we had food around you liked. And the right laundry detergent and all that."

The right *laundry detergent*? Erin's chest, which hadn't fully recovered, began to hurt again. "I'm not particular. And I honestly don't eat at home often."

"Yes, but you should. We take turns cooking, and we're both good." He held up his hands. "We don't expect you to cook."

Erin's cheeks heated. "I do know how to cook."

Why were they talking about cooking and laundry detergent? Why wasn't Erin explaining how this was a misunderstanding?

Because right now I'm a little too busy imagining terrible things and hoping like hell they aren't true.

Owen helped himself to a cup of coffee. His cheeks were pink from the cold, and Erin could smell the crisp winter air on him with a hint of engine oil. "Well, that's fine. I mean, you can cook if you want. My point was you don't have to. Do you need help getting situated in your room? Simon used to have shelves in there, but he took them. We can go get whatever you need."

Erin was about to ask what the point was when he didn't plan on staying long-term, then decided he'd have that conversation once he wasn't haunted by public record searches. "Thank you, but I'm fine for now."

Owen turned his back to him, shoulders tensed and his hands tightening on the edge of the counter. "So, I suppose we should talk."

And here Erin had hoped his dismissal would excuse him from the conversation as well as Owen's courtesy. "Wh-what would you like to discuss?"

Though Owen had been the one to initiate conversation, he hovered silently for several seconds, and when he did speak, he rubbed a hand over the back of his head and only half turned around, smiling awkwardly. "Well, to start, I feel like I should apologize. I was more than a bit of a mess last night, and I don't know that I said the right things to you or made the best decisions. I hope I haven't caused too many problems for you. I'm sorry."

Softening, Erin raised a hand. "There's no need for that. I could use a day or two away from my father, I think. It was a strange way to go about it, but—"

"Hold on." Owen leaned over the breakfast bar toward him. "You can't be serious about staying only a few nights."

Erin's gaze darted around the room, landing anywhere but on Owen. "I… I don't want to impose…."

"There's no imposing. You can stay here five years if you want. Fifteen. I'm telling you, it's fine. It's no good if you leave right away. There's too much ahead of us. I was thinking of how we could play the fake-boyfriend angle, and it's going to be fun." Owen winked. "Good thing the no-dating-between-hospital-employees rule of yours got rescinded."

Erin stifled the queasiness in his gut. "It was never my rule, and *I* was the one who rescinded it, if you recall."

"I recall quite clearly." His eyes sparkled as he smiled at Erin. "I was completely surprised by that move. Pleasantly so."

But you don't know why I rescinded it. Erin wasn't going to tell him that, but he *had* to clear the air about the bachelor bid right now, even if he looked like a fool. "About… about the auction. I didn't bid on you because of my father."

His face was red, and he wanted to crawl under the table and die, but he'd said it, and he waited for Owen's disdain, or laughter, or whatever he was going to do. None of that happened. Owen only remained standing close to him. When he spoke, he was quiet, his tone full of surprise.

"Then… why did you?"

He clutched the too-hot mug, letting the heat sear his hand. "Because I wanted to."

He had to let go of the cup because his hands trembled so much he was going to spill the coffee. Every cell in his body was braced for impact, for Owen to blink in surprise, then laugh, then mock him. He tried to put up a mask, a good front, but it wasn't possible.

He shouldn't have moved out.

He shouldn't have placed that bid.

He shouldn't have—

Owen turned Erin's face to the side, keeping hold of his chin, staring at Erin so intently it felt as if he were peering directly into his soul. His voice was cool, laced with the kind of command he used with patients. "At the fundraiser, after you placed your bid and your father came up to you, he grabbed your elbow, and you became very pale."

Erin frowned. Yes, he supposed his father had gripped him a little roughly. And Erin probably had blanched, given he'd been anticipating how much more furious his father would be in private.

"Has your father grabbed you that way before?"

Erin opened his mouth to say no, of course he hadn't, then stopped, his heart beating too fast. Well… he had. Often. His mind, the traitor, pulled up the recollection of the time when he'd returned to school and people laughed at the bruises at his elbow. He remembered feeling ashamed that he was so skinny that every mark showed on him. Those marks, and the ones at the back of his neck.

He'd forgotten about those. Except the thing was, he bruised easily. Frequently he discovered large ones on his arms and legs with no memory of when or where he'd acquired them.

"It's okay." Owen's words wrapped around Erin's troubled heart. "You don't have to explain anything to me. I understand."

Well, that was all well and good, but Erin certainly didn't understand. Owen seemed to be implying something that Erin couldn't understand.

Because it sounded like he was saying Erin's father was abusing him.

The breath in Erin's lungs caught, unable to move past his throat, and his mouth tasted like ash.

His mind replayed his father's furious face as he grabbed Erin's arm, countenance promising a sharper, more terrible nightmare at home.

No. No, he wouldn't have beat me, he would have only yelled at me.

Are you sure?

Erin pressed a hand to the side of his head, drawing in a desperate, terrified breath on a gasp.

Owen put a hand on his shoulder, gentle and comforting. "I meant what I told him." Owen's voice was quiet, but it felt like grating chains. "I won't let him grab you again. I'll pretend to be your boyfriend, stay by your side, and I'll protect you."

This was a nightmare. On the one hand it was what Erin wanted, Owen touching him, making vows to him. But he wasn't supposed to be talking about *this*. He wasn't supposed to be suggesting these things about Erin's father, wasn't supposed to be planting these thoughts in Erin's mind….

No. This wasn't what he'd wanted at all.

Dislodging Owen's hand as he rose from his stool, he turned to him and made a small, polite bow. "Thank you. But I can take care of myself."

After hurrying out of the kitchen, he escaped up the stairs to shut himself in his room.

He leaned against the back of the door, staring at the strange new space. It was a nice room, large, with big windows overlooking the street. It was cozy.

It was uncomfortable, and wrong, and awkward, and Erin wanted to be anywhere but here.

Except neither did he want to go home.

Crawling into the bed, Erin pulled the covers over his head and willed himself to sleep until it was time to meet Nick.

CHAPTER FIVE

When Nick showed up at the house, Erin practically ran for his friend's car, acutely aware of Owen's glare behind him the entire way down the walk.

Nick turned up the heat as Erin got in, an automatic gesture born out of years of friendship, since Erin was always cold. "So start talking. What in the *hell* is going on?"

Erin put his bag on the floor, snapped his seat belt in place, and huddled forward, staring at the dashboard. "I behaved a bit rashly, I'll admit."

"*A bit rashly*. You were completely unhinged, Erin. Emmanuella and Grandma Emerson have both called to lecture me because clearly something about you isn't right. I agree with them."

Despite the fact that he'd steeled himself for this lecture, it still stung. That Nick and his family were concerned only made matters worse. "I didn't know the others intended to bid on Owen, and I panicked."

"You dropped enough on the man to buy a new car, and then you moved in with him. Are you okay? Are you out of your mind?"

Erin pinched the bridge of his nose. "I'm *fine*. I got away from myself a bit. How often do I have to say it? Do you want me to admit I'm a complete fool who can't do anything right?"

"Yes, that'd be a fine start."

Nick was the same, tough love as always. Erin's cheeks flamed. "Yes, well, I already know all that. I've made a mess. I'm sorry."

"It's my fault too. I've known you were in a funky place for a while now and should have paid closer attention." Nick swore under his breath. "You were in panic mode. You make terrible decisions in panic mode."

Nick feeling bad only made Erin feel worse. "You're not responsible for me. I had a silly whim and got caught up in the moment."

"You went off the chain trying to get your crush's attention."

Now Erin was in panic mode. "I don't have a *crush* on him."

Nick gave him a long look.

Erin averted his gaze. "Fine. I… like him a little. But there's no point in telling him."

"Why the hell not? Why spend so much money on him? And why did you move in with him?"

"I *told* you, it got out of hand. And now he's misunderstood—" Erin pressed his fingers against the side of his head. "Never mind. The bottom line is that it's a mess, as you said."

"What I want to know is why you're making it messier by moving in there."

"Obviously I'm not going to stay. I was getting away from my father for an evening is all."

"Yes, because he's really going to calm down once the rumors about the two of you dating are inflamed." Nick raised an eyebrow. "Unless you actually *are* dating?"

"*No.*" Erin tapped his bag with his foot. "Can we please talk about something else?"

Sighing, Nick nodded. "Sure. How about we discuss the fundraiser totals, which are more than double last year's take."

Erin pressed his hands to his mouth. "You're kidding."

"Nope. Record-breaking income and rave reviews, even of your stunts with Owen. However." Nick's lips thinned. "When I put the numbers into the spreadsheet this morning, it still wasn't enough for the cardiac unit to start breaking ground."

"What? No. That can't be right. It should have been fine if we only met our target, but to double it—"

Nick jerked his thumb at the back seat. "I brought the records with me. You and I are heading to the cabin, where we're going to go over them. Because it's as you say. The money should be there. It's weird that it isn't."

Erin frowned absently at the dash, his mind whirring. "It doesn't make any sense."

"I didn't tell anyone I took the records, by the way. Not even Wendy. Let's keep this between the two of us. In case there's something funny going on."

Oh no. Not again. Erin held up a hand. "Look, they *fired* the embezzlers. You and I have their jobs."

"This board has been in power for decades. That never happens. The few times others have slipped in, they don't simply get them kicked out, they ruin them. They warrant a little double-checking. Especially now that they have a new member. The first thing they'll do is try to pin things on her."

The thought made Erin queasy. "You really think so?"

"I *know* so." Nick kept his eyes on the road, but his jaw had a tic in it. "My grandmother is at the cabin with Emmanuella and my mother, by the way. Waiting to talk to you."

"Oh dear." Erin shrank into his seat.

"What, you thought you could pull a stunt like that and they wouldn't say something?"

All three women came out to the porch as the two of them got out of the car, giving Erin a look that made him want to crawl behind the vehicle. Nick's sister as well as his mother, Aniyah, stood flanking the family matriarch and most formidable of the three, Pearle Dinah Emerson.

Drawing a slow, steadying breath, Erin approached Mrs. Emerson and inclined his head. "Emmanuella. Aniyah. Grandma Emerson. It's good to see you. If I'd known you were going to be here, I'd have brought something from the bakery."

Emmanuella swatted Erin on the arm. "Twenty-five thousand dollars, Erin? Seriously."

Aniyah folded her arms tighter and regarded Erin much the same as she had when he was thirteen, as if he were a small, strange bomb that might go off at any second. "Mama, he doesn't seem like he's gone crazy, but I just don't know."

Though Erin tried to wait the encounter out, Grandma Emerson's thin yet strong hand caught his chin and kept it level with her gaze.

"Are you getting enough to eat?" she asked, her dark eyes kind but firm and tolerating nothing but the truth in reply.

"Yes, ma'am."

"Are you sleeping? At least seven hours every night?"

"Yes. Most of the time."

She huffed, indicating she expected to hear a better answer the next time she inquired after him. Then she continued. "Is my boy here treating you properly at work and sometimes sitting down with you as a friend as well?"

"Yes, ma'am. Nick is a wonderful employer and CEO, and I couldn't be happier to work under him. And yes, we have coffee together at least once a week outside of work."

This seemed to please her, and she cast an approving nod in Nick's direction before asking Erin one last question. "Are you happy, young man?"

Erin hesitated. She asked him this every time, and every time he faltered. Once he'd lied and said yes, and his attempt at circumvention had earned him several hours of lectures about what happiness truly was as he escorted her to sit at her husband's graveside.

Happiness isn't something you find or receive, it's something you decide to claim. He still didn't know what she meant, but he didn't want another lecture.

"I'm trying to claim it, Grandma Emerson."

She nodded but looked disappointed. "I've left a plate of egg salad sandwiches in the fridge and a chocolate cake on the counter," she called as she followed her daughter and granddaughter to their car. "Bring the rocking chair by for me anytime tomorrow, Nicolas. I'm not in a hurry to have it."

"Yes, ma'am," Nick called back to her.

"Thank you for the food," Erin added.

As soon as they were gone, he hurried inside and wolfed down two of the egg salad sandwiches without pausing.

They finished off all the sandwiches and a decent section of the cake with a full pot of coffee as they pored over the files. Erin didn't know where to start, there was so much information.

"This goes back *decades*." Erin held up a stack of paper to Nick. "Some of this was from before we were born. Why did you bring all this if we're looking at a budget for right now?"

"Because when I started messing with the budget, and I mean really messing with it, I couldn't make it work. So I started going back one year, then two, then further and further, and I realized all the years were like that. It felt like I was trying to unravel a knot in a ball of yarn and somehow traveling deeper into a snarl instead."

"You figured this all out this morning?"

"I started yesterday afternoon before the fundraiser, and I got about an hour of sleep last night."

Erin took in the sea of paper in front of him, completely overwhelmed. "I don't know how you thought we were going to solve this in an afternoon. It'll take months to figure out what I'm looking at, let alone find anything."

"But you see what I'm talking about, right? There's something fishy in these numbers. Something more complicated than that flat embezzlement our predecessors were supposed to have taken."

Erin could see it. Or rather, he couldn't see it, but he understood why Nick had grabbed the files, collared Erin, and hidden them both in a cabin. Except it truly was going to take months to go through this. Months outside of work. He supposed he should be ready to spend a lot of time in this cabin.

Nick glanced at his watch. "We need to be mindful of the weather. It's supposed to snow again, and this road is a mess with even the slightest drifting. Usually we plow it ourselves, but the tractor is broken."

Okay, so apparently they would only work here when it wasn't snowing. Which at this time of year was basically never. Erin put down the papers in his hands. "Nick, how are we going to investigate this? Should we turn it over to someone?"

"I don't trust anyone in town. They're all connected to the board in some way."

"Rebecca, then."

"I don't want to go to anyone until I have something solid." He ran a hand over his face. "I'd hoped we could find something today, but you're right. This is too difficult. The problem is I don't want to take much of it home because if my family sees it, they'll get upset, and I'm not putting them through this again."

Again? Erin wanted to ask what Nick was talking about, but something on his friend's face stopped him.

Nick regarded Erin earnestly. "Did you really move out of your dad's house? How long are you staying there? Do you think you could talk Owen into making it long enough for you to go through these files? Without telling him about these files?"

Erin's mouth fell open, and he couldn't make a sound.

Nick pressed on. "You can't go through these files at home, not with your father. But Owen and Jared won't get into your space. Plus you're already there."

"I can't do that."

"Why not?"

"Because it's using him. I was trying to ask him out, not give myself cover!"

Nick put his hand on Erin's. "He kissed you, and danced with you, and took you home. Maybe he likes you and this will work out."

"It was all fake."

"Maybe not all of it was. Even if I'm wrong, fake it until you make it real."

Erin shut his eyes.

Nick squeezed his hand. "I don't care if you do anything about the crush or not, but we have to pursue this embezzlement issue. This is serious stuff. Lives. Every day we don't have that cardiac unit, people die. I want to know why."

Nick was right. What else could Erin do?

"Okay," he said, hoping he wasn't making a terrible mistake.

I CAN take care of myself.

All day long Erin's parting words echoed in Owen's mind, sending his temper into a slow, confused boil. He was a bear as he prepped for the few surgeries that hadn't been cancelled, and he was sour as he chopped vegetables and dressed a roast in the oven for dinner. Jack and Simon were coming over to help ease Erin's transition.

Which was interesting, as Erin had yet to return from his coffee date with Nick, five and a half hours later.

"Who in the hell goes out for coffee for five and a half hours?" He shoved the curtain aside at the living room window and glared at the street. "Where did he *go*?"

Jared, who had dealt with cranky Owen all afternoon, ignored him, but Simon and Jack, who had just arrived, tried to calm him. "I'm sure he'll be here soon," Simon assured him.

"What time did you tell him dinner was?" Jack asked.

Owen pursed his lips. "I was annoyed with him, so I forgot. But he said *coffee*. That implies a few hours at most. Where would he go?" His heart seized, and he put a hand on the glass. "Would he go back to that house?"

At this, Jared finally spoke. "He's probably at the hospital and you missed him."

Owen headed for the door. "I'll be right back."

Jared caught his arm and held him fast. "*Sit*. Eat. If he's not here by eight, I'll track him down personally."

He didn't appear all through dinner, nor while Jack and Jared did the dishes and Simon rubbed Owen's shoulder and said ridiculous, soothing things. At seven thirty, when Owen started to pace, Jared pushed Owen's coat into his hands and turned to Jack and Simon.

"Will you please take him for a walk while I deal with this? Take him to the grocery store or something. Or dump him in the bay. Don't bring him home until I text you."

Jack rounded on Owen. "Speaking of. Why haven't *you* texted *him*?"

Owen clenched his hands at his sides. "Because I don't have his number."

At the grocery store, Jack and Simon shopped for their own groceries, and Owen took a small cart and picked up a few odds and ends of things he knew Erin would like. He got the half-and-half, some sugar cubes, some better, easier elements for salads and a bento container to take them in, and some Dijon mustard, extra mayonnaise, and more eggs so he could make a set of deviled ones. He also picked up a carton of whole milk, since he knew Erin preferred it.

Jack watched him fill his cart with interest. "How do you know so much about what Erin eats?"

Owen paused with the half gallon of milk halfway into the cart. "Is that a serious question?"

Simon turned to him as well. "I've been wondering it too."

They didn't? How weird. "I watch him eat. I know things about the two of you too. I remember details about people. I thought everyone did."

Jack didn't blink. "What's my coffee order?"

"You switch it up a lot, but you prefer black coffee when it's good or when there's no milk. Occasionally you go with a plain black or green tea, but that's usually at home. Simon drinks green tea at home, chai lattes or black tea at the hospital, and Royal English Breakfast Tea Lattes on the rare occasion he can find a Starbucks. Though he will drink coffee sometimes, with milk, if it's *very* good." Owen set down the milk and leaned on the handrail. "What's *my* order?"

Jack and Simon looked at each other uneasily. Finally Simon shrugged. "I have no idea."

Owen's mouth fell open. "Si. You lived with me. We went to high school together."

Simon blushed. "I mean, it's… coffee? You drink it black at home, I think. But at Starbucks or the hospital… I don't know."

Jack held up his hands. "I wouldn't have known about the black part."

Owen couldn't believe this. "I order vanilla lattes with skim milk at Starbucks and work, and at home I take my coffee with a whiff of sugar. It's not complicated."

They apologized, and Owen sighed and tossed in the brand and flavor of yogurt he remembered seeing Erin eat before.

He'd relaxed somewhat at the store, but as they approached the house, he tensed up. Simon, thinking to help, texted Jared and discovered Erin was back, but somehow this only made Owen more upset. He didn't know what he was going to say to him. He was incredibly annoyed but also confused beyond belief.

I can take care of myself.

Owen punched the seat beside him. "God, he pisses me off."

He was fully ready to hear Erin had retreated to his room, but no, he was sitting in the living room when Owen arrived. Owen got the idea Jared had parked him there, especially since Jared stood in the kitchen with his arms folded. When Erin saw Owen loaded down with bags, he rose and hurried over to help.

"You can put these in the refrigerator," Owen said, handing him the insulated tote.

Erin took the bag, set it on the counter near the fridge, and began unloading. "Oh." He held up the yogurt. "This is…? Did you…?"

Owen busied himself with stacking the produce by the sink to wash. "It's the kind you like, right?"

"It is. Thank you."

At least he hadn't told him he could take care of himself with the yogurt too.

He wanted to ask if Erin had eaten dinner, wanted to explain to him about the salad items, but he was also still highly ticked off, so he simply washed the produce, put it into containers, and stuck it in the fridge. Erin lingered as Owen did this, looking uncertain. Eventually he cleared his throat and spoke.

"Jared tells me you expected me for dinner. I'm sorry. I didn't know."

Owen shrugged and continued to put things away. "I didn't tell you. It's my fault."

"I've written down my mobile number and put it beside your laptop. Jared's already given me his number as well as yours."

Okay. This was going a lot better than he'd anticipated. Owen leaned against the counter. "So, Monday, when we go back to work. How do you want to play this?" When Erin only regarded him quizzically, Owen began to get annoyed. "The boyfriend thing."

Erin blinked. "What?"

This guy was going to be the death of Owen, no question. "I want to know how you want me to behave at work. With you. As a fake boyfriend."

Blushing, Erin averted his gaze. "Normally, of course."

"So you want me to go out of my way to annoy you and pick fights with you? What sort of lovers have you had?"

Now Erin seemed as exasperated as he felt. *Good.* "Why *do* you fight with me all the time, anyway?"

"Because I enjoy it."

Jared snorted and settled into the couch, looking as if he wanted a box of popcorn.

Erin decidedly wasn't happy. "What do you mean you enjoy fighting with me? Why?"

"You're so good at it. Nobody else does. They run away, or they cower, or they try to calm me down. Jack and Jared come close, but you're tops. When I've had a rough day, I seek you out and pick at you like a scab until you bite back. It's the best part of my day."

Erin's mouth fell open, and he glared at Owen. "That's the most awful thing anyone has ever said to me."

Owen put his hands on his hips. "Why?"

"Because I don't enjoy fighting with you."

"That's the biggest lie I've ever heard."

Erin's chest puffed up, and he took a step toward Owen.

Owen grinned, waiting for the assault.

Erin caught on, rolled his eyes, and stepped away. "You drive me crazy."

"The feeling is mutual." Owen shifted his arms and raised an eyebrow. "Seriously, though. We need a narrative. Why are we lovers? It can't be because you bid twenty-five grand on me and you've had a crush on me this whole time."

Erin stiffened, and for a moment Owen thought Erin might actually hit him. "People don't need to know our business."

"People need to know something or your dad won't believe the lie. Help me invent it so we can pass it along." He tapped his ribs with his index finger. "It's almost got to be that we've been dating secretly. It's the only way anyone will buy your major spending spree and the sudden move-in together. Now this looks like a public capstone to a private story. When someone asks how all this happened, we can be demure and say, 'That's between us,' but with this air of affection. This way you can have everything you want. You don't have to tell them anything, but they can read between the lines and invent the story for us. I can continue to behave the same as always with you too, but we'll shift our tones slightly. This will make people realize they had no idea all our fighting was flirting. They'll write the romance in their heads and spread it for us. They won't ask us much, because you're not very approachable, and I'm *really* not."

Erin seemed to be struggling with something. "So… you're fine with me living here for a while?"

"*That's* why you're so fidgety? Of course I'm fine with it. So is Jared. You think we'd kick you out? No. You're here as long as you want to be. Do you want me to draw up a lease?"

"Well no, I don't need it, but I can pay rent."

"Yes, because you certainly haven't spent any money on me at all."

"I haven't paid any money *to you*."

"I don't need any money, all right? And neither does Simon or Jared. Not this damn second, anyway." Owen decided the only way to win this argument was to shift the topic. "We should probably consider some dates too, some public outings to seal the deal. Tell me where and when you want to go, get me coverage if I don't have the time off, and I'm in."

"Fine." Erin looked so… shy, and awkward. Owen wasn't used to it, and he found it oddly endearing. "I'll think about it and let you know."

"Great."

"I'll see you in the morning, then."

He disappeared into his room, and it wasn't until he was gone that Owen realized he'd forgotten to ask if he needed help setting up any more shelving or unpacking.

I can take care of myself.

Owen grimaced and flopped into the easy chair, grabbing the slip of paper with Erin's number so he could enter it into his phone.

"You two are better than Netflix," Jared said.

Owen flipped him off without glancing up. Then, because he owed him, he added, "Thanks for finding him. And making him apologize."

"He apologized on his own. I simply pointed out things he might need to know."

Owen tipped his head back and stared at the ceiling. "Work on Monday is going to be weird, isn't it?"

"The weirdest ever," Jared agreed.

Owen thought he could use the weekend to make things easier with Erin, but it wasn't much use. All Erin did was hide in his room, come down for meals, then disappear. Their conversations involved passing plates of foods and whether or not Erin needed to do anything around the house to help.

What annoyed Owen the most was it seemed Erin was more comfortable talking to Jared than Owen.

As predicted, Monday was strange from the moment Owen woke up. Normally he rose first, so he started the coffeepot while he ran for twenty minutes in the basement and did a round of weights, then enjoyed a freshly perked cup while he made his breakfast, unless Jared was feeling magnanimous and cooked for him. Once upon a time, Simon did it, but those days were done. After a quick shower, he went in to work, checked the surgery schedule, and dipped into OB to inquire about any moms needing epidurals.

Today he still woke first and heard Erin in the shower as he rounded the corner to the stairs. He knew it wasn't Jared because Jared's alarm was just going off and he was grumbling and rolling over to stop it. Owen got on the treadmill, but he didn't put on his headphones like usual, listening for sounds in the kitchen the whole time, and when he finally heard them as he began his cool down, he was so distracted trying to figure out if it was Jared or Erin, he nearly tripped and smashed his face into the deep freezer. Skipping his weights, he hurried up the stairs.

It was Erin, eating a yogurt and pouring half-and-half into his coffee. He glanced up at Owen uncertainly.

Owen wasn't entirely sure why he'd rushed up the stairs, and he didn't have anything particular to say.

He poured himself some coffee, realized he should rehydrate first, and got a glass of water instead. "Good morning."

"Good morning."

This was awkward. He should have stayed downstairs. It was leg day too.

Owen dabbed at the sweat around his brow with his towel. "Do… you work out at all? Do any kind of sport or exercise?"

Erin stared into his coffee as he stirred it far longer than necessary. "I don't."

"Ah." Well, there went that conversation. He finished the water and reached for the coffee. Probably he should make some eggs.

Erin cleared his throat. "I suppose you *do* play sports. You seem like you… do."

"Not many. Not with actual other people. I lift weights and run. I've played racquetball, but I have trouble keeping partners."

Erin frowned. "Why?"

"I told you. Everyone is afraid of me. Except for you."

"Hmm." Erin sipped his coffee. "Too bad I don't play racquetball."

"Well, I could teach you. It's not hard."

"Trust me when I tell you I have no talent for sports. I'm clumsy, I have no body strength, and I tend to injure myself."

"You have the instincts to play games and to compete, so all you're missing is skills. You might have to build up some arm strength, but your size makes you nimble, which is a big advantage. Plus we'd get to fight and yell in a small room while hitting a rubber ball. It would be like work, but with a twist."

Erin gave him an odd look, but he also smiled. "I'll give it some consideration."

"Might be good for work too. I always see the board members at the gym playing racquetball. Though I don't know if that's a perk...."

He trailed off because Erin had suddenly become focused and alert. "*All* the board members play racquetball at the gym?"

"Well... yeah, except for Rebecca."

Erin set down his coffee. "I would like to learn how to play racquetball."

"Great. We'll do that. Let me know your schedule."

"I'll email it to you. Thank you so much."

It was definitely suspicious, how excited Erin was to learn racquetball, but Owen was also pretty sure he wasn't going to get a straight answer if he asked why.

Erin had left for the hospital by the time Owen got out of the shower, which made sense, but he was still disappointed for reasons he couldn't understand. Honestly, he was mystified by 90 percent of his reactions to Erin, or most of Erin's reactions to him. Every now and again *I can take care of myself* echoed through his head and he bristled, but then he'd recall a moment from the weekend when Erin had thanked him for something minor but had acted as if it had been the greatest favor anyone had ever done for him.

The man would drive him bananas. They'd be harvesting them from him by the end of the week.

If he'd thought being at home was awkward, it was nothing compared to his first day at work as Erin Andreas's faux boyfriend. As he'd predicted, no one dared to talk *to* them, but they were 100 percent talking *about* them and their new relationship. Unfortunately, there was one subject nobody was shy to bring up.

"I had no idea you could play violin like that."

Nurses, CNAs, volunteers, secretaries, even the custodial staff felt compelled to comment on Owen's surprise talent. He'd barely been present Friday, so they hadn't had a chance to attack him on the issue then. They didn't waste the opportunity now. A select few had heard he knew the violin, but most carried on about how they hadn't known he had it in him to play like that. All day long they approached him, and he remained trapped inside his plastic smile until he was called away.

As if that wasn't bad enough, on his way to drop something off with Nick's assistant, he ran into Christian West.

It was common for Owen to see the longtime board member and former Weber Mining & Minerals executive vice president around the hospital, usually on his way to or from a board meeting or lingering in the coffee shop. Generally Owen had enough warning to escape, and on the few occasions they'd made eye contact, he'd gotten away with a murmured "pardon me" and gone on his way.

Not that day.

"Dr. Gagnon." West beamed at Owen as if they were golfing buddies and he was about to ask him when they were going to set up their next tee time. "What a show you put on for us the other night."

With Christian West, Owen didn't mind being rude. The problem was, just looking at the man made him angry. "If you'll excuse me, I'm late to see a patient."

As he turned on his heel and went to the elevators, West followed him, walking the leisurely stroll of someone who knew there was no way the elevator would be waiting and ready. "I can't say I predicted you with Andreas's son."

Fuck you, asshole. "Yes, well, surprise."

Owen beelined for the stairs. He headed straight for surgery prep, hoping to hide out and recover, but Simon assaulted him from an entirely different direction.

"There you are." Simon put his hands on his hips and glared at Owen. "Everyone's asking me about you and Erin. I keep repeating what you told me to tell them over the weekend, but I worry I'm not doing it right." He frowned as he got a better look at Owen's face. "Are you okay?"

"I'm fine." Owen wiped sweat from his brow with his sleeve, relieved to deal with the problem of how to address his fake relationship instead of dealing with Christian West or the violin. He kicked the lock on a wheelchair and sat, slouching. "I wouldn't worry about what you're telling people. I'm sure they're only hearing what they want anyway."

"How's everything going with Erin?"

Owen grunted, shrugging. "He's an odd guy." He remembered Erin's dismissal and got irritated all over again. "And he doesn't want me to help him."

"Help him what?"

"You were at his house. You heard the stories. You saw how he paled when John Jean found out what he'd done at the dance, how he grabbed him."

Simon set down the tray of instruments and turned to face Owen, eyes wide. "Are you saying…?"

"I don't know what I'm saying exactly. I only know what I saw. I tried to talk to him about it, and he told me he could take care of himself."

To Owen's surprise, Simon relaxed. "But that's not surprising, is it?"

It was incredibly surprising and frustrating to Owen. "Why not?"

"Well… what is it they say? 'Denial is a helluva drug'? If you don't admit something is true, you can pretend it isn't. Also, Erin has always struck me as an independent person who prides himself on taking control. I can't imagine he'd be excited about you trying to help him with this when most of your interactions to this point have been the two of you fighting."

"He paid twenty-five thousand dollars for my help."

"Yes, he *paid* for it. That's a lot of control. And you have to admit, this whole thing is strange. There's got to be something more to him asking you for this. Do you think he paid that much because he wanted you to distract his father?"

First Jared brought that up, now Simon. Since he didn't want to think about that, he addressed the other issue. Owen rubbed his thumb along his jawline. "I still don't get why me trying to help him is threatening."

"If you say you'll help in a way he's not ready for, yes, it is." Simon wagged a finger at him. "Remember, too, you're not exactly big on surrendering control yourself. If you want to help him, let him drive this bus for a while." When Owen's only reply was to curl his lip, Simon laughed. "I rest my case."

Now Owen had what Simon had said as well as what Erin had said ringing in his head all the rest of the day.

He was so agitated. He needed to blow off some steam.

He decided to look for Erin.

Owen moved on autopilot. He wanted a fight. He wondered if he’d get one. He wondered if he *should* get one. As he rode the elevator to the third floor, he fidgeted, unsure of what he was going to do or say when he arrived.

Maybe he shouldn’t go.

Probably he shouldn’t go.

When the elevator doors opened, he didn’t exit, allowing the three other passengers who had ridden with him to get off, and he remained on. Two new people got on, and the doors were starting to close to take him downstairs again when at the last second someone slipped inside—it was Erin, holding too many binders. On instinct, Owen reached for the stack.

Erin shifted and moved them farther away.

Owen glared at him.

“Would you press the first floor for me?” Erin asked.

Owen did, glancing at the stack. “You carry too much.”

Erin pursed his lips. “I’m fine.”

“You’re not. You’re clearly straining. You’re going to get a hernia.”

The two women in the back of the elevator exchanged a knowing look. Owen thought one of them hid a smile behind her hand.

The woman closest to Owen turned toward him, and before she opened her mouth, he could tell what she was going to say by the look in her eye. He froze, ready for impact.

“Dr. Gagnon, the other night, when you played the violin—”

Stepping in front of her, Erin thrust the stack of binders at Owen. "Fine. Take them, if it will stop your nagging."

Stunned, Owen moved cautiously to accept the folders. He was more surprised when Erin's gaze lingered on him.

That had been on purpose. Erin had cut her off so she couldn't comment on his playing.

He'd just been *rescued.*

Goddamn if Owen wasn't about to blush.

Erin was blushing, actually. It was super cute.

Owen cleared his throat. "It's you and me for dinner tonight. Jared has the ER shift. What do you want to do?"

Erin became interested in an ad near the button panel. "Whatever is fine. I can make something if you want."

For a second Owen's heart skipped a beat. Then he realized this remark, like the binders, had probably been a performance for the women in the elevator.

If you want to help him, let him drive the bus for a while.

Owen shifted the binders in his arms. "Sure. Sounds great. I'll do the dishes after."

As he followed Erin out of the elevator, he heard a small chorus of happy, feminine sighs.

For the rest of the day, if Erin was around, no one was able to finish so much as a sentence about Owen's playing, either.

CHAPTER SIX

ERIN'S FATHER hadn't contacted him in almost a month.

John Jean had come by the hospital as usual, but instead of stopping by Erin's office and scolding him about the fundraiser or moving out, or anything at all, he bypassed his son entirely. Erin was honestly more unsettled by this complete silent treatment than he would have been by being shouted into a corner. He'd expected *some* pushback. The silence made Erin feel uneasy and honestly, quite abandoned.

Did his father not care that Erin had removed himself from his life?

Owen, meanwhile, saw a great deal of John Jean, because anytime the man showed up at the hospital or anywhere within Owen's radius, Owen appeared as if out of thin air, aiming the most irritating version of his personality at John Jean. Owen wasn't inappropriate, but he also wasn't deferential or frightened, which was what Erin's father preferred. At first Erin tried to tell Owen this wasn't necessary, but Owen seemed determined to continue, "To keep him out of your hair," he kept saying. Erin supposed his father's inattention did have the side benefit of allowing him to go through the files Nick had given him in peace.

It had ended up, too, that Erin kept the files. Nick promised as soon as his schedule cleared they'd book another long Sunday at the cabin, but the truth was Nick didn't have the time. The files were a tedious task requiring a keen eye and many consecutive hours.

Erin often stayed up late trying to make sense of the documents, but the job was so overwhelming, he hardly knew where to start. What was he looking for, anyway? What if he found it and missed it? What if they found something and they couldn't use it because the board was such an iron wall?

Erin's anxiety simmered in him, a festering cauldron he couldn't stop filling daily with every doubt and fear rising inside him. On the outside he projected confidence and competence as best he could, not letting anyone know how much despair he felt.

Everyone seemed to buy the act except for Owen.

He stopped by Erin's office more frequently, dragging him into the cafeteria "for the performance factor" whenever Erin had a free lunch period that matched with his. If lunch didn't work, he'd steal Erin for coffee. Protesting did him no good.

"You paid a lot of money for this," Owen would remind him. Then, inevitably, he'd add, "Are you sure you're okay? You seem tense. Morc so than usual."

Every time, Erin would lie and insist he was fine. At the house, he'd do his part of the household chores before retiring to his room. He tried to stay at the office late enough to avoid dinner, but they tended to hold meals until he got home, so he put up with the communal table, did his stint with the dishes, then disappeared to sort through his papers some more.

Four weeks from the day Erin had moved out, Owen burst into Erin's office, shut the door, and loomed over his desk, arms crossed over his body. "Okay, I'm done waiting. Tell me what has you so upset, and tell me how I can fix it."

Blinking, Erin sent his chair rolling away several inches. "What?"

Owen glowered. "You're upset. Don't lie and tell me you're not. If it's me, tell me what I'm doing wrong. If it's someone else, tell me what they're doing so I can stop them."

What in the world…? Erin did his best to compose himself, but he hadn't seen this coming, and he *was* upset. And exhausted. "I…. You can't…."

"We'll take this one piece at a time. Am I the one upsetting you?"

No, Owen wasn't upsetting him. Only in the sense that he'd tipped him off his axis. "No. This has nothing to do with you. Which is why I wish you—"

"It's your father, then."

Startled, Erin opened his mouth, then closed it, frozen in place.

Grimacing, Owen sank into one of the chairs opposite Erin's desk. "You're going to tell me it's none of my business, aren't you? Or that there's nothing I can do."

Erin smoothed his hands over his trouser legs and stared guiltily at his knees. "Both."

"Is he hurting you?"

Erin recalled the way John Jean had ghosted him in the hallway that morning as he passed by with Christian West and another member of the board. Something sharp stabbed his heart. "I'm fine."

"You're not, though. You look miserable, so much so people besides me have noticed. They're also noticing other things, by the way. Like how we never do anything but sit in the cafeteria together. If you frown much more, Simon's going to get asked if *I'm* hurting you, and let me tell you how that is not going to—"

Erin cut him off before he could continue. "Why don't we go out on a date, then?"

Owen stared at Erin. Erin stared back.

Owen recovered first, a slow smile spreading across his face. "Good. I'd been wondering when we'd get to one of those. What did you have in mind?"

Erin heard himself speaking, but it was as if from far away. "We should go out to eat somewhere in town."

"Tonight?"

"If you're free."

"I'm free." Owen's smile widened, making Erin's heart skip a beat. "We could go to the Italian restaurant in campus town. Get a booth by the window. You can see the bay from there."

It sounded nice. And terrifying. Erin cleared his throat. "Shall I make the reservation?" Damn his voice for breaking at the end.

Owen waved a hand at him. "I'll do it. You concentrate on relaxing."

Erin couldn't concentrate, though, not on relaxing, not on work, not on anything.

Why? Why had he asked Owen on a date? He should be focusing on the files, but now he was going off to flirt with Owen, who'd agreed because he thought this was all to anger Erin's father—Erin's father who didn't even care that Erin existed. This date served no purpose.

I asked him out because I wanted to be with him.

Much as Erin hated to admit it, he knew this was the truth. Suddenly he was seventeen, standing on the ridge above the bay, Owen staring at him and waiting for him to confess his feelings.

He was the Erin of last October, holding the memo rescinding the dating policy.

Abruptly too warm, Erin tried to distract himself, but he was useless until the door opened to his office at five and he startled, drawn out of his thoughts.

Owen's hair was a tousled mess from being under a surgical cap all day. "Hey." He nodded at Erin and raised an eyebrow. "You done? I'll walk with you to your car."

Erin dropped the file he was holding and shuffled through the items on his desk. "I—I'm fine. I still have a few things to do." He didn't, but he felt suddenly awkward about walking out with Owen.

"I'll wait." Owen plunked into the chair opposite his desk. "You know, we should ride in together."

Owen's hair was a serious disaster. He'd clearly been running his fingers through it. There—he put his fingers into the mop while Erin looked on.

How was Erin supposed to work like this?

"Why are you staring at my hair?"

Erin cleared his throat and rubbed the back of his neck. "There's no reason." He stared at his desk instead, three stacks of color-coded folders full of work he theoretically knew how to do but at the moment couldn't begin to sort out for the life of him. He sighed and pushed to his feet. "Let's go home."

Home. His home with Owen.

He stumbled as he rounded the corner of the desk. Rising, Owen caught his elbow and stabilized him.

Erin blushed. "I'm fine."

Owen kept his face blank. "Never said otherwise."

All the way down the elevator to the first floor, neither of them spoke a word, but where Erin felt uncertain and uneasy, Owen seemed annoyingly content.

As they exited the elevator, Owen gestured to the underground parking area. "You parked here, or on-the-surface parking?"

"I'm here." Erin prayed Owen was on the surface and would need to take the opposite exit.

"Same." Owen fell in step beside him. "What time do you want to go to eat? I forgot to ask before. Is seven thirty okay? I know it's a little late, but we can pretend to be cosmopolitan, and anyway, you look tired. Rest a bit."

He was so solicitous it made Erin dizzy.

Back to the house. Why was he considering Owen's house his home? This was the second time this afternoon alone. He was truly losing his mind.

He thought perhaps he should rescind the dinner invitation and go to bed, but as he pulled into the driveway, Owen waited near the garage, waving as Erin arrived.

"I called Café Cuore and got a reservation, and I asked for the front table by the window too." Owen held open the door from the garage leading into the kitchen. "You go ahead and take a nap. How much time do you want to get ready? I'll wake you up."

Erin touched his cheeks, which he was sure were burning. "I don't need a nap, thank you."

"Well, do whatever you do in your room. You can finish putting some of your things away. I notice everything is still in boxes. Go relax, however you want."

Though Erin retreated to his room, he didn't relax at all. He pulled out a stack of documents and tried to go over them some more, but everything scrambled in front of his eyes as his mind whirred at ninety miles an hour. The slow buildup of anxiety from the day hit him full force, and he couldn't escape it now, no matter what he did. Erin paced the room, his heart beating so fast he had to press his hand against it.

Calm down, calm down. What's gotten into you? When scolding himself didn't work, he crossed the hall to the bathroom, shut the door, and splashed water on his face. Lifting his head, he saw his tortured expression, and it twisted his stomach, so he opened the door to the mirrored medicine cabinet to make it go away.

That was when Erin saw the bottle. A burnt-orange prescription pill bottle from the St. Ann's Hospital Pharmacy. *Alprazolam. Owen Gagnon. Take 1-2 tablets three times daily as needed.*

Still clutching his rapidly beating heart, Erin frowned at the label. Alprazolam. What was this for? He knew he shouldn't be snooping, but the idea that

Owen was sick on top of everything else made *him* sick, and—

He saw a smaller line at the bottom of the label. *Generic for Xanax.*

Oh. Erin bit his lip and clutched at the edge of the sink.

He shouldn't. He honestly shouldn't. It was illegal to take someone else's medication, to start, and dangerous, and immoral, and…

And this drug will stop the endless tide inside my head, if only for a little while.

Erin stared at the label, suddenly unable to look anywhere else.

Dimly, he heard some part of him objecting, banging on glass and shouting panicked warnings. *Don't you remember how he behaved at the auction? Do* you *want to behave like that? Wanton and uninhibited? Making a fool of yourself?*

Yes, Erin did. He'd admit it, at least to himself, alone in a bathroom, staring longingly at someone else's prescription. He'd never even been drunk. How pathetic was he? Thirty-three-year-old virgin who'd never been drunk, whose first kiss was part of a stunt.

As he shook out two of the pills, his hand trembled. He felt like Alice in Wonderland, and despite being mildly terrified, he couldn't wait to see what discovery this little bottle led him to.

His heart still beat too fast as he crossed the hall to his room. If anything, he felt more anxious now that he'd done something so reckless. Once he was behind the closed door, however, he was able to calm somewhat. The drug would start working soon. He only had to keep himself occupied until it did.

Nothing like his endless task of sorting through the printouts to do that.

Ten minutes into the records from 2004, Erin knew the drugs had hit his system. He'd reached for another stack of papers when his arm felt lighter, and the room seemed to spin slightly. When Erin sat on his haunches and considered himself, he decided, yes, he was calmer. Mostly he felt fuzzy. It was difficult to worry about things when you were so disoriented.

Also tired. He was abruptly so tired he wanted to lie on top of the papers and pass out. In fact, the urge was nearly overwhelming.

Erin wasn't sure he cared for Xanax.

Though he attempted to keep working, it was almost impossible. Erin had hoped to feel euphoric, easy, to have his anxiety melt away, but instead he felt as if he were fighting a room full of cotton, and a great deal of it had worked inside his body, particularly in his head.

No getting around it. He'd need to lie down for a moment.

He wanted to lie on the bed, but when he tried to get up, he was so dizzy he fell to the floor with a *thunk*, landing so hard on his right hip he cried out.

This is bad. For several seconds or possibly half a minute, Erin sat there, the room spinning as he attempted to figure out what to do. A distant, casual thought occurred that he wasn't having a good reaction to the drug and probably shouldn't have taken it. He also noted how calm he was about that fact.

It really did work on anxiety. Somehow Erin had missed the part where he'd be too dizzy to enjoy his freedom from the squirrel cage inside his mind.

Oh well.

He was debating whether he should simply nap on the documents or try again to stand up when a knock on the door startled him.

"Erin?"

Owen. Owen was at the door. Erin winced and let his head fall forward. The room adjusted its axis accordingly and continued to spin.

"*Erin.*" The door opened, and Owen appeared beside Erin, touching him. "What happened?"

Erin would have had difficulty with this situation on a good day, but he couldn't manage it with this cotton in his skull and his sense of balance on a Tilt-A-Whirl. Still, he had to do his best. Above all, he had to protect the investigation.

He braced himself against the floor with one hand and gestured at the mess of paper. "Don't look at any of this."

"I'm looking at *you*. What happened? I heard something fall, and you cried out." When Erin only hovered there, listing with his eyes half closed, Owen raised an eyebrow. "Have you been… drinking? You don't smell like it."

Erin wanted to lie, but he'd begun to fear he'd harmed himself. He opened and shut his mouth a few times, then huffed in despair as he crumpled. "I can't do it. It's too complicated, and I'm too dizzy."

Gone was the amusement from Owen's voice. He was in doctor mode now, running his hands over Erin, checking his vitals, pulling Erin's eyelid open wider to examine his pupil. "Your pulse is fine. More than fine, in fact. You're a little flushed, your speech is slurred and different than your usual pattern, and your pupils are slightly dilated. You're high. On what, Erin?"

Well, Erin had nothing to do but confess now. If he tried to dance his way out of this, Owen would drag him into the hospital. "Your Xanax."

Owen startled. "You—what? You took some of my Xanax?"

Erin nodded—carefully. "Two."

"Have you ever taken a short-term anti-anxiety medication before?"

No more moving of his head, Erin decided. "No."

"Then… why…." Owen ran a hand over his mouth. "Okay, let me regroup. I'm sorry you didn't feel you could ask for help getting a prescription if you needed it. I'll do better to make you feel you can trust me. Because as I suspect you're learning, these drugs are not one-size-fits-all, nor are their doses. I would never have prescribed Xanax to you, and never that dose. If you needed a short-term situational anxiety crutch, I'd go with one milligram of Ativan to start, letting you go up to two milligrams if you needed it. Especially given your reaction to Xanax. But if you're having generalized anxiety overall, I'd refer you to the woman I see in Duluth and let her set you up with a long-term antidepressant."

"I don't need an antidepressant."

"Hmm." Owen's half smile made Erin's insides flutter. "Are you the HR director of a hospital, but you have a bias against people who take antidepressants? Don't make me think less of you, Andreas."

Oh no. Erin's face screwed up in concern, and he reached for Owen, but he seemed so far away. He gave up and let his hand fall. "I don't have a bias. I…." Oh, words were so impossible right now. Owen's mouth was so beautiful, though. His bottom lip was shiny and slightly plump, and Erin wanted to bite it. He'd be brave enough to do it right now if he could lift his damn head.

Owen tweaked his nose. "What are you thinking about so hard? You look like you're trying to stare a hole through my face."

"I'm thinking I'd take your antidepressants if you'd lean down so I could bite your lip."

Owen gaped at Erin, eyes wide.

Erin marveled at how the drug melted away the terror that had rushed in after his confession.

Eventually Owen spoke, though his voice quavered a bit, and it cracked toward the end. "If you weren't high, I might take you up on your offer."

Erin sighed. "If I weren't high, I wouldn't have the courage to say such a thing. This isn't fair. I shouldn't have told you I'd taken the drug."

"Oh, so you think I'm the kind of man who would take advantage of someone compromised?"

He made a good point. It was just…. This time Erin managed to find Owen's face, to touch the beautiful, lush lip for himself. "I've wanted to kiss you since I was thirteen."

This time when Owen startled, Erin felt the gasp of air rush into Owen's mouth because his fingers were still there. He felt Owen tremble too. This was delicious.

"You—what?"

"I said I wanted to kiss you. Didn't you hear me?"

"But—but we didn't know each other then."

"We met. In fact, I saw you two other times after that, though the second time I don't think you saw me."

"Erin." He took hold of Erin's wrist, gently moving his hand away. "Believe me when I tell you I'd love to have this conversation with you, to hear everything you want to tell me. But I want to do it when you've come off this drug and won't hate me for listening to you when you have no filter."

Without question, Erin knew Owen was right, but in this moment, Erin refused to be reasonable. "You don't have any idea what it's like. To have so much inside your mind you can't think, but to have nowhere to put it, no one to tell it to. To want to share things with someone but to have no courage, let alone words, to open your mouth. Now I have the courage and the person to confess to, and you're telling me no."

Owen laced his fingers through Erin's, holding them fast. "I know exactly what it feels like, every bit of what you just said. For the record, it's part of why I've been on long-term antidepressants and have seen therapists and psychologists regularly since I was eighteen. So yes, I understand. Better than you can possibly comprehend."

Erin could barely breathe. He wanted to cry, but the tears wouldn't come. "Everything is a mess. I keep trying to fix it, but I think I'm making a bigger disaster."

Owen's other hand grazed Erin's cheek briefly, then retreated. "I can help you, if you want me to. I'll help you with more than upsetting your father. I'll help you with anything you want."

"Why?"

Owen's eyes fell closed slowly. Turning his head, he pressed a soft kiss against the tips of Erin's fingers reluctantly, as if he couldn't help himself.

"Because I like you, Erin. Because every day I get to know you better, I realize I misjudged you when I first met you. I thought you were an extension of your father, but you aren't. The day you undid the no-dating policy…." His grip on Erin tightened. "You're incredible. You're amazing. You're fascinating. I want to get to know you better. I want to help you. You never had to bid on me. You only ever had to ask me."

It was a lovely speech, but Erin couldn't stop fixating on one part. "But I didn't tell you the whole story about how I met you. I want to tell you *everything*."

Owen's thumb brushed the inside of Erin's palm. "Can I hear it when the Xanax has worn off?"

That was fine too, he supposed. Erin felt so soft and suggestible. Also, the thumb against his skin felt wonderful. "Is that all you want? To hear the stories?"

"If you're referring to the kisses, I'm happy to accept those too."

"But I have to initiate them. I don't like it."

Owen's thumb slid to the heel of Erin's palm. "We'll make a deal. You sleep this off, and if you come up to me after and touch my face, rubbing your thumb along my chin like you're doing now, I'll do the kissing for you."

Sleep sounded so good. Except there were so many problems with it. "I can't get to my bed. Plus we were supposed to go to dinner. And I don't want to be alone when everything is spinning."

"I'll call and cancel dinner. I don't think you're up to going tonight." He smiled as he pushed back Erin's hair. "As for getting into bed, I'll carry you. I'll stay with you until you fall asleep too."

"I don't want to sleep in here. I want to sleep with you."

Another catch of Owen's breath. Erin decided he enjoyed making him do that.

"You want to sleep with me?" Owen's voice broke at the end. "In my room?"

"In your bed," Erin clarified, in case Owen had any funny ideas about a couch.

He waited for more arguments, but the next thing Erin knew, he was being scooped from the floor, cradled to Owen's chest, and carried from the room.

Erin huddled against Owen, inhaling as he clung to his neck. "You should carry me more often."

"You're far more adorable high than I ever would have predicted, for the record."

Erin snuggled deeper into Owen's arms. "I'm not adorable. I'm highly skilled and competent, and a savvy business individual."

"You're adorable," Owen repeated, whispering into Erin's hair.

Everything became so fuzzy. Erin felt as if he were floating, surrounded by the warmth and smell of Owen, but too soon he fell slowly into bedding that smelled the same, only more faintly so.

"Don't leave," Erin called out as Owen's arms moved away.

"I won't." The bed shifted as Owen lay beside him, bringing his heat once more. "I'll stay right here."

He didn't put his arms around Erin, though. *Hold me*, Erin tried to call out, but the billowiness of the pillow, the weight of the blanket, and the feeling of Owen's breath hitting his face from the space beside him lulled him too sweetly into the sleep his body needed.

Sometimes, Erin thought, *when I look at you, I still hear the music, and I wish I could ask you why it makes you sad.*

Something brushed his forehead, something soft and warm and slightly hesitant. Or perhaps Erin was already dreaming, sliding deeper into the folds of the drug and the peaceful arms of sleep.

OWEN STARED at Erin's quiet, serene face in slumber, glad he didn't have to try to hide how stripped he felt right now.

Sometimes, when I look at you, I still hear the music, and I wish I could ask you why it makes you sad.

Erin's words had been slurred, but Owen had understood them and known exactly to what they referred. The damn violin. Except unlike the people at the hospital and around town who occasionally felt compelled to comment on it, who made Owen freeze up and want to curse Ram for getting sick and dredging this crap up in the first place, Erin's whisper made Owen ache in a different way.

Sometimes, Erin, I wish I could tell you.

Clearing his throat, Owen rolled onto his back, pushing away thoughts of the hated instrument, focusing instead on sorting out how and why Erin had ended up on the floor high as a kite when he should have been napping. Erin completely unlaced, saying the damnedest things.

I've wanted to kiss you since I was thirteen.

It took every ounce of restraint Owen had to not reach over and smooth the errant curls away from Erin's face. When had they met when Erin was thirteen? Owen had a nearly eidetic memory. How could he forget Erin, especially if they'd met with enough of an impression that Erin had wanted to kiss him?

And apparently still did….

Owen kept himself from touching Erin, but he wasn't able to drag his gaze away from Erin's plump, slightly parted lips. Would Erin have actually bitten him if Owen had let him? It had to have been the Xanax talking. If Erin remembered saying all that, he'd be embarrassed.

If he did remember, if he called Owen's bluff….

Owen stared at the ceiling, suddenly overly warm.

He got out of bed—carefully, not wanting to wake Erin—and tiptoed out of the room. He didn't know what to think about what would happen if Erin's Xanax-fueled confessions were more than chemical nonsense. He did know, however, he needed a better peek at why the man had been so stressed he'd gone hunting for pills.

Erin's first words when Owen had entered the room had been *don't look*, and he seemed to mean the piles of paper strewn everywhere, so naturally it was the first place Owen searched. Crouching in the center of the sea, he took it in, frowning.

It looked like financial printouts for the hospital, going back some time. Picking up a stack with neon flags sticking out the side, he saw Erin had made some preliminary notes on them. Erin was trying to find something. What, though? Errors? Irregularities? Missing money? After plunking himself down, Owen sifted through the stacks until he found the earliest one and began to see if he could figure out the puzzle.

When Jared stuck his head in an hour later, he had to knock twice before he got Owen's attention.

"Hey. What are you doing in Erin's room, and why is he asleep on your bed? Also, I thought you were going to dinner?"

"Dinner got cancelled." Except Owen realized he forgot to do that. Oops. He continued scanning the ledger in front of him. "Erin was tired. I let him sleep."

Jared raised his eyebrows as his gaze swept over the piles. "What are you doing?"

Oh good Lord, he couldn't let Copper Point's biggest gossip gain an inch on this, not when Erin didn't even want Owen looking at it. "Erin's taxes. He doesn't want his father's accountant to do them, so I said I would." Owen frowned at the final column, noted it on the scrap paper he had beside him, then glanced at Jared. "Everything good with you?"

Jared shrugged. "Good enough. Since you didn't eat, want me to make something?"

"If you would, that'd be great. Leave a plate for Erin in the oven. I don't know when he'll wake up, but he'll be hungry when he does."

For a second Jared appeared to want to say more, but eventually he shook his head and pushed off the door. "I'll bring your food up when it's ready."

Owen waved him off absently, absorbed in his work. There were so many documents. Why did Erin have them? Why so many years, why so far back? All Erin's notes chased the total from one year to the next, in each budget line. He'd picked up tiny inconsistencies, what had been written off as bad record-keeping and then corrected. Audits? Except Erin didn't seem to think so. He was going line by line, doing calculations of his own.

For every single year.

This wasn't seeking a needle in a haystack. This was searching for four-leaf clovers in a field of wheat spanning to the horizon. The thing was, Owen could easily see what Erin was trying to do, and Owen was quite good at this sort of thing—better, he suspected, than Erin. *He should have asked me to do this, not pose as his boyfriend and piss off his father.*

As Owen ran his finger over a tally of numbers, Erin's words echoed in his mind.

I'd take your antidepressants if you'd lean down so I could bite your lip.

Owen snapped the lead on the automatic pencil and tugged at the collar of his shirt.

Sometimes, when I look at you, I still hear the music, and I wish I could ask you why it makes you sad.

With a hollow pit in his belly, Owen paced the length of the room for several minutes before settling into his task again. When he had an impulse to put a particular artist on Spotify, he didn't let himself question it, nor did he dwell on it, simply letting the music fade into the background as he worked.

At some point Jared brought in a tray with soup, bread, and tea, and Owen ate absently, sipping the tea as he entered the blissful trance of numbers.

Jared glanced at Owen's phone. When he spoke, his voice had a careful quality to it. "Interesting… music. What is it?"

Owen picked up the phone long enough to read the title of the song. "Roxane's Veil."

"I mean the artist…."

"Vanessa-Mae." A violin virtuoso he'd been particularly fond of back in the day. Owen stared at the numbers. "If you don't mind, I'm trying to focus on these figures."

"Yes, right. Sorry."

Jared left, and Owen got back to work.

Something fishy was going on here. It was buried deep, but he knew he could find it. Owen pushed up his sleeves and got serious, spreading several of the year-end totals on the bed beside his own added columns. No question. Oh, it was *subtle*, and carefully, craftily done, but someone had shaved off quite a chunk of change each year. Since 1992 and possibly earlier. Hell, *probably* earlier. How and where it happened varied, but money continued to leak out in a steady stream. Thousands and thousands of taxpayer dollars.

Gathering up the most recent stacks representing the years he'd been at the hospital, Owen applied the same keen eye to these columns as he'd given the others, his heart beating faster and faster as he went. Oh, they were *really* sly about it now, because there were too many computers doing math and trying to catch you cooking books, but since he knew to look for it, he didn't need long to find it. The skimming was still happening, as if this were a Las Vegas casino, not a northern Wisconsin county hospital.

If they'd stolen consistently through the years Owen hadn't tracked yet—and Owen had no reason to believe they hadn't—someone had embezzled over twenty million dollars from the hospital. It might even be closer to twenty-five.

"Holy shit," he whispered to the papers spread in front of him.

He didn't hear anyone enter the room until the floor beside him creaked, at which point he startled and turned toward the sound, dropping the pencil. His heart fumbled all over again as he saw Erin standing beside him, sleep-rumbled and groggy, but decidedly less high than he'd been previously.

He stared at the papers spread across his bed, frowning.

Owen switched off the music and pushed to his feet, scrambling to explain. "I know you told me not to look, but I wanted to know what you were so upset about, and then when I realized what you were doing, I kind of got caught up, because I love number puzzles, and… well, I got carried away, I suppose. I'm sorry."

Erin's frown had disappeared, replaced by shock. "You couldn't have cracked it. Not in just a few hours."

"The embezzlement, you mean? It took me a bit longer than it would have because I didn't know what I was looking for, but yeah, I figured it out." He sighed in satisfaction as he stared at the strewn paper on the bed. "You laid a lot of it out for me, so it didn't take long, and once I had the pattern, the rest of the years fell into place."

Erin staggered backward a few steps, his hand rising to his mouth. "You… you solved *all the years*? Impossible."

"Well *yes*, I'd need another four hours and a good Excel program to finish the rest. The years when they were remodeling have got to be a disaster. But I have all the eighties, the start of the nineties, and the last few years figured out. I jumped to the end because I wanted to know if it was still happening, and I was right." He held up the sheet with his own math on it to show Erin. "The amount of money varies per year, and it increased as time went on, but you can find it if you look closely. No idea where it went, but you can absolutely track its disappearance. Someone worked to make sure it seemed invisible, and if you weren't looking for it, you wouldn't see it at all. I assume this is what I was supposed to distract your father from?" He frowned. "I hope this doesn't mean you think we're done, because I'm still not letting you—"

He stopped talking because Erin had closed the distance between them… and placed his right hand on Owen's cheek. As Owen's heartbeat kicked into overdrive, thundering staccato in his ears, Erin ran his thumb along the thin strip of his beard, heading for his chin.

Fighting to keep from swaying on his feet, Owen drew a breath. "So. You remember."

Erin didn't look away from him. "I remember everything."

"I thought maybe it was the Xanax, that even if you did remember, you'd tell me to forget about it."

The barest stain of a blush enhanced Erin's cheeks. "Will you mock me if I tell you it was all true? Every word I said?"

Sometimes, when I look at you, I still hear the music, and I wish I could ask you why it makes you sad.

Owen swallowed hard. "I would never mock you."

Erin lifted his chin, so brave and terrified at once Owen could barely stand it. "Will you keep your promise, then? Or will you tell me it was all a line to placate the—"

Erin wasn't able to finish his sentence, because Owen kissed him.

CHAPTER SEVEN

OWEN'S LIPS were as soft as they were the last time they'd kissed, except now they tasted slightly of basil and peppermint. Mostly, however, they tasted of Owen, that drugging, lightly spiced sweetness Erin hadn't gotten out of his mind since the night of the auction.

When those lips were on his, Erin didn't think about anything else. Once they left, however, a rush of doubt and fear surrounded him. He lowered his head, drawing his hand away from Owen's face as he stepped away.

Catching his wrist, Owen laced their fingers together. "Now why are you closing up on me? Are you telling me my kisses are bad?"

He spoke with a tone making it clear he knew his kisses weren't the issue. When Erin frowned and tried to back away again, Owen stroked his arm.

"Easy. You want to tell me why you're upset?"

No, Erin didn't. *I'm afraid you're humoring me.* Owen said he wouldn't mock him, but… well, there were gray areas. "I don't want to hear any teasing because I admitted I've wanted to kiss you since I was a teenager."

Now Owen looked affronted. "I wouldn't ever do that. I mean, I'm embarrassed I made such an impression without remembering it." He grimaced. "But then, in those days, I didn't notice much, and I've done what I can to forget a lot of things."

All the lightness left Owen's face so swiftly Erin was sorry he'd brought any of it up. "I'll tell you, but first I need to make sure you understand you can't tell anyone about what you discovered in these files. Not even Jared."

Owen waved a hand at Erin. "Way ahead of you. Someone's embezzling money from the hospital and they've done so for a long time. I'm assuming they're on the board, or connected to them. That's not information you want slopped around. Now it makes sense why you want your father distracted too. But no, I won't say anything. Obviously I'll help you however you want. You should use me more for stuff like this, though. I'm good with figures. I can make you a great spreadsheet showing where things are missing."

So it truly was another embezzlement problem, their worst fear realized. And Owen had solved the puzzle in one night. "That seems like a lot of bother for you."

"Not in the slightest. I'll input the data tomorrow morning before work while I finish some laundry."

Which meant after Erin had beaten his head against this since the auction, Owen would have this entire mess solved within twenty-four hours, complete with a result Erin could hand to Nick. Then they could narrow down suspects and hopefully get enough evidence Nick would feel comfortable turning this over to the authorities. The thought made him dizzy.

Smiling wryly, Owen smoothed hair from Erin's eyes. "You should never play poker, hon. Everything shows on your face."

Erin pressed his palms to his cheeks, but his fingers trembled as Owen slid his hands over them. "What—what are you doing?"

"I was thinking about kissing you again, to be honest. Unless you decided you've had enough?"

"I… no, I…."

Owen's fingers were in Erin's hair now, making it difficult for him to keep his eyes open as Owen spoke to him in a low, soothing tone. "Maybe I didn't notice you when we were younger. Maybe I misjudged you when we first met. I'm paying attention now. Though I have some bad news." When Erin only blinked at him nervously, Owen tweaked his nose. "I'm considering this fake dating arrangement officially over."

Erin couldn't breathe.

Ghosting his fingers down the side of Erin's face, Owen caught Erin's chin. Owen's smile could have belonged to an otherworldly creature. A dark fairy or a demon come to spirit Erin away.

"I want to date you for real, Erin Andreas."

Shutting his eyes, Erin tried to punch Owen in the chest, but at best he managed a swat. "I hate you."

"Mmm-hmm."

Owen kissed Erin again.

This one backed Erin into the bed, threatening to buckle his knees. Erin held on tight to Owen's shirt, but the feel of the hard muscles under his palms distracted him, and his hands kept slipping down. When his thumb grazed Owen's nipple, Owen moaned into Erin's mouth and briefly lifted his head to gasp.

Then he pushed Erin onto the bed, sending the stacks of papers flying.

"I'll clean it up," Owen whispered into Erin's neck, kissing his way along it as Erin panicked over his disturbed documents. "Right now I need to get closer to you."

Erin thought if they got any closer he might explode. He'd never experienced feelings like this—never this strong, never this intense. Never with another person. He ached everywhere, couldn't stop trembling. He needed to tell Owen, needed….

"Erin." Owen's kiss below Erin's earlobe sent echoes of sensation across his body. "Erin… don't be offended if I read this incorrectly. But… is this… your… have you not had much experience with sex?"

Owen's sweet, hot mouth would drive Erin insane. Erin clung to Owen's head, tipping his own back as he swallowed his embarrassment. "I… haven't had… any."

He waited for the teasing, for the shock. *What, at your age? You're thirty-three and you haven't had sex? You haven't even kissed? That's not normal. Are you not interested? What's the problem?*

The kiss Owen placed on Erin's collarbone was almost reverent. "Is this all right? You did ask to be kissed, but maybe… is this too far?"

A sudden tornado, twisted euphoria and doubt, tumbled Erin around. “Why… why are you asking all this? I’m such a freak, to be this old and to not have—”

Owen’s face loomed over his. “I want to get to know you better. I can’t quite decide if you’re shy, inexperienced, have a low libido, or some kind of combo platter of all that, but whatever the answer is, I don’t want to assume anything or force you, so I’m asking.”

Erin’s hands had ended up on Owen’s shoulders. Now they slid along his neck. “I… I am. Inexperienced and shy.” He felt as dizzy as he had on the highest throes of the Xanax. “I haven’t had much interest in sex before, but I would like to… explore. A little. With the right partner. With… you.”

“So I need to pace myself. Got it.” Owen teased his fingers into Erin’s hair. “Will you date me, though? For real this time?”

What kind of question was that after everything he’d confessed? Embarrassment gone, Erin pursed his lips. *So infuriating.* “Of course I’ll date you.”

Owen laughed. “You don’t sound happy about it.”

“Well, I’m not sure *you* will be. I’m not much of a catch.”

Placing a quick, dry kiss on Erin’s chin, Owen pushed off the bed, then offered a hand to help Erin rise as well. “Come with me. Jared left some dinner for you, and you have to be hungry.”

He was, now that Owen brought up the subject. It was late, and though Jared was awake, he was in his room, the door shut with his television on. Owen held

Erin's hand as he led him down the stairs, not letting go until he had him seated in the kitchen.

"I love the way Jared fusses over meals," Owen said as he prepared a bowl of soup from a small Crock-Pot and pulled a sandwich with plastic over it from the fridge. "I don't think it's a big deal to him, but it is to me. I miss having Simon around because we always felt like a family. It's lonely with two of us. I enjoy having you around, making the house lively again. When I grew up, you see, I didn't have that. Coming in the door always felt like gearing up for war. If I wasn't walking into a fight, I'd be witnessing the carnage of the aftermath, or the buildup to something. Or I'd be caught in the crossfire. If we had food, I got nervous when it was hot. It was too likely to be thrown."

Erin froze, not knowing how to respond. What was he supposed to say to that?

Owen pushed a glass of water in front of Erin. "Go on. Eat your soup."

Erin ate, grateful for the distraction as Owen continued his story.

"I keep trying to remember where I might have been at thirteen—I guess I would have been fourteen—for us to meet. We weren't in the same class, because you were off at the boarding school. Was it at some kind of town function? I avoided going to them, but sometimes I couldn't help it."

"Mayo Clinic," Erin prompted. "You were visiting someone with your dad. I saw you in the hall. You helped me find my way, then our fathers ran into each other later. I met Nick that day too, and he told me who you were. I thought you were handsome."

Owen rubbed his chin, then sat up as he remembered. "*Oh, that.* My dad wanted to kiss Christian West's ass and insisted I go along for some reason, then was pissed because I didn't perform properly. I feel like I should remember you, though." Eyes going wide, he aimed a finger at Erin. "*Wait.* The fuzzy-haired kid drowning in awkward clothes… that was *you*?"

Erin threw a bread crust at him. "No." Except of course it was absolutely him.

Owen grinned. "I completely remember you now. I almost thought you were a girl at first. You looked like a hostage. Part of me wanted to ask you if you were okay, but I had my own problems. Then you were gone, and my dad found me. As soon as no one was around, he started yelling."

If *that* was how he'd remembered him, Erin was glad. "Did your father yell at you often?"

"It was the only way he spoke to me—in private. In public, he was Mr. Perfect." Owen cleared his throat. "You said you met me another time. Two other times."

"Oh." How much of this should he admit? He didn't want to make Owen upsct. "I… saw you play once, at the mansion. From the shadows, I mean. I wasn't supposed to be there, but it was so good, I—" He realized it was the wrong take and cut himself off, focusing on the soup. It was good soup. So was the sandwich. He wanted to switch topics by offering a banal remark about the food, but instead something else came out of his mouth. "You said your father was perfect in public but awful in private. I can't stop thinking about it, wondering if I'd rather have had that or not. My father belittled me in public and ignored me in private. I suppose each treatment has its up- and downsides. I can't help noticing, though, that you seem so much more put together than me. I'm still being shoved around by my father. I'd like to think his tactics don't bother me the way they used to, but…."

His chest having grown uncomfortably tight, Erin went quiet.

After the silence went on for a few seconds, Owen spoke, his voice quiet, kind. "I've always wondered. Why did you come back to Copper Point? I assume you worked somewhere else between graduation and now—"

"Oh—I've worked for my family this whole time, don't misunderstand." Erin sipped the water. "I also took quite a while to finish school, both undergraduate and graduate. My father didn't like how poorly I performed in his business tracks of choice. I kept telling him I wasn't cut out to be in hospital administration, but he didn't listen. When I needed a break, I'd spend a summer or a semester with my mother, interning with one of her organizations, but that wasn't for me either. Eventually I found my own path. My father learned how poorly I perform in higher levels of administration during my stint at a nursing home our family owns, but during that time I also reconnected with Nick postcollege. I convinced my father if he hired the two of us for the open positions at St. Ann's, it was almost like getting what he wanted. Except now I'm disappointing him again. In ways he's only beginning to comprehend."

"Are you disappointing yourself, though?"

Erin glanced at Owen, stilling when he saw Owen watching him—quietly, but with intense focus. Erin cleared his throat. "I… don't know?"

"Are you happy?"

Had he been speaking to Grandma Emerson? "Sometimes?"

"Why are you answering all my questions with answers that sound like questions?"

"I don't—know?" God, Erin tried not to make the last word tip up, but he couldn't help it.

"Are you afraid of giving the *wrong* answers?"

Erin schooled himself before he replied. "Perhaps." There. A declarative at last. "But I don't know why. It's not as if I need your approval for anything in my life."

Owen's face was a complicated mix of relief, sorrow, and exhaustion. "Good. Because if I found out you thought I required that from you, I'd have a really rotten day."

Erin lifted an eyebrow at him. "No, the only thing you require from me is that I live with you."

"Not anymore. That was a condition to our previous arrangement. Now it's simply a passionate entreaty." He focused on the edge of the counter as he ran his finger along it. "I don't want you to live in the attic room of the mansion any longer, in a housc you can't use. I want you here. Eating dinner with me after you've taken a nap. Plotting schemes with me in your room. Making out with me."

Erin's heart was a yearning, fearful butterfly in his chest. "I've never dated before. I don't have much social experience." *Or sexual.* He couldn't say the last part out loud, though he'd already confessed it.

"My work schedule is terrible. I'm too exhausted to set up so much as a hookup online half the time. I'm temperamental, and even my close friends, of which I have precious few, find me frustrating. You keep trying to warn me away from you as if you're some sort of danger zone. I'm not sure you've looked closely at the subhuman doing the flirting."

"You're not subhuman."

"And you're not an unattractive wallflower." Owen nudged Erin's foot. "The other time we met was before I went to college, wasn't it? I remember now. At Bayview Park, the greenbelt along the bay, you came up to me. I was about to ask for your number when Jared called me away. I kicked myself for six months for chickening out, because I never saw you again. I put it out of my head in all the chaos of that time, but now that you told me we'd met, it came back to me."

Erin, having taken a bite of sandwich, patted crumbs from his lips and chewed before answering. "Yes. Though I'm sure I was as messy then as when I was thirteen."

"No. You were ethereal. Shy, but ethereal. If I hadn't been going through so much of my own stuff, I wouldn't have hesitated. I'm not hesitating now." Owen leaned beside him. "Can I get your number, Erin Andreas?"

Erin swatted him. "You have it already."

"Will you date me, then?"

"I already told you I would."

"Will you stop scowling and acting like dating me means I'm going to eat you, and maybe smile as if you think it might be fun at least part of the time?"

Blushing, Erin pressed a shy kiss against Owen's cheek. "I think it might be fun. At least part of the time."

Owen grunted and kissed the top of Erin's hair as he rose. "Okay, then."

OWEN WHISTLED to himself as he walked through the parking garage into work the next morning, and he doffed an imaginary hat at Rebecca when he met her at the elevator.

She laughed. "What has you in such a good mood?"

He waggled his eyebrows. "What are you here for? Board stuff?"

"What else?" Sighing, she glanced at her watch. "I got here early because I wanted to go over some files, but now I'm wishing I would've grabbed a coffee first."

"I've got some time. Let me get you some."

"Seriously, *who* are you? What happened to my Grouchy Gagnon?" Her eyes widened. "Wait. Don't tell me this thing with you and Erin…?"

Owen put his hands on his hips. "Rebecca. We've been publicly dating for a month."

"Yes, and I didn't believe it for a minute. Not until this one, anyway."

"Believe it."

Smiling, she shook her head. "I'll work on it. Though, say, speaking of things that are difficult to believe—I've meant to tell you, I had no idea you could play the violin so well—"

Owen shooed her out of the elevator onto the third floor. "Hush. I don't want to talk about that. Go get settled. I'll be up in a minute."

In the coffee shop, he smiled at the barista, who blinked at him as she handed him his order. He nodded good morning to a few CNAs he saw in the hall, said hello to the oncologist up from Eau Claire who joined him at the second floor on his way to a specialists meeting upstairs. He wanted to say hello to Erin, but he wasn't in his office, so Owen left the coffee on his desk. When he made it to the hospital library where Rebecca had set up shop, he presented her beverage with a flourish and a bow.

"Enjoy your caramel latte, darling. Come by for dinner with Kathryn sometime."

Owen collected Erin's coffee since he still wasn't in his office, and he began the hunt for his errant boyfriend. He also placed his call to the restaurant, making an apology for skipping out, and securing a new reservation. He was just hanging up when the elevator doors opened onto the second floor and revealed Erin holding a stack of binders as he spoke to the head of nursing.

"Pardon me." Exiting the elevator, Owen swiped the stack of binders deftly with one hand as he passed Erin the cup of coffee with the other.

The head of nursing frowned at him in confusion, and Erin started to protest, then simply blushed. "Good morning."

"Good morning yourself." Pressing a kiss on Erin's cheek, he slid his lips closer to Erin's ear to speak words for him alone. "I finished. It's on the drive on the end table beside your bed."

Erin drew back, regarding Owen with wide eyes. "Seriously?"

"Yep. I remade our reservation for tonight too, so make sure you're home and ready to go by seven." Winking at him, Owen headed into the elevator. "I'll put these on the table in the conference room for you. I assume that's where you were taking them?"

"Yes, thank you." Erin smiled at Owen, watching him go.

Until abruptly the smile died. It went under with a momentary flash of fear, replaced by Erin's cool mask.

Owen turned to see what had caused the change, but he already knew. His own expression changed too, transforming from light to feral. "John Jean. Here for the meeting, I assume?" Owen held the doors to the elevator. "Come, I'll go with you upstairs." When it looked like John Jean was going to refuse him, Owen added, "You can give me progress on the cardiac unit on the way, or explain to me why there isn't any progress on one. Again."

John Jean narrowed his gaze at Owen, but Owen knew he was also taking in the others around them, everyone watching their exchange. Owen kept smiling, telegraphing, *I can do this all damn day, and I don't mind a scene.*

Then, because those spreadsheets were so omnipresent in Owen's mind, he added, "What, are you going to tell me we still don't have the money?"

Something changed in John Jean's gaze, and he returned Owen's smile, nasty for nasty as he entered the elevator. "I'm happy to discuss the future of the hospital with you at any time, Dr. Gagnon."

Owen caught a flash of Erin's worried expression as the doors closed, but Owen tossed him a quick wink before he vanished. *It's all good, babe. I got this.*

"So," John Jean said as soon as they were alone. "You're taking this fiction with my son to some interesting lengths."

Owen cut a glance at the elder Andreas and wasn't surprised to see him adjusting his jacket cuffs and staring at the floor readout panel. He rolled his eyes and fixed his gaze straight ahead as well. "Wrap yourself in whatever delusion gets you through the night, old man."

It was funny—Owen had said as much to John Jean before, but whereas previously the hospital board president had simply looked annoyingly smug, now he huffed and squirmed as if Owen had landed some kind of blow. "I'll give you this one warning. Your appearance in this foolishness only provides me somewhere else to shift the fallout. I'll protect my son. But I'll bury you."

Was Andreas admitting he knew about the screwed-up books?

The jury was out on what "this foolishness" was, but one thing was certain. Owen had done what everyone said was impossible: he'd gotten at least a tiny bit under John Jean's skin. He didn't want to trust that instinct, because Jack got pale and swore as he told the story—usually after a few drinks—of how Andreas had pulled a grandpa act on him and gotten him to talk about Taiwan, then yanked the rug out from under him and tried to blackmail him. This didn't seem to be a bait and switch, but… well, the bastard could try. What the hell could he possibly have on Owen, anyway?

John Jean curled his lip, still tugging at his shirt cuffs. "Don't glare at me like that. You look too much like your father as it is."

Every drop of blood in Owen's veins ran ice cold—then just as quickly became boiling hot.

Dropping the binders, Owen hit the stop button on the elevator and backed John Jean into the corner.

Blinking, John Jean went, his bravado replaced by confusion and wariness as he got a look at the wildness in Owen's eye. "Gagnon, what in the world—?"

"*I'll* protect Erin." Owen didn't touch John Jean, but he came so close he nearly brushed their bodies together. He felt as if he were on fire, burning with decades-old rage stoked to life by John Jean's high-handedness and sleazy comparisons. He bore down on John Jean, who remained completely frozen, too stunned by Owen's transformation to move. "Erin's done living in garrets and hiding in his room, working overtime and organizing your events instead of having a social life. He's staying with me."

John Jean continued to stare.

This felt so amazing. "And if you think you can so much as toss a spoonful of dirt at me, you go ahead and try."

It was strange. He waited for John Jean to get angry at him. He expected sneering, shouting, derision. He was ready for it. He *wanted* it. All John Jean did, though, was stare at Owen, speechless and disarmed.

Owen's fists tightened, rising for the other man's throat. *Fight back. Fight, so I can—*

Realizing what he was thinking, what he wanted to do, Owen practically leapt away, swallowing horror.

No rage. No fighting.

Taking a few deep breaths, Owen managed to center himself, but he was still left with confusion as John Jean blinked at him, stunned and… well, not behaving like John Jean.

Owen picked up the binders, righting the pages that had slipped out of place after he pressed the button to start the elevator. "Keep your threats to yourself," he said brusquely, focusing his eyes on the door. Before he stepped onto the third floor, he fixed his glare squarely at John Jean. "And if you so much as look at Erin sideways, it's *me* coming after you now. Remember that, *Dad*."

His parting remark cost him a little too much. He got the binders to the conference room, but he had to hide out in the stairwell after, pressing his head into a cold air return pipe and breathing deeply for several minutes until he stopped shaking.

He's not your dad. You're never going to see your dad again, or your mom. You got carried away with John Jean. You're definitely projecting, and you need to slow your roll. You absolutely have to keep your anger in check, and you can't lash out at him or anyone else like that.

He soothed himself for several minutes, breathing slowly and deliberately from his diaphragm until he was calm once more. Then he ran his fingers through his hair, put his cool, collected mask back on, and opened the door to return to his day.

CHAPTER EIGHT

OWEN HAD been flirty with Erin while they were fake dating, but now somehow everything was different. The *way* Owen looked at him was different. Erin supposed his reactions weren't the same either. When Owen entered a room, Erin centered his attention on the man, breathless. Owen always smiled at him, a gesture for Erin alone. It required reciprocation, though Erin's smile lingered long after Owen left, and he had to cover his mouth to force it down.

Erin of course wasted no time updating Nick on the new development with the file, not hiding Owen's accidental drafting onto their team. "I hadn't meant to involve him. It just sort of happened."

Nick pursed his lips. "Well, so long as he keeps quiet. He *can't* tell Jared."

Erin held up his hands. "He *especially* wouldn't tell him."

The promise of the files and their contents proved to be distracting for Nick, but unfortunately Erin couldn't remain focused on his work, constantly wondering when Owen might drift into his orbit and make him feel euphoric.

"You're serious about him, aren't you," Wendy remarked as they collated files together.

Erin couldn't resist touching his hair. "Of course. We moved in together, after all."

"*That* was strange. How you behave lately, though." She shook her head, smiling. "Well, I guess it's one way to romance somebody. Move them in, keep them close."

Erin frowned at her. "You do remember I'm the one who bid on *him*?"

She waved this idea away. "Oh, you two have argued since you took this job. We all figured it was foreplay. It's nice to see you finally settling in together, is what I'm saying. I'm not going to pretend I understand how you lovebirds worked it out."

Erin considered her remark a lot as he finished for the day and went home. He wondered what Wendy would think if she knew their relationship had been sealed by a Xanax confession.

After grabbing a yogurt, he went upstairs to his room to find the thumb drive, and his heart beat faster as he pulled up the files on his laptop. There it was, just as Owen had said it would be. All the evidence organized and irrefutable.

Someone had stolen from the hospital for decades.

Erin remembered the sea of faces from the most recent hospital board meeting. Every single one of the members, except for Rebecca, could have done it.

Ed Johnson, a local businessman and veteran. Mike Leary, currently the treasurer, who used to own the hardware store. Keith Barnes, the secretary, the retired president of Copper Point State Bank. Ron Harris, the board vice president and CEO of Weber Mining & Minerals. Christian West, the retired executive vice president of Weber Mining & Minerals.

And of course John Jean Andreas, board president, local leader and philanthropist, investor, retired health care director. Any of them was potentially the guilty party.

How could Erin smoke them out? He had the gun, but who had fired it?

He had no idea how to find the answer, and he was tired of thinking about it, at least for the night. He had other things to worry about, such as getting ready for his date. Owen would be home any minute, and they'd be leaving in less than a half hour. What was Erin supposed to wear? The clothes he'd worn to work felt uncomfortable, and he didn't want to go out looking like this. What would *Owen* wear? Technically Erin knew he could ask him, but he didn't want to.

So many of his nonwork clothes were still in his suitcase or boxes. He'd been so focused on the printouts, he hadn't unpacked, which meant he stood in his T-shirt, sifting through things, trying to locate something suitable to put on. Something comfortable. He had a particular sweater in mind, a cashmere coral one he hadn't worn since he'd gone to his mother's family's ski vacation three years ago. He wanted to wear that sweater with the oatmeal mock turtleneck underneath, with a pair of khakis and patterned socks. He had the khakis, but not the socks. He'd never owned anything but plain socks in his life. Why he wanted to wear them now he couldn't say, but patterned socks were an abrupt and powerful obsession.

What is wrong with me? What am I doing?

I want to look good for Owen. I want him to see me in something other than my work uniform for a change.

The knock on his door startled him. "Everything all right?"

Erin dropped the stack of shirts in his hand. "Y-yes. Fine. I'm sorry. I can't find…." Giving up, he picked a shirt at random. "It's fine. It doesn't matter."

He clutched the shirt to his chest as the door opened and Owen entered the room.

"What can't you find? Maybe I can help." Owen frowned at the mess on Erin's bed and across the top of the boxes and inside his suitcase. "Why haven't you put your clothes away?"

Erin cleared his throat. "It doesn't matter. I'll wear something else. We're running late."

"Tell me what you're trying to find."

Erin wanted to tell Owen to forget it, but he knew from experience it would be more difficult to dissuade him than to search for the clothing. "A coral sweater and an oatmeal mock neck. And a pair of khakis to match."

"Got it." Owen moved the suitcase to the bed and began shifting boxes. "You double-check the suitcase, and I'll go through these. I know the sweater you're talking about. I remember packing it and thinking it would flatter your complexion."

Erin rifled through the suitcase, knowing full well he'd find nothing, though he did single out a few pairs of khakis that might work and a handful of brown socks. When he turned to check how Owen was doing in his search, he saw him holding both the sweater and the mock neck, grinning proudly.

"Got them both. And here, you've got the khakis. I like the lighter pair for these." He frowned. "None of those socks will do, though."

Erin accepted the clothes from Owen with a sigh. "I know, but I don't have many great choices."

Owen nodded at the door. "Come with me. I have a ridiculously large sock collection."

This Erin balked at. "I can't borrow your *socks*."

"Why not? They're not my dirty socks. In fact, some of them—*many* of them—haven't been worn. Come on."

Once again, Erin had little choice but to follow Owen, and so he did, all the way to Owen's room.

Owen opened two drawers at the top of a tall dresser, then stepped into his closet and pulled down a cloth basket overflowing with socks, which he set on the bed. "Anything in the drawers or the basket is fair game. Oh—we forgot the sweater so you can match properly. I'll grab that while you go sock shopping."

Erin ran his hands over the neat lines of socks in the drawer and stared at the basket, amazed. He hadn't looked at Owen's feet before. Well, he'd noticed his socks a few times, he supposed, and he remembered a nice argyle and a novelty pair once, but he hadn't known the man was a walking sock meme. He had every color of the rainbow, every pattern, and more fun, wild socks than Erin had known existed. There was a pair of blue socks sporting random medical items such as stethoscopes, pill bottles, and syringes.

Others had tacos, dinosaurs—one that was dinosaurs who were *also* tacos—sloths, hamburgers, pieces of sushi, busts of Alexander Hamilton, and the *Creation of Adam*. Another pair had some sort of molecule all over them, and the ones beside that had, upon closer inspection, Cthulhu.

"So what do you think?" Owen returned with Erin's outfit in his hands. "Wild, huh? I had a few cool pairs of my own, but Simon's the one who started the insanity. Now Jared gets in on it too, and Jack handed me a pair for my birthday. So take whatever you like, and keep them. Well—okay, there are a few I have to have you borrow, if they're what you choose. But most of them I can part with. Knock yourself out."

Erin honestly had no idea where to start. He glanced at the sweater and khakis, scanned the sea of socks, and picked up a striped pair that complemented his chosen clothing without going too crazy. "I'd like these, if that's all right."

"A conservative choice, but I'm not surprised."

Erin couldn't say he wanted to choose the *Le Chat Noir* socks. For one, they were red, and two, they were too much for him to pull off. "I should get dressed."

"Go ahead and get dressed in here. I'll wait in the hall."

It was strange to take off his clothes in Owen's room, stripping to his T-shirt and underwear in a place full of another man's things. In fact, since he wasn't wearing a button-down, he removed the T-shirt and stood for a moment in only his underwear, leaving him vulnerable and uncomfortable. He climbed into his clothes as quickly as possible, though he felt awkward all over again once he sat on Owen's bed to put on Owen's socks. Sitting on the comforter dislodged clouds of the man's scent over Erin, and he couldn't get out of there fast enough.

Owen was indeed waiting in the hall, holding a pair of Erin's tan loafers. "I thought these would do. Oh, you look nice."

Erin blushed and accepted the shoes. "Thank you. I just need to drop my things in the room, and I'm ready to go."

They drove to the restaurant in Owen's car. Since campus town wasn't far from Owen's house, they had parked and were walking inside the restaurant within ten minutes of leaving the house. Finding the parking spot had, in fact, taken up most of the time.

The hostess seated them with an easy smile, handing them menus and assuring them their server would be with them momentarily.

Owen grinned as he leaned on the edge of their table and craned his head to look around the restaurant. "Great atmosphere, not very big, lots of cozy nooks and crannies." He indicated the window with a nod. "And the view is fantastic."

Smoothing his hands over the tablecloth, Erin followed Owen's gaze. The view *was* quite something. Someone had clearly taken pains to ensure this particular table's occupants could see out even at night, that the glare from the restaurant wouldn't cause the glass to become a mirror. Because the café was situated slightly on a hill and clear of any trees, they could see into the whole of campus town and some of the Main Street district, and of course the greenbelt park that lined the bluff over the bay. The old-style lantern streetlights, the winding sidewalks, the evergreen trees and bushes hugging the gazebo split by footlights... yes, it was quite the sight. Music played softly too, from speakers tucked discreetly behind planters and affixed in corners at the ceiling, piping in elegant classical music.

Erin wondered if the violin-heavy concerto was upsetting Owen.

A bright young woman, someone from the college, appeared to take their drink and appetizer order. Owen declined alcohol since he was on call, but he insisted Erin order a glass of wine. "You look like you could use one. You're working too much."

"You aren't slouching yourself," Erin said when their server had left them to bring Erin his chardonnay. "Is it stressful to be on call all the time? I wish we had the funds to hire a full-time nurse anesthetist, but we don't."

Owen shrugged. "It's not my favorite thing, being on call, but I manage. I don't have it as rough as Jack, let's put it that way. My problem is the same as always. St. Ann's is technically too small to support an anesthesiologist. Honestly it shouldn't have more than a nurse anesthetist or two. But then, St. Ann's should be busier than it is, given the size of the area and the lack of medical care in the region. It all comes down to our funding, doesn't it?"

Erin kept his gaze averted, though he could tell from Owen's casual tone he had no idea he'd stepped directly into the heart of the matter. Erin should change the subject, he knew. And yet.... "It's actually more a product of the direction of the hospital. I believe St. Ann's could grow quite significantly with the right leadership."

Sipping his water, Owen leaned back in his chair. "We should get rid of the dead weight in the board, then."

Erin glanced around nervously. "Hush."

"There's no one at any table near us. But fair point." Owen pitched his voice so quiet Erin had to strain to hear it. "You don't share your father's vision for the hospital?"

Erin traced his finger around the rim of his glass. "I don't."

Owen tapped his thumb against the table, a nervous tic of a gesture more than something done for emphasis. "You should be a vice president, not in HR."

That made Erin laugh. "I already told you I'm terrible with administration."

"I don't think that's true. I think you're quite good at your job, in fact. With the right support system, especially, I suspect you'd flourish."

"Says the man who does nothing but challenge my authority whenever we're at work."

"I'm not challenging you. I'm arguing with you. I told you, I love our arguments. I don't ever want you to stop fighting with me."

You're the only one I fight with. Erin couldn't say that, so instead he asked, "Why?"

A shadow passed over Owen's face. "Because it shows you're not afraid of me."

Stunned, Erin didn't know how to reply to that, and was saved from having to do so by the server returning in an attempt to take an order they weren't ready to place in the slightest.

What does he mean, it shows I'm not afraid of him? Of course I'm not afraid of him.

Pushing the thought out of his mind, Erin focused on the menu. He was tempted by the salmon crepes, and when he said as much, Owen confessed he was leaning toward the ravioli butternut squash. They decided on an order of fritto misto and arancini as starters, which was probably too much because their meals came with a basket of hot Italian rolls and garlic butter.

It felt decadent and good to sit with a man in the window of a restaurant for the entirety of Copper Point to gawk at. With *this* man, whom so many feared, who kept smiling at Erin and touching his foot with his own beneath the table. Who had loaned Erin a pair of patterned socks and helped him find his sweater.

Who thought he was good at his job, the only one besides Nick to ever come out and speak so emphatically to him on the topic.

The restaurant hushed enough Erin could hear the violin drifting over the top of the music again. It rang in his head as he stared at Owen, who raised an eyebrow when their gazes held a little too long.

Leaning on his elbows, Owen regarded Erin over his interlaced fingers. “Everything all right?”

Smiling, Erin rested his hands on the table, close enough to brush the fabric of Owen’s arm. “I’ve never been better.”

OWEN ENJOYED sitting in public with Erin.

He liked the way people watched them, as if they were a pair of princes up on a dais, dining on display. He appreciated in particular their expressions of surprise. Somehow everyone regarded them differently today. He wondered what they noticed.

Maybe it was Erin. He looked so much brighter, so much more… Erin. Owen shifted his arms so he could rub his fingers together over the cuff of Erin's sweater. "I like this outfit you have on. It's better than what you normally wear."

Erin reclaimed his arm and stabbed a piece of salmon crepe with a wry smile. "Thank you, but I can hardly wear sweaters to work."

"You could wear brighter colors is my point. Even just a tie. You make me crazy the way you're so dreary." Owen aimed his fork at Erin. "I'm going to buy you new ties. And socks. You can keep the rest of the dowdy stuff, but we're going to accessorize you. If anybody raises an eyebrow, blame your boyfriend."

He'd expected Erin to refuse, but he only shrugged. "I can't wear socks as wild as yours."

"I didn't say socks as wild as mine." Though Owen didn't miss the note of longing in Erin's voice, either. Did he relax this much with one glass of wine?

Or is this all due to the kiss?

The kiss had been some time ago, so probably it was the wine. Well, regardless, Owen intended to kiss the man more, and soon.

He sipped his mineral water, trying to think of something other than kissing Erin, because that way lay only self-torture. "So what was life in boarding school like?"

Erin shrugged. "It wasn't that bad."

"But wasn't it lonely?" Owen leaned on his elbow and regarded Erin with naked awe. "You were so *young*. Weren't you scared?"

"Of course I was scared. But as soon as I discovered I had nothing to fear but a bit of isolation until I made friends and learned how to navigate the system, I was fine. In many ways it was a gift. I can rely on myself. I don't need anyone else, and I never have. I'm completely capable all on my own."

Owen couldn't deny that was true, because Erin Andreas was the poster boy for competence porn. Even so…. "Everyone needs *someone*, at least part of the time."

Erin sipped his wine. "I don't."

"You need me right now to distract your father." Owen rubbed at his jaw. Now he understood what Simon had said about letting Erin drive the bus. "That can't make you happy. I'm sorry."

Erin smoothed a hand over his hair and ran his index finger around his salad plate. "I don't mind needing you so much."

Owen grinned and nudged Erin's leg with his knee. "That feels like a high compliment."

Erin cleared his throat and rubbed his salad plate so hard it shifted an inch. "Since we're discussing school… haven't you been friends with Jared and Simon since your elementary days? I suppose if I'm jealous of anything, it's that."

"We weren't close in elementary school, no. They went to South Elementary and I went to North, to start. It took us a while to get to know one another in middle school as well. But yeah, I guess since then we've pretty much been together. You have to have friends from boarding school, though, right?"

"Not like the three of you." Erin had drained his wine, so he shifted to his water glass. "You went to college together, then *bought a house*. I can't fathom that."

"Going to college with friends, or buying a house?"

"Both. I mean, I knew Nick at college, but it wasn't as if we hung out together."

No, that wouldn't be Nick's style. Owen bounced his fork on the side of his hand, tapping it against his remaining ravioli. "I guess it's a little different. We went through a lot. It felt weird to let go, so we didn't."

Erin looked confused, shaken, and wracked with longing. "I couldn't do it."

Owen smiled. "You have us now, though."

He couldn't decide if that made Erin happy or nervous. Probably both.

Owen was about to launch into another line of questioning about school when a familiar voice called out across the restaurant. "Owen—oh, wonderful, and Erin too."

Ram Rao approached them with a wave. Owen waved back, though his gut was already knotting. He knew where this conversation was going to go, and he wasn't ready.

Ram stood at the edge of their table, beaming. "I've wanted to run into you both. Owen, thank you so much for filling in for me at the fundraiser. I feel terrible that I couldn't be there, but I hear you were incredible."

Owen focused on his plate, pushing the remainder of his food around. "Not a big deal, don't worry about it." *Don't bring up the quartet. Don't bring up the quartet.*

"It's a huge deal, and I'm so grateful. But you know, we'd love to have you join us—"

Owen held up a hand, a sharp gesture full of finality. "Absolutely not. You know I have no interest in joining the quartet or making it a quintet."

Ram sighed. "Owen, you're so talented. I'd heard you were a strong player, and now that you've had a taste of coming out of retirement, I admit I'm hoping I can talk you into making that return permanent."

Fear, sorrow, guilt, and panic swirled around Owen in a hot rush. Dammit, this wasn't how he wanted tonight to go—

"Ram, thank you so much, but one of Owen's conditions of filling in for you was that he not be asked to volunteer or play again, and as the organizer of the event, I need you to honor the terms we agreed to."

Ram, not at all used to managerial Erin's clipped tones, began to fumble. "Oh… oh, I'm so… I'm sorry, I didn't realize… I…." He inclined his head awkwardly in Owen's direction. "Please, excuse me, I didn't know…."

Owen nodded gruffly, unsure of how to respond. Erin, still in full HR mode, offered a polite, lukewarm, but definite *this conversation is over, thank you* smile to Ram. However, instead of waiting for Ram to leave, Erin filled the silence by asking Ram about his upcoming concerts at the university, coaxing him into more comfortable subjects. Owen didn't join in, focusing instead on running his thumb down the side of his water glass.

Once Ram finally left, Owen pursed his lips, then let out a sigh. "Sorry."

Erin waved a hand. "You're fine."

It wasn't fine, though. Owen felt jagged. "You shouldn't have had to rescue me."

"I told you. It's not an issue."

Their server appeared with their check, and Owen paid it over Erin's objection. At one point he'd planned to suggest dessert, but now he only wanted to get out. He'd also intended to take Erin on a walk along Bayview Park, but it wasn't simply cold, it was windy with lake effect snow, so he forgot about that too.

Intellectually he knew there wasn't any connection between Ram's approach and the way everything felt sour now, that this was all his decision to dwell on things he knew better than to think about. Emotionally, however, it was as if Ram had broken the spell, and Owen was helpless to stop himself. The more he tried to push the darkness down, the more it billowed around him. By the time he reached the car, his vision had narrowed to a tiny path before him, as if this weren't a simple flurry of snow but a blizzard, amplified by his emotions.

At his car door, Erin blocked him. "I'll drive us home."

Owen snapped out of his funk enough to give Erin a good once-over. "You had wine at dinner."

"One glass. I'm not so much of a lightweight I can't drive us." He nodded at the passenger door.

Though Owen felt he should argue, he didn't want to. He was raw and shaky, and Erin was a godsend right now. He got into the car.

He tensed as they left the lot, and he could tell Erin was winding up to talk. God, was he going to bring up the violin?

"That was a lovely evening. Thank you for the meal, and for the socks."

Owen couldn't help a half smile. "Oh, so you're claiming them?"

"You said yourself you had more than you knew what to do with."

That wasn't quite what Owen remembered saying, but he didn't mind. "You're welcome to keep some of the others."

"Maybe I will."

The exchange relaxed Owen significantly, though that made as little sense to him as the business with Ram making him worked up. He was still trying to figure it out as they pulled into the garage and Erin cut the engine, then turned to him in the harsh silence of the car.

"I want to say one thing to you."

Owen glanced at him, distracted by his muddled head. "Hmm?"

Erin looked prim and poised and slightly nervous, a bit like he did at work but without the stiff posturing he always gave off. He kept trying to meet Owen's gaze, but he couldn't manage it and ended up focusing at the level of his chin and shoulder instead. "I don't mind needing you. It still feels mildly terrifying, but I'm getting used to it. That said… you could stand to need me sometimes as well. It would be good for you, and it would help me."

All Owen's walls went up again. "If this is about the violin—"

"It isn't about the violin. Not specifically. I'm saying, I'd be happy to listen to you talk about it, if you needed to. But I'd also be happy to listen to you talk about something else. Or help you do a task you couldn't do on your own. I just want to be part of what—" He withdrew. "Never mind. The more I talk, the more ridiculous I sound."

He didn't sound ridiculous at all. He sounded vulnerable and sweet, and Owen couldn't stand it.

Reaching across the console between them, he captured Erin's hand, squeezing it as he stared straight ahead. "Playing the violin makes me feel sick and violated."

He braced himself for Erin to ask *why*, and he was trying to decide how he would reply when he heard instead, "I'm so sorry. That's terrible. And wrong. Because you're so talented. Though… did it always make you feel that way? When I heard you play when you were younger, I didn't get the impression you hated it."

"I didn't always hate it, no." Owen shut his eyes, holding fast to Erin's hand. "Something happened when I was getting ready to go to college."

What an understatement. He'd never so much as attempted to tell the story to anyone. They either knew, they'd guessed, or they didn't ask. Or they were Owen's therapist, which was something else entirely. It left him raw to say this much to Erin.

It also felt good. Freeing.

I want to say more.

Erin squeezed his fingers. "I'm sorry. Sorry it happened to you. Sorry whatever it was took something you once enjoyed away. Sorry it still affects you."

He's not asking me what happened. He's not trying to fix it. He's just listening. Owen sagged, leaning over to rest his head on Erin's shoulder. Then he pressed a kiss on the same spot. "Thank you."

"Thank you for sharing with me."

A rush of emotion consumed Owen, flooding the last of his edginess, replacing those feelings with slow-burning need. “Erin, I want to kiss you.”

Erin’s hand slid up Owen’s arm as Owen moved his mouth closer to Erin’s face. “I… would like that.”

“I want to kiss you in my room. With both of us wearing only our socks.” When Erin’s breath caught, Owen kissed the edge of his collarbone. “Is that too much?”

“I… don’t know.”

“Want to find out if it is, together?”

Erin shut his eyes and pressed his forehead to Owen’s. “Yes.”

CHAPTER NINE

THE HOUSE was silent as Owen led Erin to his bedroom. Jared was conspicuously absent, leaving Erin alone with Owen, his rapid heartbeat, and his raging doubts.

It wasn't a question of him wanting this. He'd dreamed of making love to Owen, fantasized about being with him since forever. He'd never thought of being with anyone else. This was such an epic moment for him, and he felt as if he were made of butterflies. Puberty had come late and slowly to Erin, to the point he'd thought something must be wrong with him, because when his body did finally begin to react, it didn't behave the way everyone else's had. His orgasms were so much quieter, to start, and never focused on anything. It was more that sometimes he had a tiny flare of sexual excitement, reacting to random stimulus. He'd never had fantasies, either…

except for ones of Owen, and even these were vague and nebulous. Colors and images in his mind as his body chased release.

This would be completely different, and he wasn't sure he was ready.

Sex, with Owen Gagnon. That he was having sex with anyone was enough to send him reeling, because he'd assumed he never would. That it was happening, and it was *with Owen*.... Here he was, almost at the door to Owen's room, where Owen would kiss him, touch him, take off his clothes—

"You okay?" They were inside the room now, and Owen touched Erin's face, regarding him with concern. "You're pale as a sheet and rigid as a stone." His crooked smile turned sad. "Look, we don't have to do this."

Erin shook his head, trying not to be wooden. "No, I do want to. I'm apprehensive, is all. I'm sorry."

"You have nothing to apologize for." Owen slid his fingers to Erin's nape, threading them into his hair. "Seriously, we can go slow, or if you don't want to, if lower contact isn't your thing, I'm okay with it. We can table sex for now, or... you know."

Erin couldn't breathe. "What do you mean? You're okay with what?"

"I mean I want to be with you in whatever way is right for you. Why is that upsetting?" Owen pursed his lips. "Arc you afraid of me?"

Though Owen asked this with a teasing note in his voice, Erin could also see the shadows in his face, echoes left over from the ones from dinner. Why was he so obsessed with worry about Erin being afraid of him? "I'm not afraid of you."

Owen relaxed. "Okay. Are you nervous because you're trying to tell me you don't want to go all the way?"

"It's not that, it's…." Erin considered his reply carefully. "It's so much, to let someone past my defenses this far."

Owen brought his fingers to Erin's face. "You've been alone for so long. I want to be with you, if only for a little while."

The hard, cold ball of fear inside Erin rolled forward into his hand, and he clenched it tight. "This is the problem. Once I let someone in, I won't want it to be only for a little while."

Owen's countenance softened, first in surprise, and then in an almost boyish brightness that stole Erin's heart. "Then I'll be with you as long as you'll have me."

He kissed Erin again.

They'd kissed several times now, and this kiss was slower, easier, quieter than any of the others, but so much sensual promise lurked behind it Erin could barely maintain his grip on Owen's shoulders and hold himself upright. The sleek, lazy way Owen's tongue explored Erin's mouth left him gasping for air. He wished he had a wall behind him, or a bed. Owen's hands roamed across Erin's shoulders, down his arms, up the sides of his body, eventually coming to the edge of the sweater.

Oh, but Owen was so good at this.

Let him lead. Surrender to him. Let him play you like an instrument. Erin could imagine it in his mind, being the violin in Owen's arm, his hand sliding over his body….

Erin shuddered, melting into Owen's embrace.

Owen broke the kiss and whispered into Erin's neck. "Can I take off some of your clothes?"

Mindless, boneless, Erin held up his arms as Owen removed the sweater and mock turtleneck. He shivered in the chill of the room, then trembled for different reasons as Owen took him in his arms again. Owen didn't resume the kiss, however, guiding Erin's hands to his own shirt.

"Undo me too."

Erin wasn't exactly adept at removing Owen's shirt, but it was thrilling to watch his skin appear, to see Owen tremble the same way he did. When Owen murmured, "Touch me," into Erin's ear, Erin did, skimming his palms across the beautiful, defined expanse of Owen's chest, loving the way Owen responded to each stroke. Owen had such *beautiful* skin. Soft, then fluffy with dark hair trailing toward his abdomen. The only place it was marred was on his left side, where a series of thin, faintly red lines outlined in white lashed across his skin in odd patterns. Old scars.

Something told Erin to go nowhere near those marks.

He focused on Owen's nipples instead, pale pink circles below that crown of hair. They were erect, rising and falling with Owen's slightly labored breaths.

Kissing Erin's hair, Owen chuckled and drew one of Erin's hands up so his fingers touched the bud. "Put your hands on me as much as you want." He kept his hand close to Erin's, showing him how to tug at the nipple as he sought Erin's mouth once more. Instead of kissing, though, Owen whispered against Erin's lips. "Want me to touch you too?"

Dizzy, lost, Erin nodded.

Owen did kiss him then, deep and openmouthed as they explored each other's nipples, teasing until they made each other moan, until they stumbled together toward the bed, their legs hitting the mattress. Rather than lie down, Owen had Erin help as he undid his own trousers, sending them to the floor. When he slid Erin's fingertips inside his waistband, Erin broke the kiss and buried his face in Owen's neck.

Owen ran a hand along Erin's naked back. "Do we need to slow down?"

Yes? No? Erin ran his thumb along the elastic of Owen's briefs, nuzzling Owen's jaw with his forehead. "It's happening so fast."

"Then we'll stop for tonight."

"But I don't *want* to stop, this is the problem."

Owen skimmed Erin's ass, cupping it lightly. "How about we compromise. How about we lie on the bed and make out. That's it, that's all we'll do. You decide how much clothes we're wearing and when we stop."

"Why do I get to decide everything? How is this fair?"

"Because it's not *my* first time, it's yours. And besides." He sent his touch traveling up Erin's side. "For me, it truly is enough to do anything with you. I've wanted this for a while."

Erin pressed his hands to Owen's chest. "Liar. You said you didn't like me before."

"I said I thought you were the enemy. I still respected you, and I still wanted you. I dreamed of hate-sex with you." When Erin laughed, Owen stole a kiss. "Kind of disappointed I'm not going to get it now, actually."

"I'm sure we'll fight over something. Though I don't think I'll be good at any kind of sex."

"I'm telling you, we don't have to do this if you're not interested. Or we can stick to just kisses and touches if it's what you want."

Erin didn't know what to do with all this accommodation. "It's not… that, precisely. I definitely have a lower interest in sex than most men I know, which always left me feeling awkward. But sometimes I'm—" He cut himself off, abruptly embarrassed.

Stroking him, Owen rocked him gently as they stood. "Don't stop. I want to hear what you feel."

Erin shut his eyes and gave over to the sensation of being held by Owen. *Let go* into the feeling, did his best to trust in it. To believe it was okay to open this part of himself to someone else, to simply be. "Sometimes I'm interested in sex. Curious, impatient, desperate to be with a partner in ways that feel incredibly wicked, at least to me. But it's felt too dangerous to let someone in. To know the things I want and feel, to see me naked. To touch intimate parts of me and look at me while I'm losing myself to lust." He opened his eyes to stare at Owen's shoulder. "I've never understood how other people do it."

Owen's hands were on Erin's waist as he spoke into Erin's neck, his cheek on Erin's hair. "It's so funny, because at first I couldn't get enough. I wanted to be seen. Touched. I was so lonely and angry and sad, and sex was often the only way I could control myself. Except it was like trying to stay warm with a match. Satisfaction only for a fleeting moment, and then I was scrambling to find someone to strike against once more. Until I listened to my therapist and sat with the emotions. Let myself feel empty until I could understand how and why I needed to be properly filled."

He spoke so freely about having gone to therapy. "I've never had a therapist."

"Nobody offered? Or you're too proud?"

If he'd heard any teasing in Owen's voice, Erin couldn't have answered. "Both, I suppose."

"It's good stuff, if you find the right one. Someone to listen to you barf up your feelings. Someone private, someone you don't know, who doesn't know you, who doesn't have anything to do with your life except for your confessions. There was some fairy tale I read when I was little about a princess who whispered her worries to the oven—I think she'd been captured or something, I forget the details—and eventually the king hears her and marries her. I'm messing it up, probably. The part I always thought about was the idea of whispering to the oven. That's what a good therapist is, except they talk back but don't propose marriage. They let you get your feelings out, and sometimes they reflect them back to you in a meaningful way that helps you sort yourself out. Mostly, though, they're an elaborate barf bag."

Erin smiled at the image. "I wouldn't know how to go about getting one. It would be such a scandal in town."

"Oh hell no, don't go in town. Didn't you hear me say mine's in Duluth? If you ever were serious about therapy, let me ask my lady for a recommendation for someone in her office, and we'll go to our respective therapists at the same time."

Erin couldn't believe a minute ago they were kissing and now they were talking about therapy. Or rather, Owen was, and he was excited about it. Erin kissed his ear. "I want to let you in," he whispered.

"There isn't a rush," Owen whispered back.

They ended up lying on the bed together, Owen in his underwear—and socks—with Erin simply missing his shirt. They held one another and kissed, languidly now, the sort of slow, unhurried mating mouths do when it's not a prelude to another act. Erin liked it. Loved it, even. It felt heady and sweet, terribly intimate, and fantastically safe.

"Let's have another date soon," Owen said when they finally broke for air.

"Yes, let's," Erin agreed, and went in for another round.

OWEN FELT like he was fifteen years old again, except this time his life wasn't a trash fire.

Though he woke alone, his pillow still smelled of Erin, and lovesick fool that he was, he cradled it to his face, trying to capture as much of the scent as possible. He lay in bed for a long time, replaying the highlights of the evening over and over, allowing himself to be… well, giddy.

Erin was so *sweet*. Not on the surface, but deep down, past the prickly, prim layers. Who would have thought? Nobody. But now Owen knew the truth. Erin was a tender, hesitant man who wanted to approach sex cautiously. He was embarrassed about his lack of experience, but he bloomed like a shy, beautiful flower when allowed to lead lovemaking. No way was Owen confessing he considered that adorable. The man would clock him. It *was* adorable, though. Utterly and completely.

His private Erin Andreas. Owen couldn't be happier.

He was the first one awake as usual, but he was still smiling as he emerged from the basement after his workout, where he found Jared in the kitchen waiting for him.

"From the look on your face, it was a good date." Jared passed Owen a cup of coffee. "I'm glad."

"Very good date." Owen didn't feel like elaborating, but he still couldn't stop his smile as he added some sugar. "Where'd you go last night, by the way?"

"Jack and Simon's. I ended up watching the first episode of some Korean romantic thriller with them. It wasn't bad." He raised an eyebrow at Owen. "Please don't chase me out of the house all weekend, though."

"Nah." Owen took a sip. "I think we should keep it chill this weekend. Probably do a lot with the three of us. We could cook something together, then watch a show. Maybe have Jack and Simon over, if they aren't on shift."

That was exactly what they ended up doing. Jack and Simon both worked Saturday, so the group get-together was set for Sunday afternoon, and Saturday was an in-house hangout. After shopping for the ingredients for stew and getting everything prepped in the kitchen, Owen, Jared, and Erin watched home improvement reality television while the meat marinated.

Erin had a weakness for those kinds of shows, it turned out. He especially loved the ones where people had their houses or any parts of their lives made over. Once Owen figured that out, he did some hasty online searching, and while the stew simmered in its final phase, he set them up with the rebooted *Queer Eye*.

Erin needed tissues. He also leaned into Owen to the point Owen got brave enough to put his arm around his lover's back. *Thank you, Fab Five.*

Sunday was a different type of great day. Jack and Simon coming over meant more cooking, but Owen had his usual rivalry with Jack to look forward to, which began as soon as they went on their group shopping expedition. He and Jack sparred over what to cook, who would make it, and who was better at every aspect of everything from the second the man walked in the door to the minute they got in the parking lot of the grocery store.

Erin shook his head at Owen as Simon drew Jack away and murmured about not making a scene. "You weren't kidding. You do love to argue."

Owen rubbed his hands together. "Gets my blood moving." He waggled his eyebrows at Erin. "Want to pick up where the surgeon left off?"

Before Erin could answer, a stooped, gray-haired woman stepped in front of them and turned to Owen, smiling. He knew where this was going even before she opened her mouth, but he couldn't do much but stand there and listen.

"Young man, I wanted to tell you what a pleasure it was to hear you play at the fundraiser last month."

Once again Erin came to his rescue, deftly deflecting her, but this time Owen wasn't frozen, only thoughtful. As Erin soothed him after she left, Owen kissed Erin's hand, then held it, drawing him forward into the produce.

Owen had a wonderful time with his friends, and he enjoyed watching Erin fold seamlessly into their group, but the woman intruded into his thoughts all night long.

She was still on his mind the next morning as Jared greeted him in the kitchen.

Owen set aside his coffee and pulled the ingredients for an omelet out of the fridge as he spoke. "You have regular clinic today?"

"No, I'm only seeing patients in the afternoon because I have an ER shift tonight, but I'm going in early for a meeting and to catch up on some charts. What about you?"

"Well, theoretically it's a light surgery day, but Kathryn has a mom who's a likely candidate for cesarean who I think they're going to add to the schedule today. She wanted to try natural, but if inducing her doesn't work, into the OR she goes." He tossed half an onion in the air before setting it on the cutting board to dice. "If there's time, I wanted to take Erin over to the gym after work."

"The gym?"

"Yeah. He mentioned before that he wanted to learn racquetball, and when I brought it up again, he was still interested, so I thought, why not."

"Cool. Well, have fun."

Owen paused with his knife over the onion as the woman from the day before drifted abruptly into his thoughts. She'd been doing so ever since they'd left the store, and he'd pushed her aside every time, but now he let her words linger, tasting his reaction to them, allowing it to settle onto his tongue and eventually fall out of his mouth.

"People keep talking to me about the performance. Ram came up to us at dinner the other night too, and tried to get me to join the quartet." Owen waited for Jared to reply.

Silence hung in the kitchen before Jared said anything. "I'm sorry if it's bothering you, everyone bringing it up."

Owen's thumb brushed the side of the onion as he stared so hard at it his eyes blurred. "I called and made an earlier therapy appointment, so hopefully it helps."

"Hopefully so. Again, I'm sorry."

He hadn't pierced the onion yet, but it was in half, so its pungency still wafted up, making his eyes sting. "I… I feel like I should tell… him. Erin, I mean. About my past. But maybe that's selfish."

Another long pause. "How is it selfish to want to tell him?"

He pushed the knife through the first segment of the vegetable, let the odor fill his sinuses, distracting him. "I don't know. It feels selfish."

"Does he seem as if he doesn't want to know those kinds of things about you?"

A second cut, more sting. "I don't know."

"Why do you feel you *should* tell him, then, if I can spin this interrogation differently?"

So I can find out now if he would react badly, before I get into this too deep.

Owen set the knife on the cutting board. That wasn't right. He didn't really think Erin would react badly. This was just old darkness creeping in. He was glad, though, he'd identified it now, so he could face it instead of projecting it onto Erin.

Drawing another breath, he let it out and resumed slicing, this time more calmly. "I think it's something people this close to me should probably know, if they're going to stick around."

He felt Jared move beside him before the gentle hand pressed onto his shoulder. Glancing to the side, he saw the sad smile Jared always wore when Owen talked about this part of his past.

"It's not selfish." Jared squeezed Owen's shoulder before letting it go. "And I agree, at some point you should talk about it. But I also don't think it's a rush. Do it when it feels right."

Owen nodded, relaxing. "Thanks for the free therapy."

"Anytime." Jared filled his thermos with what was left in the carafe. "You want me to start some fresh before I take off, or you got it?"

Owen waved him off with the knife. "Go on. I'll see you when I see you."

When Owen heard the sound of footsteps on the stairs, the first omelet was coming off the pan. Owen's heart fluttered as he waited for Erin to come around the corner.

It was the first time he'd appeared sleep-rumpled instead of getting dressed first, and Owen decided this look was his favorite. Vulnerable, peeled back, the same as Erin had been Friday night. Shy too, hovering at the edge of the kitchen, ready to bolt for his room at any second.

Putting his best foot forward, Owen set a fork beside the first plated omelet and reached for what he knew had become Erin's favorite mug. "Have a seat, and an omelet. I'm about to start mine, and then I'll join you. Fresh pot of coffee just finished too."

As Erin sat, Owen put the mug of black coffee and the half-and-half with a spoon in front of him. He would have dressed the coffee himself, but he worried it would have looked too over-the-top. Anyway, he figured they both needed something to do with their hands right now.

He focused on getting the second omelet in the pan, though he kept a careful watch on Erin out of the corner of his eye. Once he had it cooking, he started the conversation up again. "Sleep okay?"

"Yes, thank you." Erin sipped his coffee. "You?"

"Like a baby." He glanced over his shoulder. "Say. I know we talked about getting you hooked up with racquetball lessons. If we both have time and I can get us a court tonight, are you interested?"

Erin paused with a bite of omelet halfway to his mouth. "Oh—yes, that sounds wonderful. Except I'm not sure I have proper clothes or gear."

"We'll stop by the sporting goods store on our way." Owen busied himself with flipping his omelet. "We could drive in together, so we could go first thing when we're done with work. Though it might mean you waiting for me if the surgery schedule runs long."

"I don't mind waiting. Lord knows I have enough work to keep me busy."

"Good, good." Owen shifted the food onto his plate. "Everything taste all right?"

"Wonderful."

They did the dishes together, hurried through getting showered and dressed, and then they were off.

"You're practically beaming." Simon elbowed him with a cheeky wink as they got ready for the first surgery. "Both of you. You're both so different all the time now. None of the nurses can stop gossiping about it. You're not cranky, and Erin isn't as ironclad."

Owen didn't know what to say. *I hope it lasts* felt too fatalistic. So he only smiled and shrugged and ducked his head. Which wasn't like him.

Except it didn't feel wrong. Only strange.

Kathryn's patient didn't need a cesarean after all, so Owen hung out in the third-floor lounge, content to play games on his phone while Erin finished a meeting. He was deliberately avoiding the news because no way was he letting anything depressing ruin this day.

When Nick Beckert passed through and gave him a wave, slowing as if he wanted to talk, Owen happily put his phone aside and rose to greet his childhood friend turned boss. "Nick. Something I can do for you?"

Nick's smile didn't quite reach his eyes, and he looked as if he hadn't gotten enough sleep. "If you've got a few minutes, I wouldn't mind getting some fresh air."

Owen couldn't remember the last time Nick had asked him to get some fresh air with him. Something was up.

Nick led them to the roof, an unexpected move, and produced a set of keys to unlock the door. "This is kind of my private getaway right now. It's been slated to be a rooftop garden for fifteen years, but there's never the money to finish the project, and if they leave it unlocked, people sneak up here to smoke."

"Classy move at a hospital."

Nick used his shoulder to push the door open. "I learned not to expect much from people a long time ago."

Owen couldn't begin to guess why Nick had brought him here, but he didn't push to find out, and he didn't panic. As CEOs went, Nick was pretty chill. Too much so, if you asked Jared. Owen agreed to a point, though he thought most of the problem was thc leadership around the man. How was he supposed to be aggressive when he was so hamstrung? Jared argued Nick was too cautious, too eager to play the middle. "He's somewhere between Obama and Aaron Burr" was Jared's favorite complaint.

He didn't look hesitant now, more like a patient predator. Nick leaned on the edge of the barrier and stared at the ground, leaving Owen waiting.

Owen joined his employer at the crumbling wall. "When we're done here, I'm taking Erin to the city gym to learn racquetball."

This broke Nick out of his concentration loop, tripping him into mild alarm. "Erin? Playing racquetball?"

Nodding, Owen brushed a few pieces of loose gravel onto the clinic roof below. "He wants to have matches with some of the board members eventually. First he has to be able to hold his own in a court, though."

The way Nick's expression shuttered at *board members* told Owen Nick was in on the hunt for the embezzler too, which made sense. Good. It meant Erin wasn't doing this on his own.

Was this what Nick had brought Owen up here to talk about?

Nick tapped his thumb on the ledge as he cut a glance at Owen. "So you're actually dating him now?"

"I'm actually dating him."

Nick grimaced. "I shouldn't have told him it was okay to stay with you. I should have brought him to our place. My mother and Grandma Emerson wouldn't have blinked, if I'd asked."

Hold on. "What do you mean, you shouldn't have told him? What do you have to do with any of this?"

"I told him to stay with you so he could work on the files without his father getting in the way."

"You mean the ones I solved for him?"

Nick pursed his lips. "Yes, those. The ones you weren't supposed to have anything to do with. Just like you were only supposed to *pretend* to date him."

Owen leaned one elbow on the wall and studied Nick more carefully. "Is there something wrong with me dating Erin? As for the files, all I did was solve a little math problem."

"It was well more than *a little math problem*."

Truth. "Erin asked me not to talk about it, so I haven't. Not even with him."

"You also made a public scene with him in front of the town. Nothing about any of that was in his character, and you started all of it."

"Did I miss something where you were Erin's nanny that made his decisions for him?"

"You're no good for him. You rile him up and confuse him. And while I know you're a good man, when you wander off because this lark doesn't work out, it's him who's going to have hell to pay."

"Who says I'm wandering off? We've been fake dating a few weeks, legitimately dating for a few days. Could you give me a little credit here? I think I'd look creepier if I already had a wedding ring out, don't you?"

"I've watched out for that damn kid since I was fifteen. If I didn't, my grandmother would skin me alive. As it happens, though, he's also a friend."

What in the hell? "You're telling me you're giving me the big-brother talk because your grandmother told you you'd damn well better?"

"Yessir."

He said it so automatically and with such a straight face Owen was inclined to believe him. Plus, he'd met Nick's grandmother. She was ninety-three now but still living at home, and she was the only one the nursing staff feared more than Owen. Shaking his head, Owen turned his back to the wall and stared across the roof. "I'll be damned."

"You might well be. She wants you to stop by. I recommend bringing that lemon meringue you're so proud of. Leave the jokes about wedding rings at home." Nick ran a hand over his hair with a sigh. "She's never liked how Erin doesn't have family, how John Jean set up his life to keep him from ever finding one."

Owen's hands closed into fists. "Let him try now."

"Don't go poking that bear. You saw how he bested Jack without so much as lifting a butter knife. That was over a surgeon position. This is about his *son*."

No way was Owen leaving this alone. "It's absolutely about his son. The son he's neglected. Abused. Toyed with. Tricked."

"Tricked?" Nick's expression became stony. "Are we talking about Erin's father, or yours?"

The air left Owen's lungs. For a moment he felt helpless, cold.

A rush of anger filled him, sweeping through him like a vortex of fire starting at his feet, familiar heat and power from that tempting emotion. *Take this, and you won't have to feel scared anymore.*

Shutting his eyes, Owen drew air into his body, ignoring the invitation to anger, sitting with his feeling of helplessness. "I'm talking about Erin. And if this was your way of testing me, it was a dick move."

The silence went on too long, and when Owen opened his eyes, Nick regarded him with an expression even Jared couldn't criticize: the cool, composed, confident, but ultimately kind countenance of a leader.

"It's not cruel to test you when I'm trying to protect Erin. You and I haven't ever been close, and I have too many memories of you blowing your top at everyone when we were in school. Of course I'm going to poke you a bit when I find out you're seeing my friend." Winking, Nick clamped a hand on Owen's shoulder as he headed to the door leading into the hospital. "Good job, though. You passed."

Owen stared at Nick, then shook his head. "I don't know you that well either, and I've let Jared's stories about you color my opinion. I'm realizing I should have formed my own."

"You definitely should have done that."

Owen straightened the hem of his shirt as he cleared his throat. "So. Want to tell me about any of Erin's favorite foods I might not know about?"

Nick thought a moment. "Egg salad sandwiches. You'll want to get the recipe from my grandmother."

Own nodded. "Will do. Thanks."

Nick indicated the door, smiling. "Shall we go back inside?"

Nick didn't wait for Owen to answer, and Owen followed him, quickly trying to catch up, making a mental note never to let Jared's perceptions of the CEO lead him astray again.

CHAPTER TEN

ERIN WAS surprised to learn how much equipment he needed for racquetball.

He peered into his basket. "I didn't realize I'd need new socks, and knee pads, and *goggles*. The goggles make me concerned."

"Well, there's a two-and-a-quarter-inch-round rubber ball flying around in there, and the fastest recorded one went 199 miles an hour. Did you want that coming at your eye without something in the way to stop it?"

Erin startled and covered his right eye reflexively before lowering his hand. "The goggles sound fine. But perhaps we should pick up some armor as well?"

Laughing, Owen kissed Erin's head. "You'll be fine."

The city gym was full of people, particularly in the locker room. The men were loud and overly familiar, and it reminded Erin of public changing areas in boarding school. Owen helped him out, herding him into a quieter changing space that had larger lockers they could share.

The racquetball court was a narrow, tall, echoing chamber they had entirely to themselves. Owen explained the rules to Erin, showed him the service area and foul lines, where he was meant to stand and why, and then they began to play.

Erin was terrible. Owen was patient with him, except when Erin became frustrated and swung too wildly.

"Careful. You'll hurt yourself." Owen put a hand on Erin's shoulder as he stood behind him, using his other arm to lead Erin through a swing. "Like I taught you. I don't want to take you to the clinic with a separated shoulder."

It wasn't the first time Owen had fussed over Erin, worried he might harm himself, and Erin couldn't decide if the instinct was annoying or charming. "The way you can't stand people in pain is one of the reasons I like you."

Owen lowered his racquet, looking blindsided. "What do you mean?"

Erin enjoyed the disarmed expression on his boyfriend's face. "Everyone misunderstands you, thinking you're so harsh and intense. You are, and you can play ogre when you want to. But you would never actually hurt anyone. You'd scare them away, but that's not the same thing. I don't know why everyone has such a difficult time understanding the nuance of that. I mean, the clue is right there in your profession, for heaven's sake. You didn't simply become a doctor. You became the doctor whose sole job it is to remove pain."

Owen stared at Erin, openmouthed.

Feeling abruptly awkward, Erin switched the subject. "So, will you teach me now?"

Owen did, but Erin soon learned he hadn't magically developed a talent for sports since high school, and it was clear acquiring racquetball skills would take some time. Owen's patience only managed to annoy Erin more.

He tossed his racquet to the floor. "I'm terrible at this. We should give up."

"You've just started. Give yourself credit for what you're getting done. Let's do a few more back-and-forths against the front wall, then take a break."

They never managed to begin a game, but when their time was up, he elbowed Erin with a cheeky grin before tugging him to his side.

"You did fantastic. You'll do even better as soon as you stop telling yourself you're bad at it."

Erin rubbed his cheek, embarrassed at having his internal monologue called out. "I'm sorry. I was never good at sports when I was young like you."

"Who says I was good at them when I was young? I didn't participate in anything until college. When I was in grade school—" Owen's face clouded, and he abruptly stopped talking.

Erin wondered if this was about the violin or Owen's father. He wished he knew how to be supportive without being intrusive. He fished for something decent to say. "I suppose I'll have to follow your example, except as usual I'll be a late bloomer."

"It doesn't matter when you bloom. Only that you do."

They parted long enough to rinse off in the showers, but soon it was the two of them headed for the sauna, wrapped only in towels at their waists. Technically Erin should have felt self-conscious, being this naked next to Owen, but he was so focused on what was coming, he couldn't be bothered with shyness.

"I love saunas." Erin eased against the wood slat walls and shut his eyes, letting the heat envelop him. "My mother had one on the property I usually stayed at when it was my turn to visit her, and I always sneaked into it. Alone, which was dangerous, but I couldn't get enough of that warm feeling."

"Do you get along well with your mother?"

What a question. Erin opened his eyes and stared up at the ceiling. "I don't have much of an opinion of my mother either way, I suppose. I longed for her a lot more when I was little, craving her attention, but as I grew older I realized not only was I never going to get it, but I didn't really want it. We're somewhat friendly now, but she's not a good parent and never was. She was hot and cold when I was in grade school because she felt she should look the part, but as soon as I was grown, she shifted her focus elsewhere. I'm welcome to ask for favors, and I suspect if I ever did anything noteworthy, she'd mention me to people. But much like her marriage to my father, I think she views motherhood as a mistake she would prefer to forget happened."

He noticed how quiet Owen had become and glanced at him. Owen appeared… oh, sad wasn't the right word. Pained?

It's as if he wants to slay your dragons for you, but he's found you miles from the battlefield, battered and singed instead.

The thought was ridiculous, and yet Erin couldn't shake it, nor could he remove the lump from his throat.

A group of men entered the sauna, ending their conversation, but the awkwardness hung in the air between them. It was also during that time the soreness kicked in, and as they got into the car, Erin couldn't wait to get to a bottle of ibuprofen.

"Drink a lot of water." Owen passed him a bottle before starting the engine. "When we're at home, have one of your yogurts to get some protein. Tomorrow we'll make sure we warm up more first. Maybe we'll start off in the sauna."

Tomorrow. The thought of going back made Erin shudder.

The next morning dawned with a snowstorm, enough to keep the commuters and out-of-town specialists from arriving. It was a slow day for them both. More than half the scheduled surgeries cancelled, but of course none of the babies changed their delivery plans because of the weather. Erin was meant to interview three prospective hires, but only one could make it because they'd closed the road from Eau Claire. It was a fast-moving system, however, already gone by noon.

Which meant the sidewalk and driveway would need the snow removed. They'd had a few light storms, though whenever it was Erin's turn, Owen tended to take it outright or help. Whose turn was it?

Oh, dear. Owen was up. They'd received at least five inches too, and with the wind, some of the drifts were a foot high. The car had struggled to get out of the garage that morning, and the driveway would be worse now.

After pursing his lips for several seconds, Erin picked up his phone.

When the two of them headed home, Erin drove because Owen was finishing up a phone call with Jack, trying to work out an adjusted surgery schedule. He finished a block from the house with a sigh.

"Tomorrow is going to suck, that's all I can tell you." Owen rubbed the side of his face. "So will doing this damn driveway. I should have made our court time later."

"Ah. About the drive." Erin tried to work out how to explain, but as they rounded the corner to their street the visual spoke for itself.

Owen sat up in his seat. "What? Did Jared do it? Except wait, he's still at the clinic." He gave Erin a hard look. "*You* didn't do it, did you?"

Erin kept his eyes on the road. "I hired a service. It was too much snow for one person at the end of a long workday."

Why was he nervous? Erin didn't know, except he truly was. Once he killed the engine, he dared a glancc at Owen.

Owen took Erin's face gently in his hands and leaned across the console to kiss him sweetly on the mouth. "Thank you."

Erin kissed him back. "You're welcome."

They got their things ready to go to the gym, only pausing to collect their clothes from the dryer and eat a snack standing in the kitchen. When they arrived, it was windy, and the walk from the parking lot to the door was a long, cold one. Owen sheltered Erin with his body, drawing him close with an arm. Erin didn't object, glad for the warmth. He wasn't eager to strip to put on shorts once they were inside.

"We're definitely sitting in the sauna before we play today." Owen pulled towels from the bag and tugged his shirt over his head. "It'll be good to warm up your muscles, but with this cold I think we need it to heat us up literally too."

Erin couldn't deny he was chilled to the bone, and he wouldn't ever say no to the sauna. "Sounds good. Let's go."

Owen tossed a towel at Erin.

The day before, the locker room had been full as they'd gotten ready to shower, but tonight it was only the two of them, and Erin was acutely aware they were baring their bodies beside one another. He distracted himself by unbuttoning his shirt and stepping out of his pants, folding them neatly and placing them in the locker. Out of the corner of his eye he could see Owen doing the same next to him.

Owen's naked chest. Goodness, he *did* work out, didn't he? Erin had brushed against him enough, felt him when they'd danced, when they'd made out, seen the man in T-shirts, but he hadn't *looked*....

He cleared his throat and all but put his face into the locker as Owen tucked his thumbs into the waistband of his underwear and pulled them down.

The showers at the gym were stalls, actual stalls with curtains, for which Erin was eternally grateful. He rinsed off his body, basking in the warm water, splashing it on his face, letting the heat sink into him. When he pushed the curtain aside, he saw Owen waiting for him, wearing nothing but a towel cinched and hanging low around his waist.

Erin tried not to focus at the V the terrycloth made, or think about how beautifully defined and sculpted Owen's abdominals were. He tried, but he failed.

Owen indicated a small hallway. "Shall we?"

Erin followed him, clutching his own towel, worried it might fall. "You know your way around this gym well. Do you come here often?"

"Not as much as I used to. Over time I've set up my basement gym to be pretty much exactly what I want it to be, but sometimes I come here for variety. I mean, I don't think I'm ready to commit to maintenance on an endless pool."

"Endless pool?" Erin couldn't begin to wrap his head around the concept.

Owen walked backward, miming swimming as he went down the hall. "You know, one of those lap pools where you set the current you can swim against? It's basically as long as your body, and you swim in place."

Erin was tired simply thinking about it. "No, thank you."

Laughing, Owen pulled open the door to the sauna. "We'll stick with racquetball for now, then."

Erin went through the door Owen held open—and saw four members of the St. Ann's board sitting there as if they'd been waiting for him to arrive.

All Erin's instincts kicked on as he stepped inside the small, hot space and swept his gaze across the lineup of men. Ron Harris sat in the corner, chatting idly with Christian West. Mike Leary lounged beside Keith Barnes. They were the only men in the sauna, because any other men who opened the door wouldn't dare intrude on such a collection of local power.

Erin had no such qualms. He smiled at the board members in greeting. "Hello, gentlemen. What a surprise to see you here."

Harris, after an eyebrow lift at the others, chuckled. "I think that's our line, son. What brings you to the gym this evening?"

Every board member's gaze raked Owen, making it clear they were fairly certain they knew what had brought Erin there and they weren't entirely sure they approved.

Erin breezed forward. "Oh, well, Owen pointed out I needed more physical activity in my life, and I realized he was right. I'm taking up racquetball."

"He's a real natural." Owen took Erin's hand and led him to the last remaining space on the bench. "Here, hon. Sit and relax."

Erin appreciated the way the board members' feathers ruffled at Owen's use of the word *hon*. Except now Erin wasn't sure if Owen had said it because he meant it or because he wanted to get a rise out of them.

I want him to mean it. I want everyone to know we're actually dating. Erin let his hand linger in Owen's slightly longer than necessary.

"So it's true, is it, the rumor?" Barnes leaned on his elbows. "You've moved out of your father's house?"

Oh, *this* is what they wanted to focus on? Erin smoothed a hand on his towel. "Yes, well, it was time." A lame response. "I thought perhaps we could get along better with some space."

Owen said nothing, but he rested a hand between Erin's shoulders and rubbed in small, supportive circles.

Leary chuckled. "I suppose we should have seen it coming, that you were... *that way*."

Beside Erin, Owen's whole body tensed, though when he spoke, he used the same tone he did for scolding nurses. "What way is that precisely, Mike?"

Everyone in the sauna went quiet, the board members glancing at one another for direction. Erin did a silent fist pump in victory. *Yes.* He knew this was what would happen if he got the board members alone, because without his father they didn't have any leadership—

"The two of you certainly are entertaining." Christian West lounged casually against the boards, the only member of the four to not appear uncomfortable in the face of Owen's aggression. "I thought your performance at the fundraiser was something, but I didn't realize I was going to get a front-row seat at the gym as well. Will there be any more public displays of affection, I wonder?"

Owen withdrew his hand from Erin's and leaned forward with a coldness in his expression that unsettled Erin. Wanting to lighten the mood, Erin smiled as he replied. "We have been a bit of a to-do, haven't we? I imagine that's not what people generally expect, particularly from me."

The board members laughed, nervously—once again, everyone but West, who continued to regard Erin and Owen coolly.

Odd. Erin hadn't considered West to be a leader in his father's absence before. Of course, he'd never seen the board members interact without his father. He wasn't sure it helped him get any closer to discovering who had embezzled the money, but it was certainly interesting information.

The only thing Erin didn't care for was the tension between Owen and Christian West. They must know each other from the days when Owen's father had worked as an executive at the mine and so had West, but something about the way the two men faced off unsettled Erin. Worst of all, West was getting under Owen's skin, but the reverse wasn't happening.

Erin hadn't seen this before.

When the board members left the sauna, Erin breathed a quiet sigh of relief. Owen and Erin waved them goodbye, and when they were alone, Erin considered asking his boyfriend about his relationship with West. As he turned to do so, he got a good look at Owen's face, which had become a rigid mask.

No, it wasn't the time to ask questions.

After smoothing his hand down Owen's forearm, Erin took hold of his wrist. "Would you like to sit for a moment, or are you ready to play?"

Owen's expression relaxed only slightly. "I want to slam a rubber ball against the wall."

Erin pasted on a smile. "Let's get dressed then, so we can."

They left the sauna and went back to the locker room, where the board members were clustered at the other end, carrying on a low conversation full of the occasional guffaws and *you knows* Erin associated with boardroom chatter. Erin didn't focus much on them, though, too aware of Owen's tension.

Erin hurried into his clothes and shoes. "I'm ready for my lesson." He kept his voice at a pitch to be buried under the board members' conversation. "I was too busy looking around yesterday and can't remember. Do we need to check in anywhere, or can we go straight to the court?"

"I checked us in when we arrived. It's ours for the next hour and a half." Owen finished lacing his shoe, then stood, grabbing his racquet and the canister of balls. "You bring your racquet and the goggles."

It didn't surprise Erin to discover Owen's tension remained as they entered the court, though he knew his partner's bad mood wasn't because of or directed at him. Owen was doing his best to shake it. Erin wanted to support him, and he tried to read Owen, staying out of his way, putting on a bright face, doing his best to show he didn't mind that Owen was grumpy.

"The videos you sent me to watch were quite helpful." After tucking the case to his racquet in the pocket of the door, he took a ball to the red rectangle in the center of the room. He bounced the ball with his racquet, startling when it went wild and landed dangerously close to the still-taut Owen. He forced a laugh. "Unfortunately, while I can memorize rules and the names of the lines, my coordination is something you'll need to be patient with—"

The rest of his words died on a soft gasp as Owen came up to him and swept Erin into his arms. *Tenderly*. So carefully, so reverently, that Erin's eyelids fluttered closed. His small body wasn't crushed inside Owen's larger frame. He felt protected. Cherished.

Safe.

"Don't." Owen's voice was a broken, tortured whisper into Erin's hair. "Please don't ever do that again."

Owen clung to him now, almost shaking. Erin stroked his hair. "I'm sorry. I don't know what you're talking about."

"I know. That's what makes it worse." Owen let out a ragged breath. "Please don't walk on eggshells around me and smile like I'm not being a bear. Fight with me. Call me an idiot. Walk out of the room in a huff. Ignore me. Just don't look at me as if you might have woken a monster."

Erin's stomach twisted and fell in a sick knot at his feet. *Monster?* He wished he understood where Owen's reaction came from, but he knew he couldn't ask for explanations, not now. So he reached for comfort instead. "I'm sorry. It wasn't what I meant, but I promise, I won't do anything remotely like that anymore."

Owen seemed a hairsbreadth away from weeping. "I miss our fights," he whispered.

People were watching them over the edge of the balcony, so Erin shuffled them to the back wall, out of the onlookers' line of sight. "Well, then I'll do my best to find something to argue with you about. I still don't understand why you want me to do that, though."

"Because it reminds me you're not afraid of me."

Erin drew Owen's head down and nuzzled his cheek. "Dr. Owen Gagnon, I am not now, nor have I ever been, afraid of you."

Owen wrapped his arms tighter around Erin.

Now it was Erin who had to fight off a quaver in his limbs, but he managed, brushing a dry kiss on Owen's jaw as he pulled away. "Am I going to get my lesson, or not?"

Owen pulled Erin back for a longer, more substantial kiss. "Absolutely."

ON THE drive home, Erin didn't ask Owen what had upset him, which Owen both appreciated and worried over.

He certainly didn't want to talk about it, but something about how Erin avoided the topic made him uneasy. Normally Owen had no qualms about shutting down lines of questioning about his past, but Erin didn't even know this was centered on that. Which meant he was back to not wanting to upset Owen.

This wasn't good. Particularly because the only way out was Owen volunteering to talk about this himself.

Owen kept his eyes on the road, but his focus was entirely on Erin. "You know I don't mind how long you stay with us, or if you move in permanently. I can't help but feel I should do more for you, though. I hope if there's something I can help with, you'll tell me."

He wasn't sure what he expected from Erin, but more silence wasn't it. When it went on too long, he considered apologizing, then worried that would make it worse. As they pulled into the garage, he'd almost worked out an awkward topic shift, when Erin finally spoke.

"You know, I may have swung the racquet a bit too hard. My shoulder is somewhat sore. Would you mind giving me a massage?"

Owen turned sharply in his seat. "You hurt your shoulder? Why didn't you say something?"

Erin glared at him. "I said it's *somewhat sore*. If you're going to be like this, I'll ask Jared for help."

Owen scowled. "The hell you will."

"Then will you give me a massage *without* attempting to encase me in bubble wrap after?"

Owen flattened his lips and reached into the back seat for the gym bags.

Erin sighed. "Honestly, little old ladies worry less than you."

"Yeah, but they don't give massages the way I do. You're going to be *amazed*."

"I have no doubt."

Jared was in the kitchen, and he waved hello with his knife, pausing in chopping vegetables for their salad. "Dinner will be ready in forty. I left the washer free, so dump your smelly things in there, please."

Owen shouted around the corner as he loaded the washer and started it up. "Hey, Jar, do we still have that bottle of massage lotion, or did Simon take it with him? I was going to work on Erin's shoulder."

"Hmm. Not sure. If it's anywhere, it'll be in the upstairs hall closet. In the basket with the travel bottles. That was the last place I saw it."

Owen could hear the lilt of teasing in Jared's voice, the lewd comment he wanted to make about what else Owen could massage on Erin, so Owen took Erin's hand and led him toward the stairs as quickly as possible. To his surprise, he didn't find any resistance. Erin blushed, though only faintly as he glanced at Owen's door. "My room is still in a bit of disarray, and it doesn't feel the most relaxing. I mostly just sleep there."

No kidding it was in disarray. It had become the same haphazard mess as the one they'd removed him from. "I'm happy to help you, you know."

"Perhaps another time. Right now, could I come to your room so you can work on my shoulder?"

Owen's heart skipped a beat. How ridiculous that he kept behaving this way, like taking Erin into his room was some kind of forbidden act. Especially since he'd asked to have his shoulder rubbed, not his dick. "Yes. Please, come in."

While Erin sat on the bed, Owen did a circuit of the perimeter, picking up a few stray clothing items and closing a drawer. "So, uh, you want to take off your shirt?" He waved the lotion bottle in what he hoped was a casual gesture. "I mean, if you'd rather, I could skip the lotion and massage through your clothes." Seriously, what was with him? They'd sat in the sauna naked but for towels twice, and changed and showered right beside each other. Hell, they'd made out. Everything about being with Erin felt different now, though.

"No, it's fine." Erin kept his gaze on the closet as he pulled off his red-and-white-striped rugby. It was one of the few old and ragged articles of clothing the man owned, and he tended to wear it when they were at home lounging. As if it represented home.

Owen was incredibly fond of that rugby.

The shirt rose, exposing inch after inch of skin until Owen had to look away, lest he reveal himself watching when Erin's head was freed.

Erin set the shirt on the bed and huddled against the chill in the room. "How do you want me?"

Owen kicked his libidinous thoughts to the curb. "Why don't you lie down however you're comfortable, and then I'll sit on the bed beside you? Save me some space, and I'll be good."

Erin situated himself, and Owen enjoyed the sight of the man he couldn't stop thinking about wiggling around on his bed. Once Erin declared himself ready, Owen heated a dollop of lotion in his palms. "I should've warmed this in a bowl of water."

Erin smiled with his eyes shut, head turned to the side on the pillow. "It's fine. It'll warm up soon enough as you use it. You worry too much about these things."

I don't like people to hurt, he started to say, then remembered what Erin had said about why he'd gone into anesthesiology. "Is it so wrong to be conscientious?" He applied his hands to Erin's skin, grimacing when Erin jumped from the cold. "See?"

"A little discomfort is hardly something I need to be protected from. Plus your conscientiousness is so strange. You never want any credit for it. In fact, I think it would bother you to take credit."

"Well, I was raised Lutheran."

Erin's eyes flitted open, and he stared at the closet door. "I'll be honest. While my shoulder is a bit tight, the biggest reason I asked for this is because I thought if we were here in the quiet like this, in your room, with you touching me but without me having to look you in the eye, perhaps I could talk to you about some things I have difficulty saying. I thought maybe you could do the same."

Owen's hands stilled, his quickening heartbeat catching up with him. He cleared his throat. "Sure."

Erin shut his eyes again, and Owen massaged for almost a full minute before Erin continued to speak.

"You know someone is embezzling, because you did the figures from those documents. What I've wanted to tell you, but didn't because Nick asked me not to, is that Nick and I are trying to figure out who is stealing."

Owen paused. "Ah. Well, he told me a little of it."

Erin glanced over his shoulder, surprised. "Did he really?"

"Yes. But I got the impression he only wanted me to know so much. Is it okay, you telling me all this?"

Erin faced down again. "I don't know what he thinks, but I don't like keeping this from you, especially since you're already involved."

Resuming his massage, Owen nodded. "All right. But don't tell me something I shouldn't know. I understand your job means there are things you can't share with me."

"I want to share this, though, because I feel like we're getting nowhere. I gave Nick the spreadsheets you made, and he's studying them, but we're not sure how to proceed from here. That's why I want to talk to the board members, to see what they know. We think it has to be a board member."

"Makes sense, since it's happened for so long."

"It's a serious problem. It's keeping us from hiring specialists and building the cardiac unit. If I stop and think about all the things that money could have done over the years, I feel sick. I want to find out who took it, but I also want to stop them from taking more. But I don't know how." His shoulders sagged under Owen's hands. "And I'm afraid my father might be in the center of all of this."

Owen hadn't even thought of that. He'd been so focused on John Jean and Erin's personal relationship, he hadn't considered their professional one. His hands tightened on Erin's muscle, and Erin gasped. Horrified, Owen let go. "I'm so sorry."

"No… that wasn't bad, just a bit *too* much."

Owen smoothed his hands down Erin's back. "I'll help you. I'll do whatever you need. I want to protect you."

Beneath his hands, Erin startled. "I… I know. And while I appreciate it, I need to explain some things about myself." He relaxed as Owen resumed his massage, but he was tense in a way that had nothing to do with racquetball. "I'm not accustomed to having someone protect me. To be honest, I'm more comfortable isolated and ignored than I am supported and cared for. I'm embarrassed about it, but I can't change who I am." The color rose on his cheeks, and he shut his eyes tighter. "I've never had close friends, let alone any kind of romantic relationship."

Smiling, Owen ran his fingers into Erin's hair. "I know what you mean. If it helps, until Jack came along, Jared and Simon were the only friends I've ever had."

Erin's color was still high. "No… I'm *that* bad at dealing with people. I think my father thought it was funny, putting me in the position of human resources. Possibly it was his revenge, his punishment after all the years he tried to make me a successful administrator. I said I wasn't good with people, so he put me in charge of people, period. I admit, at first I was terrified." Erin let out a heavy sigh. "You mentioned how important our fights were to you, and I think it's the same for me. You came for me as soon as I took the job. You didn't shy from me because I was John Jean's son. I was so shocked that I didn't know how to respond and panic-fought, which only fueled you, and everything spiraled from there. I assumed you hated me, though."

Owen's heart lurched. "I admit, I didn't like you because I thought you were the same as your father, that you wanted the same things he did, but not anymore. And as I've said, I don't think you should be embarrassed because you haven't had a relationship."

Erin huffed. "It wasn't because I didn't want one. I didn't know how to approach people."

"You approached me fine." Owen's fingers slowed, and the moment hung between them, suspended.

Erin glanced over his shoulder. "I've told you some things about me. Will… will you tell me some things about you?"

Owen drew back. Not even the vision of Erin rolling onto his side and looking up at him, half-naked, heavy-lidded and quietly pleading, could penetrate the fog of fear that had risen to choke him. He'd told Jared he wanted to confess to Erin, but now, with the prospect in front of him, he couldn't bear it.

Not yet. I'm not ready yet.

Erin's hand on his knee quieted him. "How about we switch positions?"

How about we not? Owen swallowed and glanced at the door. "Dinner has to be ready by now."

"I asked Jared to hold it for us." Erin's grip tightened. "Please."

Owen couldn't say no, but he was terrified. "What… what do you want to know?"

"Anything. Literally anything. I just told you more about me than I've ever told anyone, even Nick, who I always thought I was fairly close to. Being your pretend boyfriend felt more real than most of my actual life, and knowing this makes me feel so alone sometimes I can't breathe."

"I'm your real boyfriend now."

"I know, but…." Erin curled into himself. "I don't need to know all your secrets. But if you could tell me something to help me feel… connected… I'm sorry, I probably don't make any sense."

Sagging, Owen shut his eyes.

Then he tugged his T-shirt over his head, lay face-down across the mattress, and buried his face in his arms.

Walking closer on his knees, Erin touched the center of Owen's back tentatively. "Where… where do you want me to focus?"

"Anywhere is fine." Owen swam in his thoughts, then rode the wave. "I enjoy touch. I like to touch people I care about. That's one thing you can know about me."

Erin's hands felt so good as they skimmed hesitantly across his skin. "It's not something I would have guessed about you, before I moved in with you."

"It's not a detail I advertise. In fact… outside of Simon, who's almost a little brother, I *don't* touch anyone."

"You touch me. A lot."

"I know. I'm… glad you let me." Owen stopped talking for a while, but he wasn't as nervous anymore. "You're right. The massage helps. How did you think of it?"

"I told you. I enjoy it when you touch me. It relaxes me. It seemed a logical extension."

Owen let Erin's touch infuse him with strength for a few minutes, then treaded carefully into waters that might drown him. "My mother used to rub my back this way."

He held his breath.

Erin skimmed his hands across Owen's shoulders, down the center of his spine. "I hope it's a good association."

A difficult answer. Owen considered how to reply. "Bittersweet. But I like your massage."

He could hear Erin's smile in his words. "I'm glad."

Owen was so far out at sea he didn't know how to return to shore. He decided the only way home was with Erin. "I like you. Having you here. Teaching you racquetball. Going to work with you. Going out with you. Helping you. Taking care of you. Being with you." His breath came out in a shudder. "I like it a lot."

Across Owen's skin, Erin's fingers trembled. "But I'm so awkward. There's so much wrong with me."

"You're perfect. There's nothing wrong with you."

It should have been a moment of opening and accepting. Owen should have turned over, and they should have kissed, eased into lovemaking. Even before Erin withdrew, though, Owen knew that wasn't how they would go. Erin had already explained. It was difficult for him to see himself this way, and the more Owen attempted to draw him in, the more Erin would shut him out.

Unless you show him you're as awkward as he is.

You want to tell him. You need to tell him. And despite your fear, you know damn well this is the best time. At least get the conversation started.

Owen swallowed his fear and let the waters close over him.

"When I was young, my father used to hit me."

He didn't let himself notice what Erin was doing, only recognized he was there, anchoring. Owen simply kept talking.

"Never so much it left marks—well, there are a few, but none anyone saw and thought they should report. But he taught me to be afraid of other people, to be reluctant to trust them. It wasn't what he did to my body so much as what he did to my mind. Eventually I figured out what he'd done, but I couldn't change who I'd become. Sometimes I would want to connect with people, but it was as if my hand would only go out so far, and then there was glass. I couldn't break it."

Down, down, down. How deep would he go? Would he go all the way to the violin? He didn't know. He didn't care. He could feel Erin's hands on him, which meant he could still breathe. He did so now, a long, slow inhale. "But I could reach you so easily. Even when I thought we were too different, when you were too like your father, I could reach you. So I guess that's why I see you as perfect. You're perfect… for me."

He heard a soft gasp, and Erin's hands stopped.

Owen's skin came alive as Erin brushed a tentative kiss on his shoulder.

The room spun, or perhaps it was just the bed. Owen's lips parted so he could take in air but move as little as possible, preserving the moment. "I'd wanted to ask you out long before you bid for me at the auction. I haven't been able to look away from you since you showed up. Even when I thought you were nothing more than your father's pawn."

Erin tensed, then surrendered. "You're not lying."

Owen drew Erin's hand to his mouth and kissed Erin's fingernails. "I'm not lying."

Erin rested his forehead on Owen's shoulder, Erin's hot, hesitant breath rushing over Owen's skin. After a long pause, Erin spoke.

"You liked me, but you were still going to leave."

The hurt in Erin's voice cut him, but Owen didn't understand. He let go of Erin's hand so he could roll slightly to one side. "What do you mean?"

"Last fall. You said you liked me, but you were going to leave."

Oh. When he was going to follow Jack and Simon with Jared. "Well… yeah, but as I said, I thought you were the same as your dad, so I didn't—"

"I reversed the policy for you."

Owen's heart beat in his ears as he rolled all the way over and sat up.

Worrying his hands, Erin stared at the bed with flushed cheeks.

Owen couldn't have heard correctly. "You reversed the policy for Jack and Simon. So they could be together, so they would stay."

"I reversed it for you." Erin cut a glance at Owen, sharp and clear, then looked down again. "I tried to explain it to Simon, but I couldn't get the words out. I tried to convince him to lie low and settle for less, but he refused. In fact he didn't simply refuse, he called me on the carpet, implying I was doing less than I should. I realized not only was he right, but also that you would never be with someone who behaved like I was. I didn't know how to stop you except to make the policy go away. I knew my father would be furious, but I wanted you to see me do it, so you'd know. I wanted you to see I was that kind of person after all. Someone who would stand up." The worrying of his fingers became intense. "Except it went so sideways. It worked out, I suppose, but it wasn't quite as I envisioned. I certainly didn't get to show you anything, and you didn't—"

Erin couldn't finish the rest of his sentence because Owen stopped it with a kiss.

He kissed Erin reverently, taking his face in his hands, Erin's reveal shaking him in slow, sonic waves.

"Tell me," Owen whispered against Erin's lips. "Tell me what you want. I'll do anything for you. Now, tomorrow—always."

Erin clung to Owen's arms, pulling him closer as he wrapped his legs around his body. "I don't ever want you to go."

Owen kissed Erin's jaw, cradling him close. "Then I'll stay."

Erin's hands were in his hair, sliding along his scalp. "I also want you to make love to me. Right now."

"I'll do that too," Owen replied, trailing kisses down Erin's neck.

CHAPTER ELEVEN

THE THINGS Owen Gagnon could do with his mouth should be illegal.

Obviously Erin didn't have anything to compare it to, but he was confident Owen's lovemaking skills were exceptional. Every time Owen's lips slid down his skin toward an erogenous zone, Erin thought he might combust. Aware he'd given consent to go all the way, Erin shivered to his core with each brush of Owen's mouth.

"Shall we do what we did with the massage and take turns giving each other pleasure?" Owen's tongue flicked against the erect tip of Erin's nipple. "Or should we be impatient and enjoy each other at the same time?"

"I don't think I have the mental composure to be touched by you and do anything else."

Owen chuckled. "Now you're flattering me."

"No, I'm telling the truth. *Ah*." Erin shivered and threaded his fingers in Owen's hair as his mouth closed over a nipple, not quite sucking, but lacing the sensitive area with so much sensation Erin felt the electric charge in every pore.

Owen traveled down his sternum, his abdomen, aiming for Erin's waistband. He kissed the skin along it as he unbuttoned and tugged, taking the fabric all the way to Erin's feet, then away from his body. "Is this okay?"

Nodding, Erin kept his hands in Owen's hair as much as possible, not guiding so much as anchoring himself. "Yes. It's absolutely fine."

"You do understand my aim is to put your dick in my mouth."

The mere mention of the idea made said dick significantly more erect. "The thought had occurred to me, yes. Please, continue."

Laughing, Owen pressed a kiss on Erin's hip. "I love you."

The words hung in the air. Neither of them moved.

He didn't mean it, Erin whispered to himself, quieting his silly heart. *It's a turn of phrase. It fell out of his mouth. Change the subject.* But the same fool part of him that liked to bid wildly on bachelor auctions said, voice cracking, "Oh?"

Abruptly, Owen's face hovered over his. He looked nervous. Serious. Terrified. "Is it too early to say that? Sorry. Though I suppose this is another confession I can make to you, one you can figure out on your own if you look hard enough. I love pretty easily. All the more reason not to let people in, because if there's anything the world has taught me, it's that this isn't a safe thing to do."

Why did Erin's heart feel as if it were beating permanently in his throat? "I'll be a safe place. A safe person."

Was that ridiculous to say?

If Owen thought so, he didn't bring it up. He only kissed Erin sweetly… and took his naked cock gently in his hand.

Erin gasped into Owen's mouth, unable to think any longer. He could only surrender to sensation. Owen had felt him up a little through his clothes, but never touched him like this. Not until now. And as he broke the kiss, still stroking, he trailed his mouth across Erin's body, and—

This time when Erin gasped, the sound was so dirty he shivered.

Wet, so *wet*—Owen slid up and down his shaft, tongue playing against the hardness, mouth sucking at the tip. Erin had thought of this, of Owen's mouth on him, but it had always been so ephemeral, smoke passing through his mind. The reality rattled Erin's core and made him feel like jelly. Electric jelly.

Sliding. Sliding. Wet, sucking, sliding…. He could hear the suction from Owen's mouth. Feel the pull along his skin, his groin. *So much touching.* Hands on his thighs, holding his legs open, thumbs at the base of his cock. Erin tried to watch, but it was too much. He was going to come, right in Owen's mouth, right in—

His orgasm came out of nowhere, a shivering rush, a wet sigh. He *did* ejaculate into Owen's mouth, but Owen didn't seem to mind. With a gentle brush against Erin's thigh, Owen rose, wiping his lips with his fingers.

"I'm sorry—" Erin began, then stopped because Owen leaned over him, a satisfied grin on his face.

"For what?" Owen parted Erin's lips with his thumb. "I enjoyed myself. Didn't you?"

Enjoy was far too simple a word. "I came so quickly." His face flamed. "I always do. I usually try to get it over with. I didn't want to this time, but it felt so good and it just happened—"

Now he couldn't speak because Owen kissed him, slow and sweet, tasting oh so faintly of Erin's ejaculate. Whimpering, Erin slid his hands along Owen's chest, then up his neck and into his hair as Owen's tongue ventured farther into his mouth, taking up a rhythm that stirred heat in Erin's groin. His cock couldn't answer the call, but he responded to Owen all the same, spreading his legs and giving Owen a silent invitation to grind against him.

He accepted, though he moved with a slow deliberation that melted Erin into the sheets.

"Oh my God." Shutting his eyes, Erin let his arms fall above his head and arched his body into Owen's. "I feel like I'm going to explode into a million pieces."

"Go on and explode." Owen kissed beneath his ear. "I'll put you back together if you do. I'll hold you close. I'll never let you go." Though even as he said this, one of his arms released to push down his jeans, his underwear, and then—

Erin hissed and whimpered as Owen's cock touched his. Skin to skin, velvet heat to velvet heat. Erin couldn't go all the way erect, but he wouldn't stay that way for long.

"This okay?" Owen kept his focus on Erin. "Not too sensitive?"

Holding on to Owen's shoulders, Erin nodded. "It's fine. Good. Perfect."

"How about I add a little lubricant and take this up a notch? Still good?"

Taking deep breaths, Erin dug in his fingers. "Yes."

It was more than good. As Owen gripped him with slick fingers, Erin forgot his self-consciousness about his lack of experience, forgot this was Owen Gagnon, the only person he'd ever fantasized about, and simply surrendered to this sense of safety Owen gave him. When Owen cradled his head to come in for another kiss as he thrust, Erin lifted his chin and his hips to meet him. He wasn't holding anything back anymore. No more nerves, no more hesitation. Not now while they made love, and not when it was over.

Not if he could help it.

Erin didn't come a second time, but he nearly did, a sort of mini, mental orgasm as Owen came on his abdomen. He accepted Owen's slow, openmouthed, postcoital kiss, then lay languidly on the bed, waiting for Owen to come back with a warm washcloth to clean him.

Owen gave him a wicked but pure-hearted smile as he returned to the room. "You're beautiful when you've been debauched."

Erin threaded his fingers in Owen's hair as soon as he came close enough. "Only when I've been debauched by you. Though to be fair, you're the only one who's done it."

Owen nipped playfully at Erin's palm. "I don't want anyone else to have the privilege. I'll do my best to keep you from wanting to inquire after other debauchers."

I don't have any interest in anyone else. Erin let his hand fall to the mattress. "I look forward to that."

After tossing the washcloth across the room into a laundry basket, Owen tucked himself into the space beside Erin. "Stay with me tonight. I'll make you breakfast in the morning, if you do."

"You usually do anyway."

"It'll be an extra-amazing breakfast. I'll bring it to you in bed."

That gave Erin pause. "I've never had breakfast in bed."

Owen nuzzled Erin's neck. "Stay."

Erin turned his face toward Owen, closing his eyes. "Okay."

THE BREAKFAST Owen brought Erin truly was exceptional: ham and cheese soufflés in individual ramekins, paper-thin Swedish pancakes with berries, and honeyed hot cocoa. Better yet was how they ate from the same tray, and once Owen fed a bite to Erin, they ended up feeding most of their portions to each other, then kissing for so long they were nearly late for work.

Erin couldn't quit smiling or touching his face and hair as he rode the elevator alone to the third floor. He was still having difficulty erasing the silly grin from his face when Nick knocked on his door at eleven.

Nick didn't look pleased. "Jared just bullied me into being his doubles partner in some sort of upcoming tournament against you and Owen. I knew you were learning racquetball, but I didn't realize I was going to get involved."

Now Erin felt bad. "I'm sorry. I told Owen I wanted to practice before we had games with the members of the board. I thought it might be a good way to get to know them one-on-one, perhaps get more insight into who might have done the embezzling."

Rubbing a hand over his face, Nick sank into the chair opposite Erin's desk. "That's not a terrible idea, though I'm not sure they'll give us much intel."

"I'm open to ideas if you have them. I want to approach them, but if I try to make lunch dates with them, my father will get wind of it and intervene. He doesn't play racquetball, though. Anyway, I drew up profiles for each of the candidates, trying to guess who might be the culprit before we start talking to them. Except, honestly, no one stands out. We don't have a gun, let alone one that smokes."

"You may have to accept we won't find the person who's done this."

"Nick, if we give in now, we'll never get out from under them. The board will keep hindering you and every decision you attempt to make."

Nick didn't meet his gaze. "They'll retire eventually. At some point new people will join the board."

"They don't intend to let that happen. My father told me how they plan to start grooming their successors. His sole purpose in life is to keep his iron fist over the board and this hospital, and apparently they all agree. We have to fight for this."

"I know. *I know*." Nick pinched the bridge of his nose. "You sound like Emmanuella."

"I've always liked your sister."

"There's no foothold to make here, Erin. They've sewn everything up too neatly. And I don't like how your father hasn't contacted you. It makes me uneasy, because it's not like him. It makes me worried he has some kind of scheme we haven't thought of."

"If he does, we'll undo it." He thought of Owen's angry reaction to his father and added, "And trust me when I tell you Owen won't let my father so much as get close to me."

"That's supposed to reassure me? I'm still not sure I like you dating him."

The memory of Owen lying on the bed rose in his mind, Owen's broad, muscled back exposed under Erin's as he massaged him, as Owen confessed how his father had abused him. Erin searched for a way to politely sidestep the question, but he couldn't locate a safe path.

Ogre. Dragon. Demon. Except now all Erin could see was the softness that was Owen lying on the bed, letting out the pain of his past.

I will protect you too.

Erin smoothed his hand over the folders in front of him. "He's a good man. People judge him unfairly."

"You're *smitten.* I never thought I'd live to see the day. Well, be careful. And let me know what you need." Nick rose, brushing his suit. "Don't let your father get to you. If Gagnon makes you happy, then let him make you happy."

Erin considered what Nick had said all morning. Owen did make him happy. Whatever Erin worked on, his thoughts always managed to land on his boyfriend. He remembered the night before or mused about the days to come. If he was in a boring meeting, he imagined how Owen would crash it and make it interesting.

The only time conjuring Owen didn't work was when he saw his father in the hallway. This cold treatment still stung. Erin did his best to imagine how Owen would tell him it didn't matter, but the mantra was impossible to hold on to with so much emptiness pressing on him.

Erin did his best to put his father out of his mind. He found his boyfriend in the cafeteria, glowering at a cluster of CNAs who hadn't yet noticed him. Frowning, Erin wondered what they were doing that might have drawn Owen's ire. Owen was so absorbed in his glaring he didn't notice Erin until he tapped him on the shoulder, at which point he straightened, smiled, and patted the empty chair beside him. "Hey. Have a seat."

Keeping one eye on the aides, Erin remained standing but put a hand on Owen's shoulder. "I can't stay. I was wondering if it was too early to set a date for our doubles tournament. Nick came by my office this morning and mentioned it."

"Oh, sure. We'll probably have to give them time to practice first, but I can look ahead. Probably sometime in April? Soon enough?"

"Sure. If you think I'll be able to handle it by then. It's a casual tournament among friends."

"I think you'll do fine."

One of the CNAs giggled loud enough to draw their attention, and Owen glowered again.

Erin frowned. "What are you staring at them for?"

Owen's scowl stayed in place. "They're gossiping about staff they don't like."

Now Erin straightened. “Did you hear any details?”

“A few. I’m going to write up the people I heard talking, but I’ve been trying to decide if I go over and scare them until they can’t see straight, or if I take down their names and get them in trouble.”

For heaven’s sake. “I don’t want to hire an entirely new department of CNAs. We’re going to end this now.”

Owen pursed his lips. “All right. I’ll go put the fear of God into them.”

“This is my department. Literally. You may sit here and look fierce if you like, but you will sit, and you won’t interfere.”

Leaving Owen at the table grousing quietly, Erin drifted to the cluster of gossipers, though he deliberately kept himself behind a pillar and stayed at enough distance so they’d need a few seconds to realize he’d moved closer if by some miracle one of them was smart enough to pay attention, which none of them were. This was typical behavior of these types of gossipers, he’d noticed during his tenure at health care facilities. There were plenty of hardworking professionals in every department, but there were also always those who hardly worked at all and chose to treat the hospital as some bizarre extension of their local high school, only working when nagged or threatened and never passing up an opportunity to form a herd and whine about their lot in life and who they felt was responsible for it.

The group at the table continued to talk loudly, laughing and speaking over each other, allowing Erin to hear everything they said. They were in fact running through a litany of the staff, nurses, doctors, and administration. In a moment of perfect timing, one of the aides glanced at Erin's hiding place as a particularly chatty woman in the center shifted the topic of complaint.

"Oh my God, but Mr. Andreas. He's about as stiff as they come. I don't believe he's actually dating Dr. Gagnon for a *second*."

A round of urges to shush washed over the group, and the woman who'd referred to Erin as stiff paled, pressing herself into the man sitting beside her as Erin revealed himself. He gave them his cool, nothing-can-affect-me smile and swept his gaze across the group slowly, engaging each one of them in eye contact.

"Good afternoon. Such a boisterous break we're having here."

He paused to let them squirm. No one could look at him. A few appeared as if they wanted to make an excuse, but one glance at him and they gave up.

Erin lifted his arm and checked his watch. "Either you're about to be late for your next shift, or you're loitering in the cafeteria breaking hospital rules flagrantly and loudly enough that hospital guests and other staff can clearly hear you. Dr. Gagnon, in fact, has recorded everything you said for the past twenty minutes. Is there some reason in particular you have chosen to do this? Do you have a complaint about hospital policy or your working conditions you wish to discuss with me? Or are you enjoying sitting in the open, tearing apart your fellow employees in a manner that amuses you?"

The aides mumbled unintelligently around garbled apologies, keeping their heads down.

Erin waved at them impatiently. "Go, all of you. Learn to think. Because next time, I'll simply leave the cafeteria and let Dr. Gagnon come for you."

They scurried to their feet and hustled out of the room, a few of the braver ones daring to glance at Owen, who stared daggers at them from his table in the corner.

Erin returned to Owen once they'd left, eyebrow raised. "Will that do, Dr. Gagnon?"

Owen grimaced at the place where the aides had disappeared. "I would have preferred if you'd let me have them for lunch. I haven't eaten."

After checking the clock, Erin took in the empty lunch line, which was closed because it was two thirty in the afternoon. "I suppose you had a full surgery schedule. Why didn't you bring something from home?"

"Forgot it on the counter. Somebody distracted me."

Though the idea that he filled Owen's thoughts brought him pleasure, Erin regarded his boyfriend sharply. "Are you implying your lack of a meal is my fault?"

Owen held up his hands. "It certainly wasn't me who left the house wearing the brand-new blue-gray suit I bought you with the pastel plaid shirt and pale pink tie. And to think those fools dared to call you stiff."

Erin sighed, but he also had to hide a smile. "I haven't eaten either. Do you have time to wait for me to order something?"

"If it's quick. I need to make rounds with Kathryn. She's got a mother in delivery who needs an epidural, and she wants me to soothe her first."

This remark made Erin do a double take. "I thought you were known as Owen the Ogre."

He winked. "Only to the nursing staff. To mothers hoping for a pain-free delivery, I'm the King of the Good Drugs. They don't talk about my good looks or my bedside manner the way they do Jared or my string of accomplishments like people do Jack, but any of the moms who are nervous get talks from their friends about how they shouldn't worry, Dr. Gagnon will make sure they don't feel a thing."

Somehow this was the most Owen thing Erin had heard all day. "I'll order from China Garden. What do you want?"

Owen gestured vaguely with his hands as he stood. "The noodle thing Jack always orders for Simon. I can't remember the name."

It was a good thing Erin didn't have much on his docket this afternoon. "I'll see what I can do."

Owen placed a kiss on Erin's cheek. "Thanks, hon."

Erin did his best not to blush. The cafeteria wasn't entirely empty. "Where will you be? Your office?"

"Probably roaming the floor. Listen for the screams of the CNAs."

"For heaven's sake," Erin murmured, as on older woman eavesdropping on them chuckled.

Erin had to ask Simon the name of the noodle dish, which meant finding him in the OR where he was cleaning up after the last of the day's surgeries. Simon smiled and waved as Erin entered. "Hello, Mr. Andreas. What can I do for you?"

Erin frowned. "You can call me Erin, I should think."

"Not at work. The same way Owen is Dr. Gagnon, Jared is Dr. Kumpel, and even Hong-Wei is Dr. Wu when I address them. The last thing I need is the rest of the nursing staff murmuring about how I'm uppity." Simon set aside the medical equipment he was wiping down and picked up something else Erin didn't know the name of. "So. As I said, what brings you up here? I doubt it was to chat. Though I do want to hear about this doubles tournament sometime. Hong-Wei won't admit it, but he's put out he wasn't asked. Apparently I have to learn how to play now."

Erin liked the idea of playing against Simon and Jack, actually. "Owen missed lunch, and he asked me to order the noodle dish Jack always orders for you. I can't remember the name of it."

"*Tsao mi fun*. If you ask for Dr. Wu's stir-fried noodles, they'll get you what you need."

Erin decided he might as well get them for himself too. It dawned on him if Owen missed lunch, Simon and Jack probably had as well. "Did you want anything while I'm placing an order?"

"Oh, do you mind? I packed us lunches, but at this point we're both so hungry we're ready to eat dinner on top of it all. Here, I'll write down what to ask for. Thank you *so much*." He glanced at Erin as he dried his hands and reached for a notepad. "I like your outfit. It suits you."

Placing the order wasn't difficult, and as soon as the hostess learned part of the delivery was for Dr. Wu, the tenor changed. Erin had the feeling they'd be eating a lot faster because Jack was involved. Ever since he'd saved the life of the owner, Jack was a hero at China Garden, but he'd charmed the entire staff long before then. Sometimes it seemed as if they were looking for an excuse to come out to the hospital to bring him things.

As he'd expected, it was Mr. Zhang himself, China Garden's owner, who brought the delivery, though Erin could also see his disappointment that it wasn't Jack picking up the order. His English was improving, Erin thought—he suspected Jack was giving him lessons, but he wasn't sure. Erin thanked the man, tipped him profusely, and made his own deliveries.

He saved Owen's for last, assuming he was in the doctor's lounge, but he was at the nurses' station, hovering over the counter and making everyone cower. Stifling a sigh, Erin held out the bag as he approached.

"Dr. Gagnon. Please stop harassing my staff and eat your lunch."

Owen turned toward him without letting go of the edge of the counter, his gaze hooded by the untidy overhang of his hair. He did look rather like an ogre sometimes. "I'm not sure if I can. After all, I'm nothing but a wild monster who could snap at any moment."

Erin stilled, his stomach dropping. His glare cut to the quaking cluster of staff, confirming this wasn't a random quip from Owen. He was repeating something he'd overheard.

Setting the bag of food on the counter, Erin considered the staff coolly, then shrugged. "I'm afraid I can't help you. I'm about as stiff as they come."

Owen broke his glower to snort a laugh. "That's the most ridiculous thing I've ever heard."

"As is the wild-monster remark about you."

Owen nestled his elbows more firmly on the nurses' station. "I don't know. I'm feeling pretty monstrous right now. I've stood here for the last ten minutes hoping someone would give me an excuse to *snap*."

Erin shook the bag near his nose. "Yes, it's all very well, but in the meantime your noodles are getting cold."

Owen made a purring noise that sent goose bumps across Erin's skin. "Tempting. I don't think it's enough, though. If only I had a boyfriend who was a handsome prince and could break my evil curse with a kiss."

Erin rolled his eyes. "You are *completely out of hand*."

Owen grinned and leaned closer, running a finger under Erin's tie. "Come on. A guy who'd bid twenty-five grand on me to get my attention can certainly spare me a kiss at the nurses' station."

Erin felt his ears go scarlet. "This is sexual harassment."

"Nah, I'm just begging." Owen tugged Erin closer with the tie. "Please, Erin?"

Dimly, Erin was aware two nurses and three aides watched them from the other side of the station as if this was the finest entertainment they'd seen all day, which undoubtedly it was.

Erin let go of his inhibitions as best he could, grabbed hold of both sides of his ogre's face, and kissed him gently on the mouth.

This was the second time Owen had kissed him in front of an audience, and it was so brief and chaste one could argue it was barely a kiss at all, but as Owen's fingertips brushed his cheeks, Erin's heart filled with want and his stomach danced with butterflies. The nurses murmured, and Erin transported to the hallways of his school.

You were just kissed in front of everyone who teased you, who ignored you, by the handsome, successful, powerful doctor. If they dare try to strike you or laugh at you, he'll tear them apart and present you their livers to please you. He'll walk you to class and hold your hand.

He'll heal every horrible fissure in your soul, if you let him. Because he's perfect for you, Erin Andreas.

"*What's going on here?*"

The sharp, familiar sound of Erin's father's call shot through him and pushed him away from Owen as effectively as a hand.

Well. His father was talking to him now.

Cold fear ran across Erin's skin like ice water dumped over his head, and for a moment he was so disconcerted and ashamed for what he'd been caught doing he didn't know how to school his reaction. *He's displeased with me. He's angry.* Thirty-three years of habit, of trained obedience, made Erin cower into himself, moving away from Owen and into the shadows.

All this happened in the flash of a second—he only pulled a few inches away before Owen slipped an arm around his shoulders and drew him flush to his side as he faced John Jean, who stood at the other end of the hallway. Erin couldn't see Owen's face, but when he spoke, he could hear the deadly smile.

"Good afternoon, Mr. Andreas. I'm about to enjoy a late lunch with my boyfriend. Would you care to join us?"

Oh God.

No one breathed unless they were on a ventilator and didn't have a say in the matter. Several patients peeked out of their rooms, eyes wide as they slid their gazes between the two men staring at each other icily from either end of the hall. Despite Owen's words, there'd been no invitation in his ask, only a steel gauntlet laced with barbed wire.

John Jean narrowed his eyes. "Another time, perhaps."

Owen inclined his head in a bow that did nothing but mock. "I look forward to it."

Erin's father disappeared, and Owen picked up their bag of food and ushered Erin toward the doctors' lounge with a hand on the small of his back. Erin went with him in a daze, stomach feeling as if someone had disconnected it from its tethers to let it bounce around inside his body.

Why? Why was his father treating him this way?

Why did his father's coldness seep across whatever happiness he was able to find?

Owen drew him close again and kissed his hair. "Don't worry. I told you, I'll protect you, no matter what happens."

Erin said nothing, because he couldn't. All he was capable of doing was following Owen into the lounge, doing his best to reconstruct his walls so Owen was the only one who knew how close he was to falling apart.

CHAPTER TWELVE

THOUGH IT wasn't on his workout schedule, that night after dinner Owen donned a pair of shorts and a sweat-wicking shirt and went to the basement. Putting his earbuds in, he adjusted the treadmill settings and started his run, knowing immediately where his mind was going to wander.

John Jean Andreas.

He hadn't expected the man would appear to witness their kiss, but if he had, he would have made it more of a spectacle. It'd given Owen icy pleasure to shelter Erin, to stare the man down. It felt so good to win.

Finally.

He wiped sweat from his brow as he fought the incline, but he pushed on, fueled with the rush of victory. He had no doubt a retaliation was coming—a man like John Jean would insist on it. No matter. Owen was ready.

John Jean couldn't hit Owen with anything he couldn't counter. Money? Owen had enough nobody could threaten him. Power? He had what he needed and didn't crave anything further. Owen could protect his friends, or they could protect themselves.

Bring it on, bitch. I'm hungry.

The wild card, he acknowledged as he rinsed off in the basement shower, was Christian West.

Owen would put all his money on West being the embezzler, but this was because Owen hated the man and wanted him responsible for everything evil in the world. West had been a friend of his father's. Owen could still hear the sound of the asshole's guffaw drifting up the stairs of his childhood home, could hear the way his voice had pitched low the night he'd advised William Gagnon how to best cover everything up, to keep from *making a scene*.

Owen had too much of an emotional reaction to West, and he needed to keep himself in check. He couldn't let the man get to him. He had to focus on Erin, who was rattled from the day, and who definitely deserved a better kiss than the one he'd received in front of all the nurses. Owen hoped he wasn't mad. Or he was the kind of mad that would result in a refreshing fight.

Erin didn't seem angry when Owen found him on the couch in the living room, watching another home makeover show with Jared. He was completely engrossed in it, his face twisted up in longing, and when Owen came up behind him, he didn't react, not until Owen touched his shoulder.

"Oh—hi. How was your run?"

"Good." Owen plunked into the space beside him. "What have you two been doing?"

Erin didn't look away from the television. "We just started watching this after the dishes. Do you want to watch with us?"

Owen sat with them, though mostly he watched Erin. The naked need in his boyfriend's face tugged at him. After an hour, he suggested they go upstairs, and Erin didn't fight him.

Owen rubbed idly at Erin's neck. "We still need to put your room in some kind of order."

He expected Erin to bristle, but he only sagged deeper against Owen. "Can I stay with you tonight?"

"Anytime you want." Owen kissed Erin's hairline and led him down the hall.

When he was alone in a room with Erin, Owen felt like a teenager whose limbs didn't work right. Though as soon as he focused on his lover, his doubts fell away. Particularly tonight as he saw how much Erin needed him. Erin looked lost, descending inside himself. Owen took Erin to the bed, where he arranged his boyfriend on the pillow and spooned behind him, wrapping him in a cocoon.

Owen ran his free hand through Erin's hair, tangling his fingers. It was one of his favorite sensations. "Talk to me."

"I feel… cold. Sharp, as if there's a knife against my stomach, but I can't get away from it no matter where I turn. It's so stupid. What do I have to be afraid of? I don't understand. I *hate* this. I feel so out of control."

That's what you're afraid of, love. Losing control. Owen pressed a soft, lingering kiss at the back of

Erin's neck, drinking in the scent. He descended into the feel of Erin's hair, the smell of it. If he died right now, his heaven would be Erin's hair.

He let out his breath and gathered Erin closer to him, shutting his eyes.

You need to tell him everything. You need to let him know exactly why you understand.

Owen was terrified. But he was ready. He wanted to tell Erin everything.

How should he start?

Maybe he should simply dive right in. His stomach lurched at the thought, but after one more whiff of Erin's hair, a deeper tangle of his fingers, he was all right.

"I told you before about my dad." *Exhale. Inhale.* He could do this with Erin. "There's more to the story. It was bad when I was younger, but it slowed around fifth grade. It was right—" He swallowed, anchored himself, drew on Erin's hair again. "It was about the time my mom signed me up for private violin lessons. They were with this professor at the college, but she wouldn't give me a ride there. I had to practice there as well, in a special practice room, and I always had to walk to and from the college. One time someone gave me a ride, and she was furious with me. I never accepted another ride."

His whole body tensed, trapped in the arc of the story.

Erin stroked his arm, and eventually Owen could continue.

"My dad slapped me around sometimes, and the two of them always fought. Sometimes he'd come home from work parties, and my mom would get angry at me and send me to my room, locking me inside. My dad would bang on the door, but she must have hidden the key. I was scared. I wanted him gone. When she wasn't around, I fought with him, trying to get him to hit me so I could turn him in, but he'd never do it so it left marks, not enough. By the time I was in high school, they divorced, and he left town. It didn't get any better, though. We pretended we were fine, but at home everything felt heavy, like I was choking.

"My refuge was violin. I had the same teacher and practiced at the college. I practically lived there after school. I applied for scholarships, and I got every one of them. I picked the best school for music, one far away. I was getting out of Copper Point, and I couldn't wait. And then."

He shuddered, not sure he could do this after all.

Erin lifted his hand to his lips and kissed it. Held it there, waiting.

Owen focused on the warmth of Erin's breath on his fingertips, let it carry him away. "Two weeks before I was supposed to send the deposit for college, she confronted me. I came home, and she was sitting at the piano. She'd been drinking. She told me she didn't want me to go away for school. She told me I owed her and had to do what she asked." His throat became thick, and he felt flat, not wanting to finish, knowing he had to. "I was angry and didn't understand. I told her no. So she explained that the reason I had lessons so often, why I had to walk to them, was because she'd used the time to make sure he beat her instead of me. Beat her and did… other things. She told me more than I should ever have heard, in a way that stripped off pieces of me I can never get back. She made it clear my escape, my solace, my joy, had been at her expense. And now she wanted repayment."

Erin clutched his hand. "*Owen.*"

Owen couldn't return his grip. He could only forge ahead. "She apologized the next morning when she was sober, but she didn't say I could go wherever I wanted to college. It was clear I was still supposed to stay. I don't think she truly meant the apology either, only knew she shouldn't have said it, much as she was secretly glad she had. It didn't matter anyway. I knew I could never play the violin again. I wanted to smash it, but I couldn't bear to because it was a gift from my instructor, so I returned it and asked him to contact the college to decline the scholarship and my admission. I moved out of the house the second I was eighteen, got a job while I went to college in Madison, and as soon as I had money, I sent it to my mother. I calculated the cost of my lessons over the years, and with part-time jobs, I gave it to her. When I told her the only way I would speak to her was if she went to a therapist with me, she went back to drinking. Once I was a doctor, I found her the best therapist in the city she was living in at the time—she'd moved away by then—and told her I'd pay for her therapy. She's never gone. I haven't spoken to her since. I haven't played violin since the day she got drunk and told me what she'd done, not until the day of the auction. I never told anyone why except my therapist, not even Jared and Simon. They only knew it was something serious and I didn't want to talk about it."

He could breathe now, so he did, a lungful of the sweet smell of Erin's hair. "That's the story of me and the violin."

He felt better. Lighter. He kept breathing, holding Erin close, letting the dark memories slough away.

Eventually he realized Erin trembled in his arms. Owen stroked his back, trying to soothe him. "It's okay."

"That should be my line. Why are you the one comforting me? What happened to you is *awful*."

"My parents are broken people with significant flaws. My mother did her best, which in the end wasn't good. She should have left him and taken me with her when I was young, but she didn't want to abandon her position and give up her status. My father was under a lot of pressure, which is no excuse to behave the way he did, and I'm fairly sure his father beat him far worse than he did me. I've done what I can to stop the cycle they set up for me. I went to bales of therapy in college. I still see someone a few times a year to make sure my thinking is on straight. I take my meds. I undo the bad patterns of thinking when I recognize them." He wrapped his legs around Erin. "I'm doing my best to open up to you."

Erin turned around so he could nestle into Owen. "I hate the idea of you bearing this all alone. Of her taking something you loved so cruelly away from you. No wonder you looked the way you did at the auction. Except… you're so *good*, Owen. I know hearing those words is painful for you for some reason, and I'm sorry if my saying so rubs salt in a wound, but it's such a sickening thing for you to have your talent stolen like this. It would be different if you didn't enjoy it, but I know you once did. I *saw* it, I swear. Am I wrong?"

"No, you're not. I did enjoy it—which is the trouble. Her one sentence poured acid over my joy and ate it away, made sure I could never enjoy it again. The concert on Valentine's Day proved it. Every note was pain. Every time someone says I played well, I see my mother's drunk, twisted face, describing the things my father did to her, letting me know this was the price for my joy."

Warm, wet drops fell onto Owen's neck—Erin's tears. "It's not right. She should never have said such things to you. It's wrong. Utterly wrong. You shouldn't have to feel that way."

Closing his eyes, Owen leaned into Erin, tangling his fingers into the hair at Erin's nape.

You shouldn't have to feel that way.

The words kept echoing in his head. Other people had told him the same thing in different ways, different orders of words, but Erin saying this, with his heart so broken, healed Owen as nothing else had.

Drawing a long breath, Owen curled his body around his lover. "Intellectually, I understand she didn't have the right to say such things to me. My emotional comprehension of this, unfortunately, is something else entirely."

"I remember how you looked when you were young, playing in the mansion, as if the violin was the most important thing to you in the world. I hate how she stole it from you. Her cruelty is as bad as your father's abuse. She invalidated your solace. She took away your protection—your mother and your violin. I can't stand it."

"Thank you. I appreciate it." Owen's whole soul eased at Erin's outrage on his behalf. "Part of why I told you this story is to say I empathize with the feeling of knowing something doesn't need to bother you while at the same time acknowledging that's all it does."

Erin smoothed invisible wrinkles on Owen's T-shirt. "I'm afraid my father will take you away."

"He can't. No one can. And I have no intention of going unless you ask me to leave."

"I understand it… in one sense. But as you said, another part of me can't stop being afraid." Erin buried his face into Owen's chest. "I thought I'd made my peace with how I grew up. However, the more I spend time with all of you, particularly with *you*, the more I realize my peace was incomplete. I hadn't admitted to myself how lonely I was. I can't pretend I'm fine anymore, and now I'm terrified."

Owen stroked Erin's hair. "Did your father frequently take things he knew were important to you?"

"That's the thing. He didn't do it as deliberately as you're implying. I mean… sometimes it felt like it. But it wasn't as if I was living out *Oliver Twist*, or *The Little Princess*."

Erin seemed uncomfortable, as Owen was when people pushed him about the violin and he couldn't handle it. Owen softened his tone. "Tell me more about the loneliness. Or tell me whatever feels right. I don't want to make *you* talk about something you don't want to talk about, either."

"I don't know. I don't remember much of being at home or school when I was younger than thirteen. Everything is grayed out, only these vague concepts and fragments. I'm not saying I can't remember what happened to me. It feels as if it's a film reel from the 1970s, run too fast with poor sound quality. It doesn't feel threatening, but it also doesn't have much detail."

"Some of this is your brain's defense mechanism. I have the same kind of film reel effect over holidays and birthdays, all the things Simon and Jared remember so fondly with a warm glow. Mine feel flat and mostly invented, which is eerie since usually my memory is so strong. It bothered me until my therapist helped me accept it was maybe a good thing I didn't remember everything clearly, that this was my brain doing its job. It's the same thing as the way mothers who go through childbirth without anesthesia will talk about the pain and remember it in this abstract sense but not actually remember the pain itself. They remember they had it, but the pain gets erased. Some of it is helped by the postnatal hormones, but a lot of it is the brain."

He wasn't surprised this didn't comfort Erin much. "Then why did I have the reaction I did today? Why does it make me think about being young, about being afraid to go home from school?"

"I don't know. But I'd love to hear about it. Any of it."

Erin snorted derisively. "What, my days at school? Going home for break? Which pathetic tale do you want? I hated my boarding school, where I didn't have friends, but at least there I was alone among people. When I went home, I was alone in silence. For the first few years, I kept hoping my father would notice me, that if I kept my grades up and joined the right aetivities, he would praise me and take me to dinner, but he never said a word. The only time he paid me any attention was… oh." Erin's fingers stilled. "I'd forgotten."

"What had you forgotten?"

"I can't believe I didn't remember this before. I made a friend, and he happened to be from a town a few hours away. I was so excited and proud of my accomplishment I told my father while I was home on break. Except for some reason my father didn't care for the idea and told me not to speak to the boy anymore. I think he didn't care for the family. I was stunned, and though I told him I wouldn't speak to the boy, I knew I wouldn't obey my father. Benjamin was the only friend I'd ever had. I wouldn't turn him away. Except when I went back to school, Benjamin had already abandoned me. Somehow I knew my father was behind it. I was never so devastated in my life."

Shutting his eyes, Owen held him close. "I'm sorry."

Erin curled his body tighter to Owen's. "I hid everything from my father after that, and when people attempted to befriend me, I was so paranoid about hiding them they tended to drift off on their own. When my father introduced people to me because of business, I knew they were only paying attention to me because he wanted them to." His inability to speak to Owen the day on the ridge made sense now too.

Owen lifted Erin's face to kiss him lightly. "You know, I've thought this before, but though we both may be in our thirties, it's as if we're a pair of teenagers. That's what you make me feel like, at least."

Erin smiled. "So the hospital is our high school hallway?"

"Convince me it isn't."

Erin laughed, and Owen did too. Erin nuzzled his nose, ran his hands down Owen's face.

Owen's mind raced. "We should do the things with each other we didn't get to do in high school."

Erin lifted an eyebrow. "What do you mean?"

"I mean let's get a do-over. What were the things you missed out on that made you regretful or sad? I know you have things. I sure do. We should tell each other what they are, then try to do those things together."

"Hmm." Erin laced his fingers behind Owen's neck. "I'm embarrassed at how boring I am. I always dreamed of a date. Being picked up at my house, driven somewhere fancy, taken to a nice dinner when dressed up, having my heart flutter over a set of candlesticks."

"Nothing embarrassing or boring about that. I'm in." Owen rolled onto his back, drawing Erin into the crook of his arm. "I dreamed about Valentine's Day. I think they've banned it now, but Copper Point High used to have flower deliveries at school, and I was always the one who didn't get anything. Even Simon and Jared got friend flowers from girls."

"They didn't get you anything?"

Owen laughed. "We were out, but we weren't suicidal. The administration wouldn't have permitted gay deliveries back then anyway. They would have been too afraid of someone complaining."

Erin traced the line of Owen's sternum. "Some of the things I wanted had nothing to do with romance. I simply wanted to have friends over to my house. To have friends I *could* invite over."

"You have them now."

"It still feels strange to me, though. They feel borrowed."

"Then you should practice doing more things with them without me so they feel like yours."

"It makes me nervous."

"I know. But it's okay to be nervous." Owen kissed Erin's hair, lingering in the curls. "Your dad can't take me away. I'll tell you as many times as you need to hear it. I'll never be impatient with you for being worried about it."

"I'm also worried my awkwardness and clumsiness will chase you away."

"The more awkward and clumsy you are, the more I love you."

Erin climbed onto his knees, swinging one over Owen so he straddled him. Bracing one hand on the mattress beside Owen's shoulder, he stroked his face. "You aren't an ogre, or a dragon, or any of the names you call yourself. Don't ever do it again."

Owen attempted a rueful smile, but he couldn't maintain it. "You have your evil curses, and I have mine."

Erin tugged on his forelock. "Yes, and I know exactly how to break your spell."

Owen wrapped his arms around Erin's shoulders, eager for the demonstration.

CHAPTER THIRTEEN

OWEN HADN'T been this nervous for a therapy session in a long time.

He fidgeted the whole drive to Duluth, unable to settle on a podcast or audiobook to keep him company, disgruntled by total silence. In the waiting room, he fussed with his phone, grimacing at the news, flipping between mindless games and distraction apps, curling his lip at the politicians and celebrities on the magazines displayed on the coffee table. When he was finally called back to see Jeannie, he was grumpy, edgy, and wound up.

As usual, she accepted his agitation in stride. She smiled at him from her seat on the couch, wearing her usual coral cardigan, paired today with a light teal T-shirt and flowing pink skirt. Her dark hair framed her face in a perfectly smoothed bob. The room around her was decorated in colors complementing her clothing: terra cotta and peach, with hints of bright red and teal. Healing crystals and stones were placed in various—and particular—zones around the room, and the walls were filled with wooden carvings, hangings, some framed bits of wisdom. Her desk was full of photos of her husband, children, and grandchildren, at birthdays and quinceañeras and weddings, everyone smiling and hugging each other.

Jeannie folded her hands in her lap. "It's good to see you, Owen. Why don't you take a minute to get comfortable. Can I make you some tea?"

Owen shook his head, rising. "I'll make it. Would you like some too?"

"That would be lovely, thank you. I'll have the herbal blend in the box on top, in the blue cup with orange flowers."

Focusing on the ritual of filling the electric kettle with the jug of water, preparing mugs with tea bags, Owen began to speak. "A lot has happened since I last saw you."

"I'd love to hear about it."

Why do I feel so anxious? Owen stared at the kettle, watching the condensation forming along the water fill line. "It's difficult to know where to start. I wish I could hand you the backstory and begin with the things… pressing on me."

"I think it's a fine idea. Let's jump right in, and when I don't understand enough to follow or would like to know more because it seems important, I'll ask you questions. How does that sound?"

"Wonderful, actually." The water finished boiling, and he poured it into the cups. Bringing them over, he set them on the table and took his seat again. "I ended up having to play the violin, in public. I knew it would stir things up in me, but I didn't anticipate how long it would linger, and I didn't expect I'd want…." The panic returned, and he stared into his mug, not able to breathe.

Jeannie didn't touch him, but she leaned forward and spoke gently. "It's okay to tell me what you want, and it's okay for you to want something. This is a safe place to talk about it. Take your time, and when you're ready, I'll listen."

Owen shut his eyes, drawing in air, letting it out. He felt the words in his head, felt their terror, but he also knew he couldn't bury this feeling. Gripping his knees, holding on, he allowed the confession to fall out.

"I want to play," he whispered, his stomach twisting, bile rising. More air fueled the rest of the confession, this part easing the sick feeling. "I want to play… for Erin."

The admission rattled him, his tears falling as he battled sobs and a sense of sickness inside him. *I want to play for Erin.* He hadn't articulated it out loud before this. He'd simply known something ate at him, clawing, pulling at a curtain he didn't want drawn open.

I want to play for Erin.

He let out a ragged breath on a sigh.

Jeannie's words were a caress. "I'm so proud of you, Owen. To be able to want such a thing, even for a moment, is a major step for you. I hope you feel pride in that. I hope you can recognize what an achievement simply thinking this is for you. Good job." She patted his hand. "Now, I have a question, and I suspect you can guess what it is. Would you mind telling me about Erin?"

Where did he start? Owen smiled. "Well, he bid twenty-five thousand dollars for me at a charity bachelor auction."

"My goodness, that's certainly something that doesn't happen every day. So he's bold, this Erin?"

Bold? Not a word most people would use for him, no. But Owen supposed he was, if he sat down and thought about it. "He's… forceful when he needs to be. He can take charge. But he's soft inside, and lonely, and needs someone more than he wants to admit most of the time. He can argue, though. I love arguing with him. He calls me out when I need it, and doesn't back down even if I'm grouchy."

"And he makes you want to play the violin, does he?"

From anyone else, in any other conversation, this would have felt like an attack, but with Jeannie, in her space, it was okay. Owen sipped at his tea, nodding. "When I told him about my dad, he was upset for me, but when I told him about what my mother did, he… transformed. He was angry but full of sorrow too, and he looked like he wanted to go get vengeance then and there. He said it was almost worse, what she did. *You shouldn't have to feel that way*, he told me."

"This Erin seems to have left a powerful impression on you. Now you want to play for him. Is it because he gave you permission to let go of those negative feelings?"

"I don't… think so. Erin had a different childhood than me, but there are places where we recognize each other. His father—the president of the hospital board—was always distant and controlling with him, and he grew up isolated. He's confessed things to me about his past, and I think I feel a connection with him that makes me feel safe enough to play for him."

"Wait." Jeannie sat up, eyes wide. "If his father is the board president… is this Erin the HR director you're always complaining about?"

Ducking his head, Owen smiled ruefully. "Yeah."

He told her everything, about the embezzlement, about him doing the math on the figures, about their date, about how different things were at work, about the quartet and why he'd gotten dragged into it—he talked and talked and talked.

As he wound down, Jeannie sipped her tea. "You *have* had a lot going on. If it's okay with you, I want to go back to the quartet and this pull you have toward playing. Because at first you sounded as if it was something you wanted to confess and bury, but now I'm getting the idea you might be exploring it as an actual possibility."

He had no idea. But he could think about it now without panicking. "I don't want to join the quartet and make it a quintet." He paused, then corrected himself. "Well, I don't know. Right now, I can't think about joining it. I can't imagine playing at all most of the time. For some reason, though, I want to play for Erin."

"Let's start there. Imagine you could play for him. You get to arrange it however and whenever you want. The setting, the date, the time, his arrival, the way you both look. What's this feel like for you?"

Owen shut his eyes, trying to sense it. "Intimate. Just the two of us, somewhere no one else will come. But not… not my house. Somewhere that when I play, I won't hear or feel the echoes of it later. Not yet."

He tried to see it, him standing above Erin, playing… "Somewhere elegant. We look fabulous. It's a beautiful moment. Something out of a storybook. There are candles and deep wine colors everywhere."

"It sounds lovely. Does it feel good to you?"

It did. It felt more than right, it felt… it felt like something Owen needed. He drank deeply of his tea, seeking fortification in its now-lukewarm heat. "I want to do it. I want to actually do it. I want to find somewhere private, create the beautiful moment, and play for him. The perfect moment for him as much as for me."

"You don't sound hesitant when you say this."

He didn't feel hesitant, either. It couldn't possibly last, but for now…. "I'd have to practice. And borrow a violin. Which means I'd have to talk to someone else about this."

"Do you feel there's someone you can confide in?"

Considering his sea of friends, Owen smiled to himself. "Yeah."

"Good. Well, it sounds as if you have a goal, and the start of a plan, and your work cut out for you. How are you feeling about all of that?"

To his surprise, when Owen looked inside himself and examined his emotions, the answer was simple, and not the one he was anticipating. "Good. I feel really good."

ON WEDNESDAY morning, Erin was calmly eating his breakfast and mentally indexing his day at work when Owen said, "Next weekend, let's have Valentine's Day."

Erin put down his fork. "Next weekend is April thirteenth. Valentine's Day is well behind us."

"I know. This is exactly my point. We missed one of the prime dating experience holidays, and I think we should make up for it."

"On April thirteenth."

Something was going on, because Owen was more than nervous. He was… apprehensive. "Yeah. I want to have a special day with you. I'm off next weekend, and I already booked somewhere absolutely perfect. I hope it is, anyway."

Concerned, Erin turned to face him. "Owen, is everything all right?"

"Couldn't be better." Owen kissed him, holding Erin's face with both hands and lingering over his lips. "Save next Saturday night for me, okay? And plan to dress up."

This was all Owen gave him before disappearing, insisting he needed to drive in on his own. Erin couldn't find him much the rest of that day either, which wasn't entirely uncommon as it was a busy surgery day, but usually Owen found ways to stop by.

Something was decidedly up, but Erin wasn't going to figure it out easily. He had bigger problems on his hands now. Erin had a date he was supposed to wear *something nice* to. If it was a makeup Valentine's Day, then he needed a gift too.

Oh God.

Owen had bought Erin three new work suits and a handful of ties, which Erin could technically wear to his date, but it felt wrong to mix business and pleasure. Except without them he had nothing original to wear. He also had no fashion sense with which to make selections.

The task of purchasing a gift was worse. He'd somehow ordered the worst gift ever, except it was the only thing he could think of every time he tried to shop, as if the common sense part of his brain shut off whenever he went online. He'd have to get something banal instead, he supposed.

The matter of what he should wear was not as easily solved. Unwilling to end up with another online disaster, on Thursday Erin left work early, went to Rebecca's firm, and begged her for assistance.

She regarded him with amusement as she set a stack of files on her desk. "I can't decide what about this surprises me more. That we've somehow become the kind of friends who shop together, that you think I would know how to pick out clothes for you, or that Owen is inventing a substitute Valentine's Day."

Frankly, Erin was shocked by the same things himself. "I can't explain the substitute holiday. As for who I asked to help me with shopping… Simon would help, but… I don't want to ask him. He'll have a million questions."

She raised an eyebrow. "You don't think I will?"

"No, to be honest, I don't."

She smiled. "You're right, I won't. Only a few here and there. Mostly I want to observe the two of you at this point. I am curious about the need for new clothes, though, and why I leapt to mind."

Erin gestured to her outfit, which was professional yet full of color. "You always look neat and tidy, but not gray, like Owen always says I am. I don't know how to pick out things. I want something vibrant.

Something that says *date*. Except I don't know what this something is. *You*, though, have been on all kinds of dates."

"Yes, dear. Lesbian ones."

She wasn't shaking him this easily. "You always look amazing no matter what, even if you're in casual clothes. I don't need a miracle or a makeover. Just an outfit and maybe a little schooling so next time I know how to do this myself." He tugged at his tie. He'd gotten permission from Nick for this, but he was still nervous. "Also, I thought we could talk about board business."

Rebecca's gaze sharpened slightly. "This is an interesting twist." With a sigh, she folded her arms. "Well, as luck would have it, my wife is working late tonight, and I just finished a trial. Let's go shopping."

They agreed on a time and that Rebecca would pick Erin up at Owen's house. He worried she'd arrive once everyone was home and he'd have to explain too much, but he escaped into her vehicle before either Jared or Owen returned, and he sighed in relief as he snapped his seat belt into place.

She regarded him with interest. "You're different since you moved in with Owen. I approve. I wasn't sure what was going on with the two of you at first, but I like what you've done for each other."

"It's certainly been an adventure."

He was still working out how to broach the subject of the board, treading carefully around their investigation as he'd promised Nick, when Rebecca went straight for the jugular. "So when you said you wanted to discuss the board, I assume you wanted to talk about the messy books?" When Erin froze, she laughed. "What, you thought I wasn't looking into it myself? The whole setup is fishier than the bay. Literally no hospital board anywhere, ever, has so little turnover as this one does for so many decades, with members practically beating people down who attempt to join their ranks. They're trying to play their resistance to me as misogyny and white supremacy, and there's plenty of that, but it's not so simple. I could tell they were hiding something from day one. So I smiled, pretended to struggle with them on the surface, and began digging. Then I saw Nick accessing the same files I was, and I thought, well, it's about time. Unfortunately, they saw him too. I've been trying to keep them focused on me as much as I can, but they've been at this for a long time. They can divide their attention easily."

Erin didn't know where to start, his head was spinning so much. Rebecca had suspected trouble this whole time. Of course she had, the more he thought about it. She was a prominent lawyer who had only been in Copper Point since she married Kathryn. Small-town embezzlement was probably child's play.

He decided it was time to make sure they were on the same page. "We have proof of embezzlement, but no lead on who the embezzler is. Do you have any further leads you can offer us?"

"Unfortunately, no. I was hoping you'd find something when you went through the files." She raised an eyebrow at Erin. "You did get through all of the files, right?"

"Yes, but I had help." He explained about Owen finding his notes and solving the problems he'd been banging his head over.

Rebecca was so taken aback she nearly ran a red light. Then she laughed self-deprecatingly. "Oh, but Kathryn is going to have so much fun with this. She's nagged me to get the boys involved since this started, Owen in particular. 'He's good with numbers,' she kept saying. Now I see why."

"Why *didn't* you go to your friends, if you don't mind my asking? They're all part of the hospital."

Her smile made him shiver. "Because I don't like too many people involved in these sorts of things, especially in a small town. The more people who know, the easier it is for leaks to spread. And once I knew you and Nick were involved, I stopped my personal efforts because I didn't want to get in the way of handing the two of you a lever to hoist yourselves into the real power you deserve. You should be a vice president, to start, and Nick should have more authority. Believe me, I'm ready to dig my fingers in if it comes to it. But I'd rather let the two of you handle it your way, to let you have the win and the power that comes with it. It'll only benefit me in the end, after all."

"I think I want you on retainer as my personal lawyer, Rebecca."

"I'll have my secretary send over an invoice and some documents." She straightened and angled the car toward a parking space. "Here we are. I thought we'd start at Engleton's."

There were two adult clothing stores in Copper Point, Engleton's Fine Clothing and a chain department store in the slowly dying mall on the far side of town. Erin did most of his shopping online, or he took care of things when he traveled or visited his mother. He'd never gone to either of the men's stores in town.

Engleton's had a nice feel to it, Erin decided as they entered. It was larger than it looked from the outside, deeper and wider than the facade led him to believe, and a glance told him they carried men's and women's clothing, as well as shoes. The walls were dark brown, though the place was well lit, giving an aura of elegance Erin hadn't anticipated. Everything was arranged in a pleasant, enticing manner, inviting customers to explore and touch the bright colors and wander into the displays.

They hadn't gone seven steps before a clean-cut young man with gleaming golden hair and impossible blue eyes approached Rebecca with open arms, smiling as he welcomed her. "Rebecca. I thought you'd started shopping somewhere else. How have you been?"

"Busy." She returned the embrace, then drew back, indicating Erin. "I've actually brought you a new client today. Erin Andreas has a date he'd like to impress."

Erin barely had time to blush before the man was before him, eyes alight as he extended his hand. "My, *my*, if this isn't something. Mr. Andreas, it's my pleasure to welcome you to our store. I'm Matthew Engleton, general manager. I'll personally assist you in finding something that will suit you. If you'll follow me?"

Matthew Engleton was a force, Erin quickly learned, and forty minutes later he had a stack of clothing, two pairs of shoes, and several pairs of bold socks ready for purchase. Of course, everything Matthew had talked him into buying was far more assertive than what he usually wore. He hadn't simply picked up casual clothing, either. He had several new dress shirts as well, and three new ties Erin thought Owen would appreciate.

All Erin had said was, "I'd like to try a little more color."

The items were excellent, and while the bill was high, it wasn't unreasonable. The quality of the clothing was higher than he'd expected, rather on par with the boutiques his mother took him to. If anything, the prices were slightly lower.

He was still in a daze as he walked with Rebecca toward the restaurant she'd chosen for dinner.

She nudged him with her elbow. "You seemed to find things you wanted. Are you satisfied?"

"Yes—only a bit overwhelmed."

"Matthew is an excellent salesman. His father owns the business, but he's stepped back since his son has taken over management. They were doing poorly for some time, but Matthew has turned everything around." She dusted her hands. "So, now you have the clothes for your date. We've had our business chat. Is there anything else you want to discuss?"

Erin shook his head. "Only to confirm I'm the one picking up the tab for the meal."

Smiling, she held the door open for him. "After you."

Nodding acknowledgment, he allowed her to usher him inside.

IN THE end, the only person Owen could go to about the violin was Jack.

He approached him after surgery on Thursday and asked if they could talk sometime, just the two of them. He'd worried Jack would want more of an explanation, but all the surgeon had done was nod and say he'd text him some times he was free.

They ended up meeting at Jack and Simon's place that evening, and as Owen removed his shoes at the door—a hard-and-fast rule at their place—Jack said, "Simon is at a church fundraiser for his mother. He's out for at least two more hours, so we're alone."

Owen lined up his shoes on the rug at the bottom of the stairs. "Thanks."

"Not a problem." Jack inclined his head toward the kitchen. "I started some coffee. Would you like some?"

"Please. Just a little sugar."

Jack smiled wryly. "I remember."

Simon and Owen lived in a tidy, nicely appointed condo not far from Jared and Owen's house. The first floor was essentially one room, the living room taking up most of the space, with a dining area tucked beside the kitchen. Owen had spent many happy hours at their table, eating Simon and Jack's cooking, sometimes cooking with them. He hated to admit they had superior knives and owned some killer cookware.

On the far side of the sitting area stood Jack's violin, free from its case and hanging from a music stand, the bow tucked into another catch beside it.

They sat in the living room, sipping coffee as silence expanded between them. Though Owen fidgeted, Jack remained calm, waiting for whatever Owen had to say. Jack's composure helped Owen significantly. They'd been friendly rivals since the moment Jack had arrived, and Owen had always thought if they'd gone to high school together, Owen would have spent those years chasing Jack's academic prowess while also backing him up however he needed it.

Ironically, in the one area he thought he had good odds of trouncing his rival, he had no motivation to compete.

Eventually the silence got to Owen, and he confessed what he'd come here to ask. "I wanted to know if… I could borrow your violin."

Jack raised an eyebrow. "I see. I take it you don't want your activities advertised, since you asked to see me alone?"

Why did Owen want to fidget so much? "Not a secret as much as a surprise for the person I'm playing for. That and…." He ran a trembling hand through his hair. "It's pretty significant I'm attempting to play at all, but you don't know why, and I doubt you're going to push me to tell you the story, which I appreciate. I was hoping you'd let me borrow your instrument, maybe coach me so I don't fall on my ass, and keep this between us."

"I won't push you to explain yourself, no, and I won't tell anyone we're doing this, not even Simon, though I hope at some point *you* do, because he and Jared care for you a great deal. As do I. As for coaching you…." Jack pursed his lips. "I heard you at the fundraiser. Though I hate to admit it, despite the fact that you hadn't touched an instrument in years and were clearly battling some sort of inner turmoil as you played, you were still far superior to me. What you think I can offer you, I'm not sure."

Owen stared into the inky depths of his coffee. "Every note I played at the fundraiser felt as if it were pieces of me falling onto the floor. Not one note came from joy or passion, only from sorrow and cold, white terror. When people tell me how wonderful it was to hear me play again, every compliment is an axe taking another chunk out of me. I don't want those feelings to crop up when I perform, but they aren't something I can shake my shoulders and dispel. You *don't* know the story, which means you won't look at me with pity as I try to battle this. You're a phenomenal musician and a good friend. I was hoping you could bully me out of playing from fear and nudge me toward playing in a better space."

Jack sat listening quietly as Owen spoke, then nodded. "Of course I'll help you. For this performance and for any others you decide you'd like to attempt, now and in the future." His long fingers curled around his mug. "For the record, I wouldn't pity you even if I knew the story. I'd respect your struggle and do my best to honor it as I helped you move forward."

Funny. Owen had known that too, deep down, but it warmed him to the depths of his hollow soul hearing Jack's vow out loud. He smiled, some of his shadows lifting. "Maybe I'll tell it to you sometime."

"I'll be ready to listen whenever you feel like talking. Though I have one condition."

Owen raised an eyebrow. "Oh?"

Jack regarded Owen sternly. "If I do this, you let me in on the racquetball tournament."

Laughing, Owen opened his palms. "Of course."

"Excellent. I'll make sure Simon is game ready. In the meantime." Jack indicated the violin. "Shall we get started?"

Setting his mug down, Owen stood. "Absolutely."

CHAPTER FOURTEEN

OWEN CAME to pick Erin up for their date squarely at seven.

Though Erin protested repeatedly it was silly to be picked up when they lived in the same house, Owen insisted. "This is part of our teenager experience. You should get picked up like a real date."

Erin wasn't sure if it was the getting-picked-up factor or what, but his nerves consumed him as he stood in the foyer watching for Owen's car. He wore one of the outfits Matthew had helped him pick out, and he'd thought he looked okay as he'd gotten ready, but now he doubted himself. He held his gift in a bag, hating how pedestrian it was, and he kept touching the pocket of his coat where *that* gift remained hidden, the one he couldn't decide if he should give Owen.

After Owen parked at the curb, he rushed up the stairs to meet Erin at the door.

"You're supposed to let me knock." Owen waggled his eyebrows at Erin. "You look good."

"Thanks. So do you." Owen's coat was zipped up tight, which seemed excessive. It was warm out, and Owen had to be hot.

Erin was going to remark on that, but Owen took his face and kissed him so hard on the mouth the thought fled.

"Thank you for the flowers. They were beautiful."

Oh, yes—in his nerves about everything else, Erin had forgotten the flowers. Owen had gone in this morning to help Kathryn with a baby, so Erin seized the opportunity to have flowers sent to him at the hospital. Erin touched his hair self-consciously. "I'm glad you enjoyed them. I couldn't deliver them to you at a high school, but since you said the hospital was like a high school hallway, I thought it might be close enough."

"It was *absolutely* close enough. They sat at the nurses' station forever waiting with my name on the tag, and nobody could stop talking about them or the fact that I was the recipient. I felt like I carried a billion dollars to my office."

Flush with pleasure, Erin smiled. "Good to hear." He regretted he hadn't gone to witness the scene. He played it over in his mind, and he was in the middle of one of his imaginings as he got into the front seat of the car when Owen produced a blindfold.

"I'm going to need you to put this on."

Erin drew away from the black mask. "Why?"

"I don't want you to know where we're going until we get there." Owen slipped it over Erin's head.

"But—oh, it's so dark." He patted the blindfold, then fumbled for the seat belt, which Owen helped him click into place. As the car pulled onto the street, Erin clutched at the door. "I feel as if I'm being kidnapped."

"Not kidnapped." Owen captured his hand. "I like your outfit. You went to Engleton's?"

"How in the world could you know that?"

"I know Matt's style. I approve. But next time, let me come, okay? I'd enjoy shopping with you."

Erin's heart fluttered. "All right."

Even if Erin had wanted to guess where they were going, he couldn't have managed it. Being in the blindfold was so disconcerting. He felt adrift without a tether. Except all the while they drove, Owen held his hand, keeping him anchored.

When the car stopped, Owen let go of Erin's hand, but he recaptured it just as quickly, squeezing it. "I'll come around to your door and guide you, so hold on, okay?"

"Okay." He didn't take the blindfold off because he could tell it was important to Owen. The only request he gave when Owen helped him out of his seat was "Please grab the gift bag on the floor, but don't look into it."

Erin heard the rustle of paper. "What is it?"

"You said it was our substitute Valentine's Day. I got you a present. But I don't want you to open it while I'm standing blindfolded in the parking lot or wherever it is I am."

He startled as Owen pressed a kiss on his cheek. "You're so perfect. Come on. Now I can't *wait* to give you your present."

"Don't get too excited." Erin clutched at Owen's arm as he followed him across an asphalt lot and up a set of stairs. "It's not much of a present. I didn't know what to get you."

"I'm excited for any present from you. Watch your step here, this one goes up higher."

Erin stopped talking and paid more attention to his footing because the steps had become irregular, old wood creaking beneath his feet. As Erin's focus was solely on movement, his brain began to whirr.

This feels quite familiar.

There was no question. Erin had walked up these steps before, and he found if he stopped worrying about the next foot placement and allowed automatic memory to tell him where to go, he was fine. Where in Copper Point was he that he knew how to walk up the stairs this well? Technically he was from one of the oldest families in Copper Point, but he was one of the most uneducated about its landmarks. There weren't that many options for him to be this familiar.

Then Owen opened the door, and Erin understood. The scent of the building hit Erin like a train, choking him until he couldn't breathe. Old wood, antiques, and the aged, slightly musty smell that, for better or for worse, had surrounded Erin all of his life. This was the Andreas mansion.

Home. Owen had taken him home.

He tightened his grip on Owen's arm and managed to draw a breath, but couldn't speak.

Owen put an arm around him and kissed his temple. "No one's here but us. I rented it for the night."

Erin's legs were lead. "My—my father—?"

"He's out of town. Remember?" Owen stroked Erin's back. "Diane isn't here either. We have special permission to stay the whole night. But we don't have to if you don't want to."

Erin didn't understand. What was going on? He reached up to push away his blindfold.

Owen stayed his hand. "Not yet. Will you trust me a little longer? Please?"

What else could Erin do but let Owen grip his hand and lead him forward into the mansion?

Erin was home, inside the museum part of the house. He'd gone in the front door. When was the last time he'd walked up the front steps of his home, opened the door, and come inside to use his own space? He had no idea. His only memories of doing so were so old they blurred, wiped away by the mystical swish of his mother's skirts as she led him through the rooms to play.

What were they going to do in the mansion? Why had Owen done this? What was he thinking—?

Fingers tugged at Erin's blindfold, and for a moment the scent of the mansion was overpowered by Owen, sharp and peppery and hinting of wind. With the fabric peeled away, Erin blinked to adjust his vision to the light as Owen stepped aside.

For the second time that evening, Erin lost his breath, except this time his hand flew to his mouth, a reflexive gesture to stop his bursting heart from escaping.

Owen had made over the mansion.

The parlor at least—it was the room they stood in now, the only room Erin could see, but if Owen had given this treatment to any other space, Erin didn't think he would survive. Owen hadn't done anything worthy of sending Diane into the rafters. The antiques and vintage furniture were all in place, as well as the damask curtains. However, in the spaces around the untouchable objects were Erin's treasures.

Owen had gone into Erin's room, sifted through the mess, and somehow zeroed in on the items Erin cherished. Things from school he'd tucked away in trunks were set out on display. Old artwork, science projects, ribbons he'd won. Class photos from years when he'd still been attempting to make friends. The stick and stone collection he'd amassed one summer when he was particularly lonely—that was the centerpiece on the side table, all the usual knickknacks tucked elsewhere.

The uncomfortable ancient furniture remained, but strewn across them were blankets and pillows from Erin's room, and others from Owen's bedroom. And everywhere were candles, tiny battery-operated tea lights set up in all the nooks and crannies, flickering softly to cast the room in a comforting glow, while above their heads hundreds of fairy lights created a soft net of white extending down, here and there, along the gauzy sheers framing the room.

It wasn't the mansion's parlor any longer. It was Owen's magical bower, into which he beckoned Erin forward.

Breathless, Erin followed him inside. He couldn't help noticing Owen appeared nervous as he led Erin to the couch, encouraging him to sit, arranging him against the pillows and covering him with the blanket.

Before Erin could ask him if he was all right, Owen spoke. "You told me you never spent time in the nicest part of your own home, so I thought I'd give you an evening to enjoy the space, adjusted for your personal taste. I have dinner waiting in the other room, but there's another part of your present I want to give you first."

Erin wanted to ask if Owen had redone the dining room as well, then decided it was a silly question. Of course he had. "What is it?" He glanced around for his bag. "Oh, I should give you my present too." Except he felt ridiculous over how lacking his gift was in comparison to this.

Owen held up a trembling hand. "If you could wait, I'd appreciate it. It's taken me a bit of courage to get to this moment, and I don't want to lose my focus." He reached up to run his fingers through his hair, then stopped, rubbing his neck instead.

This was when Erin got a good look at Owen, who was finally removing his coat. Erin's mouth fell open. "You're wearing a *tuxedo*? With *tails*? You didn't tell me to dress up *that* much."

"Yes, well, for what I'm about to do, it's the right uniform to wear." After tossing his jacket onto a chair, Owen kissed Erin's hands, and Erin's irritation bled away as the last of Owen's walls fell, revealing his naked unease and disquiet.

"Owen." Erin tried to keep hold of his hands, but Owen had already pulled away.

"Please stay where you are, and listen." He crossed to the piano. "You're about to hear something no one else has for seventeen years."

The small service door on the far side of the room opened, and to Erin's surprise, Jack Wu pushed through the gauzy curtains. He too wore a tux with tails, but whereas Owen stood at the far end of the instrument, Jack went to the bench, elegantly flipping his tails as he sat on the seat. A wordless exchange took place between the two men as silence bore heavily onto the parlor, and Erin watched with interest, wondering what was about to happen.

Owen lifted a violin from some secret void behind the piano and settled it into his chin.

Erin clutched a pillow to his chest and sat up straight, staring at his boyfriend in disbelief.

Smiling back at him, Owen tuned against the piano. The tuning finished. Jack and Owen took up more serious positions.

Owen looked at Erin. "This is for you, Erin. Only for you."

The song began with soft arpeggios on the piano, and Erin thought he recognized the tune from some pop song. He stopped attempting to place the artist or title, though, once Owen's violin entered the music. Clear, sharp, piercing, captivating. Much like the man himself.

So beautiful. So completely, achingly beautiful.

Erin didn't know a great deal about music and what made it good or bad, but he could recognize the incredible skill in Owen's playing, the control he had over the instrument. The way such intense power came from it, so much sound. Yet sometimes he played so quietly Erin held his breath, in case this allowed him to catch the music. He added flair and spin to the notes, extra things that likely weren't in the original song, yet not to the point the additions were ridiculous. There was something, too, about the way he sometimes traded the melody with the piano, stealthily becoming the accompaniment. To Erin, this told the story of Owen more than anything. For as much as he liked to boast and brag, especially with Jack, here he was, gracefully handing over the lead.

The most remarkable aspect of all, of course, was that Owen played, full stop. It didn't look as if playing caused him pain. This time, at least, Erin was sure the music came from joy.

As the song came to a close, Erin rose off the couch and moved toward Owen, pulled by invisible strings, unable to go anywhere but into his lover's arms.

Owen clutched the violin, staring at it, an inscrutable expression on his face. Erin did his best to decipher it. Was it pain? Anguish? Disappointment? Relief? Happiness? Something too complicated to name?

Erin touched his face with great care, so as not to break him. "Owen?"

Are you okay? My darling Owen, my love, are you okay?

A single tear escaped down Owen's cheek, and almost immediately Erin felt one follow onto his own.

"I've missed this so much," Owen whispered at last. "It still hurts, but I've… I've *missed this so much.*"

Erin began to understand. This part of the gift wasn't for Erin, not completely. This was for Owen, the gift he didn't know how to give himself. So Erin didn't tell Owen how well he did, how beautifully or perfectly he'd played. Instead he pressed a tender kiss to Owen's forehead.

"You deserve to play like this whenever you want, for whoever you want. You deserve to be happy. No matter what she said to you."

Shaking, Owen set the violin on top of the piano and wrapped his arms around Erin.

Erin's gaze met Jack's briefly, catching his nod as he picked up the violin and disappeared through the service door. Alone with Owen, Erin let himself dissolve into Owen's embrace and spoke louder this time.

"You deserve happiness, Owen Gagnon. You deserve to have it however you find it, however you need it. However you want it. Anyone who tells you otherwise is wrong."

Weeping, Owen sank to the floor, and Erin went with him, rolling him over the Persian rug and against the leg of piano, cradling his cracked-open lover to his chest. Erin rested his head on Owen's unruly hair and shut his eyes, inhaling the tangled draughts of the Andreas mansion and Owen Gagnon, whispering a silent declaration of his own.

You deserve happiness, Owen, and I deserve it too.

IT WASN'T part of Owen's plan to fall apart.

He hadn't had a specific visual for the end of his performance, but collapsing to the floor, clutching Erin as he wept, wasn't how he'd imagined this going. Still, there was no denying he'd needed to hear the words Erin spoke to him.

You deserve happiness.

Why was this sentence such a revelation? Why did something so basic, something he could easily say to anyone else, pierce him so deeply? It literally brought him to his knees, emptying him until he was spent, until the rushing in his ears quieted and he was aware once more of Erin gently stroking his hair.

"Feeling better?"

Owen lifted his head, wiping his eyes with his thumbs. "Yes. I do feel better. Thank you."

Producing a handkerchief from his inside breast pocket, Erin dabbed at Owen's eyes as if grown men fell apart in his arms every day. "Thank you for playing for me, for making over the parlor. No one has ever done anything like this for me in my life. You certainly know how to sweep a man off his feet."

Owen was about to reply, then stopped as he saw something peeking out of the lapel of Erin's jacket. "What's that?"

Glancing down, Erin blushed scarlet. "Your present."

Owen frowned. "I thought my present was in the bag out with your coat."

"That's a silly present." Erin handed Owen the thin, flat object wrapped in red tissue paper. "This is the one I wasn't sure whether I should give you. I'm certain now."

The present was soft, and as soon as Owen had it in both his hands, he knew what it was. "This is a pair of socks." What would Erin have to be unsure about with socks, though?

Pulling away the tissue, Owen understood, and his heart caught. It was indeed a pair of socks—one covered with tiny, dancing violins.

"You have socks with everything imaginable on them, I swear, but you don't have these." Erin's knee touched Owen's as they gazed at the cotton.

"I love them." After kicking off his shoes, Owen removed the socks he was currently wearing. "I'm putting them on right now."

Laughing, Erin held up the discarded pair. "*Plain black socks?* Who are you and what did you do with my boyfriend?"

"It was a concert. I was taking it seriously." Sticking out his legs, Owen wiggled his toes and admired his new footwear. "They're cute. Where did you find them?"

"An online strings boutique shop in Canada. I had them expressed to me at work."

"Thank you. I love my present." Owen kissed Erin lingeringly on the lips. "I have a favor to ask you, though. Before we eat, will you give me a tour of your house?"

Erin smiled. "Of course."

Technically Owen had already received a tour when he'd booked the house. That had been from Diane, however, not Erin, and he quickly learned there was a world of difference. As they moved through the rooms, Erin relayed story after story, not about the legacy of who had lived there and where the antiques had come from, but what the place meant to him.

"This is the foyer, obviously. It didn't used to have these antiques in it—they were brought in for the museum. It was fancy, but we had our things in it when I was young. When I went to the Catholic school in town, I'd come home and set my backpack on a different antique bench we had here, but my mother took it with her when she left. The parlor has always been too precious to sit in since that and the dining room were where events were held, but this room here was our family room, and we had modern furniture in it instead of these antiques. This is some sort of tribute to famous figures of Copper Point now, but it was where I watched cartoons when I was young. There was more yard as well, because they hadn't poured the parking lot. We had a wonderful housekeeper too, who baked the most amazing things. She was so kind to me. She'd bring me things to eat in my room, though my parents said food should be kept in the kitchen. Oh, do you want to see where my room was? It's nothing like it used to be, but I can still show you."

"I'd love to see it." Owen followed him, mystified. This was an Erin he hadn't known existed. He didn't want to say too much, lest he break the spell.

Erin hurried up the main stairs, cheerfully leading Owen on. "The room is all done up in vintage style now, but when I used it, it was all pink. My mother wanted a girl. And yes, since you've been kind enough never to ask, that's why my name is spelled the way it is."

"They didn't think to use the male spelling?"

"With my mother, it's always difficult to tell what the actual thought process is. I suspect I was originally going to be called an entirely different, distinctly feminine name, and Erin spelled the traditional girl's way was the compromise. Ah, here we go."

He opened the door to a large room on the second floor, which was indeed decorated in dark, late-Victorian colors matching the rest of the house, featuring heavy drapes. On the far wall was a large bay window filled with elegant pillows.

Erin gazed fondly at the space. "I spent so much time curled in that window seat. Reading, playing, staring out at the bay. You can see it perfectly from there, all the way to the horizon. Sometimes I could see ships coming in, and I watched them for hours. It was so peaceful."

As Owen took in the wistful remembrance on his boyfriend's face, the thought that had crept up slowly on him bloomed into a full realization.

Erin wants to go home.

He couldn't get this revelation out of his head as Erin led him through the rest of the tour. This was why Erin wouldn't unpack, why he lived in boxes at Owen's house, why his room in the attic was a disheveled mess despite the way he kept the rest of his life. Whether he admitted it or not—possibly whether he was consciously aware of it or not—Erin cherished memories of this place and wanted to return. Not just to the house, but to the house the way it had been, the way it should be.

"It sounds so lovely, growing up here," Owen observed as they sat down to the lasagna and bread he'd kept warm in the oven. The dining room still felt formal and stiff despite his attempts to decorate it with tea lights and photos he'd found in Erin's room and the few that had been taken while Erin lived with him, but now he took in every photo, looking for a clue to Erin's past. "You must have been so sad to leave it and go to boarding school."

"Oh, I always knew I'd end up there, though I hadn't anticipated it happening so soon." Erin dabbed his napkin at his mouth after a bite of pasta. "As for growing up here being lovely… well, it had its moments, but let's put it this way. My parents didn't belong together, and in hindsight, I think they stayed with one another longer than they should have. My mother fell out of love with my father and being a mother long before she left. She enjoyed playing house in the mansion and being a lady of town, and that was all. Only when I was older and listened to the two of them talk about one another did I realize how harmful it was that they stayed married as long as they did. My mother is better with me as an adult, but she's still distractible and flighty, and she says many casually cruel things. Despite what people believe about my father, he wounds easily. I think she did a great deal of damage to him."

Was it something about this house allowing Erin to speak so calmly? Owen didn't want to break the spell, but… "Yet he makes you cower so much."

Erin laughed. "Oh, yes. He was the only parent who attempted to care for me at all, and I've always wanted, despite my best efforts, to win his approval. I know I remind him of her because I look like her, because she can be manipulative and play innocent right before she laughs and dismisses you. I think he's waiting for me to behave that way. Meanwhile, I've been waiting for him to tell me I'm doing a good job, if only once. We're some kind of sad Broadway play. Lin-Manuel Miranda should set us to music."

Owen couldn't get his head around this idea of a vulnerable John Jean. "You do know everyone calls your father manipulative and calculating?"

"Yes, I suppose he is. Whether he or my mother was worse, I don't know. I guess that's the vise of memory, isn't it? Your father smiles at you once, holds your hand, and tells you you're good at something and can't wait to see what you can do, and you feed off the compliment for decades, all the while standing before the stranger he's become, waiting in vain for that kind man to return." He pushed cheese around his plate. "Pathetic, isn't it?"

It took Owen a moment to climb out of his own fog of memory, drawn there by the lure of Erin's words. "I can't remember my father's kindness anymore. I had to shut it all off, the darkness and the light."

Erin's face was soft, melancholy in the low light. "Do you regret that? Or welcome it?"

"I don't have thoughts about it most of the time. It wasn't a choice I made. It ended up some kind of consequence, once I realized I'd never see them again. If either of them showed up now, trying to make amends, I'd need to send them away. I had panic attacks over seeing them for years, but my therapist helped me give myself permission to say no, I don't want to see them, that it's healthier for me not to. Which is why I think my brain quietly erased as much as it could. I didn't forget I had parents. I can't touch on many of the details. Mostly I remember tension and pain, always worrying about what was going to happen. Fury and confusion as I wrestled with my orientation. The joy and release music brought me, and what it felt like to have it shattered to the core of my being. The latter in particular isn't something I can wipe out no matter what I do."

Putting down his napkin, Erin moved his chair closer and rested a hand on Owen's thigh. "I wish I could take that pain away from you."

"I hate thinking about your loneliness, how you have so few memories from your youth, and how you were made to feel solitary and invisible by your school and your father, pressed up to the wall until you weren't a wallflower, you were part of the paper itself."

Erin ran a finger over Owen's nose, unable to look him in the eye. "Do you hate that I still wish I could have a relationship with my father?"

Owen considered. "I don't… no. I don't understand it, but I don't hate it." He tugged at the end of a piece of bread. "Actually, I understand it in a way. I guess my reaction is more I fear you're chasing after something that isn't there."

"If it makes you feel any better, I've often worried about the same thing." Erin took a long drink of wine, sighing after he swallowed. "Sometimes I feel as if I'm dragging my feet with this embezzlement investigation because I'm afraid of what I'll find."

"You think your father might be behind it?"

"No. I know he'd never do it personally. I don't have any doubts about that. I am afraid, though, he'll shatter the last of my hope. I'm afraid I'll find the culprit, take measures to expose them, and then there will be my father, not only standing in our way but cutting the last threads of my ties to the parent I yearn for." He swirled his finger over the glass's rim. "I can't let it stop me from doing what needs to be done, however. Before I got to know you better, you and Jared and Simon and Jack, I couldn't let go of him because I was too worried about being truly alone if I turned away from him. But I'm not concerned about that any longer."

"Good." Owen caught Erin's wrist lightly. "Because you're not alone."

Erin left his hand in Owen's, twining their fingers together, letting them duel gently as he spoke. "You taught me I can make friends. I can make my own place for myself. It's a bit pathetic to have taken so long to learn such a lesson, but I feel as if I've grasped it, finally." He kissed Owen's nose. "Who knew what I needed all this time was to be kidnapped?"

"*Kidnapped*? You came here voluntarily. At best I was a bit pushy. In any event, you were the one taming me. I don't know if I can go to the ogre meetings anymore."

"I told you." A glint in his eye, Erin stroked Owen's face. "You're not an ogre."

Owen should have let it go, because it was such a perfect moment, but that was part of the reason he couldn't. "I think at best my ogre is only tamed. This isn't *Beauty and the Beast*. The monster doesn't vanish with a kiss. He's always here, part of me. I fear, sometimes, the ogre is what will make me like my father."

Erin moved so quickly he stole Owen's breath. "You aren't your father." Erin held Owen's face tightly, tipping his chin higher when he tried to avert his gaze. "Look at me. *You aren't your father.* You'd never treat me the way he treated your mother. You'd never treat anyone the way he treated people. Your fear is simply that: fear. Your rage is your own rage, and you're entitled to it. You're also man enough to know how to keep yourself in check. Doubt isn't the same as doing. If you were to strike someone out of anger, once calmed, you would bend in half to make amends. Even to your greatest enemy."

Owen fell forward, resting his forehead on Erin's shoulder. "How do you know?"

"Because I know you. And I love you."

Owen could only cling to Erin and accept his love.

Erin stroked his back, his hair. "The meal was lovely. Is there dessert?"

"Handmade pistachio cannoli. Oh, and egg salad sandwiches."

Erin's hand stopped. "Egg salad sandwiches? For dessert?"

"No, they're just for whatever. In case we get hungry later. It's Grandma Emerson's recipe, so I know you'll like them." Owen kissed Erin's neck. "But first I want to take you to the parlor and make love to you."

Erin softened into him as Owen slowly nibbled his way up Erin's body. "In—in the parlor?"

"Yes. I seem to recall you saying you wanted to roll around naked on the antique rugs someday. I thought, why wait?"

With a sigh, Erin surrendered, sliding his arms around Owen's neck. "I said I *could* roll around on them, when I owned the house."

"Are you telling me you don't want to test them out now?"

Though Owen didn't get an answer, he did get a long, deep, and rather dirty kiss.

This was reply enough.

Some of the tea light batteries had gone out when they returned to the parlor, meaning the greatest source of lighting now were the twinkle lights on the ceiling and the periphery of the room, making it seem as if they were making love in a fairy bower.

"Do we need to take down all these lights and put the house back to rights after?" Erin asked between kisses as Owen helped him out of his shirt.

"Simon, Jack, and Jared are taking care of that." Owen pressed a kiss in the center of Erin's chest as he crouched to help him out of his trousers. "These really are nice clothes. You should wear them to work."

"No, I want to keep them for social occasions."

"Then I'll be sure to take you out as often as possible." After shedding his tuxedo jacket and tugging at his tie, Owen eased Erin to the floor.

Erin looked beautiful, ethereal, a captured prince. A happily captured prince. Smiling, he stroked Owen's thighs. "I dreamed of this, you know. Maybe not this exactly, but of being with you. As I lay upstairs in my attic room, wishing my life were different, I dreamed you would come through the window and be with me."

Owen laughed. "Through the window, huh?" He glanced around.

Swatting him, Erin drew him closer by the open lapels of his shirt. "Don't even think about it."

Nuzzling Erin's jaw, Owen couldn't hold back a smile. "But you dreamed about making love to me, did you?"

"Yes, in my own naive, idealized way, not knowing much about you except that the way you looked at me, the way you played your instrument, made my heart beat faster. I longed for you helplessly, because your very existence made me want things I didn't know how to contain."

"And now?"

Erin nipped at Owen's earlobe, sending a shiver down his spine as he tugged him onto the rug. "I'm not so naive any longer."

CHAPTER FIFTEEN

THEIR FIRST official doubles match was set for the Monday after Erin and Owen's replacement Valentine's Day date.

Owen told Erin this as they sat together in Owen and Jared's kitchen Sunday morning, feet tangling between their footstools as they picked food from each other's plates. "It'll be a tournament of sorts, because Jack and Simon are coming too." He fed Erin the last bite of his french toast. "I'm off to soothe one of Kathryn's patients who is probably headed for cesarean. I'll see you later?"

"Of course."

After a lingering, syrup-flavored kiss, Owen put on his coat and went out the door.

Grinning knowingly into his mug, Jared slid into the seat across from Erin.

"I enjoy this high school sweethearts thing you two have going on." Jared reached for the last piece of bacon on the platter. "Except between you two and Simon and Jack, I'm starting to feel like the odd man out."

Erin had worried about this himself. "Well, you *are* Nick's doubles partner. Maybe it will lead to something."

Jared paused with the bacon halfway to his mouth. He had a strange look on his face. "Has Nick… told you he's gay?"

Erin blushed. "Well—ah, no. But I guess I always… assumed. I don't know why. Maybe it's because his sister thinks he is."

"I didn't know you knew his family that well."

"When I was younger, my mother made the exchange for my father's custody turn at the Mayo Clinic while he was visiting a friend. Except she simply dropped me off at the front door of the building, and I got lost."

Jared regarded him with horror. "At the *Mayo Clinic*? Grown adults need maps to navigate their way around there."

"Well, yes. This is where Nick's family comes in, specifically Emmanuella. She adopted me, as did her grandmother. Nick and his mother weren't as sold on the idea, as they knew full well whose child I was and didn't want trouble."

Jared rolled his eyes. "Jesus, sounds just like them both."

"It wasn't off the mark, because my father was horrible when we were united. I was so embarrassed. The Beckerts took me under their wing after that, I'm sure at Grandma Emerson's edict. Emmanuella embraced me more than Nick at first, always saying hello to me when I was home over the summer, sometimes stopping by to make me come out of the house. I got to know Nick when we ended up at the same undergraduate university."

Sighing, Jared gazed out the window. "I've known Nick and his whole family since I was young and my mother brought me along to her book club meetings, some of which were at Nick's house. I loved the ones at Nick's because there were kids to play with. Eventually Nick asked me to stay over, and I felt like I'd hung the moon."

Erin frowned. "You don't seem as if you're as close anymore."

"I wonder what makes you think that." Jared's smile was decidedly forced. "I'm looking forward to the doubles matches. I think they'll be good for Nick, don't you? He could stand to get out of his own head a bit."

"Well, it will be nice to have so many people involved. I'm eager to hone my skills with people I'm comfortable with."

"I never got a clear answer on why you suddenly need to know racquetball. Is there some hospital tournament coming up?"

Erin hesitated. "I… have my reasons. The short version is once I'm good enough I want to play people who may not be as forgiving of the fact that I recently began learning and who I need some information out of. So I need to learn how to lose, but with a certain bit of grace."

"Ah, one of those situations." Jared dried a glass thoughtfully. "I remember when you were the guy we all tiptoed around, like Roz from *9 to 5*. Though I suppose to be fair, Owen didn't tiptoe around you. He's always had your number."

Thinking of how intimately and exquisitely Owen had possessed Erin's number last night, Erin hid his blush with the curtain of his hair as he poked at the vestiges of his breakfast.

Miraculously, Monday's workday went by smoothly, meaning everyone was able to arrive at the gym without getting called away for an emergency, and by five thirty, Erin and Owen faced off against Nick and Jared in their first match. Erin was clumsy at first, making dumb mistakes that sent him into spirals. Owen was patient with him, telling him to shake it off, kissing him on the lips and smiling as he winked and reminded him this was all for fun.

Jared and Nick won by a landslide, sending them into battle against Simon and Jack. Because the whole point was for Erin to get in practice, he played everyone again after the mini tournament. Though he and Owen lost every time, by the end of the third game, Erin felt he was starting to get the hang of it. Before he could suggest they hit the showers and go to the sauna together, Jack aimed his racquet at Owen.

"Gagnon. You and I are going one-on-one."

Owen bounced the ball idly against the floor, then reached for his water bottle. "By all means."

Erin couldn't fathom playing for another second, but he went above to watch with the others as Jack and Owen began their match, making it clear they were out for blood. Erin spent most of the match with his mouth open, too stunned to speak.

"I had no idea Owen could play so well," he said to Simon. "I knew I was holding him back, but I didn't realize it was to this degree."

Simon looked equally stunned. "I feel the same way about Hong-Wei."

Jared snorted. "Please. Those two live to outdo the other. It's a caucus race of pissing contests, with a true friendship behind it all. Bless their bizarre hearts."

Nick came up to stand on the other side of Erin, wiping sweat away from his chin and watching the display below with mild confusion. "Why is Gagnon still playing? Ah. Wu."

Jared held up a hand in a *there-you-go* gesture. "See? Even Nick knows."

Nick raised his eyebrow. "What do you mean, *even* Nick?"

Jared rested his chin in his hand and returned his focus to the game. "Ah. Jack scored. Now Owen's all fired up."

Nick grumbled under his breath and continued to wipe sweat from his facc as he walked away.

When the two of them finished their game—Jack winning—all of them showered and headed for the sauna, where Nick waited. Jared didn't look at Nick, and Nick went out of his way not to have any interaction with Jared, either. How odd they were such seamless doubles partners but cold to one another off the court.

"This was fun," Simon said as they left the sauna. "We'll need to do this again sometime."

Erin glanced at Nick, waiting for him to say he wouldn't. To his surprise, Nick nodded. "I'll have to check my schedule, but yes, I'd bc open to a rematch."

In the parking lot, Erin broke away from Owen and the others to follow Nick to his car. "Thank you for coming. I hope you had a good time."

"It makes sense to approach the board members this way. That's all this is."

Was it? Erin wanted to press Nick, thought better of it, then watched him drive away instead.

"What was that about?" Owen asked him as they drove to the house.

"Nick's in for using games to flesh out the embezzler."

"Well, good. I just hope he understands you already have a partner. If he wants to join the fun, he'll have to bring his own."

Exercise-weary, heart full of happiness, Erin leaned on his boyfriend's shoulder as he drove them through town.

THEIR FIRST opportunity to play two of the board members happened purely by accident.

They were having their second tournament with the others, and during a break between sets, Owen saw Keith Barnes and Mike Leary coming out of the locker room. A glance told him all the courts were taken and the board members were waiting for their turn, but they were early for the time change by fifteen minutes.

Catching Erin by the sleeve, Owen nodded as casually as he could in the board secretary and treasurer's direction. "Go over and strike up some conversation. I'll come along in a second. The goal is to get them to come do a quick, casual match in our court while they wait for theirs. Bait them with a wager that the loser buys the winner drinks after. Get them to up the ante for a full game with dinner on the line in their court once it opens. Obviously we want to lose."

Erin smoothed his hands over his shorts. "Do I look messy?"

"You look like you've been playing racquetball. Go get your targets. I'll clear our court."

While Erin hurried away, Owen slipped into the room and stopped the game, and while Jack and Jared complained, he pulled Nick aside. "Erin's about to lead Barnes and Leary over here. We need the room."

Though Nick's eyes widened in interest, he also frowned at the others. "I don't know what to tell them."

"I think you punt for now, but to be honest, the two of you need to consider coming clean with the Scooby gang. Why turn down help when you've got it right here?"

Nick blinked at him. "The Scooby gang?"

"Yes. You're in the club, Mr. President, in case you didn't notice. We want you to stay." Owen patted Nick's biceps and headed for the door. "I need to catch up with Erin. Leaving this to you, Fred."

Nick scoffed. "I am *not Fred*."

Owen grinned over his shoulder. "What, you're Velma? Don't tell me you're Daphne."

Nick flipped him off as Owen ducked out in time to meet Erin, Barnes, and Leary. The two board members waved at him, and Leary extended his hand.

"Good to see you, Gagnon." Leary glanced at the door. "Erin mentioned a quick doubles game—I take it you'll be his partner?"

"Of course. They're clearing out of here now—we were having an informal tournament."

Barnes smiled. "Ah, yes, we used to play like that, back in the day. Always late to dinner."

If Owen recalled correctly, Barnes's wife had passed away in the early 2000s after a prolonged fight with cancer. *Could be reason enough to steal money, to pay those bills.* Except it didn't explain the amounts taken in the eighties and nineties.

They made their way to the room, and Erin and Owen took their positions against Barnes and Leary.

"Highest points when the buzzer calling time sounds wins?" Leary suggested.

"Sounds good," Owen said, since Erin was apparently too focused on where he should stand to answer.

Owen had no need to throw the game. Leary and Barnes had played together for years and went for blood. Erin's coordination was poor, and he and Owen were still finding their rhythm together against opponents. But they put up a decent struggle, enough that when the buzzer sounded and the four of them shook hands, Barnes winked at Erin. "Want to come with us next door and have a rematch?"

Erin didn't miss a beat. "Yes, but this time the losers have to buy the winners dinner."

Leary's eyes lit up with glee. "Deal."

Owen and Erin were roundly trounced, and after an evening of play, completely exhausted. In the sauna afterward, Owen wanted to pull Erin to him and prop him up, but he had to let him do his job. Which he did quite well.

"It's nice to see you outside of board business." Erin leaned against the sauna slats and ran his hand down his racquet arm, massaging it lightly. "I see several of you together around town often. I suppose after so many years working together, friendships must form naturally."

Barnes chuckled. "We've had each other's backs so many times, I've lost count. We're there for each other in the good and the bad."

Owen thought he should do his part for the conversation. "You all grew up in Copper Point, right? All the board members?" He deliberately didn't mention Rebecca. Leave her off, lure them into feeling like he was on their side.

"Oh yes. Point of pride how we could all trace our lineage to the area. Well, until that woman." Leary pulled a face.

Erin gave them what Owen thought of as his HR smile, the one he got right before he turned other people's words inside out. Except this time he didn't. "I've only been a member of the hospital administration for a few years, but the more I absorb the history of St. Ann's, the more I realize how deeply the board has been a part of making the institution what it is. And what incredible longevity you have, most of you members since the eighties. You must have done this while you still held jobs, many of you at high levels. I can't fathom it."

Owen nodded, clear in his role now. "I didn't appreciate it as much as I should have until Erin drew my attention to it. The level of public service you've given us is unreal."

Boy did they reel in the right fish, because Barnes ate this up with a spoon. "Well, yes, it's trying at times, but what is a community without health care? Despite what *some* people think, we care about Copper Point and what happens to it."

Leary gestured grandly. "The worst was before you came, Erin, when we had the corruption problems in the administration. We had our bumps when Beckert was on the board for a brief time in the nineties, when West had his cancer scare. Collin was a good man, and perhaps in another time he could have joined us longer instead of filling in, but his people don't fit the image of the board. In any event, you and Nick are doing a good job. You had your wobble last year, but it's worked out all right, so we've decided to look the other way on it for now."

There was so much offense in that speech Owen didn't know where to start. The implication they'd allowed Collin Beckert to serve on the board as a stand-in for *West* of all people, then kicked him out because, what, the nineties hadn't brought racial equality to Copper Point? Then the quick reprimand to Erin for rescinding the dating policy—*their* policy. What was this, a test?

If it was, Erin passed. He nodded at Leary as if he understood him completely. "St. Ann's has had its struggles, hasn't it? But I agree, it all comes down to unity, taking care of one another. I'm grateful you'll overlook my transgressions the same way you will those of the others." He paused, withdrawing and covering his mouth in embarrassment. "I'm sorry. I overstepped. I didn't mean to imply any of you have had any transgressions."

Barnes and Leary exchanged a glance holding constellations of meaning. "Oh, there have definitely been transgressions," Leary said.

Well done, Erin.

There were no more tidbits after that, and neither Erin nor Owen pressed. They endured the men's company through the showers and a dinner at the steakhouse, which Owen paid for. The conversation was often painful, full of casual racism, sexism, general bigotry, white supremacy, and classism, but Owen and Erin endured it, waiting for the prize Erin needed, the one he received in the parking lot as they went their separate ways.

"We should do this again sometime," Barnes said.

"Yes," Leary agreed. "Erin, bring your partner and meet us tomorrow. More of us will be playing then, around six. Are you free?"

Erin smiled. "I am, and I'll be there. Thank you for the invitation."

As soon as they were in the car, Erin unloaded.

"They were so obnoxious, I could barely stand it." Erin turned to Owen as he buckled his seat belt. "I can't believe you were able to keep quiet. They had to be testing us."

Owen shrugged. "Maybe, maybe not. Though I wanted to ask you. What are you looking for in these interviews?"

"I'm not sure. I get this idea I'll know it when I hear it. On paper, any of them could have done it, but none of them have an obvious motive. They took significant amounts, but still in small enough bites it could have been several people or different people at different times."

"Maybe. Someone organized it, though. That's clear. Someone good with books, which points at the treasurer."

"Then the one person we can rule out is Christian West. How could he possibly have embezzled from the hospital bed?"

"Who's saying he hadn't set something up that was running like a machine even while he was out of commission? I'd put all my money at that bastard being in the thick of all this."

Erin took Owen's hand. "What is it with you and West? You're tense whenever he's mentioned."

"He worked with my dad. They were close friends. He was always over at our house, and he made me feel uncomfortable from the moment I met him. Why I get upset around him, however, is because he's the reason it took my parents so long to divorce. He bullied my mother into staying with my dad when she shouldn't have, and I heard him sit up with my dad nights after Mom had gone to bed, the two of them at the table chuckling as West gave my dad advice on how to control his family and manage his life. He's a creepy, slimy bastard."

"You want him to be the embezzler."

No point in lying. "I do. I'm doing my best not to project onto him, but yeah, I'd love to see him go down for this. Only if he actually did it, though."

"It's all right. We'll find the right person." Erin kept his chin high, shoulders back. "I want to win this."

When they got home, Jared was waiting for them in the kitchen. He didn't look happy. "I heard from three different people the two of you were out at the steakhouse with Barnes and Leary. I want an explanation of where you've been and what you've been doing, or at least a better one of why Nick *won't* tell me anything."

So Nick hadn't decided to play Fred after all. Damn. Owen gestured to Erin. "I defer to you."

Erin tugged at one of his curls. "Well, it's complicated, and I probably shouldn't go into much without Nick's say-so. The bottom line is we're investigating something regarding a new embezzlement issue, and to that end we're getting close to board members."

"Who's we?"

"Nick and I—well, and I guess Owen, since he's accidentally ended up part of the investigation."

Jared folded his arms over his chest. "You do know I'm one of the biggest gossips in Copper Point? I know everything about these guys. You should bring me in. Jack and Simon too, but at least me."

Erin rubbed his neck. "I understand. Let me talk to Nick, all right?"

Owen hadn't realized Erin meant he'd talk right then and there, but Erin pulled out his mobile, and as he walked up the stairs toward his room, he'd already begun the conversation. This left an annoyed Jared with Owen.

Jared glared at Owen. "So you've been in on this the whole time?"

"I wouldn't say I'm *in* on anything, but I know what they're talking about, yes. It's complicated and delicate. Give both of them a break, okay?"

Jared huffed. "It was the way Nick rebuffed me that got under my skin. I should have expected as much from him, but it smarts."

Where was he supposed to start on *this* subject? "You know the two of you don't end up well together."

"Well, nothing's happening, so stand down. All I wanted was to be civil with him, but apparently that was too much to ask."

Owen distracted Jared with compliments on his playing style, taunting him with the prospect of some one-on-one in the future, and just when he was thinking he'd have to come up with another conversation distraction, Erin returned, phone in hand.

"Nick is coming over. He wants us to call Jack and Simon and see if they can join us too." Erin glanced at Owen. "He wants to tell everyone everything."

Jared pulled out his phone.

It only took Jack and Simon ten minutes to arrive, and by then Erin and Owen had a full pot of coffee ready and hot water for tea. Jared had laid out a tray of cookies and set it in the middle of the coffee table, and when their first two guests arrived, he brought them beverages. They chatted idly as they waited for Nick, but as soon as he arrived the mood sobered, and they took their places in the living room, Nick standing in front of the fireplace.

"Someone on the board has been embezzling money since the eighties, and they've taken close to twenty-five million dollars over the years," he began, cutting directly to the chase. "Rebecca knows about this too, but she's deferred to our investigation, ready to offer support. We're trying to find the culprit so we can take them down and use that maneuver to have a stronger position in the administration. Erin's idea has been to get closer to the board members, but he's hampered by John Jean. Right now Erin's father is out of town, so we have a small window where we can access them without interference. Playing racquetball is an innocuous way to find hints of who to dig into."

Jack frowned. "This isn't a solid plan."

"No, it isn't," Nick acknowledged. "I'll admit I've allowed myself to be intimidated by this board. I don't know how much intel we'll get from casual conversations, or how we'll get them squirming. This is a start, though."

"We could leak the books to the paper," Simon suggested.

Jared held up a hand as Erin and Nick drew back with a wince. "That tactic is a nuclear bomb, and the real embezzler will immediately hide their trail."

Rising to his feet, Jack stared at the floor as he paced, lost in thought. "The trail is the key. All those years, someone took money. Is *still* taking money. It left the hospital's accounts. Where did it end up? The amounts were paid out to someone in the form of a check."

Owen couldn't believe they'd missed this. "You mean, look backward?"

"Do we still have those kinds of records?" Nick asked, tentatively optimistic. "This is the part that frustrates me. The hospital only recently started doing its own bookkeeping, and I can't get access to the old years."

"Those records have to exist somewhere." Jared had a wicked light in his eye. "I say, though, we stick to Erin's play. Keep talking to the board members. Who knows, we might learn something, but if nothing else, this is our distraction. Meanwhile, we find out where and how the records of payouts are kept and what figures match the ones on the sheets."

Jack shook his head. "That's an insane amount of data."

Owen grinned. "I got this. Trust me."

Simon rose, taking his fiancé's hand, then Erin's. "No. *We've* got this."

CHAPTER SIXTEEN

FOR TWO weeks, all Erin did was hunt for files and play racquetball.

It was all any of them did—that and their actual jobs, which were no afterthought. They searched for the files and kept up a regular rotation of games with the board, then fell into their beds at night, exhausted. Most of their searching had to happen at work, because they couldn't think of where else that information would be located. Simon was the least able to search while on duty, as nurses were expected to pick up each other's slack when they had downtime. The last thing they needed was someone noticing what he was doing and drawing attention to their scheme. Jack and Jared didn't get much further, since searching meant either invading file areas off-limits to employees—a task Nick and Erin took on—or making inquiries, a tricky prospect to do without rousing suspicion.

Owen had the worst luck of anyone, because no one wanted to talk to him.

Jared was the one who found success in the end—with his bachelor auction date.

Gretta had elected to save her coupon, as she called it, for her granddaughter's wedding in May, and Jared wasn't halfway through the evening before he started sending red alert texts telling the others to gather at the house. When his car finally pulled into the drive at the end of the night, he parked haphazardly and ran to the kitchen.

"I know where the records are, and they almost certainly have everything we need." Jared gripped the edge of the kitchen counter, vibrating with excitement. "You won't *believe* the things this woman knows. I'm starting to think St. Ann's was run by the mob until you came along, Nick."

He told them the story of how, after an evening of charming the bride and dancing with every female relative Gretta had, his conversation with his date turned to her recent retirement from Shaw Accounting.

Owen perked up at this. "Hey isn't that the firm that handled hospital payroll before Nick became president?"

Erin nodded. "Yes. We had an internal review when he arrived, and Nick had them stop because it was unnecessary to use outside contractors for so many things."

"I'm sure that's how the former president's financial shenanigans began," Nick added. "I only wish I'd asked for the old documents when I was first hired. When I called the other day, they told me they'd been destroyed a long time ago."

Jared held up a hand. "According to Gretta, that's not the case. She says there are boxes of files in the basement full of payroll stubs and other things."

Erin couldn't believe this. "Why are they hiding this? Why didn't they bring these out when the former president and HR director were investigated? They could have made a stronger case."

"She made it sound to me like the elder Shaw, who has since passed away, was in on the scheme with the old president. She stumbled across the files one day by accident, and Shaw forced her into retirement, giving her some hush money on her way out the door. She kept quiet at the time, but she loved sharing gossip with me because I'm good at getting people to talk, and now it all feels like ancient history." Jared grinned. "She swears Shaw's son, who currently runs the firm, has no idea what he has in his basement. The elder Shaw told his cronies on the board he got rid of everything, but he didn't. Apparently he hated destroying documents. The basement is a sea of crap, and she doubts the son got rid of anything when his father died last year. It's not his style."

"So you're saying no one but us knows these documents are there?" Simon asked.

"That's exactly what I'm saying." Jared held out his hands. "What a find, eh?"

Nick folded his arms over his chest. "I knew my predecessor and the other members of the administration were less than ethical, but this could confirm a whole new level of corruption. And our answers might be lying in wait in those files."

Jack raised his eyebrow. "I'm finding it difficult to believe the board president didn't know about this, with the way he keeps such a tight hand on things."

Erin focused his gaze on the floor. Did his father know? Had he known about all of this and turned a blind eye? "I don't think we can know anything for certain until we see what they contain, until we know which board member was working with the CEO."

Please don't let it be my father.

"How do we get into the files, though?" Simon tapped his finger thoughtfully on his cheek. "Nick could possibly ask to see them, but thcy could just as easily tell him no, especially since they likely won't believe they have them. They already told him once the documents had been destroyed."

"We have to get Owen inside." Jared rubbed his hands together. "He's the one who can scan through the files the fastest and find what we need."

"I want to be there too," Nick said. "This is my hospital."

"I'm not being party to any breaking and entering," Jack declared.

Owen scratched his chin. "No, I think you'd be a better decoy, Jack. All I need to do is get into the basement and start on the files. The second we find something incriminating, it's over. Even if they kick us out."

Simon grimaced. "We need a better plan."

Jared nodded at the calendar. "So everyone is aware, John Jean returns tomorrow. He remains our biggest obstacle to exposure. Be on guard. I say let's table this for now and plan to regroup soon."

Everyone agreed, and after saying good night to Jared, Owen and Erin went to Owen's room, where they ended up holding one another in bed, Erin resting on Owen's shoulder.

Owen stroked Erin's hair, tangling his fingers in the curls. "Nervous about your father coming back?"

Erin had been nervous for over a week. "He wasn't talking to me before, so I doubt he will now."

Owen brushed a kiss across Erin's forehead. "I know you wish he *would* talk to you."

Erin turned his face into Owen's chest, kissing the curling hair, trailing his lips slowly down.

Owen's grip on his head changed.

They didn't make love every night, many times simply touching bodies in the dark. Some nights it was like this, a slow, languid exchange of mouths and touches. Tonight Owen drew Erin's mouth to his own and rolled Erin under his body, sliding their cocks together in sensual concert as he thrust his tongue inside Erin's mouth. Without a word, he stole away Erin's worries and fears over what the next day might bring, of what the investigation might reveal about his father. For the moment it was the two of them, steeped perfectly in pleasure.

The next day Erin dressed in his blue-gray suit with a bright orange-red tie that made him feel good, and a pair of Owen's socks, ones with shooting stars all across them. He ate his breakfast and drove in alone, since Owen had already gone in for an early surgery. After greeting Nick's assistant and retrieving his mail, Erin went to his office, determined to have a good day no matter what.

His father waited for him in his office.

Erin stopped in the doorway, so startled he almost dropped his mail. He glanced at Wendy, who by rights should have warned him if he had a visitor. She averted her gaze guiltily.

"Come in and close the door."

Erin complied, unsure of what else to do. He couldn't hold on to a thought, everything pinging through his mind and bouncing around. Was his father involved in what they were investigating? Was his father here to stop him? Had his father done something illegal? Were his actions about to send his father to jail?

Had his father stolen all that money from the hospital? Was that how Erin had gone to school?

John Jean pushed off the edge of Erin's desk and glowered at his son. "I'm done waiting for you to come to your senses. I assumed I'd return to discover you'd tired of this farce with Gagnon's son, but instead I hear you entertained him in our home."

Gagnon's son? What a strange way to refer to Owen. Erin wanted to protest this wasn't a farce, not remotely, but before he could gather his words, his father spoke again.

"Now I hear you and his friends are sidling up to the board members, and that excuse for a CEO is doing it too. I'm not certain what game you thought you were playing, but it's over now. Leave that house and return home. Stop seeing Gagnon. Stop snooping around the board. Do the job I told you to do the way I told you to do it, or there will be hell to pay. Have I made myself clear?"

No.

The denial wouldn't go past his tongue. His father's presence froze him, stole his words, pinned his gaze to the floor.

John Jean stepped closer, his voice pitched low. "You can't begin to comprehend what you're messing with. Keep your head down and stay out of trouble." A curl of derision entered his tone. "I don't know how much of this with Gagnon was serious and how much was a joke, but it's absolutely over."

No. You can't take him from me. He's not yours to command. Neither am I. But the words remained locked inside Erin as he cowered before his father.

The door opened at the same time Nick called, "Erin."

Nick's voice at the door broke his father's spell. He backed away, still rattled. "Y-yes?"

Ignoring John Jean, Nick stood in the doorway, regarding Erin as if he hadn't walked in on them while John Jean was intimidating the hell out of his son. "I want to go over the personnel files you put on my desk last week as soon as possible." He nodded curtly to Erin's father. "John Jean. I hope you had a pleasant trip."

Nick departed, keeping the door wide open in his wake.

Aiming a finger at his son, John Jean started to leave. "I'll be waiting for you at home. You won't like the consequences if I don't see you there tonight."

Making no reply, Erin watched him go. Once the coast was clear, he melted into the chair in front of his desk.

Nick came into the room, shutting the door before crouching in front of Erin and regarding him intently. "Are you all right?"

Erin nodded, rubbing his temple as he leaned into the desk. "I wasn't ready. I couldn't say a single word to him."

"I'm going to give Wendy a severe reprimand for letting him in." Nick's features hardened. "The more we learn about this embezzlement, the deeper we learn this corruption goes, the less I can stand sitting back and waiting them out. I'm tired of everyone thinking *he* runs this hospital. I'm done playing cautiously. If I take decisive action and lose my job, then I lose my job. I'd rather do that than be the puppet they laugh at. That's not who my family raised me to be."

Nick's words haunted Erin the rest of the morning as he tried to reclaim his headspace and go about his day. *That's not who my family raised me to be.* What had *he*, Erin, been raised to be, then? Who had raised him?

What moral pillar from his upbringing was he supposed to hold on to? The sad memory of his loneliness?

He was preparing to go to lunch when his door opened again, this time admitting an out-of-breath Owen, who was still in scrubs with a surgical mask pushed down to his chin and a cap askew on his head.

"I heard he was here." Owen rushed to Erin's side, kneeling as he took both of Erin's hands in his. "Are you okay? What did he say to you?"

The tears Erin had fought all day threatened to fall at last. He wiped at his eyes in case they escaped anyway. "I'm fine. He told me to stop snooping around the board, to stop seeing you, and to come home."

Owen gripped Erin's hands tighter. "I won't stop seeing you, and I don't want you to go home."

Erin smiled, and one of the tears did escape then. "I know." He stroked Owen's cheek.

"I'll talk to him if you want. I'll tell him to back off and leave you alone. I'll go right now. I have time before the next surgery. I heard he's still in the building."

Heart swelling, Erin realized the answer to his question from earlier. This, this was what he'd hold on to. Not just Owen, but the emotions and the personal strengths he'd learned from being with Owen, the ones that wouldn't go away no matter what happened between the two of them. Self-confidence. Self-love.

Myself. I'll just hold on to myself.

Erin held Owen's face in his hands. "I love you."

"I love you too." Owen kissed his palm. "Does this mean you want me to tackle him?"

Erin kissed his nose. "It means I want you to go back to work and not get arrested."

Owen grimaced. "I promise you, Erin. I'm going to make sure nothing happens to you, that no one hurts you ever again."

Erin slipped off the chair and into Owen's arms, letting him roll them both to the floor.

I promise the same to you, Erin vowed silently, as he lost himself in his lover's kiss.

IT TOOK them a few days to iron out their plan, but by the tenth of May, they had one. Owen thought it was a bit of a mess, but so long as it got them results, he would go along with anything.

Jared came up with their working draft as they sat around the table at Owen and Jared's place. "Distraction is the key to getting Owen into that basement. If Jack and I and Simon go in to talk about getting personal accountants for ourselves, we can occupy Shaw and at least a few of the office staff. Now, Nick, if you come in with Erin at the same time and say you have some questions about how things were run when Shaw managed the hospital accounts, this should put the rest of them in a tailspin."

Jack frowned. "But won't it tip them off?"

Jared held up a finger. "Ah, see. Here's where it gets interesting. I asked Gretta for a layout of the office. All we have to do is get Owen down the hall toward the bathrooms and he can slip into the basement while the rest of us buy time for him to finish. We're going to stay upstairs and have a serious conversation with the son, who will keep denying he has any involvement. If Owen doesn't find much, or only the start of a new trail, he comes back out and we move on. If he finds the jackpot, we have a big reveal and call the police."

Simon's eyes went wide. "The police? Seriously?"

"Sure. This is embezzlement." Jared's eyes were flinty. "This can't stand."

Erin looked green as Nick held up a hand. "I don't know if we need to have the two different schemes going, Jack and Jared talking to an accountant and me coming in to ask questions."

"I think he's saying that so we have an excuse to be present," Jack suggested.

Jared shrugged. "Guilty."

Simon tapped his finger on the table. "All that matters is getting Owen into the basement. I say have Erin go with him so he's not managing everything alone. I'm not sure what excuse we give for Owen to be there—maybe he's after an accountant too? Maybe we say the doctors are all looking into it and you're representatives? It's flimsy, but if Jared sells it, they might bite. Basically then Nick comes in and gets everyone upset, and hopefully shortly thereafter Owen has the smoking gun."

"There's no way it's going to be this simple," Jack said.

Owen agreed. But it was a plan, and better than no plan at all.

Jared got them an appointment sooner than they expected: May thirteenth, which by some miracle they could all get away from the hospital for.

"It's fate," Simon decreed.

It was something, but Owen wasn't sure what yet.

On the evening before the appointment, he was restless, and he went out to drive and think.

He knew Erin was nervous his father might be incriminated by the files. Owen felt he should be comforting his lover, but wasn't sure how. He didn't understand this desire to redeem John Jean.

Or rather, he admitted as he drove along Bayview Park for the third time, if he was truly honest with himself, perhaps deep down he too longed for a parent who could come back from the darkness. Maybe despite all his therapy and careful packing away of anger and feelings, making new family and telling himself he didn't need the monsters who had destroyed his childhood… maybe what gutted Owen the most was he still wished sometimes they were with him, at least the idea of them. That sometimes his phone would ring and he'd have a parent to talk to, or he'd be called away to help with a community function or move a couch. That at holidays he would be pulled to some primal core he belonged to out of blood.

Family. It didn't matter how much you damned them, tried to forget them. Thosc who raised you—or failed to—for better or worse, were with you forever, clawing at your heart.

That was the ache tugging at his violin, he realized. This truth, the unshakable knowledge, sucked him dry every time he played. He wondered what would happen if he gave in to it. If he let himself yearn. For what he'd lost, for what he wished for and knew he would never get back again. It seemed insane, to hold on to such pain.

Except maybe I wouldn't keep it with me. Maybe I'd tap into it and send it out through the strings.

He wondered what that would sound like.

Owen wanted to go play right now, but he didn't have a violin, and he was, ostensibly, supposed to be picking up milk and eggs. He headed for the grocery store, and after sending a quick text to Jack to see if he could borrow his violin for the evening, Owen went inside to finish his errand so he could go home.

He didn't make it to the door before he ran into Christian West.

Owen skidded to the side, stopping the collision, but West sidestepped as well, meaning though they'd both come to a halt, they faced one another. West regarded Owen with a mildly amused gaze. "Well, well. In a rush, are we?"

Owen did his best to swallow his bile. "I just want to get my groceries. I'm sorry for nearly running into you."

West held out an arm, keeping Owen in place. "Don't run off so fast. I'm glad I caught you. I've been meaning to talk to you."

Owen did his best to school his reaction, but it was difficult. He folded his arms over his chest. "About what?"

"So combative. There's no need for that, young man. I've known you since you were a baby bouncing on your father's knee."

Owen tried to leave again. This time West blocked him with his whole body, speaking directly into Owen's ear.

"You'll never be good at these games, boy. No sense of planning. No organization. No cool head. You let other people control you instead of controlling yourself. You react too easily, give in too quickly to your anger." West's chuckle was dark. "Not unlike your father."

Owen gave up on the store, striding so fast to his car he was practically at a run. His hands shook and his vision was blurry, but he had to get away, go somewhere West wasn't.

He ended up at Jack and Simon's, arriving at their door in a daze. He hadn't bothered to check his phone to see if Jack had replied, but apparently he had because when the door opened, Jack appeared with the instrument in hand, safely tucked into its case.

"You didn't reply, but I had a feeling you'd want to take it with you and so—" Jack cut himself off as he got a better look at Owen's face. "Are you all right? Do you want to come in?"

"I'm fine. I just… need to borrow this for a few days."

"Not a problem." Jack passed it over, still regarding Owen with concern. "Let me know if you need anything."

Nodding, Owen cradled the instrument to his chest as hc hurricd down the sidewalk.

He ended up back at the park, standing on the spot not far from where he'd encountered Erin at seventeen. The day he'd officially decided to go to school in Madison with Simon and Jared, when he'd first thought about being a doctor instead of a violinist. He remembered Erin now—from when he was seventeen, not when they'd met in the hospital. That day at the park, he'd thought Erin was ethereal and handsome, a mystical unicorn, a boy whispered about on the wind for years as "Andreas's son." Then he'd faded with the rest of Owen's youth, until one day he was installed in Owen's life as the HR director at the hospital. Owen had regarded him as the enemy, a clone of his father, and he'd vented his anger on the man.

In reply, Erin had pushed open the windows of his prison tower and invited Owen inside.

The restlessness in Owen was so acute now it was painful, driving him to the edge of the park where he could look out at the bay, the water black and dangerous in the thin moonlight.

You let other people control you instead of controlling yourself.

You react too quickly and give in to your anger. Just like your father.

Owen let West's words cut him, bleeding into the soft place he tried never to go. Let the blood wash over the monster inside him, waking it as he fitted the violin to his chin.

Let's hear what you have to say, ogre of mine.

He let the tears stream down his face as he played—what the song was, he didn't know. Perhaps he'd heard it somewhere, perhaps it was the composition of his battered, lonely heart. He didn't try to stop it, didn't fear it, didn't censor a single note. He didn't hold his breath on a hope that tapping into this pain would free him. He didn't accept that he was his father, nor did he say he wasn't. He didn't muzzle the whisper of regret that perhaps his furious response to his mother's outburst had been too much, that if he hadn't packed his feelings away, he could have had his music all along. He didn't reply to the counter another part of him offered, saying her betrayal had hurt so much it was only now, here, he was healed enough to reclaim it.

Owen performed for himself, without fear or hesitation, to see what playing was like now when he held nothing back.

It sounded more resonant, more poignant, than he remembered. Brighter, but with deeper echoes tugging at his heart telling the story of his pain. He felt the ache of loss, the longing and the regret. But he felt the endurance as well. The beauty that came with survival.

I'm not my mother or my father. I miss them and the life I should have had. Yet I'm someone different than the man they tried to make me. I made this for myself, with the help of those who love me.

I have people who love me.

I love myself. Ogre and all.

Letting out a shattered sigh, Owen played on long into the night, into the darkness, into the winds of the bay and the space between his present and his past, for all the music that should have been, for what was about to be.

CHAPTER SEVENTEEN

WHEN OWEN returned to the house, Jared and Erin were in the kitchen. They both rose as he entered, clearly concerned. "We were about to send out a search party," Jared said.

Owen shifted the violin on his back. "I ran into Christian West. We need to be ready for the possibility they've beat us to the punch."

"Given what Jared told us, can they really know about the files at Shaw's?" Erin's gaze lingered on the violin.

Owen gripped the strap tighter. "I don't know."

"We'll find out." Jared pushed to his feet with a weary sigh. "I suggest we head to bed, as we have a big day tomorrow."

Alone in Owen's room, Erin and Owen prepared for bed in silence. It wasn't until they were both beneath the sheets, shrouded in darkness, that they spoke.

"Is everything all right?" Erin's fingers whispered over Owen's naked shoulders in a quiet caress. "You looked upset when you came in the door."

Owen caught Erin's hand, lacing their fingers together. "I'm okay. West got under my skin, but I—" He tightened his hold on Erin. "I went to the bay and played for a bit, and I feel better."

It was dark, but Owen could see Erin's eyes widen. "You played?"

Owen nodded. "A lot. It felt good."

Erin smiled. "I'm so glad."

"What about you? Are *you* okay?"

Erin nestled against Owen's chest. "Of course I'm not. If my father was involved, it's going to hurt, and I don't know what to do about it."

With a kiss on Erin's hair, Owen stroked his back in a rhythmic motion. "If he was involved, you'll face it, you'll mourn, and you'll get through it. We'll be there for you, every step of the way." Closing his eyes, he steadied himself and reached into the wisdom he'd found through playing. "And if it turns out he's done something terrible, if he breaks your heart into a thousand pieces, it's all right if you want to love him, if you wish he could be the father you need him to be. There's nothing wrong with that."

Erin made no reply, only buried his face deeper into Owen's chest and held him tight.

Morning came too early, too bright, too sharp. Owen couldn't get into the rhythm of his workout, and his breakfast didn't taste right, like someone had stripped the sensors from his tongue. No matter how he doctored his coffee, it tasted too bitter, as if it knew the task ahead and insisted on forecasting the outcome in his mug: *you will discover only bitter dregs.*

Work offered small salvation in that he was incredibly busy, keeping his mind occupied. They had surgery after surgery lined up, and Erin worried they wouldn't be able to leave on time to make the appointment at Shaw's. By a miracle they managed, and Jared got out of clinic on time as well. Then it was five thirty, and the six of them stood behind the shrubbery in the parking lot, metaphorically synchronizing their watches.

"Remember." Jared adjusted his tie as he addressed the group. "Jack, Owen, Simon, and I are heading in first for our appointment. Nick, you and Erin come in *right away*. We'll create enough chaos for Owen to slip away, and if you have to, Erin, ask where the bathroom is. One of you ask, obviously, and the other one follow. Once you get to the file room, look for a set of white cardboard file boxes with pink inserts in the front with the initials *SA*. They'll be way in the back, likely buried under other stuff, but there will be a ton of them. At least twenty-five. Owen, you start hunting for the figures we need and any name that can give us a link."

Nick grimaced as he fidgeted with his cuffs. "If the basement has been remodeled into a break room instead of storage for ancient files, you realize this whole operation is a bust."

"Not going to happen." Jared had a fire in his eyes Owen wasn't sure he'd seen before. "I believe in Gretta and the power of our Scooby gang. Now let's go, everybody, and get the bad guys."

"Yes, Fred," Jack murmured, but with a smile.

Owen had seriously thought the distraction plan was weak, but it worked surprisingly well. Basically, Jack and Jared tag-teamed the charm, Simon came in for the assist, and when Nick entered with his CEO lights turned on full blast, it went as Jared promised: the whole office emerged to watch the show. Owen and Erin could have whistled and done a tap dance routine down the hall to the basement and no one would have paid them any attention, they were so riveted on what was going on in the lobby.

On the stairs, Erin took Owen's hand. "I hope we're not here for nothing."

Owen hoped so too. He held his breath as he opened the door to the basement file room.

It was, as Gretta had promised, full to bursting with boxes of old documents, and in the southwest corner were the piles of white file boxes containing the past accounts of St. Ann's Medical Center, including payroll and payments made from several other accounts.

Erin crouched beside Owen, scanning the files with him. "I can't make heads or tails of this. Does it say anything that helps us?"

Owen held up a hand, silencing him as he slid under his data trance. So much information, so many numbers, so many accounts. But there were names too. Lots of names. Names he knew—it was a time capsule of Copper Point, a trip back to his youth, his first days of working at the hospital, the years he was away at school, the decade before he was born… all he had to do was open a different box and he landed in a new window of time. Doctors and nurses coming and going, secretaries, cooks, janitorial staff… the people who made the hospital run. CEOs… only two, the corrupt weasel they'd run out on a rail and Nick.

And the board. In every file, there was the board, holding St. Ann's tight within its fist, never changing, never letting go.

Owen paused. *Hold on.*

He picked up a paper, then another from another box, then another, then another… and as the pieces of the terrible puzzle fell into place, he let out a heavy breath, carrying the weight of his shock.

Jesus. They didn't even use fake accounts. They were that brazen.

They were that brazen. He couldn't believe it. It wasn't one person. It was—

"Owen."

Blinking, he turned to find not only Nick, who had called out to him, but Jared, Jack, Simon, and Erin. Several members of the staff were there as well, and Shaw looked ready to blow a gasket. He didn't say anything, though. Everyone looked at Owen, waiting for the final act in the show.

Yes, well, you certainly have quite a number to end this on, don't you?

Simon leaned forward. "Did you find anything, Owen?"

This unmuzzled Shaw, though all he did was murmur under his breath. "This is ridiculous. There's nothing to find." He looked a little worried, however.

Owen ignored him, answering Simon. "Oh yes. I found the embezzler. Or rather, the embezzlers. It was all of them. Every last one. The former CEO, every member of the board, including my father when he was still in town. They were all in on it together, and Shaw helped them do it."

Shaw the younger stepped forward, eyes wide, mouth agape. "My father would never—"

"Your father left behind acres of evidence right here, damning himself and every one of them." Owen lifted his gaze to Erin, who had frozen on the spot. "All of them, except for John Jean Andreas. His is the only name missing, the only one who never took a payment."

Jared's eyebrows lifted into his hairline. "You're kidding. Does that mean he didn't know it was going on?"

Nick huffed. "Didn't know, or didn't tell on them? He's been a member of their exclusive club for how long, and you honestly think he didn't know what they were doing?"

Erin, who still hadn't said a word, crumpled quietly onto a file box and stared at the floor. Owen wanted to reach for him, but he was buried in paper. He started to dislodge himself, but before he could get very far, Shaw came out of his shock and started raving, waving his arms and almost stepping on Owen.

"What do we do now?" Shaw cried. He looked at the files like he thought, perhaps, he could dispose of them.

Owen drew them protectively to his side.

Jack pulled out his phone. "What else is there to do? We call the authorities."

Nick put his hand on Jack's arm. "This isn't Houston. We don't exactly have the kind of authorities you're thinking of. They might well be on the side of the board members. We need the county district attorney, whose number I don't have handy. In the meantime, we need to make sure Shaw here doesn't destroy the evidence."

Shaw bristled. "I wouldn't—"

"*Wouldn't* you?" Nick's voice was tight with controlled fury. "I'm almost positive my father was onto them during the time he was on the board and tried to take them down. That's why they didn't simply run him off the board when West's cancer was clear. They attempted to ruin his business and gave him the heart attack that put him in his early grave. So I don't want to hear *one word* from anyone about what will or won't happen or how this is going to get handled. *I'm* handling this. And we aren't the damn Scooby gang either. Update your metaphor. This is *Brooklyn Nine-Nine*." He punched furiously at the screen of his phone. "And I'm calling in Rosa."

Shaw looked around in confusion. "I'm sorry, he's calling who?"

"Rebecca," Jack explained for Shaw, tucking his phone into his pocket. "He's calling Rebecca Lambert-Diaz."

With a whimper, Shaw backed into the wall.

As Nick retreated into another part of the room to explain the situation to Rebecca, Owen crawled over the file boxes, pulled Erin into his lap, and folded him into his embrace.

HOURS LATER, Erin sat with Owen, Nick, Jared, Simon, Jack, and Rebecca around the table at Owen and Jared's house, going over the boxes of files Shaw had released to them. The county attorney, away on a family vacation, was returning the next morning to collect the file boxes, but he'd agreed to leave them in Owen and Jared's care in the meantime. Which meant the boxes were here, surrounding them in the dining room, the living room, and part of the kitchen, smelling of dust and old paper and buried crime.

My father's crime.

"There's no way John Jean didn't know," Rebecca agreed, "but there's also no tangible proof in either the files Nick and Erin had or in Shaw's to prove he's involved. The only way to implicate him for sure is if one of them turns on him or he confesses, and I can't see either outcome happening. I wish we could find a way to expose him. If we catch them by surprise at this board meeting Nick's called tomorrow, I think maybe we can get them to reveal something in front of the county attorney he can use."

Jack shook his head. "That's a long shot."

"It's all we have," Jared pointed out.

"I still don't see how we can be sure Shaw or his employees don't talk," Simon said.

Rebecca's smile was a little evil. "Shaw will comply. Nick, Jared, and I did a triple-team on him, and the short story is he's working with us, eager to assure his father goes down as someone who helped put away the embezzlers instead of acting as their accomplice."

Owen snorted. "Even though he was practically their ringleader?"

"I think ringleader is stretching it." Rebecca smoothed her hand over the paper in front of her. "Shaw's father is dead, and he left us a gift. We can't prosecute a dead man. If his son's assistance comes at the cost of allowing him to believe his father will look pure, then so be it. Once the full narrative is on the table, it won't be so easy to control. The point is, we want the members who are still with us. *They* can go to jail."

Jail.

Erin rose and headed for the door.

He wasn't surprised Owen followed him, but he didn't know what to say, didn't want Owen to ask if he was all right. He wasn't.

Owen didn't say anything, only stood beside him on the porch, staring into the night.

"I needed some air," Erin said eventually.

"Me too." Owen tucked his hands in his pockets and looked up at the stars. "Nobody is going to fault you if you sit this out, by the way."

Erin's laugh was bitter. "Yes they will. The whole town will talk about it."

"Fair enough. All right, let me try again. Nobody *here* is going to blame you if you basically show up and make sure you're seen and nothing else. You heard Nick. He's taking the reins and not letting go. Rebecca's on point beside him. You don't have to sit in that room and take body blows because this involves your father. You don't have to let anyone know how much it hurts, and you don't need to hide it, either. You don't owe anyone anything. You can do whatever you want. I'll be beside you as well, every step of the way."

Erin wanted to cry. He wanted to fall into Owen's arms, wanted to go upstairs and let Owen make everything go away. But he could only stand there, numb and hollowed out, stuck in the same frozen state he'd been in since Owen had told them what was in the files.

"I want to be alone for a while." He felt as if someone else had spoken, someone far away.

Owen squeezed his arm gently and kissed his cheek. "I'll be inside if you need me."

It wasn't simple enough to say Erin felt out-of-body. He felt he belonged to many bodies. One of them was numb, unable to think, feel, or move. One wanted to pace and swear, to rage and tear at his clothes and hair, knocking over any and everything in his path. One longed to sob, collapsing into a useless heap, spending his sorrow. One was determined to take the keys to Owen's car and drive away into the night.

Before he had a chance to second-guess himself, he did just that.

Erin returned to his right mind at a downtown stoplight. Where exactly did he think he was going? The answer came faster than he expected. *To see my father one last time.*

Rage, sorrow, and numbness swirled like the three winds of a deadly storm, and Erin surrendered to them, his body moving on autopilot toward the Andreas mansion.

As he approached, a voice of reason pierced him. *You can't tell him what you know. You can't destroy everyone's work because of your pain.* For one breathless moment, Erin almost shoved it aside. He couldn't, though. Not when he remembered Nick's anguish as he described *his* father. What *if* Erin's father had caused that? *Then my father has to pay.* It wasn't a question.

I want to see his face.

The plan unfolded perfectly in Erin's mind. He could sneak into the house without his father knowing he was there. He could move without being heard, linger in the places he wasn't supposed to be without being seen. He'd done it all his life. The only reason Diane had caught him the night he'd come to collect his things with the others was they didn't move as silently as he did. Erin could come up the service road and park behind the garage the way he had to do when the events at the mansion required too many parking spaces.

The moon was high in the sky, and Erin killed his headlights as he rounded the last curve of the road to the house. It was a cool night, but he could smell late spring on the breeze as he closed in on the kitchen door, sending a silent thanks to the gods that Diane had already left as he reached into his pocket to turn off his phone. This was going to be as easy as breathing.

As he put his hand on the knob, he paused, catching sight of something out of the corner of his eye. A strange car was parked in the front visitor's spot.

Who was here at this hour?

Taking greater care as he moved, Erin opened the door.

The entire first floor was silent, meaning his father was entertaining the guest in his private study on the second story. Leaving every light off and hugging the wall, Erin inched his way up the servant stairs, until three-quarters of a way to the top, a familiar voice made him freeze.

"—even if she did get the second set of books, there's nothing to link it to us. None of us keep it anywhere incriminating, and Mike makes sure to never keep anything that can tie us to any charges."

Christian West. It was Christian West in Erin's father's office. Talking about the embezzlement.

Erin didn't move a muscle, focused entirely on listening.

John Jean sighed in annoyance. "I'm telling you, they're about to make a move. Not Lambert-Diaz, *them*."

West laughed. "What, your son and his band of Robin Hoods? Yes, well, we've had this crop up before, haven't we? Everything old is new again, don't you know, J.J."

"You won't do a thing to my son."

"Oh, I'm afraid we're going to have to break his heart. His dashing boyfriend will be the first to go." West made a clucking sound with his tongue. "Gagnon is still hung up about his father. One good push, get him to rage in public, and then it's a matter of planting evidence to frame him for… well, anything violent, really. Tell me what you'd like and we'll get it done. As for the other doctors—malpractice is such an ugly reality these days, and it destroys careers. The nurse isn't worth considering. I can have him fired tomorrow. And the CEO?" West chuckled darkly. "Good for the goose, etc."

John Jean wasn't laughing. "I don't like this."

"Yes, well, you never have cared for the ugly side of management. Which is why you turn a blind eye and let us run the show."

"You've nearly run it into the ground!"

"It was a dark time with the stock market, is all, and you got nervous and meddled. *That's* when it nearly ran into the ground." West's voice was deadly. "I'll remind you you're neck-deep in this with us now.

You may not have dipped your hands in the till, but you watched us do it, and that's still a crime. We let you get rid of Albertson and Lamb without dirtying your hands, but you've used up your chances there. So unless you're ready to rush off to the county attorney, sit back and do as you're told, the way you're supposed to."

Erin listened intently, but he couldn't hear his father say anything.

When West next spoke, he sounded quite self-satisfied. "That's what I thought. My goodness, but you're a lot of work lately, J.J. I miss the days when William was around. He knew how to keep you in hand." West sighed, and Erin thought he could hear the smile. "I'll see myself out."

Erin remained where he was until he heard West's car pulling out of the driveway and the only sound remaining was the tick of the grandfather clock in the hall. Then he finished ascending the stairs, crossed the landing, and opened the door to his father's office.

John Jean glanced up, his expression changing from weariness to shock. "Erin?"

Erin wasn't conflicted in his desires any longer, nor did he feel hollow inside, aching for something he didn't know how to name. He was filled to the brim now—overflowing, in fact—with rage and pain. It took him three surefooted strides to reach his father.

"*Monster*." His nostrils flared as he clenched his fists at his sides. "You've known all this time. You *knew* it was going on. Your precious hospital, the institution you've made me sacrifice my life for, *you* have let them rape since before I was born. *You*. When others tried to stop them, you allowed the thieves to tear them apart like wolves. You must have had quite a laugh when I suggested Nick as the CEO, after what you did to his father. Here I was encouraging him to take more risks. *Me, whose father helped destroy his own.*"

John Jean held up a hand. "Now hold on, I didn't know what they'd planned for—"

"*You knew they had plans.*" The force of Erin's rage sent his father into stunned silence. "You knew they were a mob, you knew what this town was like, and you did nothing to stop them. Not for the sake of Nick's father, his family, or anyone else." The white fury that gripped his belly unleashed a single finger, and he felt as if cold fire whispered from his lips as he spoke his next words. "But what you're going to answer me right now, *Father*, is how much you knew about William Gagnon."

Frowning, still stunned, John Jean sat up slightly. "William?"

Another bit of the fury unleashed, exploding on his teeth—it tasted of bitterness and cold, of dead dreams and iron. "If you so much as look as if you were aware of what he was doing to Owen, the second this mansion is mine, I'll burn it to the ground. I'll spend every penny of your money on things I know you'll hate."

John Jean's face crumbled, and for the first time since Erin was small, father regarded son with a glimmer of yearning. "*Erin.*"

Hot tears ran down his cheeks, and sharp laughter choked from his throat. "Except that's the problem, isn't it? It doesn't matter what you say to me, there's no way I can trust your words. Because all you are is a manipulator. A nasty cheater and a liar. An enabler.

You let the most evil men in town steal twenty-five million dollars from the hospital, you made everyone who ever wanted to love you afraid, you destroyed families, including the one family in town who's ever been kind to me, and you turned the house I loved into a forbidden palace I couldn't enter. I'm done with you. I disown you and everything to do with the name Andreas for the rest of my life."

"*Erin.*"

He paused at the door and threw his father a cold, withering glare, the mirror of the one he'd cowered from. "And if you or any of your weasel-minded cronies try to touch Owen, I'll take you out myself."

Ignoring his father's cries, Erin went down the grand staircase and exited out the front door.

He didn't look back.

CHAPTER EIGHTEEN

WHEN AN hour had passed and Erin hadn't come inside, Owen stepped out to search for him, but his boyfriend wasn't anywhere.

"Hey, guys?" Owen interrupted the heated plans at the dining room table. "Any of you seen Erin?"

Jack glanced around. "I thought you went outside together."

Owen didn't like the feeling in the pit of his stomach. "Yeah, a million years ago. I left him alone at his request. Which I'm now realizing was stupid. He's not outside anymore, and I swear I didn't see him come in."

Discussion ended immediately as they searched the house, the yard, and the garage, and it was during the search of the latter Jared discovered Owen's car was gone. Owen called Erin's phone, and it started ringing just as Erin pulled into the driveway.

He didn't look ready to crumple into a pile any longer as he exited the car. He seemed ready to rip trees from the ground by their roots.

"My father is complicit in everything. He never took any money, but he knew about all of it and deliberately looked the other way, as predicted. Whenever anyone else suspected what was going on, the board members ruined them, and my father didn't stop them. They're ready to do the same thing to all of us for investigating."

The last remark sparked Rebecca's interest. "How do you know all this?"

"Because I went home to see my father and ended up eavesdropping on his conversation with Christian West." Erin's gaze flickered to Nick, and the anger buoying him began to give way. "Nick, I'm so sorry. They admitted what they did to your father. You, your family, have been so kind to me, when all along, my father—" He lowered his gaze. "You knew, didn't you. All along. I was the fool who had no idea, but you knew. All of you."

Nick remained patient, steady, with the reserved steel Owen suddenly understood so much better. "You know now. What *I* need to understand, though, is what you said to your father. Did you let him know what we were doing?"

"No." Erin laughed bitterly. "I told him he was a manipulating lying bastard I couldn't trust, I disowned him, and I threatened him if he hurt Owen."

Everyone went quiet. Eventually Simon broke the silence. "Erin, are you okay?"

Erin shut his eyes, swaying on his feet. "No. I don't think I am."

Owen supported him with an arm as he led him into the house. He wanted to take him to the shelter of their bed, but Rebecca insisted on recording everything he remembered hearing Christian West say, which for some reason Erin wouldn't do until Owen went outside.

Simon went with him.

"*I'm* not running away with anybody's car," Owen grumbled to his babysitter.

"I know." Simon linked their arms and rested his head on Owen's shoulder. "But I thought you could use the company all the same."

Probably true. Owen stared across the street into the darkness. "I've never seen him like that."

"He's protecting you."

"I don't need protecting, though."

"Everyone does, Owen. We all want to shelter the ones we love from harm."

Owen grimaced and rocked on his heels. "I know what Rebecca's doing. She's thinking she can use Erin's testimony to bring down John Jean. Which in theory is fine, but in practicality, I don't know what that does to Erin."

"Maybe it'll help him heal."

"Possibly. But maybe it'll harden him too much. I don't like it." He sighed. "It's not as if there's another way, though. Not unless one of them confesses, which we know they'll never—"

He cut himself off as a car pulled up in front of the house and killed the engine. The driver's door opened, and John Jean stepped out.

Simon started for the house. "I'll go get…." He paused. "Who should I get?"

Owen headed for John Jean. "No one. Don't get anyone."

It was as if John Jean and Erin had swapped places. Whereas Erin had arrived full of bluster, John Jean was uncertain, withdrawn, and when Owen approached him, he looked ready to get in his car and take off. He didn't, though, only lingered near the vehicle and said, "I'm here to see my son."

When hell freezes over. "Your son is busy at the moment. Not to put too fine a point on it, but I don't think he wants to see you." Owen folded his arms over his chest, studying John Jean carefully. "If this is an act to buy my pity, it won't work."

For a second, there was the old John Jean, blooming in a flare of annoyance. "I'm not acting. Why do you both—?" He cut himself off and wiped at his mouth, hand shaking. "I should go."

"Hold on." Owen held up his hand, and to his surprise, John Jean stilled. *This is so weird. It's like he's an entirely different person.* "I have more than a few questions for you." Owen nodded to the garage. "Let's talk over there. We'll move your car too, so he doesn't see it. Toss me the keys."

He said the last one almost as a joke, to see if it would make the man bluster, but he only reached into his pocket and handed over a fob before climbing into the passenger seat.

Casting a glance over his shoulder at a stunned Simon, Owen shrugged, then got into John Jean's BMW and drove it down the street so it was hidden behind the garage.

He kept the keys in his hand, and he didn't get out as he killed the engine. "What do you want with Erin? Because I think you've upset him more than enough."

Grimacing, John Jean stared at the dashboard. "I don't want to upset him. I want to apologize. I want to explain."

Jesus, good luck. "Practice on me, then. Go ahead, tell me how it's okay to do what you did."

Shutting his eyes, the man beside him crumbled. "It started so innocently. We couldn't keep a coherent board, and the hospital was in danger of closing or being taken over by a corporation. We needed strong leadership, but it's a volunteer position. No one wanted it. Your father and West had the idea that if it was a paid position, people would come, but I knew that wouldn't be possible with the political climate in town. They said they could make it so they got paid, only a fraction, and no one would know. They made it sound so innocent. They'd take it out of the foundation, and they'd make all the money back, so it wouldn't be a problem. It was an investment, they said. They promised to keep me completely out of it. Except as it went on and on, as people began to suspect and they 'got rid of the problems,' it felt more and more dangerous. When I saw how much the previous CEO had taken, I put a stop to him myself, and they were furious with me. I tried to lay out my own control for a new future. Erin still wasn't ready for leadership, but I brought him in anyway, and when he suggested Nick as the new CEO, I thought this could be it. But they wouldn't behave. I had to focus on protecting Erin."

This was bananas. "All you've ever done is belittle Erin and tear him down."

John Jean pressed his lips together. "He has so much potential. He needs to try harder."

"He needs some damn *support*, you asshole." Owen sighed and ran a hand through his hair. "So does this hospital. I can't believe how much money you let them siphon off. We're here dying for a cardiac wing, and you let them walk off with twenty-five million dollars."

John Jean cut a sharp glance to Owen. "Erin said something similar. Where did you get such an outlandish figure?"

"From math. I did the figures myself. Don't tell me you weren't aware of how *much* they took—" He watched the color drain from John Jean's face and swore under his breath. "Shit. You didn't know, did you. You just gave them the keys to the bank vault and told them to help themselves. What in the hell is wrong with you?"

John Jean looked as if he might be sick. "That can't be right."

"It's completely right. You let them take a few thousand here and there, for decades, and there are several of them doing it—it adds up to what could have been another surgeon. A nurse anesthetist. More specialists. The rooftop garden. And, of course, the cardiac unit."

"I only wanted to protect St. Ann's, the legacy of the Andreas family. I only wanted—"

"Well, you didn't. You were arrogant, narrow-minded, controlling, and foolish." Owen folded his arms over his chest. "So what now? Don't tell me you're going to talk to Erin. That will only make things worse."

Agony bubbled out of John Jean. "But I need to *explain*—"

"Explain *what*? He *knows*. Everything's crystal clear for Erin. It's you who doesn't understand."

"I need to apologize, to fix this—"

Oh, fuck this. "You honestly think words are going to do anything at this point?"

John Jean threw up his hands, some of his anger returning. "Well, what do you want me to do? Tell you what a failure I am? Tell you I'm a worthless loser who couldn't keep his wife, who didn't know what to do when she said she didn't want our son, who didn't know what to do with him either? Who somehow turned into his own father without realizing it but couldn't seem to stop? To admit I'm the Andreas who destroyed everything, who couldn't carry on a single tradition—not a family, not the festivals at the mansion, not the caretaking of the hospital? To admit I failed with my son, who I don't know how to talk to, who somehow became a mouse who won't speak up—except now he does, for some reason, for you?"

Okay. Maybe Erin should have heard some of this after all. "Yeah. You should tell me all of this. And Erin, when he's cooled down."

John Jean scoffed. "Why, so you can lord over my failures?"

"So we can accept you as a human. So *you* can accept yourself. So you can start over with your son, who has only ever wanted you to see him for who he is, to praise him, to be a true father for him."

"He won't do any of it now. He said he disowned me. He could barely look me in the eye before today, and now he told me he doesn't want to be an Andreas anymore."

"Then make the Andreas name something he can be proud of. Don't wait for someone to dig up the dirt on you. Confess it all. Apologize. Make amends. Make restitution to Nick's family and anyone else the board destroyed. Expose the rotten wood and clear it out. Let St. Ann's start over. *You* be the one to set it free, to hand it to Nick, to Erin."

Gaze haunted, John Jean stared out the windshield. "I'd end up in jail."

"Probably. But not for long, if you confessed first and helped them. And you'd go with a clean conscience. Everything you just confessed to me, all those shameful fears weighing you down—you'd lose them. You could start over. You'd have a chance, a real one, of getting Erin back when you got out. You'd be able to support him, help him do what you weren't able to do: restore the hospital and the family name."

Owen didn't think for a second John Jean would do any of it. He rested the butt of his palm on the steering wheel, waiting for John Jean to tell him he couldn't, to make up some excuse, and Owen would get out. Which was why he was so surprised when John Jean went in an unexpected direction.

"Erin mentioned something to me I didn't understand. He asked me if I knew about your father. About what he was doing to you."

Owen went completely still.

John Jean frowned, shaking his head. "Erin was so upset, but I… I truly don't know what he was talking about. I wondered if you might enlighten me."

Gripping the wheel, Owen swallowed, took a breath. Then he let go, pushed the button overhead to turn on the interior lights, and lifted his shirt on the side.

"Can you see these lines on my skin, the scars that look like claw marks in perfectly straight swipes?"

Leaning closer, John Jean peered at the faint, raised lines. "Yes?"

"Gardening rake, when I was five. My father had a bad day at the mine, was angry I'd messed up the dirt when I was playing, so he beat me with a garden implement. My mother tried to stop him, and he got angrier and beat her with a shovel."

John Jean recoiled in horror. "What?"

Owen rubbed his thumb across the lower part of the steering wheel, anchoring himself on it for support while he lowered his shirt. "Christian West showed up in the middle of it. Gave my dad a drink and told my mom to calm down and wrap my wounds carefully so I didn't end up in the emergency room, because that would be awkward for the family and the mine. Once I was bandaged, he gave her something to make her sleep, came into my room, and told me I'd better not say anything, because my daddy was an important man, and my job was to not make him angry."

Now John Jean trembled, his face twisted in revulsion, shock, horror. "He said that? To a child?"

"He said it often. When my mother finally divorced my father, he helped make sure none of the child or spousal abuse came out, that the charges against him were dropped, and he helped relocate him far away."

John Jean buried his face in his hands. "I had no idea. I had absolutely no idea."

"Few people did. That was the point." Owen watched with mild interest as John Jean folded into himself. "Are you telling me if you'd been aware, you'd have behaved differently?"

"I don't know." Lifting his head, he stared out of the windshield, an embodiment of misery. "I want to say I would have. But I don't know."

You wouldn't have, which is why you feel so sick. "Since you're cognizant of it now, how will you behave?"

A soft, sad peace settled over John Jean. "I'll confess everything. To whomever you want me to confess."

Owen paused, needing to test it. "You're letting me decide?"

"I am. You're right. I can't see Erin yet. I can't do anything but this."

Owen picked up the keys in his lap, running his thumb over the fob. "Then I'm going into the house, and I'm coming back with Rebecca and Nick."

John Jean nodded, still calm, staring at the dashboard. "I'll wait here for them. Take the keys with you. If you don't feel comfortable with me staying here, I can come along."

"Follow me, but don't come in."

They moved quietly toward the house, where Simon still stood on the porch, looking anxious.

Owen felt uneasy too. "Si, will you get Nick and Rebecca? But only them, and don't let Erin know who's out here, no matter what."

Simon headed for the door. "I'll get Hong-Wei to help me."

Owen stood in silence with John Jean beneath a tree, waiting. Two minutes later, Rebecca and Nick emerged from the house.

They came quietly, their expressions wary but their strides commanding. Rebecca wore a knit tunic and a long-flowing burgundy cardigan, looking like a warrior goddess descending to deal with someone who dared to desecrate her shrine. Nick had never changed out of his work clothes and approached with his suit coat billowing, red tie flapping against where it was tacked to his shirt. He was every inch the CEO, grim and commanding.

They stopped before Owen and John Jean, and Owen was trying to figure out how to start the explanation when John Jean bowed his head and dropped to his knees.

"I'm sorry." His voice was small, flat, and completely contrite. "I'm sorry for what I've done to you and to your families, directly and indirectly. I'm sorry for my failures as a leader, as a member of this community, as a father, as a man. I want to confess what I know about what the board members have done over the past decades, and I want to explain my part in their criminal activities. But for now, out of deference to my son's pain, I would prefer to do so away from him."

Rebecca regarded Owen with wide eyes. Nick never took his gaze away from John Jean.

"If this is part of an act," Nick said, "I'll be merciless."

John Jean shook his head. "No act. I understand this is out of character and difficult to accept. I'm willing to do whatever you need me to do, explain whatever needs to be explained in order for you to believe me. I don't have much in the way of proof, but I'll give you whatever I can. I put myself in your hands, Mr. Beckert."

It was at this point Owen decided he couldn't take any more. He held out John Jean's keys to Nick. "You got this, boss?"

Nick took the keys, a small, satisfied smile stealing over his lips. "Oh, yes."

Owen clapped a hand on his shoulder. "I'll leave you to it, then."

The walk to the house was never longer, somehow, the doorknob never heavier in Owen's hand. Owen was exhausted.

Erin met him at the stairs, looking much the same as Owen felt. Kissing him, Owen drew Erin to his side. "Let's go to bed and make the world go away."

Erin gave no answer, only hugged him back and helped hurry him up the stairs.

THE DAY of the special board meeting, Erin woke in the cradle of Owen's arms.

Burrowing into his lover's chest, he inhaled the comforting scent of him, but as he saw how bright the room was, he realized how late it must be. He lifted his head and regarded his boyfriend blearily, climbing into consciousness. "What time is it?"

Owen, completely awake, ran a finger down Erin's nose. "Seven thirty. Don't panic," he added as Erin threw off the covers. "There's plenty of time to get ready for the meeting."

"But I never went over anything last night with Nick. We passed out without setting an alarm. *Oh no.* Owen, you had an early-morning surgery—"

"Morning surgeries are rescheduled. None of them were emergencies. Jack and I talked last night, and we decided we wanted to be at this meeting too."

They talked last night? When? Had Owen gotten up after Erin had fallen asleep? Erin rubbed his head, which felt heavy. "Did I take one of your Xanax?"

Owen smiled. "No. Though in hindsight, we both could have used one, couldn't we? Anyway, I think we'll be all right today. You get showered, and I'll make us breakfast."

It was then Erin saw Owen was dressed and ready, meaning he'd been up for some time. Somehow it was only Erin who was out of the loop.

He did as Owen suggested, showering and putting on his clothes for work. He wondered what one wore to a lethal board meeting. Rebecca already had the corner on red, and anyway, it didn't look as good on him as it did her. He decided he'd go with professional but crisp, wearing one of the new shirts and suits Matthew had helped him select and a bright blue tie.

He borrowed Owen's Cthulhu socks. It seemed like that kind of day.

Owen noticed the socks right away as Erin came into the kitchen. "Destructive mood? I feel you. Though I was more tactical." He stuck out his ankle, revealing socks depicting General Leia.

Erin's eyes widened. "Those are *great*."

"Aren't they? Jared, last Christmas. I was so wrecked by Carrie Fisher's death. This is the first time I've worn them. I thought she'd find it fitting."

Accepting the mug of coffee Owen pushed toward him, Erin settled onto the stool. "Last night I was full of rage and ready for this. This morning, I'm mostly tired."

Owen kissed his forehead. "That's why I'm coming with you. Your whole family will be there for you."

When this made Erin shed a tear, Owen simply wiped it away, slid a plate in front of him, and gently admonished him to eat his breakfast.

The meeting was at ten, but Erin arrived at work with Owen by nine so he could prepare. It was so strange. Erin felt as if the hospital should be abuzz, everyone should be whispering and looking at them, but of course no one knew a thing. The revelation was still contained within their circle.

Erin was surprised to discover Nick hadn't arrived yet, but this didn't seem to surprise anyone else. "He's off with Rebecca," Jack said.

"He said to go ahead and get ready, to keep the other board members occupied until they arrive," Simon added.

Erin glanced between the three of them. "What's going on? What are Rebecca and Nick doing?"

"They're doing last-minute prep." This came from Jared, who'd just arrived in the boardroom. "Sorry I'm late. I had a few appointments I couldn't reschedule. I'm here now, ready to work. How do we set up for a board meeting?"

Though Erin didn't understand what was going on, it was clear they weren't going to explain. "Go with it," Owen whispered, and Erin trusted him, so he did. He explained how they should type up dummy meeting minutes and print them out, then distribute them around the table. Simon called for a tower of coffee from the cafeteria, as well as a tray of pastries.

Owen set out an array of pens and pencils, and that was that.

The most difficult part was when the board members began to arrive. Erin didn't want to greet any of them, but the others managed to do so in his stead, to the mild bafflement of the board. The only one who seemed bemused rather than befuddled was West, whom Jack and Jared kept far away from both Erin and Owen.

"What's this meeting about?" Ron Harris demanded, when they'd sat mingling for ten minutes. "I have other places to be this morning."

"Mr. Beckert will return shortly," Erin replied. "We're also waiting for two additional board members before we can proceed."

Ed Johnson waved the agenda sheet in the air. "All of this could have waited until the next official meeting."

"Please have patience," Erin replied, then added silently, *Hurry up, Nick.*

Five minutes later, Nick arrived. With him were Rebecca, the hospital's lawyers, the county attorney, and three state troopers.

And Erin's father.

Erin deliberately looked away from him, uncertain what this was about, not ready to be taken in by any more of his lies.

"Sit." Nick's voice was laced with command as the room broke into chaos at the sight of the troopers. Rebecca went to the far end of the table and took her seat, her countenance a cool mask as Nick continued. "Before I proceed with the agenda I had planned for today, I yield the floor to this body's president, John

Jean Andreas. I trust no one here will interrupt him. Should you do so, you'll be removed. However." He cut a glance at the troopers. "You won't get far."

No one in the room breathed. Erin gripped the arms of his chair tighter.

Owen put a hand over his.

Buttoning his suit coat, Nick stepped away from the table and gestured to John Jean. "Mr. Andreas."

Erin watched as his father, weary and rather beaten, stood at the small podium at the head of the table. Then he listened, dumbstruck, as his father confessed to it all.

Revealed everything. Absolutely everything.

It was a surreal experience. Erin's father spoke matter-of-factly, making eye contact with no one. He'd pulled a piece of paper from his pocket and read from it with pain and shame in each word. He apologized repeatedly for the suffering his actions and the actions of others had caused. He stated his desire to make things right and his willingness to do whatever necessary to make that happen.

When he finished, someone began to clap—sharp, jarring interruptions of sound that drew everyone's attention to the side of the table.

Christian West.

"Well. That was quite a performance, J.J." West's smile held no warmth. "You seem to be going through something difficult at the moment, for which I'm sorry. No doubt your son's recent antics haven't helped your mental state any. I hate to be the one to tell you, though, that your attempt to draw the rest of us into your sordid crimes won't work. Since we haven't done anything wrong, you won't find any evidence—"

"Oh, I have all the evidence." Nick's interruption was calm, but it was also clear he enjoyed this.

West shifted his gimlet glare to the CEO. "Do you now? Are you talking about some second set of books J.J. has babbled to me about? Because there's no proof—"

"I have the second books from Leary's computer, yes, showing the full amount of money stolen over the years you've all been on the board. I also have the payroll stubs showing to whom the money went. Every one of your names are on them. Each transaction saved."

West didn't move, all the blood drained from his face. The other board members, who had been conspicuously quiet, began to cough, and Ed Johnson clutched at his chest.

Jack leaned toward him. "Ah, if only we'd had enough money for that cardiac unit."

Nick glanced over his shoulder. "Shaw, this is your cue."

The doors opened, and Shaw and his staff wheeled in three pallet carts stacked high with white file boxes to the county attorney, who looked completely gobsmacked.

"These are the files Nick is talking about." Shaw opened one of the boxes on top of his pallet. "My father saved them all. You'll find what you need in here."

"Let me see that," West demanded, lunging for the boxes.

The county attorney raised a hand, not looking away from the boxes. The nearest trooper restrained West as the attorney went through the box. Nick helped him understand what he was seeing, showed him the books Owen had organized and the payrolls he had decoded, and then it was the attorney's turn to pale.

"Oh my God. Arrest them. Arrest all of them."

"I demand to see my attorney!" West shouted as the trooper wrestled him into cuffs.

"I think that's a very good idea," the county attorney agreed, still absorbed in the files.

Erin's father held out his wrists, and one of the troopers clinked the cuffs onto them. Then, in the middle of the shouting board members, Erin watched the troopers lead his father away.

Owen, who had never left his side, squeezed his hand. "It's going to be all right."

Rising out of his stupor, Erin faced him. "Did you know this was going to happen?"

"Your father stopped by the house last night, and we talked. I wouldn't let him see you. He said he wanted to do the right thing, so I gave him to Rebecca and Nick." Owen watched West get shuffled out by the troopers. "I honestly didn't know what was going to happen, what your father would end up doing or saying in the end. Which was why I didn't say anything. I didn't want you hurt any more than you already were by things he'd said or done." He lowered his gaze to the table with a heavy sigh. "I'm sorry if that was the wrong decision to make."

"No, I don't think it was." Erin held tight to Owen. "I don't know if I could have believed this until I saw it with my own eyes. I'm still not sure I do."

Owen lifted Erin's hand and kissed it, keeping it close to his chest as they waited.

It took a lifetime for the troopers to clear the room. Erin wanted to leave too, to retreat to his office and put his head on his desk. Obviously that wasn't an option yet. He couldn't fathom what came next, though. The entire board save one member was gone. What were they going to do now?

The answer to this question came soon enough. Once the embezzlers and their accomplice were gone, taking the troopers, the county attorney, Shaw, and the carts of documents with them, only the hospital's attorneys, Rebecca, Nick, Erin, Owen, Simon, Jack, and Jared were left in the room.

Nick motioned for everyone to sit, though he remained standing. "Rebecca, move closer, if you would." He cleared his throat and gripped both edges of the podium as everyone settled into place. "Now that the unpleasant business is dealt with, we still have plenty of serious work to see to. Namely, we now have six board seats to fill and a president to elect. I'm naming Rebecca Lambert-Diaz our temporary board president. On the advice of our legal counsel, I'm changing the makeup of the board. We'll still have a president, vice president, secretary, and treasurer, but instead of three additional lay members, we'll only have two. Effective immediately, the hospital board will also have three representatives from the medical staff and one from the nursing department. For the time being, I'm nominating those remaining in this room to fill those positions." Owen, Jared, and Simon began to protest, and Nick ignored them, holding up a hand. "I also promote Erin Andreas to hospital vice president and quality improvement officer."

Now it was Erin sitting forward and sputtering along with everyone else at the table—all but Rebecca, who didn't seem surprised in the slightest by any of this. Erin noticed she wore blood red from head to toe.

"Nick, what do you mean you want me to be a vice president?" Erin's face burned with hot terror. "I can't do that kind of thing."

Nick turned to him, completely collected, as if he'd waited a long time for this. "You're my right hand. You do far more than manage personnel. It's well past time you were given the position and the pay reflective of what you do."

It was difficult for Erin to speak around the lump in his throat. "But… my father…."

"Has nothing whatsoever to do with you and your work performance." Nick lifted his chin to address the rest of the room. "Are there any other objections that need clarifying, or can we move on to nominations for our missing five board positions?"

"They all accept." Rebecca rose, flipping through a notebook in her hand. "As for the other five positions, I have several suggestions."

"I had no doubt." Nick stepped aside and motioned to the podium as he took his seat. "Let's hear them."

And just like that, everything changed.

EPILOGUE

Six months later

IT WAS the day of the concert, and Owen was a lot more nervous than he wanted to be.

"You're going to be fine." Erin fussed with his tie as they dressed together in their bedroom.

Owen couldn't stop sweating. "I'm probably going to make a bunch of mistakes."

"Go ahead and make them. We'll enjoy those as well." Erin patted his lapel and kissed his lips. "Are you wearing your socks?"

Lifting a foot, Owen pointed at the dancing violins.

Erin nodded in approval. "Excellent. Do you want to do another run-through downstairs, or should we head over?"

"I don't want to run through it. Let's go."

"Very well."

It had been four months since Owen and Erin had moved into the Andreas mansion, and Owen was getting used to it. They were slowly remodeling, turning it into more of a home than a museum. They'd started, of course, with Erin's childhood bedroom, the bedroom which was now their own. A few of the more traditional spaces they'd kept in their antique glory, because Erin had decided to restart some of the long-forgotten Andreas family–sponsored festivals. They'd reclaimed a great deal of the former museum, however, and renovated it back to what Erin had known as the family living area growing up. Of course, no matter how you looked at it, they had a *lot* of space. Which was why they were doing more remodeling on the third floor, turning the attic and former servant spaces into small apartments they planned to lease to the college for artists in residence.

As Owen pointed out, they had to pay these insane utility bills somehow.

One of the rooms on the second floor, formerly John Jean's study, was now the music room. It had a decent upright piano and several music stands for when the quintet came to practice, after which they always had refreshments in the dining room. They had a new housekeeper, a team of housekeepers, in fact, from a local company who came by three times a week.

Erin had finally unpacked his things, and he now kept their bedroom and their living spaces as neat and orderly as he did his office.

He also seemed to enjoy fussing with his boyfriend, as he was now, bothering him all the way to the car, warning him they were going to be late if they didn't hurry.

Owen growled right back. "It's *early*, for heaven's sake. How can we be late if we're early? Also, they can't exactly start without me."

"I want you there before anyone arrives, or they'll start fawning over you and make you so nervous you'll bail on the entire thing, and then where will we be?" Erin's lips tightened. "Plus I wanted to talk to Grandma Emerson and Aniyah. My lawyer called to let me know my father is getting out a month earlier than originally expected. Which I think will be good for him, given his health, but I wanted her to be aware."

This was news to Owen. "How do *you* feel about this?"

"I don't know if I'll ever be ready to face him, but at the same time, part of me wants him out, wants to see if he can change. The plan is he'll live away from Copper Point at first, to give everyone space. But he's sticking with his promise to fund both the Collin Beckert Cardiac Wing and a scholarship for local minority students in Nick's father's name. My father's already settled with Aniyah, though his lawyer advised him not to, saying there's no direct wrongful death claim. Apparently he asked to meet with Grandma Emerson's lawyer, asked what she felt would be appropriate restitution, and then paid it without question. He's trying. He's asked if I would come see him once he's out and settled. I think I want to go."

Owen took his hand. "I'll go with you."

"I don't know if he can truly change."

"Well, you and I did. So perhaps anyone can."

They said nothing more on the subject, but they didn't let go of each other until they reached the venue.

As soon as Owen saw the lineup of cars at the community center, he began to panic, but Erin remained calm, driving him to the rear entrance, where Jack, Ram, Amanda, and Tim waited to collect him.

"Right, inside you go." Ram winked at Erin as he ushered Owen and his instrument away. "We'll see you once you've parked. There should be some reserved spaces on the east side."

"There are too many people," Owen murmured, hugging his violin as they led him to the greenroom.

"It's going to be fine." Jack plucked his own violin off a stand. "Come on. Play something with me and relax."

Owen tried. He let Jack bully and tease him. Jack wouldn't allow him to retreat into himself, and neither would the rest of his quartet. They kept telling him the same thing Erin had: if he made mistakes, it wouldn't be a big deal. It wasn't as comforting with the mass of people waiting for him, though.

"This was supposed to be a *small, simple* concert," Owen complained, and not for the first time.

"Well, what do you think, when you haven't played in so long?" Ram patted him on the back. "Tune out the audience. Play for yourself. For the five of us. For Erin."

"Speaking of Erin, he's finally here," Tim said.

"Sorry." Breathless, Erin hurried to the place where they were huddled. "I had to find Grandma Emerson and tell her some things."

"Like what?" Amanda asked.

"That I was happy." Erin kissed Owen's cheek. "Stop being nervous. Also, why aren't you in your costume? Why aren't *any* of you in your costumes?"

Erin was already in his. He wore a long, flowing blue cape and a large gold crown that tended to tilt to the side. He carried a scepter as well, with a bright red jewel at the top. This he set aside as he fitted Owen with his shaggy hood, his false nose, furry shoulder pads, and hairy fingerless gloves.

"By rights, you should have long nails," Erin murmured as he strapped one of the gloves onto Owen's hands.

"Well, if I did, I couldn't play a note." Owen flexed his hands once the last bits of his costume were in place. "So where's my violin going to be?"

"Simon will bring it out. I didn't trust it left on stage. He'll be in costume too, so wait for him to hand it to you, then carry on."

"Got it." Owen rolled his shoulders and flexed his neck. "Okay, I'm a little less nervous in this getup."

"Why do you think you're in the getup?" Erin tweaked his nose. "All right. Stand by. Just one more thing before curtain."

What one more thing? Before he could ask, he saw the members of his quintet and Simon—also in costume—standing beside him, and at some point Jared and Nick had joined them too. Since the latter had no part in the performance, they were in regular clothes.

Owen raised an eyebrow, which, thanks to the prosthetic Erin had glued on, was quite bushy at the moment. "Someone want to tell me what's going on?"

"Pregame show," Jared replied wryly as he leaned against the wall.

That was when Erin flipped back his cape, got on one knee… and held out a ring.

Owen's heart melted. "*Erin.*"

Erin lifted his head. "Owen the Ogre, Terror of Nurses, Fright of the Cafeteria… Stealer of Pain, Bearer of Sorrows, Owner of my Heart. Would you do this humble prince the honor of being my husband?"

Owen stared at Erin, his heart overflowing, as all around them their friends' phones clicked with photos and whose red lights told him the whole thing was on video.

I'm literally in an ogre costume.

Laughing, Owen scooped Erin up from the floor and kissed him hard on the mouth, knocking his fake nose onto his cheek.

"Say yes," Tim called out, lifting his phone higher as he kept recording.

"Yes," Owen replied, holding Erin close.

So as it happened, he wasn't nervous at all as he took the stage. He was full of joy and hope and love. His ogre roar was pretty pathetic, and the kids who made up the first seven rows of the audience laughed. Not a problem. None of this was about scaring anyone anyway.

When Erin appeared and aimed his scepter at Owen, casting a spell so he played a song instead of scaring the townspeople, Owen was itching to play instead of nervous about it. The choir began to sing and the chamber orchestra played as Simon brought him his violin. The quintet of ogres danced around the delighted children as well as the enchanted adults.

None of the ogres danced more than Owen. None of them played more enthusiastically. He could hear the audience gasping, could see them pointing—after this was over, he knew, there would be more comments about his wonderful playing than he'd ever had in his life. This was fine. He was ready for their compliments now. He was ready, he felt, for anything.

As Owen danced his way down the aisle toward the stage, he saw Erin standing in the center, smiling as he watched Owen play.

Owen smiled back, playing with all his heart, all his soul, telling his lover, his fiancé, the light of his heart, how much he would love taking the rest of his life to show him how completely he made him happy.

SEE WHAT HAPPENS NEXT IN...

www.dreamspinnerpress.com

THE DOCTOR'S ORDERS

Once upon a time Nicolas Beckert was the boy who stole kisses from Jared Kumpel beneath the bleachers, but now Jared's a pediatrician and Nick is the hospital CEO who won't glance his way. Everything changes, however, when they're stranded alone in a hospital elevator. Ten years of cold shoulders melt away in five hours of close contact, and old passions rekindle into hot flames.

Once out of the elevator, Jared has no intention of letting Nick get away. It's clear he's desperate for someone to give him space to let go of the reins, and Jared is happy to oblige. But Jared wants Nick as a lover in a full, open relationship, which is a step further than Nick is willing to go. They've traded kisses under the bleachers for liaisons in the boardroom… and it looks like the same arguments that drove them apart in high school might do the same thing now.

Jared's determined not to let that happen this time around. He won't order Nick from his shell—he'll *listen* to what his friend says he needs to feel safe. Maybe this time he can prescribe his lover a happy ever after.

www.dreamspinnerpress.com

CHAPTER ONE

ONCE UPON a time, Nicolas Beckert went to weddings without a heavy pang in his heart.

He'd attended plenty in his day, between his Copper Point cousins, relatives in Milwaukee, and friends of the family. For several years it felt like every weekend there was yet another gift his grandmother or mother picked out, waiting for Nick to amplify it with a little extra cash and a handwritten note wishing the couple a bright future. Nick had always happily gone to these weddings. As the one who had understood without being told it was his job to live up to the legacy of service and grace his father had left behind, Nick knew his duty, and he took pride in fulfilling it, never once begrudging even a penny of those cash packets tucked into the card or a second of those busy Saturday afternoons.

Lately, though, the weddings themselves underscored the fact that while he was present at these events, he was separate from them in a way he couldn't ever let anyone know.

The wedding of his third cousin at the New Birth Baptist Church in Copper Point was particularly uncomfortable, and it wasn't just because the first Saturday in June had dawned uncharacteristically muggy and hot. People were gossiping as they always did, but the topic du jour made him distinctly uncomfortable.

"Did you hear, the surgeon and nurse finally picked a date for their wedding? Coming up fast too. First weekend in October." The speaker, one of Nick's distant relations, raised her eyebrows knowingly, fanning herself with a paper plate as she stood in line for the buffet. "Going to be a big to-do, since Dr. Wu has his family coming from Taiwan."

Nick's great-aunt clucked her tongue. "The things we see sometimes."

The group around them made ever-so-slightly disapproving noises.

This whole speech was spoken a bit loudly, for the benefit of Dr. Kathryn Lambert-Diaz, whose first cousin was the bride. Kathryn was attending with her wife, Rebecca, whom she'd married years ago in a ceremony among friends and accepting family members while Kathryn was doing her residency at the University of Iowa. Nick watched them both, worried Rebecca in particular would say something, but they only continued to chat politely with Kathryn's parents. They didn't have plates of food in their hands and looked as if they were about to leave.

"The other couple hasn't set their date yet, but they're next." By other couple, his great-aunt meant Dr. Owen Gagnon and Erin Andreas. "Should have never thought to see the day."

"All of them working at the hospital too." Uncle Billy leaned around his wife to address Nick, who stood close enough to easily be drawn into conversation. "You best keep your people in line there, son."

His wife swatted Billy with her fan. "You leave the boy alone. He's had enough work, with the embezzlement scandal. He don't need your sass too."

Pastor Robert came up behind Nick and rested a hand on his shoulder. "I have faith in our Nick. He's done a wonderful job with the hospital. I daresay we've never had better leadership in place there, thanks to him. We certainly haven't had a better CEO." He winked at Nick. "If all it comes with is a bit of unusual community color, I suppose we can count that as a blessing."

Everyone at the table chuckled, and Nick inclined his head. He wanted out of this conversation. "I should go check on my grandmother and mother, to make sure they don't need anything. If you folks'll excuse me?"

They shooed him away gleefully, but Nick could hear them talking about him as he disappeared, and a perverse instinct kept him nearby but hidden so he could eavesdrop.

He's the next one we need to see married off.

Get him a wife and a couple of kids, and we'll have ourselves the Copper Point Obamas!

What's taking him so long, though? He never dates anybody.

Well, he's been busy with all those scandals.

Scandal's been done and dusted. Besides, a man's got needs. It's not right, him never dating.

You don't think our Nick....

Nick's stomach turned over. Wiping his mouth to cover the grimness of his countenance, he moved out of earshot before he heard the rest of that sentence.

He didn't get three feet, though, before he ran into the choir director, James Grant.

James greeted him with his usual wide smile. "Nick, looking good, brother." His grin faded as Nick failed to mask his unsettled emotions fast enough. "You all right? Something happen?"

Nick fished up a smile. "Nah. No worries. Too much to do, is all, too much on my mind."

James raised an eyebrow. "Things haven't calmed down at the hospital?"

"Oh, you know how it goes." Nick couldn't quite catch his groove. That last remark kept echoing in his head. You don't think our Nick….

James put a hand on Nick's shoulder. "Hey. You want to go sit somewhere for a minute and talk? You don't look so good."

Talking was the last thing Nick wanted to do. And much as he loved James, sitting with him and having an intimate heart-to-heart would only fuel the flames of what people were apparently thinking about their Nick. He held up his hands. "Thanks, but honestly, I'm just doing a little too much these days." He took a step sideways and kept walking as he spoke. "I got-ta go check in for a second. But we'll talk soon. The choir is killing it, by the way."

"All right." James waved him away, looking sad. "We'll talk later."

Nick gave himself a moment behind a bush to gather his composure before hunting down his family. His mother, grandmother, and sister were together at the table where the groom's closest relatives had gathered, Grandma Emerson holding court. She was in the middle of telling some story as Nick approached, but his sister broke away to greet him.

"Hey, you." She nudged him with her hip. "You going to get down with me later?"

"Can't. Got the reception for Dr. Amin."

She sighed. "Oh right, I forgot you had to leave early."

"Erin's covering for me, letting me show up late." He tugged at his tie and reached into his pocket for his handkerchief to dab at his neck, which dripped in the heat. "Need to go home and freshen up before I head out to the country club."

"Country club crowd." Emmanuella wrinkled her nose. "How bad will *that* be?"

"Standard hospital donor schmoozefest. Pretty dry and crusty, but they made the cardiac unit possible. I wish you would've agreed to be my date so you could meet Dr. Amin. She's amazing. You'll love her."

"I'll meet her sometime when she's *not* at one of those horse and pony shows, thanks. The dedication ceremony was more than enough for me." She punched him lightly in the arm. "Besides. It's time you get a proper date for yourself instead of hauling me around to these things."

"She wants to meet the family, though, since she wasn't in town for the ceremony."

"You should invite her family over for dinner. Mom and Grandma would love it." She leaned in closer and spoke quietly. "Did I hear right, the Ryans will be there?"

The Ryans were Jeremiah Ryan, their father's longtime friend and sometimes business partner back in the day, and his daughter Cynthia. Since then, Ryan had made quite a name for himself in the hospital industry, to the point that now he was the CEO of a corporation managing several medical centers in the Midwest. Nick nodded, stealing a careful glance at their mother. "Was she the one who mentioned it?"

Emmanuella snorted. "I can't believe she hasn't bothered you about it yet. You know she's always dreamed about Cynthia Ryan as a daughter-in-law."

Yes, Nick was painfully aware. He didn't comment, choosing to wipe his mouth with his hand and send his gazc out across the crowd. It landed on the bride and groom, who stood hand in hand as they greeted their guests two tables over. They looked so happy.

Nick fought another pang in the center of his chest.

His mother spied him then, smiling wide and waving him to her side. "Baby, come sit and eat. I made you a plate, and it's getting cold."

Though Nick wasn't remotely hungry, he held up his hands in apology, dredged up his most charismatic grin, and settled into the space beside her. "Sorry, was making my rounds." He reached across the table to shake hands with the groom's family. "Wonderful ceremony. Thanks so much for having us."

Mrs. Hill beamed and pressed her hand to her chest. "We're so glad y'all could come. Espccially since your mother tells me you have another event yet today?"

"Reception for the new cardiologist, yes."

Mr. Hill's chest puffed up at being prioritized over the fancy country club shindig. "I'm telling you, Nick, your daddy would be so proud to see the work you've done with that hospital. Not just becoming the CEO, but cleaning up all the mess those fools made for so many years. You're a credit to his name."

Nick inclined his head. "Thank you, sir."

Mrs. Hill elbowed her husband with a sly wink. "Now we have to help find *him* a lovely wife too."

Nick pushed the potato salad and baked beans around his plate, doing his best to ignore the leaden feeling in his stomach.

As the table conversation resumed, allowing him to drift into his own thoughts again, Nick focused on the sea of guests. People were happy and laughing, caught up in the festivities. It was a humble gathering, with homemade decorations and family and church members helping cook and serve the dishes in lieu of a catered lunch. It was practically more picnic than wedding, except everyone was dressed in their finest outfits and of course, in the case of many of the ladies, hats. Nick loved the children the best, in their frilly dresses and suits and ties, chasing each other and giggling as they ran about the lawn, mothers and aunties occasionally hollering at them to mind their clothes or sit and finish their food.

Everything was warm and wonderful and perfect.

Thc bride and groom glowed as they reveled in their special day. They were good people, and Nick looked forward to watching them make their family together. Except though he celebrated their union and their happiness, it pained him too. With every tinkle of laughter the couple inspired, each beaming smile they shared, the yearning inside Nick grew, until eventually he excused himself from the table and flitted around the reception once more.

When the time came for him to bid people goodbye and get ready for the country club party, he was almost relieved. As he stopped by his family to let them know he was leaving, his grandmother put her hand on his arm. "There's a bag on the table in the kitchen, a small gift for the Ryans. Give it to them, will you, when you see them this afternoon? And be sure to say hello to Cynthia. Tell her to stop by the house the next time she's through."

"Of course." With a squeeze of her shoulder, Nick went on his way.

He found the gift—locally roasted coffee and a loaf of Grandma Emerson's famous banana bread tastefully tucked inside tissue paper in an elegant bright blue gift bag—where she'd said it would be. It smelled wonderful, and he lingered to savor the mingling scents. Then, setting his keys beside the package so he wouldn't forget it, he hurried upstairs to shower.

Shutting his eyes under the spray, Nick saw the smiling faces of the bride and groom once again in his mind's eye. So happy. So celebrated. So protected. Everything laid out before them, the community ensuring their path stayed clear.

What would that be like, he wondered?

Adjusting the plain silk bow tie over the tips of his shirt collar, he stared at his reflection. He felt much stiffer in his tuxedo than he had in the tan suit and gray-striped tie he'd worn to the wedding. He tried out a few expressions in the mirror, searching for one that allowed him to remain guarded but still seem dignified.

He grabbed the gift bag along with his keys, and to boost himself on the way to the country club, he blasted The Weeknd on his stereo. He sang along, winding down the long, scenic road leading to the country club on the top of the hill overlooking the most beautiful and expansive part of the bay.

Pulling up to the gates, he clicked off the radio, put his work face on, and presented his member card to the guard.

The party was in full swing as he handed his keys to the valet and entered the crush. The women were in elegant dresses, the men all in tuxedos or suits—excepting Rebecca Lambert-Diaz. She and Kathryn had already arrived, no longer dressed in airy outdoor wedding clothes, but while Kathryn wore a simple black evening gown, Rebecca had donned a smart black pantsuit with glittering rhinestones on the collar and cuffs. They seemed a bit more at ease at this party than the one they had left, laughing and mingling with the guests.

Nick took his place in the crowd as well, moving from group to group, smiling and shaking hands, ensuring people felt welcomed. His reception here was markedly different than it had been at church. Here they were wary of him, the young upstart who had changed so much about the tidy lives of Copper Point.

As far as they were concerned, he'd broken all their rules. Nick had been hired to be a pawn. Oh, no one had ever come out and said as much, but he'd understood things with one glance. A hospital CEO, at his age? He didn't have the experience. His suspicions had been confirmed as soon as he'd come through the door. No real power, no backing. Even so, experience was experience, and it was nice to stay close to home. He'd told himself he could put up with it for a while, until it was time to upgrade.

Except part of him hadn't been able to shake the idea that he could dig under the rotten surface of the institution and dismantle the system that had broken his father's spirit and nearly ruined their family. A few years on the hospital board had been enough to catch the attention of the power players at the hospital in a way that dogged him even after he'd been voted out. They worked behind the scenes to ruin his business and nearly cost him his home—and ultimately, through his failing health, had cost him his life.

Nick hadn't really thought he'd be able to avenge his father, had only dreamed of it. But with the help of Erin and the others, he'd done just that. Now there was a new board, a new balance of power, and a new day at St. Ann's. For many of the people in this room, though? Oh, Nick was still that man. It didn't matter that the board members who'd embezzled a scandalous amount of money were all in jail and that Nick had helped put them there. These people still didn't like him. They didn't like how he'd gone out of his way to make the new hospital board reflect the diverse population of Copper Point. There was a lot of rumbling from this set about "the way things used to be," their gazes turned toward the past with longing.

Well, Nick thought as he sipped a glass of champagne he'd collected from a passing tray, if they'd rather have the crooks than progress, then screw 'em.

Jeremiah Ryan beamed when he saw Nick, waving him over. Cynthia waved too, her expression welcoming and warm, reminiscent of the faces he'd left at the wedding reception. It also carried the whiff of something more, something hopeful.

Nick smiled back, ready to make his way to this important donor, this friend of the family, this man who understood his difficult position better than anyone, this woman he admired and considered an important friend. But before he reached them, he bumped into another guest, and as soon as he saw who it was, his carefully constructed image fell apart.

"Sorry." The man, fair-haired and tall, but not as tall as Nick, held up his hands and stepped aside. As their gazes met, the man's smile fell away. "Oh. It's you."

Yes. It's me.

It's you.

Both their masks were down as they regarded one another. Nick was conscious of the heavy beating of his heart, of the ache and longing he always felt when he stood this close to Dr. Jared Kumpel. He looked devastating in his tuxedo, crisp and neat, dark-blond hair gleaming in contrast to the dark fabric, his light skin glowing in the dim light.

He was beautiful in a way that stole Nick's breath and short-circuited his brain. This man had stirred him ever since he could remember, since the moment Nick had been, at last, able to understand why he felt so different than everyone else around him.

Jared spoke first, his voice thin and forced. "How was the wedding?"

It took Nick a second to register what Jared had said, to remember he shouldn't simply stare at the seductive curve of the man's upper lip. "G-good. It was good." He cleared his throat. "Hot."

"Yes, it's a muggy day out, isn't it?" The conversation, such as it was, broke off and dangled.

Nick tugged at the cuffs of his shirt and glanced away. "I should…."

"Of course." Jared's voice was flat, dead, as if he couldn't wait to get away. "I'm sorry to keep you."

And just like that, they parted, Jared wafting over to the bar, Nick resuming his trajectory toward the Ryans, plastering on the expression he'd practiced in the mirror as the leaden weight settled all the more deeply onto his heart.

DR. JARED Kumpel wanted to find a dark broom closet, put a bucket over his head, and scream.

It was supposed to be an evening of celebration. The physicians, board members, and local donor class were gathered at the Copper Point Country Club to toast the arrival of Dr. Uma Amin, who would start work next week. After years of embezzlement scandals and a complete overhaul of the hospital board of directors, at last things were peaceful. Perfect, even.

Except for the part where Nick Beckert had a smile for everyone in the room but Jared. The memory of Nick's bright expression melting away at the sight of Jared, the way he'd hurried off as if escaping the plague, drove Jared directly to the bar, where he sipped his drink and tortured himself by watching Nick pull out the charm for everyone else.

Goddamn it.

Jared had absolutely no right to feel so proprietary, which only made him crankier. Nick wasn't his boyfriend, was barely his friend, despite the fact that once upon a time they'd been so intimate he could have identified the man by the sound of his breath. For the past four years, Nick had been Jared's employer, in a sense, though the contractual relationship between clinic physicians and St. Ann's Medical Center was complicated. For years the two of them had silently agreed to pretend the past never existed, and this strategy, while frustrating, had mostly worked out for the best.

It was just lately they'd gotten along, talking casually, playing racquctball, hanging out in the safety of large groups. Jared realized he'd allowed these interactions to engender false hope and perhaps a bit of expectation. He wasn't ready for Nick to start freezing him out.

Before the embezzlement crisis, Nick had focused entirely on work, and Copper Point had seemed willing to leave him to his monkhood. But then Nick had taken out the embezzlement ring in the old board and overseen funding for the long-overdue cardiac center, dedicated in his father's name. He was the shiniest man in town, and everyone wanted him on their arm.

So many damn *women* wanted him in their bed.

Watching yet another woman brush a manicured hand along the sleeve of Nick's tuxedo jacket, Jared told himself it didn't matter. *He's never going to admit who he is, even to himself, so who cares who flirts with him?*

I care, damn it. Turning away with a glower, Jared finished off his drink and wandered into the crowd. Except he didn't feel like mingling, so he found a table as far from Nick as possible and sat, ready to bury himself in his phone.

He hadn't had so much as a chance to reach for his pocket before someone joined him. Dr. Owen Gagnon, St. Ann hospital's anesthesiologist and one of Jared's best friends, pushed a glass in front of Jared and plunked down at the table beside him. "Doing all right? You seem off your game."

After taking a sip of his drink, Jared waved a breezy hand. "Fine. Not feeling the hospital function vibe, is all."

With a grunt of agreement, Owen peeled back the panels of his tuxedo jacket and settled in. "Jack has to be jealous we didn't throw him a party when he arrived."

Jack was Dr. Hong-Wei Wu, St. Ann's resident general surgeon. "Knowing Jack, he's indifferent. I'd think he wouldn't want the fuss but would have endured it if we'd arranged it for him. Though maybe you're right. Maybe he was quietly offended we didn't treat him better. He holds a lot of cards close to his vest."

Owen snorted. "He's all about doing things up properly. I bet he was mad we didn't give him more of a welcome. He sure as hell deserved it."

Jared felt better not thinking about Nick. He tried to keep the conversation going. "By the way, the quintet sounded great, but of course it always does. Your solo was particularly good."

As usual, Owen ignored the compliment and wrinkled his nose. "I don't love how every time we have one of these gigs I have to play Pied Piper. Sometimes I want to sit and grouse about having to show up in my monkey suit with the rest of the doctors."

"If your fiancé hears you, you'll be sleeping in the garage tonight."

"Yes, well, the good news is the garage in the mansion is climate controlled." Owen glanced around. "Still, there's no reason for Erin to have to hear."

This time Jared didn't have to fake his grin. "Have you seen Jack or Simon?"

"Jack's talking with Dr. Amin. Simon, I'm not sure."

"Probably with Jack, since he's not with us. He feels out of place at these things. Until he was Jack's plus-one, he never had to come."

"As the nursing rep on the hospital board, he'd be here anyway. He needs to get comfortable." Owen leaned in closer, eyes sparkling with mischief. "So, Mr. I-Know-All-the-Gossip. How's Copper Point's elite handling yet another physician who isn't a white male evangelical Christian?"

"Oh my God. Where do I start?" Jared rolled his eyes and picked up his drink, sipping it as he moved closer to Owen so they wouldn't be overheard. "The retired college president's wife was in a private chat group pitching a fit because the new cardiologist isn't only from India, she's Muslim. Someone pointed out there was nothing wrong with that, and the end result was the country club scrambling to find someone they could send into the women's locker room to break up a fight when the online spat went abruptly offline. Then on Copper Point People someone else—no one of note, some random MAGA—complained about how it was obvious St. Ann's had an antiwhite hiring policy."

Owen buried his face in his hands. "That Facebook group is trash."

"Wait until you hear how it got resolved. People argued back and forth for two days, but when everyone was starting to cool off, someone came in as the 'mediating' voice and pointed out at least she was straight this time."

Owen sat up slowly, drawing his fingers down his face and staring sightlessly at the table decorations in front of them. "Tell me again why we live here?"

"Because Simon couldn't bear to leave his family when we were looking for somewhere for us to get jobs together after med school. Plus now you're marrying one of the founding sons. Just because we're stuck in this crazy town doesn't mean we can't get our quiet revenge by living well, though. I think you and Erin should adopt a horde of children and raise them Wiccan. It's thc only way to hcal this placc."

Owen rubbed his jaw. "I dunno if I'm organized enough to be Wiccan. Aren't there a lot of meetings and rituals? I could do casual pagan."

"I think it depends on the type of Wiccan." Jared lifted an eyebrow. "Are you ignoring the hordes-of-children part, or is this your way of telling me you've changed your opinion on fatherhood?"

"Well. I mean, I don't know about *hordes*. But yeah, we've talked about it some, and it doesn't seem such a terrible idea, when I think about it with Erin. Oh." He straightened, his face transforming into a youthful, slightly ridiculous grin as he waved to someone across the room. "Speak of the devil. I need to go. You sure you're okay here?"

You fine being alone? That was the translation.

Jared got out the fake smile, wrestling it into something genuine. "Nowhere else I'd rather be. Go see your man."

After Owen left, Jared sipped his drink and people watched for a few minutes, telling himself everything was fine, but his gaze kept drifting to Nick. The DJ switched to a slow song, and one of the women surrounding Nick took his hands to lure him onto the dance floor. He didn't fight her.

It was the daughter of the investor from Milwaukee. Cynthia Ryan. The two of them looked stunning together, her dark hair swept up in a breathtaking style no white woman in the room could emulate, her brown skin glowing against her goldenrod evening dress.

If Nick took Cynthia home to Grandma Emerson, she'd give her blessing in the span of a sigh.

Setting his teeth, Jared finished his drink, then rose and went to get a refill.

Matthew Engleton was at the bar, collecting change for a vodka sour, and he grinned at Jared as he approached. "Dr. Kumpel. Good to see you."

It wasn't a dismissive greeting, which Jared found interesting. He knew Matt, vaguely, because you couldn't live in Copper Point and not know the Engletons, especially if you ever had to buy a suit from their family store. Matt was on the hospital board now too, so they'd gotten a bit closer.

Jared smiled back politely. "Good to see you as well. Enjoying yourself?"

"Oh, as much as I can at these sorts of things." Matt leaned an elbow on the bar and gestured at the crowd of Copper Point elite and St. Ann's higher echelon. “What about you? You aren’t with your usual crew.”

“We’re all busy networking bees. They want the doctors talking to the potential donors, so if we stay in the corner and drink, it defeats the purpose.”

Matt laughed. “Difficult to hide, I suspect, when one of you is engaged to the vice president.” He motioned to the bartender. “Let me buy you a drink, and you can network with me.”

“But you’re a board member.”

“I’m also one of the potential donors. Dad always gives liberally to the hospital, but he never comes to these functions anymore. He says he needs me to be the representative now. So I have double duty.” He raised his eyebrows. “You’ll have to charm the money out of me, Doctor.”

Oh my. Was Matt… hitting on him? A closer inspection of the man’s focused gaze told Jared yes, he was.

Well. He hadn’t seen this coming. Jared had assumed Matt hid his orientation in deference to the family business. Apparently he was wrong, or there was an exception clause for local pediatricians.

Did he *want* Matt to hit on him? He hadn’t thought of Matt as anyone but the polite man who sold clothing well before, and now was also the man who sat in boring meetings beside him. He supposed he was cute enough….

“What’ll you have?” the bartender asked.

“Old Fashioned,” Jared replied.

A familiar feminine laugh behind him made his shoulders relax. “Someone’s ordering an Old Fashioned? Dr. Kumpel must be at the bar.”

He turned around in time for Rebecca Lambert-Diaz to catch his cheek in her hand and give it a gentle tweak. He playfully swatted it away. "Hello, Rebecca. Where's your wife?"

"Hiding in a corner. She hates these things, and we already had to endure a family wedding this afternoon." Rebecca smiled at Matt. "Hello again, Matthew. How's the store?"

Was it Jared's imagination, or did Matt's expression dim a little? "Everything's going well, but we'd do better if our favorite lawyer came by and checked out our new summer line."

"Always a salesman. But now that you mention it, you're right, I haven't been by in a while." She withdrew a twenty and waved it at the bartender. "Let me get my glass of wine, we'll find a seat, and you can tell me what you have in stock. I do need a new suit."

The three of them ended up back at the table Jared had vacated, Rebecca in the middle as she and Matt spoke intensely about women's clothing. Jared sipped his drink and scanned the room, more concerned about where people were. Jack was with Dr. Amin, poor Simon appearing as lost as Owen had said. Owen was with Erin, talking with the leader of the Copper Point string quintet.

Where was Nick, though?

Jared's lip nearly curled when he found him. He was with Cynthia Ryan, and didn't they look *cozy.* Grumbling under his breath, Jared took a fortifying drink of alcohol, the burn fueling his ire.

"Don't you think, Jared?"

He snapped out of his funk at Rebecca's question. "Sorry, what?"

She gestured to herself, miming dress parts as she spoke. "I enjoy a double-breasted suit, but I think what's best on me are those single-breasted smooth pieces that don't have a crease. You know what I'm talking about?"

Jared frowned at her, his attention officially drawn away from Nick. "Well, yes, it's the most flattering option for you, but it isn't as if you can wear the same thing all the time."

Matt held out his hands. "*Thank you.* I've been trying to convince her of this for months."

Rebecca waved airily. "Whatever, I'll let the two of you dress me."

Jared snorted into his Old Fashioned. "You won't ever give up control so easily, but nice try."

"Who I'd really like to get into the store is Jared." Matt bumped Jared's arm, lingering a little longer than necessary. "It's been a while since you've treated yourself to some new clothes. Unless you've been cheating on me with other clothing stores?"

Rebecca laughed. "Jared, leave town to shop? Good luck with that."

No question about it, Matt was trying to flirt with Jared and was getting lesbian cock-blocked at every turn. Well, Jared supposed he could do worse.

He cut a glance to the other side of the room. Matt was as nice as any number of men, but Jared's attention was firmly fixed elsewhere.

Jared's gaze landed on the woman's hand sliding down Nick's arm, and his teeth set.

"Did you want another drink?" Matt shook Jared's glass, which he was shocked to discover was empty. "Or maybe you want to get up and walk around?"

Jared couldn't look away from Nick, though he knew he needed to. He felt a hand on his arm as he stood—he saw Rebecca giving him a questioning look.

"You've seemed off all evening. And honestly, you haven't been yourself lately, period. Is there something going on?"

How could he tell her or any of them the truth? He bent and kissed her on the cheek. "I'm fine, but thank you."

She caught his shoulder and kept him down long enough to whisper. "You're not. You might have fooled the others, but you haven't fooled me. Who's giving you a ride home?"

Oh, Lord, now he had Rebecca mothering him. Sighing, he patted her shoulder. "Seriously. It's not a problem. Okay?"

Matt frowned at him.

Jared squared his shoulders. He *was* fine. He was absolutely perfect, and he didn't need a babysitter. Maybe he'd start an affair with Matt Engleton, what the hell. Maybe sweet little Matt would surprise him and he'd be the next one of their group to find a happy ever after.

Sweet, boring Matt.

"You okay?" Matt asked.

God, they needed to *stop asking him.* Jared's face was going to break, he was stretching it so far for these damn smiles. "Absolutely."

Except as they rounded the corner of a group of chuckling old men, he got another glimpse of Nick as the music shifted. It was Prince of all the damn things, and not only Prince but "Kiss."

Like magnets, Nick and Jared's gazes met and locked.

You're not boring, baby. Not boring at all.

And I haven't forgotten a thing.

When two new women appeared beside Nick, giggling and tugging him forward, Nick turned away, and Jared couldn't stand it anymore.

Jared threaded his fingers through his hair in an attempt to hide his shaking hands. "Actually," he said to Matt, "I think I wouldn't mind stepping outside."

Matt beamed. "Great."

Yes, let's get out of here.

Except Jared knew from experience it didn't matter how far he ran. He couldn't get away from Nick.

HEIDI CULLINAN has always enjoyed a good love story, provided it has a happy ending. Proud to be from the first Midwestern state with full marriage equality, Heidi writes positive-outcome romances for LGBT characters struggling against insurmountable odds because she believes there's no such thing as too much happily ever after. Heidi is a two-time RITA® finalist, and her books have been recommended by *Library Journal*, *USA Today*, *RT Magazine*, and *Publisher's Weekly*. When Heidi isn't writing, she enjoys cooking, reading romance and manga, playing with her cats, and watching too much anime.

Visit Heidi's website at www.heidicullinan.com.

You can contact her at heidi@heidicullinan.com.

FOR
MORE
OF THE
BEST
GAY
ROMANCE
DREAMSPINNER
PRESS
dreamspinnerpress.com